MASTER
⊢ OF ⊢
WAR

DAVID GILMAN

HEAD
of ZEUS

First published in the UK in 2013 by Head of Zeus Ltd

9 7 5 3 1 2 4 6 8

A CIP catalogue record for this book is available from
the British Library.

ISBN (eBook) 9781781852941
ISBN (HB) 9781781850107
ISBN (XTPB) 9781781850114

Printed in Germany.

Head of Zeus Ltd
Clerkenwell House
45-47 Clerkenwell Green
London EC1R 0HT

www.headofzeus.com

For Suzy,
as always

PART ONE

THE BLOODING

CHAPTER ONE

Fate, with its travelling companions Bad Luck and Misery, arrived at Thomas Blackstone's door on the chilly, mist-laden morning of St William's Day, 1346.

Simon Chandler, reeve of Lord Marldon's manor and self-appointed messenger, bore his master's freeman no ill will. A warning to the young stonemason of the writ issued for his brother's arrest would stand him in good stead with his lordship and make the reeve appear less grasping than he was. A chance for the boy to run rather than hang. And hang he surely would for the rape and murder of Sarah, the daughter of Malcolm Flaxley from the neighbouring village.

'Thomas?' Chandler called, tying his horse to the hitching post. 'Where's that dumb bastard brother of yours? Thomas!'

The house was one room deep, twenty-odd feet long, its cob walls made of clay and straw mixed with animal dung, the steep pitched roof thatched with local reed, now aged and smothered in moss. Smoke seeped through an opening in the roof. Chandler stooped low beneath the eave to bang on the iron-hinged door. A figure emerged from the mist at the side of the cottage.

'You're about early, Master Chandler,' said the young man cradling an armful of chopped wood. He looked warily at Lord Marldon's overseer. There was no good reason for the man to be there. It could only mean trouble.

Thomas Blackstone stood a shade over six feet and, apprenticed in the stone quarry since the age of seven, had the build of a grown man who used his body tirelessly doing hard labour. His dark hair framed an open face with no meanness of spirit reflecting from his brown eyes. Lean like the rest of him, it was weathered to a colour that almost matched his leather jerkin. It gave him the look of a man older than his sixteen years.

'I'm here to warn you. There's a warrant of arrest for your brother. The sheriff's men are on their way. You don't have much time.'

Blackstone peered into the rising mist; another hour and the morning sun would burn it away. He listened for the sound of hoof beats. The horsemen would come down the rutted track; its flint would ring from the impact of steel-shod hooves. It was quiet except for a morning cockerel. The cottage lay beyond the edge of the village; if he had the desire to run he could have his brother into the forest and over the hills without being seen.

'What charge?'

'Rape and murder of Sarah Flaxley.'

Blackstone felt his stomach lurch. His face betrayed nothing.

'He's done nothing wrong. There's no need for us to run. Thank you for your warning,' said Blackstone, laying down the cut firewood next to the front door.

'Christ, Thomas, I know his lordship would not want any harm to befall your brother. You're his keeper, and his lordship has always looked kindly on you both since your father's death, but you will be held equally responsible. You will hang with him.'

'Is your cousin still seeking to farm here? It would be convenient if Richard and I took to the hills as fugitives. Our ten acres would suit him.'

Chandler was stung by the truth of the accusation. 'You're a fool! Lord Marldon can't protect you from this.'

'My lord has always said a man has nothing to fear if he is innocent.'

Chandler pulled the reins free from the post and climbed into the saddle.

'You remember Henry Drayman?'

A man disliked across half a dozen villages in the county. A brute of a man in his twenties who would gamble for any easy victory, be it cock-fight or throw of dice. Blackstone's brother had repeatedly beaten him in archery competitions, but Drayman's humiliation had been complete this past Easter when Richard had beaten the older man in the wrestling contest. Bested by a boy nearly ten years his junior, he had sworn revenge, and now, somehow, he was inflicting it.

'Your freak of nature brother will be on the end of a rope by tomorrow. He'll bray in terror. The dumb bastard.'

Blackstone took a step forward and effortlessly grabbed the horse's reins. He twisted them, trapping Chandler's hands in a leather burn. The man winced.

'I respect your office, Master Chandler. You serve his lordship with diligence, but I would beg you to assure him that neither I nor my brother have brought any shame to his great name.'

He released his grip. Chandler turned the horse away.

'They caught Drayman with her ribbons. Her body was found in her father's cornfield. That's where you used to take her, isn't it? And your brother? Christ, the whole damned village fornicated with her, but Drayman turned approver before they hanged him yesterday.'

Blackstone knew there could be no escape from the sheriff's court now. A man condemned to death could accuse his enemies by way of appeal – of implicating another in his crime by approval. Torture was illegal under King Edward III, but those with the power and authority of local law enforcement would never shy away from using it to secure a confession. After a week tied naked to a stake, soiled by his own waste, starved of food and denied water, the beating at the hands of the sheriff's men had finally broken Drayman's mind and loosened his tongue. His life was forfeit, but sufficient cunning still lingered behind the pain and suffering. He would leave this world taking another with him. An enemy. The one who had humiliated him; whose name was etched into his heart as if the stonemason himself had chiselled it there.

Chandler smiled. 'The price of wool is going up. My cousin will have his sheep on your land in a week.'

He spurred the horse away.

Woodsmoke trapped by the mist snaked away, searching for its escape. There was none. Blackstone knew the dead man had wreaked his revenge. The sound of horse's hooves clattered towards him.

It was too late to run.

Blackstone had time to warn his brother not to resist the armed men who came to arrest them. The boy made a guttural groaning sound, his way of confirming his understanding. His brother and guardian was the only source of comfort the deaf-mute boy had had in his life. He was little more than a beast of burden to anyone else and the butt of practical jokes and torment. Were it not for Thomas, Richard Blackstone could have used his strength to fight and kill his tormentors. The boy's size and that great square skull with nothing more than a down-like covering confirmed to everyone in the surrounding villages that the boy was indeed a freak of nature. His crooked jaw gave his face a permanent idiot grin.

They had cut his mother open to lift the child from her and she was dead within hours from the loss of blood. A huge child at birth, he uttered no cry and showed no sign of reaction to the torchlight being crossed in front of his face. The village midwife who helped Annie Blackstone bring this hulking creature into the world said that the silent, mouthing infant should be left in the cold night air to die. Tortured by the loss of his wife, Henry Blackstone agreed. He already had a two-year-old infant to care for. This monstrous baby would be left to nature. It was a bitter wind that blew from the east that autumn of 1332. The barley crop had failed again, the drought suffocated the land and cold air settled at night into an unseasonable frost to cramp a man's starving body. By midnight the moon's glow illuminated the sparkling ground. The abandoned child's father walked out to the corn stubble and found his son still alive. A ring around the moon shimmered, a sign of heavenly marriage between sky and earth, and Henry Blackstone lifted the child from the cold ground. His wife had taught the warrior that tenderness would not weaken him, and her love had weaned him from the brutality of war. He lifted the cold body and held it close to his naked chest, wrapping it in a blanket and settling more logs on the fire.

It was his child. It had a right to life.

The sheriff's men took the brothers, tied and manacled in the back of a cart, through the hamlets and villages to the market town. The iron-rimmed wheels rumbled across the rutted marketplace towards the town's prison cells, past Drayman's body dangling from the gibbet. The crows had already taken his eyes and the pecked flesh was down to the bone in places. His tongue had been torn away by voracious beaks.

The soldiers threw the brothers into wooden cages in the coldest corner of the sheriff's courtyard where the sun's warmth could not penetrate. The boy muttered an almost animal-like whimper, a question to his brother.

Over the years Blackstone and his father had developed a means of communicating with the blighted sibling by using simple gestures to calm and explain events. Where he should go, what he should do, and why strangers stared and children tugged his shirt. The local villagers had ceased tormenting him when the novelty wore off and the boy's strength and skill with a bow became apparent at the county fairs. They might call him the village idiot, but he was *their* village idiot and he brought victory. They lived in hovels, died young through disease, hard work and war – but Richard Blackstone, the freak child, gave them with his success the only status they would know.

There was no dulled intelligence inside the lumbering boy; his eyes and brain were as sharp as a bodkin arrowhead. The fact that he was trapped in silence was no indication that his mind was disabled as well as his speech and hearing. He kept a constant watch on his older brother and took guidance from his instructions, which was why he always walked a pace behind Blackstone's left shoulder.

Now he endured the guard's taunts as they jabbed their spears through the bars, forcing him into the corner of the cage, but he could not escape the man who urinated over him as he cowered back from the spear points. He could see Thomas's face contorting in anger as he gripped the bars, his teeth bared.

'Leave him alone, you bastards!' Blackstone yelled and earned a blow from the dull end of a spear shaft.

However, there was little sport to be had from tormenting the creature and the guards soon went back to their posts. The piss-stinking boy looked to his brother and understood the look of anguish on his face, and his helplessness. Richard's crippled jaw opened into a wider smile. These events were nothing new. He dropped his hose and bared his arse in contempt for his gaolers.

Thomas Blackstone laughed.

'You've got yourself in a shit pit and there's not much I, or his lordship, can do to save your neck from the gibbet. The court sits today,' said Lord Marldon's man-at-arms Sir Gilbert Killbere. 'You know as well as I do your brother spent more time quill-dipping Sarah Flaxley than most anyone else in the damned county.' Sir Gilbert stood outside the cages. 'I'm here to exert what influence there is, but his lordship won't pay the sheriff's bail – bribe more like – for your release and I dare say you haven't got two pennies to rub together.'

Sir Gilbert tugged his belt and scabbard further round his hip, pulling his padded jacket tighter, which emphasized the breadth of his shoulders. He was almost as tall as Blackstone, but the soldier lacked the boy's handsome features, not that he would have it any other way – Sir Gilbert's pock-marked face added to his fearsome reputation. At thirty-six he was known for his skill with the sword and the lance and there would be no man willing to challenge him for speaking to the prisoners without the sheriff's permission. Which he did not have.

Blackstone shook his head. 'My brother is innocent. He didn't kill Sarah Flaxley, you know that, Sir Gilbert.'

'Henry Drayman told the court your brother was with him when he killed her. For God's sake, boy! Don't be so damned naive. He turned approver, that's all there is to it. Justice is nothing to do with innocence; it's to do with finding someone guilty for the crime. It doesn't matter who it is. His lordship is aggrieved; the south wall needs finishing and here you are rotting in the sheriff's gaol while you could be cutting stone. And there are other matters that don't concern you – yet. You've been here a week and I've been dragged from my duties elsewhere. You're a bloody inconvenience.'

'I'm sorry, Sir Gilbert. I know you were rent collecting for his lordship.'

'Sitting on my arse behind a table – and don't think I'll thank you for relieving me from that, or from listening to every excuse under the sun why scab-ridden peasants like you don't pay what is owed.'

'I'm a free man, Sir Gilbert. I'm sorry if that is an inconvenience.' Blackstone chanced a smile. The knight had known his father and, with Lord Marldon, they had fought together in the Scottish wars.

'Aye, you'll have a different smile on your face when that rope tightens around your neck before the day is through. Christ, your brother must have shafted his arrow more times than I care to think. How often did the girl's father pay leyrwite?' he asked, referring to the fine – some called it a tax – levied by the local lord or abbot on poor women deemed guilty of fornication. 'You train a dog by thrashing it. He didn't wield the stick enough on the bitch. The whole damned county knew she was a whore – and you and your brother paid her.'

'Can you help us, Sir Gilbert?'

Sir Gilbert shook his head. 'I don't know. Rape and murder. You being free men in Lord Marldon's domain gives his enemies a chance to poke him in the eye. Sweet Jesus, it's hardly the loss of revenue from the whore, is it?'

'My brother beat Drayman at the Easter fair. That's all this is about. He doesn't deserve to die for that.'

8

'You're his keeper. You'll be held as responsible. I might be able to save you, but not him. Christ, they'd have him in a bull pit and set the dogs on him if they could. Hanging is a merciful end.'

Half a dozen guards approached; they were taking no chances with the hulking boy.

'They're wanted, Sir Gilbert,' one of the front men said.

Sir Gilbert half turned. 'Wait, I'm not finished yet.'

The guard was about to say something but thought better of it when the knight glared at him. Sir Gilbert turned his attention back to Blackstone.

'Can you read?'

'Sir Gilbert?'

'You've served a damned apprenticeship since you were seven; your father paid good money for it. They must have taught you to read.'

How many written words could Blackstone remember? He understood geometry more than any written explanation, but had had little use for reading. He needed only a good eye, a plumb line and a skilled pair of hands to chisel stone.

'A little,' he said.

'Did the cleric at the school teach you nothing when you were a child?'

The village school had taught him to write his name and a few letters. Work was more important than learning.

Blackstone shook his head.

'Sweet Jesus! What a waste of time.' Sir Gilbert kicked the bars of the cage in frustration. 'Had your mother lived she would have given you some learning. I can't help you. I'll speak for you and your grunting brother.'

Blackstone had prayed that Sir Gilbert's presence was a sign of hope, but now he realized that he and his brother would most likely be choking to death, kicking to the amusement of the crowd, before the sun climbed higher than the prison's turret. The knight nodded at the soldiers and stepped back as the brothers were roughly pulled from the cages, then prodded and kicked towards the sheriff's tourn – the circuit court that dealt with serious cases, bringing the judges to the county, keen to clear any backlog of felons so that the gaols could be emptied. Leniency was seldom recorded in the court records.

As the brothers ducked beneath the arched doorway they saw two soldiers leading away a girl no older than ten. The one soldier laughed and turned to the other. 'They dance longer at the end of rope when they're this small.'

The child looked bewildered but allowed herself to be taken towards the town square and the decaying remains of the man still hanging from the gibbet. Blackstone felt a pang of remorse for her – more than for himself and his brother.

'What did she do?' he heard himself ask. Hanging was a common enough occurrence, though he and his brother saw little of it in the village, and the guard seemed surprised that he had even bothered to ask.

'Stole a piece of lace from her mistress,' he said, and shoved the brothers forward into the courtroom.

The usual mockery directed at Blackstone's brother took up the first few minutes of the trial. That the grunting, incoherent creature in the shape of the accused was an affront to the good people of the county and that allowing such a dangerous beast loose on unsuspecting people constituted a public danger. Furthermore the responsibility for control of such a beast lay at the door of Thomas Blackstone. And as a man would be punished for the behaviour of his wife, she being his chattel, so too was this creature's keeper responsible for the crime against Sarah Flaxley.

It was little more than a monologue of condemnation and insult and would serve only to be noted on the court record as the reason for the brothers' execution.

The judge looked around the crowded room. It was to be a busy day with more than a dozen cases to hear – and after ridding this town of its felons he had to move on to the next county. 'Does anyone speak for the accused?'

Sir Gilbert pushed forward. 'I am Sir Gilbert Killbere, these are free men from the village of Sedley, which lies within the estates of my Lord Ralph Marldon. I have been instructed to inform this court that these are valued men to his lordship and he has no desire to see them punished from the approval of a turd such as Drayman.'

The judge could be bribed or threatened but it was not Lord Marldon's place to do so, and everyone knew Sir Gilbert was a poor knight and held his position through his loyalty and fighting skills.

'There is no evidence to suggest that this creature was not involved,' the judge said, knowing the sheriff had tried bribery and been refused, so there was no chance that the larger amount that he would demand to dismiss the case would be forthcoming. Bribery and extortion were common practice for those exercising the Common Law. Whether it involved a judge, a bailiff or a gaoler, at every tier of justice money could save your life. How often had a sheriff had a condemned man approve the sheriff's own enemies and then extort money from them for their lives? Sir Gilbert's appearance was purely to make Lord Marldon's standing appear more kindly to his tenants. He offered no means to buy the prisoners' necks.

'Is there any just cause why they should not hang?' the judge asked Sir Gilbert.

'You'll know of the proclamation for every man with an acre or more and who earns more than five pounds a year to provide an archer for the King's intended campaign,' said Sir Gilbert. He looked at Blackstone, whose head tilted quickly, looking at the knight. It was the first he had heard of it. A town crier would not have visited hamlets and villages, and any written proclamation would have gone unread unless a village cleric translated, and Sedley's cleric was on a pilgrimage to the Pope in Avignon, and had probably been waylaid at Calais by the nearest brothel. Was Sir Gilbert using the proclamation as a means of saving them?

'These are free men. They are not bonded to his lordship, but my lord needs men-at-arms and archers to answer the King's writ to raise an army. Thomas Blackstone is an apprenticed stonemason and earns five shillings a year. That, with his wool and crops, brings him to the required amount. His duty is clear. His life is needed by the King,' Sir Gilbert said.

'There are sufficient archers and hobelars in the region to satisfy the King's demands. I see no reason to offer him a village idiot who, by his very presence, would be an affront to His Highness. If that is the only defence it is denied.'

Sir Gilbert was not about to be cut down by a warty, pot-bellied judge, living fat from bribes and authority. 'The boy is no idiot. He's worked in a quarry all his life, he has greater strength than many grown men, and his skills as an archer are well known in three counties. It would please the King to see his skill put to good use in killing the enemies of the realm.'

The judge pointed a stubby finger at Sir Gilbert. Men-at-arms had caused him many a grievance over his years as a judge. Fighting men familiar with rape and looting on campaign often burgled and murdered at home. He would hang as many as came his way. This one was dangerous. He knew about Sir Gilbert's violent reputation and fighting skills, and wished there was a felony in place for which he too could be charged. 'The five pounds law is from the land holding alone. The fool earns nothing – he is a kept beast used for quarry work, as you have admitted. His fornication with the girl is well known. His life is forfeit.'

Sir Gilbert looked at the deaf mute whose lopsided jaw dropped his face into the caricature of a fool. The knight turned to the older brother and shook his head. He could see Blackstone was ready to launch himself across the court. Sir Gilbert quietly gripped his arm and, despite the boy's strength, held him fast. The last thing Sir Gilbert needed was Thomas Blackstone being hacked to death in court for attacking a shit-pit judge.

'Think!' he whispered urgently. 'Think of what your father taught you! He was a soldier, for Christ's sake! Lord Marldon taught your father, your father must have taught you! Think of the Benefit!'

Panic at his lack of learning gripped Blackstone's throat. Sir Gilbert had given him a chance of life.

'I pass sentence on both these men,' the judge ordered.

Blackstone pulled his arm free from Sir Gilbert. 'I claim Benefit of Clergy!' he shouted. Sir Gilbert smiled. Blackstone's life was now in his own hands.

A monk or priest accused of a felony could save his life by claiming the Benefit, and a literate man could invoke the same right. The risk was huge. If the accused was unable to read from the open Bible placed in front of him his execution would be uncontested. If acquitted he would be placed in the care of the clergy and tried in the Ecclesiastical courts. It was rumoured that, more often than not, a court asked the accused to read Psalm 51, the Psalm of Contrition. It was Blackstone's only chance. His father had beaten him with a willow switch until he memorized the verse word for word. But that had been more than three years ago. Now his memory stumbled.

'Thomas Blackstone can read. It is his right to claim,' said Sir Gilbert.

The request could not be denied.

'Bring the Bible. Where's the cleric? Where is he?' the judge demanded.

A young, tonsured monk, his black habit released from the pillars' shadows, stepped forward with a large open Bible, its corners protected by brass fittings. He presented it to the judge who looked at the chosen passage and nodded. The monk stepped forward, held the Bible open in front of Blackstone and waited.

Blackstone's eyes fell across the letter-covered vellum, the ornate twist of the first letter caged in a decorative painted tomb. There was nothing recognizable. He could read French. Not Latin. The number next to the Psalm was covered by the monk's grubby thumb.

Blackstone begged his mind to remember. His master stonemason had taught him to see the structure of a building in his mind's eye – to interpret the numbers on his drawings into reality. See it in your mind and it will appear, the grizzled master with a crushed hand had taught him.

Blackstone pictured the words his father had thrashed into him. His mind cleared of panic – the monk's thumb moved, revealing the Psalm's number: 51.

'Have mercy on me, O God, according to your unfailing love; according to your great compassion blot out my transgressions. Wash away all my iniquity and cleanse me from my sin. For I know my transgressions, and my sin is always before me...'

Line by line he went on, reciting the contrition with the pace of a man reading from the Good Book. It took a few minutes for his pretence to work. He was convincing enough for the clerk of the court to turn to the judge before committing the death sentence to the trial's records. Blackstone dared not look at the judge, or the monk who gazed into his face. Had he realized Blackstone had only recited the words from memory? After a pause, and what Blackstone took to be a faint smile, the monk averted his eyes from his and moved back into the shadows.

'The older brother is declared not guilty and committed to the care of the monks at St Edmund's. The fool will hang,' said the judge.

While Blackstone committed Psalm 51 to the court, Sir Gilbert had moved closer to the judge, his actions barely noticed as the words bounced across the granite walls. Sir Gilbert had only to lean forward. His whisper was a cold, unemotional threat.

'Hang this boy and I will slice your cock from your crotch and fry it. You'll eat it before you die. Give him to the monks at the priory of St Edmund's.'

He stepped back and waited.

The blood drained from the judge's face. Murder was common coin for some men and Sir Gilbert was not a man to make an idle threat. A poor knight without lands depended on violence to achieve any wealth or influence. The judge had no doubts about the threat. He wiped his face with an expensive linen handkerchief.

'However... the community will be better served if we commit him also to the care of the monks of St Edmund's, who will render some use of the mute and put him to work in God's name. Case dismissed.'

Sir Gilbert guided the Blackstone brothers out of the court's stone-chilled air. Richard lifted his face to the sun and uttered a braying groan of pleasure.

'He's a goddamn donkey in human form. Your father should have let him die,' Sir Gilbert said as he climbed into the saddle.

'You had that choice too, Sir Gilbert,' said Blackstone.

'Aye, and much good it would have done me. I had nags brought in anticipation of you using your brain.'

The monk led two swaybacked palfreys into view. He smiled at Blackstone and handed him the reins to one of them.

'Well recited, Master Blackstone,' he said and smiled.

Sir Gilbert turned his palfrey. 'One with a prodigious memory, the other with a prodigious member. Both mean trouble, but my Lord Marldon wanted them alive. I've done my duty. Thank you, Brother Michael. Will you turn them over to my keeping?'

'I will, Sir Gilbert.'

'Then the money shall be at St Edmund's as promised.'

He spurred his horse. Blackstone and Richard followed.

Sir Gilbert was riding for Lord Marldon's manor.

The track meandered through the trees: steadfast oaks and great chestnuts. The riders followed the curving river two hundred feet below, turning gently through the bends of the wooded valley. On the far side the grassland on the southern slopes was being harvested by half a dozen men; the occasional shouts of playful insult between them carried up to the riders. Blackstone could not help gauging their distance and the angle of trajectory needed to fly an arrow. It was instinct, something he was blessed with from the early days when his father had given him his first bow. As he grew in strength and ability so the bow became bigger and more difficult to master. His father had taught him the skill of drawing the bowstring by laying his body into the stave; more than an arm's strength was needed to pull the hundred and sixty

15

pounds draw weight and to do it repeatedly. By the time the royal proclamation was issued prohibiting, under pain of imprisonment, all games that drew men away from the butts, Blackstone had already inherited his father's cherished war bow. The ideal height for an archer's lethal weapon, the deadliest killing machine of its age, was four inches taller than the archer, and his father's bow stood six feet and four inches. Blackstone was the firstborn; it was his right to inherit. And, as his father knew, he was a better archer than his brother. His father had spoken gently and at length to explain that his younger son's skills were better than any in the county, except those of Thomas. Yet he asked that every time the brothers competed, Thomas would allow Richard the final arrow of victory. It was the only way the deaf-mute child might find acceptance in the community. Father and elder son shared their secret pact with no one.

Since his father's death, whenever he notched the hemp string over the bow's horned nocks, and wrapped his hand around the stave's four-inch belly, he sensed his father's energy in the bow. It was made of yew; bonded springy sapwood on its outside, the dark, compressible heartwood facing the archer. His mind's eye sometimes imagined the battles his father had fought. A shiver would grip his groin, uncertainty that he would ever have his father's courage if it were demanded. That time now seemed imminent.

Swathes of meadow flowers quilted the distant fields, leading the eye of the observer to the final turn of the river where the turrets of Lord Marldon's manor house appeared above the treetops.

They were in no hurry now and the landscape almost demanded that they slow the horses' pace to a walk. Sir Gilbert hadn't spoken since they left the town and Blackstone saw no reason to make idle conversation. The natural beauty of his surroundings touched something deep inside of him – a gentleness that almost suggested a mother's love. Despite the hardship of their lives his father had always said they were God's children and that nature was their comforter.

Sir Gilbert looked at him, as if reading his thoughts. 'Your mother ruined a good fighting man,' he said. 'She sucked the will to fight from him like marrow from a bone. He gave up war and worked every God's minute to be with her and then raise you and the donkey after she died.' He saw the flash of anger in Blackstone's eyes, but noted the boy's self-control. Once these brothers were sent away from the sanctuary of their own hamlet and surrounding villages, strangers would taunt and Blackstone would have to defend his brother, but he would need a cool head to do it, because the men who would do the taunting knew about killing on a grand scale.

Blackstone let the insult go. 'Why did my father do that?'

Sir Gilbert snorted and spat out a globule of phlegm. 'Because he loved her more than any man should love a woman.'

The road opened before them, the manor's gates came into view. Sir Gilbert spurred his horse.

Blackstone hoped their bad luck was behind them.

Misery was yet to unsheath her infected claws.

Once through the huge, arched entrance gates they dismounted and handed their horses' reins to an ostler. The courtyard seemed alive with servants coming and going as Sir Gilbert went ahead and spoke to Chandler, who gestured them towards the great hall. Blackstone had helped repair its walls and Lord Marldon's bridges, but had never been inside the manor house.

The brothers gazed up at the oak timbers that curved high to the apex of the ceiling. Banners and tapestries hung from the walls and freshly gathered reeds covered the cut stone floor. Two wolfhounds and half a dozen assorted other dogs raised themselves from the front of the massive fireplace where logs burned despite the heat of the day outside. They growled and barked, Sir Gilbert ignored them and they sniffed and settled. Lord Marldon sat close to the fire, his cloak gathered around him, his face gaunt from twenty years of living in pain seldom dulled by the rich red wine from his holdings in Gascony.

Blackstone bowed his head in respect; his brother, a pace behind him, did the same. His lordship gazed at them for a few moments and Blackstone could not help but look at the half-leg that rested on a cushioned support. All that anyone knew was that Lord Marldon had fought in the Scottish wars and a battleaxe had severed his leg at the knee joint. That he had survived was a miracle. The injury had never stopped him riding across his estates, with the half-leg secured to the stirrup straps to keep his balance. Once or twice over the years Blackstone had seen Lord Marldon ride past the Blackstone land and speak quietly to his father.

'You saved them from the hangman, then, Sir Gilbert.'

'He did it himself at the end of the day, my lord.'

Despite being a free man, Blackstone knew Lord Marldon still carried the authority and influence to affect his life. It would do no harm to pay more respect than was obligatory. 'My lord, it is you who saved our lives today. Sir Gilbert told me that you had told my father the value of learning the Psalm of Contrition.'

Lord Marldon laughed. 'Your father was right to devote himself to your well-being. You've intelligence and wit and there's something of your mother's beauty. A boy as good-looking as you are should never pay a woman for her pleasures. Your father would have beaten you. Perhaps I should for the trouble you've caused me.'

'I apologize, my lord. It was not my intention to be arrested,' Blackstone said, and then, risking a rebuke, added, 'and I have never paid, my lord.'

Lord Marldon laughed again. 'I miss your father. Perhaps I should have made myself better acquainted with his son.' The smile gave way to a look of what Blackstone thought to be sadness as he turned his gaze onto his brother. 'At least one who could humour me and answer when spoken to.'

Sir Gilbert had moved away from the fire and stood stroking one of the hounds that sat at his side. Blackstone glanced quickly at him, uncertain how to respond to the remark, but Sir Gilbert showed no expression to indicate that the boy should answer. Blackstone felt he was being tested.

'My lord, my brother is strong, and works long hours, so there is benefit for his lordship in his being without speech. For he labours without complaint.'

'A good answer – but the constant searching of his eyes disturbs me.'

Blackstone touched his brother's shoulder. The boy turned and looked at him and Blackstone raised a finger and touched below his own eye and spread his hand in a calming sign. The boy nodded and remained still.

'You're going to war, Blackstone. King Edward raises an army. Commissioners of array are moving through the land, contracts are being made between knights and men-at-arms and free men must go and serve their King. Sir Gilbert will muster the men from my estates and you will wear my livery.'

The straightforwardness of his lordship's comments took Blackstone by surprise. His whole world was about to change. 'Who will we fight?' was his stumbling response.

'If you paid more attention to the proclamations posted by the sheriff in town you'd know well enough. The King and Parliament have asserted that the French seek to deny him his right of lands in France. War has not yet been declared, but it'll be the French. It always is.'

Blackstone was aware of the rumours over the past months, and of the King's men purchasing grain and livestock, but the thought that he'd be taken and sent to fight had never occurred to him. His daily life was already one of survival.

'You should know, Blackstone, about your father. I gave his family my protection. That was the debt I owed him, and that was all he asked. When that axe took my leg he tied the tourniquet that saved my life. He carried me miles to safety. I was barely conscious. It was he who poured burning pitch on the stump to seal the wound. And I loved him for it. I doubt there was a more loyal sworn man in the realm.'

Blackstone found his voice. 'He never told me.'

'You did not know because he was sworn to silence. To have it known that I favoured your family would have caused greater resentment than that already shown against your brother.'

Blackstone's heart beat harder – it felt like panic – like the time a quarryman ran to tell him of the rockfall. Wild thoughts and terrifying images of his father lying crushed under rock crowded his mind. 'He always honoured you, my lord. He always offered prayers for your safety and long life,' Blackstone replied, feeling the burden of loyalty increasing its weight.

Lord Marldon nodded, his voice softened with genuine affection. 'And I honoured him as I have no other. I made him a free man and whenever the King called his veterans to war I paid his quittance. By arranging a good price for your father's wool I found a way for him to pay for your apprenticeship. When the rockfall took him in the quarry I continued my promise to him and shielded his sons from those who would have their land.'

Blackstone stood as dumbfounded as his silent brother.

'But now you must take your own chances in the world, Thomas. Your King needs you. My life will be over soon and I have done my duty. Now you must do yours.'

Blackstone looked at Sir Gilbert again, and this time he nodded. The lord of the manor was dying. His protection would die with him.

'We'll serve you loyally, my lord, as my father would have done,' Blackstone said.

Lord Marldon shook his head. 'Only you, Thomas. Your brother is of no use in a war. We'll send him to the monks, they can put him to work and protect him from ridicule.'

'The Franciscans care for dumb animals,' Sir Gilbert added.

The younger brother looked startled as Blackstone gripped his arm. 'He can fight. He's the best archer in three counties.'

'And he's fourteen years old, for Christ's sake,' said Sir Gilbert. 'He's deaf and dumb!'

Blackstone laid a hand on Richard's chest, to allay the fear he saw in the boy's face. 'He can hear well enough, Sir Gilbert. My lord, he feels the vibrations of drumbeat and the force of trumpets. The air reverberates with shouts and loud voices. He's worked alongside my father and me since he could walk. No one I know can match his strength. His eyes are as sharp as a bodkin. He looses more arrows a minute than any man I've seen draw a bowcord.'

'Fifteen is the youngest we can send men to war,' Sir Gilbert said roughly, exasperated by Blackstone's insistence.

'I am his guardian, my lord, just as you gave your protection to my father and his sons.' He knew he was running out of argument. 'Look at him. Does he look to be the age he is? By the time the harvest is in, he'll be old enough. He's big enough to be half his age again. Would any man doubt it?'

Lord Marldon and his man-at-arms fell silent for a moment.

'There's not a whisker on his face,' Sir Gilbert said finally.

'And he has goose down on his head,' Blackstone answered. 'Others will take him as he is. Better he endures the mockery of soldiers and has me at his side, than be whipped by monks for not hoeing their carrot patch to their liking.'

Lord Marldon coughed hard and long. Sir Gilbert quickly poured wine into a goblet and held his master's shaking hand, easing it to his lips.

'Sweet Jesus Christ! I wish your father and I could have ended our lives as men should. Not crushed like an ant and eaten alive from within,' wheezed the old warrior. He steadied his breathing. 'Wait outside. I'll make my decision. God bless you, Thomas Blackstone. Always remember who your father was and honour his memory. Go.'

Blackstone bowed his head, his brother did the same.

When the doors closed behind them Lord Marldon wiped the wine-mingled blood from his lip.

'Chandler wants their land and I doubt I'll be able to stop him. Do I send the boy with his brother?'

Sir Gilbert poured wine for himself. 'He's like a bullock. I doubt the rockfall that killed his father would have done the same to him. And I think he's got a temper if it's aroused.' He took a mouthful and wondered if his lord needed to hear his thoughts about Blackstone. There was little choice. Time dictated honesty. 'The oaf's an archer all right, but Blackstone's a lying shit. I've watched from the woods and seen him practise. He's the better man. He can loose enough arrows to kill a small army.'

Lord Marldon's voice was barely a whisper. 'He protects his brother at the cost of his own stature.'

'If the dumb beast is with him then at least he'll slaughter his fair share of poxy Frenchmen. I'd let him go. Why not?' He hesitated. 'But Blackstone? Loosing arrows at a straw target isn't a way to take his measure. He's not a shadow of his father. He has no instinct to kill. He shies away from violence. I doubt he'd manage to kill a suckling pig. There's a weakness in him. Like his mother corrupted his father. I think he'll be dead or a deserter after the first battle.' He swallowed the wine.

Lord Marldon nodded. Henry Blackstone had not beaten the boy enough. Sentiment and love needed to be tempered with unflinching courage in the slaughter of war. How often had he spoken to his sworn man about the boy's gentle nature? His lordship's friend had argued that in addition to the skills of war a nobleman was encouraged to appreciate poetry and the finer things in life; why, then, should a common man not have the same attraction?

'Do what you can. Even the tenderest heart can be turned to war,' Lord Marldon told him. 'And if they are to die, let it be with anger in their blood and love for their King in their hearts.'

CHAPTER TWO

Blackstone and his brother rode with Sir Gilbert and forty other mounted archers wearing Lord Marldon's livery over their russet brown tunics. The surcoats, of a black hawk on a blue field, were faded and bleached from many years of service, and from being beaten against river stones by the estate's washerwomen. Faint, speckled stains could still be seen; blood spots from older battles.

The archers' leather belts held their arrow bags, made of laced waxed linen for protection against moisture – an arrow with wet feathers would not fly straight. The bag was stiffened by withies to keep the arrows separate, which helped protect the goose-feather fletchings. As well as the bag the archers carried a short-bladed bastard sword that cost sixpence in the local town – the cheapest sword men could buy. A long dagger and the archer's bow, carried snugly in its leather case, were their only other weapons. In a small pouch was a spare hemp bowstring, which Blackstone, as his father had taught him, impregnated with beeswax to ward off the damp. Fine thread was kept for repairing damaged fletchings, a leather guard to protect the fingers of the right hand from the bowstring and a brace to cover the inside of the left forearm, the arm that held the bow. Like all archers, the brothers kept their bows unstrung when travelling to reduce the tension in the wood. Each man carried a small haversack for food. They were the lightest-armed and fastest-moving soldiers on the battlefield; and at sixpence a day they were paid twice as much as archers on foot.

Lord Marldon was contracted by the King to supply forty mounted archers and a dozen men-at-arms, all of whom would come under the command of Sir Reginald Cobham, a veteran whose fifty years made him no less able to lead his men from the front.

The invasion fleet being anchored at Portsmouth meant the roads became increasingly congested as supply carts clogged highways already packed with horsemen and infantry. It was near the end of June and the heat and dust made the going seem even slower than it was. Blackstone had never seen so many people or such a hive of activity in his life. There were thousands on the road. Craftsmen, wagoners and soldiers jostled with knights riding palfreys, their pages leading their master's destriers, the powerful war stallions whose unpredictable temperament made them kick out at those crowding them from the rear. Squabbles and short-tempered curses flew between those of equal rank, while the nobles and knights kept a haughty disdain for anyone of lesser stature. Banners, denoting the nobles and knights banneret, fluttered in the freshening breeze. Blackstone knew that a poor knight such as Sir Gilbert was not permitted to display a pennon. Instead, he wore his arms painted on his shield, a black sword, like a crucifix, startling in its clarity against an azure field, the same design repeated on his surcoat. He wanted to be noticed by friend and enemy alike.

Sir Gilbert had spoken little since they set out from the manor house, where the county's archers had gathered. Blackstone knew most of them from the market days and archery competitions. The younger men, gathered from the villages and hamlets, were of mixed humour. Most were ready to serve and take their pay, proud that their lord had provisioned them with horses and weapons. John Nightingale was not much older than Blackstone, and his good humour and stories of a drunken father, a mother who produced a child a year and the girls he had bedded kept the men amused for the day's journey to the coast.

They were mostly men of eighteen and nineteen years of age, though three or four of the men-at-arms were in their mid-twenties and had fought in the Low Countries. Some of the young men's boisterous enthusiasm for the adventure that lay ahead was allowed free rein; the veterans kept to themselves and Sir Gilbert spoke more with them than the others. Blackstone felt the exclusion from their comradeship but did not share the visceral excitement of the younger men. How, he wondered, could he protect his brother in the turmoil that was surely to follow? The quiet, uneventful life they led at home, despite the lack of comfort, gave them a sanctuary of sorts where the world seldom intruded. June was the month for haymaking, a second ploughing and sheep-shearing. Now war had ploughed a deep furrow through their lives.

His brother, by contrast, rode without concern. The sun warmed him and the freshening south-westerly wind played on his face. Released from the daily back- breaking work at the quarry, to him the freedom of riding across the chalk hills with the tantalizing tang of the sea carried on the breeze was elixir. His grunting happiness caused little rebuke from the county men who knew him, but a knight slapped him across the shoulder and told him to stay silent.

Blackstone was uncertain what to do. The man had seniority and Blackstone had no rights to challenge him, but felt compelled to offer some kind of defence for his brother.

'He cannot hear you so when you strike him he has no under-standing.'

'Then perhaps I should strike him harder to give him whatever understanding he needs. Get him to stop that snuffling grunt. It's worse than having a pig on the end of a rope. Though a pig would at least serve a purpose.'

Blackstone could not afford to antagonize a war veteran of senior rank and the nervousness in the pit of his stomach halted any immediate response. Sir Gilbert was riding ahead but he turned on the saddle and looked at Blackstone. It seemed he was waiting to see what Blackstone would dare to say in response.

'His value lies not in his deafness or with him being mute, but in the strength of his bow arm. He will be of great use to a knight on foot facing heavy cavalry.' Blackstone paused and then said respectfully, 'My lord.'

Sir Gilbert nodded and turned away. The boy's father must have told him how, when knights and men-at-arms stood shoulder to shoulder as common infantry in the Scottish wars, facing their enemy's cavalry charge, the English and Welsh archers had slaughtered the Scots. The English army had learnt its lessons from its defeats; bloody experience had taught them the value of the war bow and cloth-yard long arrows with their armour-piercing bodkin heads. It was men like Blackstone's father who had saved men like the arrogant knight in past battles. And similar men who would do so again.

The knight spurred his horse forward. 'Your men border on the insolent, Gilbert.'

'I taught them myself,' Sir Gilbert answered. The disgruntled knight rode on. In that moment Sir Gilbert had spoken for his men; defended them to an outsider. A simple lesson in leadership. Blackstone felt a surge of loyalty towards the impoverished man-at-arms.

As the long day's light began to fade the horsemen crested the high ground behind Portsmouth. Thousands of small fires burned across the hillsides, their smoke drifting on the wind. The lantern-lit armada nestled in the care of the protective harbour. Blackstone had never seen the sea – a vast field of dark water spreading to the horizon. The last of the daylight reflected on the bay showed up the black hulls of hundreds of ships bobbing on the tide. Blackstone drew level with Sir Gilbert who had reined his horse to a halt.

'Sweet Jesus, we must be going to Gascony,' Sir Gilbert said.

Blackstone looked at him, not understanding the significance.

'It's before your eyes, Thomas. Our King must be going to secure his lands in south-west France. There must be five hundred ships down there.'

Blackstone had already quartered the harbour in his mind's eye, broken the scene into accurate measurements – a mason's skill, second nature now. 'More like eight hundred,' he said without thinking that he was contradicting Sir Gilbert, who turned to him, saw his unblinking gaze. Sir Gilbert acknowledged Blackstone's calculation.

'Then eight hundred it is.'

He nudged his horse forward, past some of the thousands of men settling down for the night, towards one banner among the many, a black and white ermine-patterned lion with several small crosses on a red field, that of Sir Reginald Cobham.

An old armourer stood outside the knight's tent beating a steady rhythm with his hammer against a breastplate curved onto an anvil.

'My lord keeps you busy as always, Wilfred,' Sir Gilbert said to the armourer.

'Aye, that he does, Sir Gilbert. How many times have I advised him that the iron from the Weald of Kent is not as strong as that from the Forest of Dean, but he says he likes it well enough and doesn't want to spend the extra money. It's cheaper to have me beatin' out his dents.'

'It's more unusual that any man lives long enough to lay a blade against his armour. Is he inside?'

'That he is,' said the armourer and went back to his work.

The brothers lay on the trampled grass with the other archers in their company. The sea's chill would cramp them by morning, but nothing could dampen their spirits. As Lord Marldon's men cooked their pottage and ate the dried fish issued by one of Sir Reginald's captains, Sir Gilbert beckoned Blackstone and his brother to follow him.

'I'm to talk to the men, make sure we don't have any deserters in the night. Promise them they'll be paid. Warn them who's to fight alongside them.'

'Warn them?' asked Blackstone, keeping up with Sir Gilbert.

'Aye.' He gave no further explanation.

'Then what am I and my brother to do?'

'Nothing. I want these scab-pickers to see who you are and who you're with. I'm doing Lord Marldon's bidding, Blackstone, I can't wet nurse you once we're off those boats.'

They made their way through the campfires until they were close enough to the water's edge. Sir Gilbert turned and faced the men who would share the danger of battle.

'I am your captain, Sir Gilbert Killbere. Some may know of me, those who do not can ask their neighbour.'

A voice called from a group of men somewhere in the distance.

'I was with you at Morlaix, Sir Gilbert! We kicked their arses and slit their bellies then!'

'An archer?' Sir Gilbert called back to the unseen man.

'Will Longdon of Shropshire.'

'I remember you, Will Longdon of Shropshire! I thought the pox had taken you when you deserted with that French whore. Should I warn the men not to share the same spoon in the cooking pot?'

The men laughed.

'Can you still draw a bowcord or is your arm exhausted from self-abuse?' Sir Gilbert asked.

There was more laughter and jeers.

'That and more, Sir Gilbert. Enough to squeeze a French whore's tit.'

'Then, we shall oblige you, Will Longdon – and you know I am a man of my word.'

'I do, sir.'

'Good, because what I tell you now is as if it comes from the King's own lips. Courage will be rewarded, victory will bring more than honour. Your lord, Sir Reginald Cobham, needs no tales embroidered about him. There is no finer nobleman on the field of battle. He's our commander and we will fight with the Prince's division. Us, the Earl of Northampton, Godfrey de Harcourt, marshal of the army, and the Earl of Warwick. We're the vanguard, lads! We'll get to the French bastards first and we'll wallow in their blood!'

There was a raucous cheer. 'And the plunder!' one of the men shouted.

'That's right!' Sir Gilbert shouted back. 'The French like their finery, and they hoard coin like a moneylender. When you come home you'll be living like kings! Though you'll still stink like sons of whores born in a piggery!'

The men laughed and cheered. Ale and a full belly helped, though the food was little more than oats, barley or beans boiled with wild garlic and herbs. Nutritious and light to carry, it was a staple diet. Bread was for those who could afford it and meat only for the nobles.

'There are two men standing with me,' Sir Gilbert said. 'They are archers and I would wager there are few men here who have the strength to draw their bows. This one...' he half turned and pulled Blackstone to his side, '... is Thomas Blackstone who carries his father's war bow. He is guardian of a dumb creature, his brother.' He tugged Richard forward so that now all three men stood shoulder to shoulder in the firelight. Richard's size loomed over them both. 'A creature that God in his wisdom chose to suffer this imperfect creation in silence. Let it be known that these are my sworn men. Any act against them is an act against me.'

The men fell silent. No one jeered or called out against the lumbering, crooked-jawed boy.

'Then it is settled and no more need be said.' He waited a moment before speaking again. 'But one more thing. There's a few thousand spearmen on the other side of that hill. They're to be with us.' He paused, to lend more weight to his words. 'Welsh spearmen.'

Men shouted insults and swore in disapproval.

He raised a hand to settle the men's taunts. 'And I'm told they wouldn't leave home until they'd been paid in full. Let's not forget we're Englishmen. Those bog rats will steal your boots without you knowing it. And if you bend to take them off they'll mount you as if you were black-faced sheep.' The taunt lessened the men's animosity.

'Where are we going, Sir Gilbert?' one of the men called.

'Does it matter?' Sir Gilbert replied. 'You're paid to kill the enemies of the realm. It's at your King's pleasure. I don't know, lads, but I look at the fodder being loaded; I see hundreds of sacks of grain and all the sheaves of arrows and that tells me we are in for a long campaign. I hear there's good, strong wine in Gascony!'

A hard-looking man pulled off his leather cap and rubbed the sweat from his scalp.

'All well and good, Sir Gilbert, but I was in the Low Countries with the King six years ago and his treasury was empty then. He had to borrow money from the locals to pay us archers; he even sent the horses back home to be fed. You think this time will be any different?' he said.

'Don't tread too heavily on my affection for my King,' Sir Gilbert said coldly, his voice a warning that instilled fear without effort. Blackstone felt the threat.

The man yielded. 'I want to get paid for my loyalty is all. I'll spill blood, but I need to feed my household.'

The argument seemed set to deteriorate. Sir Gilbert stepped away from the fire. 'We'll get paid,' he said finally, 'just make sure you earn it. We'll show them what an Englishman can do when he fights for his King! *And* how much booty he can carry!'

'God bless you, Sir Gilbert,' someone shouted, and the cheer went up.

'And you too, lads,' the knight replied.

They moved a few paces from the huddled men, and Blackstone turned to Sir Gilbert. 'Is that what this fight is about? Money?'

'You expected it to be about honour? Chivalry?'

In truth Blackstone didn't know what he thought, but he sensed it was about a wrong being righted. 'Something like that. The King is claiming what's rightfully his or stopping the French King from taking it.'

Sir Gilbert stopped, and looked at the thousands of small fires burning across the hillsides. 'Everyone's here for the money. We all need to be paid. The banks have collapsed, the taxes are high. The King needs a war. I need to fight and find myself a nobleman to ransom, and then I can go home with some wealth. If you survive you go back to your stone quarry, your sheep and pigs, and you'll wait until you're called again, because war is how we live.'

'There has to be some honour. My father saved Lord Marldon.'

'Aye, he did, but that was different; that was about men fighting for each other.'

'Then that's why you're here. To fight for your King.'

Blackstone had touched on Sir Gilbert's honour. The knight chose to ignore him. 'Get some sleep. We board the boats at first light.'

He turned away, leaving Blackstone to gaze across the army. The murmur of fifteen thousand voices drifted upwards like bees swarming on a summer's day. He suddenly realized how frightened he was. Killing would be the order of the day once they landed in France. A pang of sorrow for his home squeezed his throat. 'Dear God, help me to be brave and forgive me for bringing Richard into this. I should have left him at home – in torment, but in safety,' he whispered to the buffeting clouds.

He crossed himself and wished there was a chapel to offer more prayers.

You don't need a chapel when you talk to God, his father had once told him, but Blackstone craved the sanctuary and silence it would offer, away from the crush of bodies, the stench of shit and the rising tide of violence that would soon engulf him.

The wind hissed and shrieked relentlessly through the rigging, drowning out the agonized groans of the men. The round-ships of the English fleet could not sail close to the wind and the strengthening south-westerlies from the Atlantic held them in the choppy Solent for almost two weeks. Confined aboard the rolling tubs, men would have sold their souls as easily to God or the devil if either would give them calmer water, but the torment went on. Vomit sluiced around the decks, drained into holds, ran like a sewer's slick onto the legs of men too ill to move, too far gone to care.

Misery was having its day.

Blackstone could barely lift his head to retch. Whatever food had been in his stomach had long since departed to feed the fishes.

Only one man was unaffected, and he went among the others, carrying them to the ship's side to retch blood and gall, and to hold them to the wind, the spray slapping their faces, helping to keep the next gut-twisting retch at bay. Blackstone, as helpless as the others, as weak as a child, saw his brother, the grunting deaf mute, earn himself the comradeship of men during those days.

And then the wind shifted. The fleet followed the King's flagship the *George* away from the coast and into the Channel. Blackstone stood at the bulwark, his legs steadying him against the pitch and roll of the vessel, his salt-encrusted hair matted like chain mail. The ships' banners, snaking tails of colour, were unfolded. It was a stirring sight, the undertaking of a warrior King taking his army to war. Sir Gilbert spat over the side. He was smiling, looking at the sky, watching the banners. He turned to Blackstone.

'We're not going to Gascony, boy! I can tell you that!' His face shone with a fierce joy. 'I wondered why Godfrey de Harcourt was made a marshal of the army.'

'I don't understand, Sir Gilbert.'

'You're not paid to. Godfrey's a Norman baron with no love for King Philip. Our noble liege is slapping King Philip in the face. We're going to Normandy.'

A day later, on the twelfth of July, the vast fleet filled the horizon as the leading ships swept into the bay of St Vaast la Hogue, their shallow draught allowing them to run easily aground well in to shore. Sir Gilbert had prepared his men and, with Blackstone at his shoulder and Richard a pace behind, splashed ashore at their head. A great roar came from the vanguard of archers and horseless men-at-arms. Blackstone heard himself yelling like the others, spurring himself on. All along the waterline Blackstone saw what must have been a thousand archers pounding across the rippled wet sand towards the hundred and fifty-foot escarpment. But no enemy fire rained down on them. He felt the strength return to his legs, his lungs sucking the energy into them. Everything was so crystal-clear, so bright. Every ship was etched on the sea and every man's surcoat, no matter how dulled, seemed a patch of strident colour.

Blackstone, grinning at the joy of it, turned his head and saw his brother loping effortlessly a pace behind. As they crested the rising ground, a dozen or so levies were running for their lives – fishermen or townspeople, Blackstone didn't know which – but within moments death whispered through the air. The veteran archers had drawn and loosed before Blackstone had even perceived them as a threat.

'Blackstone! Here and here!' Sir Gilbert shouted, pointing to places on the cliff top. 'If it looks like a threat kill it.' He made the same command to another fifty men, placing them in defensive positions.

Nicholas Bray, who commanded the company of archers, spat a curse at him. The climb had taken its toll on the forty-five-year-old centenar's lungs.

'You turd! Sweet mother of God, Blackstone, who's the idiot? You or the donkey? Sir Gilbert'll crack your skull!'

It took a second for Blackstone to realize it was no good facing the bay – the enemy was behind him. The blood rushed to his face, but no one else had noticed the mistake.

'You stay here until you're told otherwise, we'll be moving inland soon enough.'

'Do we get the horses?' Blackstone asked, wanting more than anything to involve himself.

'Horses'll be like mad bastard lunatics after being cooped up on ship for two weeks, 'specially them bloody destriers. They'll gallop 'emselves free of it up and down this goddamn forsaken beach. You can say a prayer of thanks that our Lord King fooled the French. If they'd been waiting for us we'd be crow meat.'

He turned and walked the line of defensive archers, cursing their mothers and blessing their King as he went. Blackstone and his brother did the centenar's bidding. They stayed in their positions and watched for a counter-attack. None came.

Ten yards away John Nightingale called, 'I'll kill more than you and Richard both when I see them!'

'If they don't see you first,' Blackstone told him, aware that the

33

older veterans were casting looks in their direction, aware that none of the village lads had ever been in a battle, other than a tavern fight with the bailiff's men. Nightingale was fiddling with his belt, testing his bow, checking the arrows as he covered his own nervousness.

One of the older men, whose bow was unstrung, squatted next to him.

'Loosen the cord, lad, it'll only take a second to arm yourself if the French try their luck. I doubt we'll spill any blood for a few days yet. Your stave'll thank you for it.'

Blackstone immediately did the same, and nudged his brother to follow his example. The veteran moved to them.

'You lads listen to your centenar. Nicholas is an old soldier and he'll keep you alive as long as he can. You just keep your eyes open, that's all that's asked of you right now.'

Blackstone nodded.

'I'm Elfred. I knew your father,' he said to Blackstone. His voice gave nothing away. He and Blackstone's father could have been either friends or enemies, but before Blackstone could ask, the man moved down the line, talking to old friends, gently advising the new recruits. Nightingale smiled nervously at Blackstone, who turned his attention towards the village and the countryside beyond. Just in case.

The hours passed and ships came and went, there being far too many for the small bay to handle all at once. Blackstone had no idea how big France was, but surely no threat could stand in their way, not with this fleet and these thousands of men.

Chaos reigned on the beachhead: horses galloped uncontrollably as horsemasters tried to gather them; wagons were reassembled, their cargoes loaded; livestock, baggage carts and supplies all needed to be organized, and, slowly but surely and with great skill, they were. As the beachhead cleared Blackstone saw smoke plumes miles inland – towns were burning.

'Infantry got there before us. Welshmen, probably,' said an archer as he relieved himself over the edge of the cliff. His face whiskered from the voyage and cropped hair beneath a leather cap made him seem more gaunt than he was. 'Nothing like a good piss on Frenchie's home turf.' He tied the cords on his hose and moved closer to Blackstone. 'I'm Will Longdon. So, you're Henry's son, eh? And the dumb one as well.'

Blackstone nodded, unwilling to be drawn by the stranger who went down on one knee next to them.

'I knew him. I was about your age when we first went north. He had a name for himself even then. He was a hard bastard, but he looked after the youngsters. He did all right by me anyways.' Longdon examined what he had just picked from his nose, and then flicked it away. 'Is he not with us?'

'He died,' Blackstone told him, not wanting to explain further.

Longdon grunted and scratched his arse. 'I hate boats,' he said by way of reply. 'That's the trouble when you have to invade the Frenchies, y'always have to do it by boat. Why the bloody carpenters can't build a bridge across I don't know. Still, here we are, not drowned or nothing. That's a good start, I always think.'

Blackstone remained silent. His natural suspicion of strangers, especially in safeguarding his brother, made him wary of an uninvited approach.

'We've a bit of a wager going. Me and some of the lads.' He tilted his head, back towards the line of archers defending the cliff top. 'See if I could draw his bow, your father's, given Sir Gilbert seems to think less of us than you two.' His grin exposed broken, brown-stained teeth; his eyebrows questioned Blackstone.

The man seemed to offer no threat so Blackstone stood and bent the stave, hooking the cord onto the horn nock. He handed his bow to the man. He was shorter than Blackstone by a good few inches, and not as broad-shouldered, but his barrel chest and muscular arms suggested he could match the boy's strength without a second thought. Longdon examined the honey-coloured wood. 'This yew came from Italy, I remember him telling us that.' He slid his hands lovingly along the war bow's curve, more tenderly than he had touched any woman. He gave a gentle, testing tug of his fingers on the cord, and then, in a swift, fluid motion, bent his torso into the bow, angled it upwards and pulled back the cord. With a straining arm he got it as far as his chin, hesitated and then eased the bow down. His look of disappointment mingled with uncertainty. He handed the bow back.

'Maybe Sir Gilbert was right after all,' he said.

Blackstone shrugged, not wanting to best a veteran. The other archers were watching.

'Or is he protecting you because of your father's reputation? You and the dumb ox here.' The grin became a sneer. Blackstone turned his back to the man. Richard could see there was trouble brewing but Blackstone's eyes told him to stay back.

'Archers earn their respect, young Blackstone. It's not given just because a fighting knight says so or because of who your father was. You earn it,' he repeated with emphasis.

The challenge could not be ignored, not in front of these men. Blackstone tugged an arrow from the bag, nocked it, turned without a word, drew back the cord to his ear and loosed the arrow in an arc towards a crow perched on the topmost branch of a tree over 150 yards away. It cawed its old-woman croak for a few seconds longer then fell under the arrow strike, the shaft's velocity forcing it right through the bird, which tumbled soundlessly onto the heads of some infantrymen.

The archers jeered at the cursing men.

Longdon spat in his hand and offered it to Blackstone, who took it in his own.

'We'll have to find some black-hooded priests for you to knock off their perches. They croak a lot better 'n that.' He walked back to the others. Richard smiled and grunted at the small victory.

The sense of achievement lasted less than five minutes. Sir Gilbert strode from the village's outlying buildings. Blackstone was about to tell him what had happened but never had the chance. Sir Gilbert struck him hard across the head, the blow so heavy it put Blackstone down onto one knee.

'Stay down! You dog's turd.'

Richard lunged forward but Sir Gilbert suddenly held a dagger in his hand; its point touched the skin beneath the boy's neck, stopping him from taking another step. 'You ever raise a hand to me again, you deformed donkey, and I'll have you dancing from the end of a rope on that damned tree!' He kicked Blackstone hard, sending him sprawling. The knife never wavered. 'Tell him!' the knight demanded.

Blackstone gestured, small signs that the boy understood. His brother stepped back away from the knife point. 'Get up,' Sir Gilbert commanded.

Sir Gilbert sheathed his knife. 'You think I give you my protection so you can sell yourself like a tavern whore? You waste an arrow on damned carrion? I'll take it out of your pay.' Sir Gilbert looked to the other archers. 'Which one of you made the boy use a good shaft that could kill a Frenchman?'

Blackstone wiped the trickle of blood from his face. 'It wasn't them, Sir Gilbert. You were right; I was showing them my father's bow. The fault is mine.'

Sir Gilbert was no fool and he could read his men. 'So, was I right? Can anyone draw that bow other than Henry Blackstone's son?'

Longdon spoke up from the ranks of archers: 'I doubt they could, Sir Gilbert, if anyone were to try.'

'Aye, if anyone were to try.' Sir Gilbert pointed in the direction of the infantrymen beneath the tree. 'Blackstone, send your brother to retrieve the arrow, then follow me.'

He turned his back and moved towards the village. Blackstone sent Richard to do the knight's bidding and then picked up their haversacks and arrow bags. Will Longdon had drawn him into making a stupid mistake of vanity, but Blackstone had learnt the lesson and kept the man's involvement to himself. He was learning. Longdon grinned as Blackstone passed him.

'You'll do all right.'

Blackstone hoped that was true.

CHAPTER THREE

The brothers trudged uphill in silence towards the village of Quettehou, a mile inland from the beachhead. Sir Gilbert spoke only once of the matter as they approached the church of St Vigor.

'You're a free man; behave like one. Those scum may be fighters but they stand in your father's shadow. You're better than they are. Start thinking and behaving like him.'

Blackstone saw heavily armed knights and their retinues, jostling in a flurry of activity. The King had landed at midday, Sir Gilbert told him. And now that they were on Norman soil the royal household and senior commanders gathered to hear him declare his campaign against King Philip VI of France.

'Is that the King?' Blackstone asked, as one of the royal party, whose quality of armour was unmistakable, passed by them in the crowd.

Killbere caught a glimpse of the man. 'Him? That peacock? No, he's Rodolfo Bardi, the King's banker. He's here to make sure the money's well spent.'

Sir Gilbert led them past the crowd to a small door at the side of the church. 'Sheath your bow and tell your brother to keep his grunting silent. He's to stay at this door.'

Blackstone did as he was ordered. Richard sat on the grass, his back against the wall. Blackstone felt a pang of regret at leaving his brother alone, but he had no wish to receive another rebuke from the knight.

Sir Gilbert leaned his shoulder against the heavy oak. It creaked open wide enough for them to ease through. They stood in the cold shadows behind the packed congregation of knights and commanders. Heraldic devices rich in colour, emblazoned on banners, shields, pennons and surcoats, filled the small church. Blackstone had never seen such a gathering, nor even imagined it. The low murmur of voices from the altar could not be heard distinctly, but Blackstone could see the man who stood facing his lords and barons.

'That's your sovereign lord,' Sir Gilbert whispered.

Blackstone felt a surge of excitement – a common man witness to a royal ceremony. The King was in his mid-thirties, about the same age as Sir Gilbert, Blackstone guessed, but he looked magnificent. He was tall, his stature and bearing made even more impressive by his armour and quartered surcoat of three golden lions on a field of red and the scattering of lilies on a field of blue. This was a King ready for war. Even from the back of the crowded church Blackstone caught the tint of blue in his eyes and the light touched his blond beard. A handsome young man bowed his head to the King, then knelt, yielding a sword before him, held like a cross. Blackstone could not hear what was said, but Sir Gilbert whispered again.

'Young nobles are to be knighted. It's good for morale. Makes them slaughter the enemy more.' He smiled. 'Chivalry. Good for killing. That's the King's son. He's the same age as you.'

Blackstone stood on tiptoe to try to see the ceremony. The young man wore the same livery as the King, except for the addition of a horizontal line with three short vertical lines below it. King Edward laid his hands on the boy's head. Chivalry was not dead – it couldn't be; Blackstone just knew it. The King's voice carried. He charged his son to behave with honour and stay loyal to his liege lord. Blackstone heard those words and knew Sir Gilbert must surely be an embittered knight not to believe in the glory that the King stood for.

The Prince of Wales, taller than his father, moved to one side. Blackstone could barely believe that a boy so young could lead the vanguard of the English army even if his guardians were to be the marshals of the army. His sense of awe eased when he remembered his own age. Caring for Richard had made him older than his years.

'Remember these nobles, Blackstone, and their coats of arms. You'll be fighting alongside them sooner or later and you'd best know who you're going to die for – other than me and your King.'

As each young man knelt before his sovereign Sir Gilbert whispered some of their names: *Mortimer, de la Bere, Salisbury, de la Warre.* Then a lame middle-aged noble limped forward, his surcoat of red and gold horizontal bars catching the rays of the July sun through the church's west window. He knelt and did homage to Edward.

'That's Godfrey de Harcourt,' Sir Gilbert said quietly as the Norman baron swore his allegiance and recognized Edward as King of France.

Then lions and lilies unfurled as the King's standard was raised.

'Now we're at war,' Sir Gilbert said and tugged the reluctant Blackstone to the door.

Sir Gilbert was pursuing his duty to Lord Marldon. He hoped that giving Blackstone his protection and then chastising him harshly would teach the boy quickly and help him find the courage needed for what lay ahead.

He took twenty hobelars – light cavalry who looked as if they could ride down wolves – attended by twenty archers, and rode south to scout the land. Sir Gilbert had chosen veterans and half a dozen of Lord Marldon's men to ride on the sortie. Nicholas Bray rode at their head. Norman forces loyal to Philip were light on the Cotentin peninsula, but every step towards the River Seine and Paris, the French capital, would take its toll on Edward's forces. There had already been brief skirmishes with other units and one of the marshals, the Earl of Warwick, had been ambushed, but had fought his way clear. The few hundred retreating French troops would harry and snap at the army's flanks.

And now Edward had made a proclamation that, out of respect for de Harcourt, and to show that these French were Edward's vassals, no Norman manor houses or towns were to be looted or burned. That beggared belief as far as Nicholas Bray and the other veterans were concerned. How was the army to feed itself? How could lowly paid men be kept willing to fight if they could not plunder? Scouring the land was accepted practice. Sir Gilbert knew it was a promise that the King could not keep, and told them so. The army was a disciplined fighting force against any enemy, but villages needed to be looted and burned – that was a fair warning to his King's enemies. This war was not about mercy.

And Blackstone needed to be blooded. For days they rode south, criss-crossing the peninsula. Villages were deserted; some had already been burned by foragers and those that remained Sir Gilbert's men put to the torch. The message was being sent to the French King that the English army was coming. As each day passed the frustration of not engaging with the enemy made Sir Gilbert more bad-tempered than usual. Like all the nobles and knights he craved the joy of battle and the glory and wealth it could bring. The dragging pace of the baggage train kept Edward's main division well behind the vanguard. And thank God for it, Sir Gilbert let it be known. They needed to get their arses out of the confines of this suffocating landscape before the French King brought up his army and trapped them with their backs to the sea. If the Prince of Wales's vanguard of four thousand troops could smash their way through to the cities of St Lô and Caen then they would be on their way to Paris. Sir Gilbert knew the land. He'd irrigated the French soil with his enemies' blood before. That's why he was leading a reconnaissance of pox-scarred, drunken, throat-slitting archers across a godforsaken landscape with nothing but the mocking crows to taunt him. And he told the archers so. Every day.

Blackstone had no idea where he was. The names of places meant nothing to him, nor to most of the others. What he did know was that the expectation of the unknown scared him. They had skirted the marshlands, moving down the narrow tracks between high hedgerows. This *bocage* was the most dangerous terrain and the men were forced to ride close together. A couple of miles to their front the ground rose to the west and then spread out into more open meadows. The burning villages were far behind them and the roving Welsh spearmen and English infantry had not yet reached this far south.

It was Richard who raised the alarm. His guttural cry alerted Sir Gilbert, who turned in the saddle prepared to issue a rebuke, but then he saw the boy explaining to Blackstone what he had seen. He halted the horsemen.

'He saw a man half a mile away push into the hedgerow,' Blackstone explained.

'A peasant?' Sir Gilbert asked.

Blackstone shook his head. 'He wore mail.'

Sir Gilbert looked at Blackstone's brother. 'Tell him if he is wrong I'll have him whipped. I need to move faster.'

'With respect, Sir Gilbert, being dead is as slow as you can go,' Blackstone said. 'If he says he saw a man wearing mail, then that's what he saw.'

Within minutes Sir Gilbert had ordered a plan of attack. Blackstone and the archers dismounted, climbed a high bank and pushed through the hedgerow. The track ahead looped to the left and the hedgerow followed the curved route. An ambush by French troops would be on that bend and the archers would be shielded as they approached their firing position, half-concealed by tall meadow grass and a drainage ditch.

'My life is in your hands,' Sir Gilbert said to Bray and the archers before they scurried away, their bows already strung.

Elfred led the way, crouching as he ran, seeking out the best position: a place that allowed them to kill the enemy without fear of their arrows striking Sir Gilbert and the horsemen. They heard the men continuing their way down the track as they prepared to draw the ambush.

On Bray's silent command the dozen archers spread out a yard apart, nocked an arrow each and waited. Stillness gives a hunter the edge over his prey, but the shadows in the hedgerow, now two hundred yards away, shuffled nervously, readying themselves to strike and so revealing their position. The memory of the men working across the valley on Lord Marldon's estate flashed into Blackstone's mind. That idle game was now a deadly reality.

Blackstone saw a gauntleted arm raised from the greenery, a command to attack about to be given. He raised his bow and, as one, the others followed his lead. Goose-feather fletchings hissed through the air and the yard-long arrows struck home moments before the ambush. Despite the distance the sound of steel-tipped arrows ripping into flesh could be heard by the archers.

The wounded enemy's screams were drowned by the attacking cries of Sir Gilbert's men. Metal clashed, more screams, horses whinnied, half a dozen figures burst from the hedgerow to retreat across the meadows, running for shelter in the woodland five hundred yards away – a distance no retreating man could make when an English archer followed his run. Hemp cords released another flurry of arrows and the helpless men fell, most with two shafts tearing through bone, cartilage and vital organs. Those who did not die instantly would bleed to death within minutes, the shock from the impact of the arrows crippling and fatal. The battle was still being fought on the track. Blackstone broke cover, running instinctively, breathless with excitement mingled with fear, but with a focused certainty that he needed a better firing position. If Sir Gilbert had advanced along the track then he and his men would be in danger from his own archers. Something blurred past his face and one of the Englishmen cried out as a crossbow bolt slammed into his chest. An archer's padded jacket offered insufficient protection against a direct strike.

'Kneel!' yelled Bray. From a dense patch of brambles half a dozen more bolts snapped over their heads; the range was down to a hundred yards. The crossbowmen had placed themselves between brambles and hedgerow, out of sight from an attacking force from the rear. Without conscious thought Blackstone and the others adjusted their bows' angle and loosed a concentrated hail of arrows into the confines of the bramble patch. The enemy's cries of pain ended quickly – the hammer-like force of a shaft striking a body stunned most into breathless pain. Except for the agonized moans of the wounded, the fight was over – the killing had taken less than ten minutes.

Blackstone and the others advanced carefully.

'Bray! Elfred! Blackstone!' Sir Gilbert's voice carried from the other side of the hedges.

'Aye!' Elfred and Bray answered.

'Yes, here, Sir Gilbert,' Blackstone heard himself say. He was gazing down at an old man, the French knight whose gauntlet-covered fist had been raised, ready to trigger the ambush. Blackstone's arrow had taken him through the collarbone into his chest and out of his groin, piercing his chain mail as if it were nothing more than a nightshirt. He lay on his back, his body contorted in a frozen spasm of shock, then death. The blood from his gaping mouth was already buzzing with flies. His jupon of pale apple green with a vivid blue swallow was darkened by the seeping stain. Blackstone couldn't take his eyes from the man's deathly gaze.

Two of Sir Gilbert's soldiers hacked at the hedgerow and then Sir Gilbert himself pushed through the gap. He was grinning. Blood splattered his surcoat and legs.

'We killed a dozen or more,' he said happily. 'Is he one of yours?' he asked, following Blackstone's gaze. Blackstone nodded.

'Well, there's a feather in your cap, lad. Your first kill a knight. A piss-poor one with no arms worth taking, perhaps, but praise God there'll be plenty more. France has the greatest host of knights in the world. They're magnificent fighters, I'll say that for them. Though not so magnificent with a yard of English ash gutting them, eh?' He laughed and touched Blackstone's shoulder. 'Well done, lad.'

Dying men had soiled themselves and the smell of ordure, together with that of copiously spilled blood, mingled into a throat-gagging stench.

Blackstone turned away and vomited.

The men around him laughed.

'First time is the worst time, lad. Get used to it. This is as much glory as you'll see in a battle,' Sir Gilbert said. He raised a flask to his lips and swilled the wine before spitting it out. He unbuckled the dead knight's scabbard and looked at the chipped blade.

'An old sword, older than him, but it has a good balance to it.' Sir Gilbert sheathed it and tossed it to Blackstone.

'Spoils of war. It's better than that bastard toothpick of yours. Attach it to your saddle, but get rid of the scabbard if you fight with it. Damned scabbard is no good to a man on the ground with a sword in his hand, it'll trip you and then you're done for.'

The wounded men in the hedgerow were quickly despatched by the hobelars. 'There's fifteen or more here, I'll wager,' Sir Gilbert said. 'Did we lose anyone?'

'Attewood,' Bray answered, as he unstrung his bow. 'Back there in the field.'

'Well, that's a poor bargain. An English archer for these scum,' said Sir Gilbert.

'Do we bury him, Sir Gilbert?' Elfred asked.

'No time. Foxes and carrion crows will pick his bones. Was he Christian?'

'He never said,' Bray answered.

'Then we'll let God decide. Get his weapons.'

Elfred nodded and turned back towards the fallen archer.

One of the wounded attackers, his lower back pierced by an arrow, was trying to drag himself away through the meadow grass. He muttered words that sounded pitiful to Blackstone – words he did not understand. Sir Gilbert picked up a cumbersome crossbow and tossed it to one side.

'Genoese crossbowmen. They're the best in the world, but not good enough today. Philip's bought himself some mercenaries. If there's half a dozen all the way back here then you can be sure there's another few thousand between us and Paris. Put the man out of his misery, Blackstone, and gather up any arrows you men can use again. Let's be on our way,' Sir Gilbert commanded, and then pushed his way back onto the track. The soldiers followed him.

Bray slit the throat of another wounded man, then turned and looked at Blackstone. 'Come on, lad, we can't let the poor bastard die like that. Use your knife. Quick now. No different than slitting a pig. And he won't squeal as much.'

Blackstone felt another horror squeeze his chest. He took a few uncertain steps towards the crawling man, felt the knife in his hand, though he had no memory of drawing it. He hesitated. It sounded as though the man's pitiful whispers were pleading to God, or to his mother. All Blackstone had to do was reach down, grab a handful of hair, pull back his head and slide the blade across his throat.

His hand was shaking. The arm that had tirelessly wielded a stonemason's hammer for hour after hour, that could pull back a mighty war bow, could not bring itself to sever the man's throat. It trembled like a virgin's body before being loved for the first time. Someone nudged him aside, stepped forward, bent down and with a quick, decisive stroke, killed the wounded man.

Richard wiped the knife blade, put an arm on Blackstone's shoulder and turned his brother towards the road.

They travelled another ten miles without incident. Nightingale chattered like a monkey on a pole, convinced he had killed more in the ambush than even the veterans. He had loosed a dozen arrows and wanted to know from the others if they had seen his targets fall. The veterans ignored him, the local lads argued back, until Bray yelled they'd best be quiet before Sir Gilbert made them ride through the night until they found themselves another scourge of Frenchmen to slaughter. Killing was thirsty work and they needed water and a soft hay barn for themselves. An hour before the light faded in the west, they came to a deserted village. The villagers would have seen smoke drift across the horizon from the torching of other towns and been told by French soldiers to move south towards St Lô and Caen. They carried away as much as they were able, but there were still a few free-running chickens for the taking.

Sir Gilbert and the men penned their horses, posted a sentry and went looking for a place to sleep. There was nothing of value in any of the hovels. The archers, preferring their own company, settled in a barn on the edge of the village where the freshly cut hay's scent reminded Blackstone of home. John Weston foraged and uncovered an apple rack covered in straw. He found what the villagers had left behind, stone jars of cider.

'All right, lads, this is the fruit of the land. We've to keep up our strength for Sir Gilbert, I reckon,' he said as he handed out the jars to the approving men. 'We keep this to ourselves. No need to let the cracked-arsed cavalry know about it.'

By the time darkness nudged away the day, Bray's archers had eaten and settled into the barn's comfort. Nightingale's stories made the archers laugh and his own escapades with village girls caused doubts about such virility. Nightingale put it down to his mother's milk and his father's skill at poaching venison.

Richard watched carefully as Elfred showed him how to repair and clean the arrows used in the ambush. The older man grunted to emphasize each stage of the task, as if Richard would understand more easily. If nothing else, Blackstone thought, his brother was being accepted by the archers.

Sir Gilbert took the best village house for himself, as was his right, but he went among the men before taking his own share of the cooked chickens and eggs.

Blackstone sat away from the others as he ate, his brother cleaning the bodkin arrowheads in between tearing mouthfuls of chicken, oblivious of the grease running down his chin.

Sir Gilbert squatted, fingering the edge of the old knight's sword.

'You need a keener blade than this. Get one of the hobelars to whet it.'

'I can do that myself, Sir Gilbert.'

'So you can. And so you should. There'll come a time when arrows won't be enough and you have to close with the enemy. Elfred and Nicholas told me you did well today. Nicholas said you were the one who moved forward.'

Blackstone shrugged, not wanting special attention above the other archers. 'I could hear you fighting. I knew you'd taken the fight to them.'

Sir Gilbert nodded and stabbed the sword into the ground. 'We could have been in your line of fire if you hadn't moved. It was good thinking.'

Blackstone felt relieved no mention was made of the wounded man, that he was not questioned further. But he also knew that Sir Gilbert's tone had altered. That the killing had raised his status in the knight's eyes.

'Do we know who the men were we killed today?' Blackstone asked.

'I wasn't on friendly terms with them,' Sir Gilbert said, and smiled. He put a stone jug to his lips, the strong Normandy brew cutting across the back of his throat. 'Spies tell us there's five hundred or so under the command of Sir Robert Bertrand, he's the Signeur de Bricquebec. That was one of his raiding parties. He's an old enemy of de Harcourt's. His force is too small to face Edward's thousands, but he'll try to slow our pace by harassment and ambush and by burning bridges across the main rivers until Philip's army gets to us.'

'When will the battle be?' Blackstone asked.

'When our King finds a good place for killing them,' he said.

He handed back the jug and sought out Nicholas Bray. 'You'll post a sentry, Nicholas. We'll leave before dawn, so save that devil's brew for another night.'

'I were going to use it for stripping the rust off this old sword of mine, Sir Gilbert.'

'That's not rust, you blind old bastard, that's dried French blood,' he answered.

'Well, I never, I must've slaughtered more o'them than I thought. You sleep tight in your bed now, Sir Gilbert, and be sure to keep a grip on your own blade,' he said, the crude reference making the men laugh.

'God help the whores when you and Will Longdon press a coin in their hand,' said Sir Gilbert.

'That won't be all being pressed in their hands neither,' Will Longdon told him.

Sir Gilbert gave him a friendly kick. 'Trouble is, Will, the whores will be giving you change from your coin.'

'That's because they feel ashamed for charging a man what gives 'em so much pleasure.'

The men jeered, letting Sir Gilbert return to his men-at-arms. Nicholas Bray pointed a finger. No need for a veteran to lose his sleep.

'Nightingale, that's enough drink. Ready yourself to stand watch.'

The men slept heavily. The sea journey, the hard riding and the ambush had taken their toll. As had the fermented cider that could strip a rat's pelt from its bones when it fell in the vat.

Nightingale felt the injustice of being chosen, but the day's killing still excited him and he knew he probably would not have slept even if he were inside with the snoring men. He would tell of the attack when he rejoined the untested archers who waited back at the coast. The tavern ale would be bought by those who had yet to face the danger. Young lads needed the advice of veteran archers – and that's what he was now. A veteran archer.

He loosened his jerkin and tugged free the stone jar of contraband.

In the early hours before dawn a group of men crept close to the barn. These men were not soldiers, but villagers resentful of the betrayal by some of the Norman barons. They had no weapons to face the English, but they did not wish to succumb without trying to kill at least some of the invading army. They had watched, hidden in nearby orchards, as the horsemen and archers ransacked and occupied their homes. They could not have guessed that the Englishmen would drink so heavily, but that realization came to them as the night wore on. A breeze favoured them as they moved downwind from the horses. The peasants would not dare venture too far into the village for fear of alerting the better armed cavalrymen, who slept close to their mounts, in a farm's courtyard.

The village men saw that the barn's doors were already closed, and only one man stood post, the Englishmen inside secure in the belief that any unlikely attack from armed men could be repulsed between the cavalry and the archers whose positions in the village created a natural ambush for any attacking force. But these villagers were not armed, except with their hatred of the English and the traitor Godfrey de Harcourt. They hesitated. Who among them would be brave enough to sneak up on the sentry and silence him? The question held them fast, none dared risk the confrontation. And then the question was answered for them. The sentry eased himself to his feet from where he had sat, his back propped against the barn planking, and took a few uneasy steps forwards. He had left his bow against the wall. The men looked at each other. The archer was young. And he was drunk.

After a few yards the boy stopped. There was the steady sound of piss hitting the ground. One of the men carried a hoe as a weapon. In a moment of daring he stepped out of the shadows and swung the metal-headed stave against the archer's head. The boy crumpled.

Emboldened by their act the dozen men quietly rolled a haycart across the barn doors to stop any attempt by the men inside to escape, and bundled crisp hay along its length. The high, dry weeds and grass around the old building would do the rest. Without a sound they spread tallow across the main doors. They sparked a flint, and by the time they had reached the safety of the woods, the summer grass and tinder-dry wood were ablaze.

Blackstone was in the depths of a dream. He had cut and laid the cornerstone for Lord Marldon's great hall. The laying ceremony was attended by the King and his son, Edward of Woodstock. The speeches praised the stonemason's skill, promised him wealth and entry to the stonemasons' guild. A great feast and tournament followed. An ox turned on a spit, flesh sizzling, fat dripping. The smoke stung his eyes.

He dragged himself awake. Thick choking smoke filled the barn and fire hungrily licked the walls. Somewhere in the distance behind the crackling sound of the burning wood men shouted and horses whinnied. He was near blind from stinging tears and each breath scoured his throat and lungs, plunging him to his knees in spasms of coughing. Pulling his jacket over his head he reached out blindly, trying to find his brother, but found his own sheathed bow instead. Like a blind beggar he used it to stab the hay around him until it prodded a body. He reached down and felt the man's face. The stubbled jaw told him it was not Richard but he kicked the man time and again until he awoke. Fear quickly sobered him and he stumbled against Blackstone for support.

'The others!' Blackstone yelled from beneath his self-made cowl. 'The others!'

Whoever it was fell to his knees, pulled his jacket across his head like Blackstone, and swept his hands in front of him. The fire took hold and in a great surge clawed towards the roof. The heat would soon kill them, if the building did not collapse first. Blackstone scrambled, felt his brother's crooked face and tried to lift him. But the bulk and weight of the boy was too much even for Blackstone's strength. His hands touched a stone jug. He splashed the fluid into his brother's mouth. The gush of liquid choked him and he sat gasping for breath. Blackstone shook him and the boy reached out, grabbing the lifeline that was his brother.

Three men stumbled into them. They huddled together for a moment, each seeking a way of escape. A farm wagon, hidden in the smoke, rested in the corner of the barn. Fire was already spreading across it, hungry for the tallow that greased its wheel axles. Blackstone pointed – to talk meant inhaling lung-destroying smoke. The cart seemed their only chance. If they could push it hard enough through the burning timber walls they might have a way of breaking out. Burnt straw swirled through the air, the fire's updraught sucking it from the floor as sparks and splintered timbers tumbled from the roof that would soon fall in. The doors of hell had been opened.

They pressed their bodies against the cart, but despite the archers' strength its weight could not be moved. They retreated beneath its broad oak planking. Blackstone covered his mouth with his hand, trying to draw air into his lungs.

'There!' he shouted above the roaring fire. 'That corner!' He pointed. The fire smothered everything, but one corner burned more slowly. 'They made repairs! That's new wood. It's the weakest part!'

There was no time left. He ran at the corner planking, his hair singeing, the heat blistering his face, and threw his shoulder against it. The freshly cut, slower burning wood gave an inch or two. He tried again and this time his brother hurled his bulk against it. The wood nearly splintered away. The other two men began kicking the planks and when Richard shouldered the loosest, it gave.

They burst through the fire into the night. Stumbling and gasping, they dragged each other but then could run no more and fell again, retching from the smoke, eyes streaming. Men ran towards them; Sir Gilbert took one of Blackstone's arms, a horseman the other, soldiers did the same with the other survivors and dragged them to the safety of the trees. Two soldiers ran from a trough carrying buckets and threw water over the choking, smouldering men. The barn collapsed, sending a fireball of sparks pluming high into the darkness.

Blackstone lay on his back. As his eyes cleared, the stars were red, glittering in the firmament, sucking up the dead men's souls. Clutched to his chest, like a priceless prize of war, was his father's war bow. The leather case was singed, but the weapon was unharmed. He needed luck to stay alive, and his superstition was strong enough to know that as long as the war bow remained in his keeping its good fortune would protect him. As dawn broke the smoke-blackened men gazed at the smouldering barn. Their comrades' remains lay indistinguishable from the charred timbers. The survivors drank thirstily, trying to ease their raw throats.

'Sir Gilbert!' one of the hobelars called.

The men turned to see where he pointed. John Nightingale was on all fours crawling from the bushes. His hair was matted with dried blood and he retched vomit into the dirt and over his jerkin. He sank back on his haunches staring blankly at the charnel house that had been a place of safety and laughter for his comrades.

Sir Gilbert strode quickly to him as two of his men hauled Nightingale to his feet. The boy squinted. His sour, dry mouth croaked. 'Water, Sir Gilbert... water. If you please.'

Sir Gilbert gripped the boy's chin. The stench of vomit and stale cider confirmed what he already knew. One of the hobelars picked up the stone bottle and tipped it upside down. It was dry.

'Give him water!' Sir Gilbert commanded, then turned to the survivors. 'Was this man posted as sentry?'

Except for Blackstone's brother, who could not hear the demand, the men averted their eyes.

Sir Gilbert would have none of it. He grabbed Will Longdon roughly. 'Did Bray post this man?' he demanded. Longdon had no choice. He nodded.

Sir Gilbert pushed him back and turned to Nightingale, who drank desperately from a waterskin. Sir Gilbert snatched it away. 'Where's your bow stave and arrow bag? Where's your goddamn sword, you pig shit? And your knife?' The knight's threatening voice was chilling. Blackstone could feel that something terrible was about to happen, something perhaps more terrible than the barn's destruction.

'Get a rope,' Blackstone commanded one of his men.

Blackstone's heart thudded with helplessness.

Nightingale mumbled, his befuddled brain still trying to grasp what had happened.

'Sir Gilbert, I don't know... I went for a piss... I'm sorry,' Nightingale stuttered.

'Fourteen archers dead, Master Bray among them. The King values his bowmen. They are the gold in his crown. And they are dead because you supped too long and hard like a suckling pig on a sow's teat. Men came and took your weapons. Men came and slaughtered my archers! Because of your neglect!'

One of the hobelars had knotted and thrown a rope across the limb of a chestnut tree. Two others dragged Nightingale towards it. The boy struggled.

'Sir Gilbert! I beg you!' He almost broke free, the fear sobering his mind, adding strength to his archer's muscles. One of the hobelars struck him across the back of the head, and as suddenly as he had resisted, he yielded to the inevitable.

'I'm sorry,' he called to the five archers who had not moved. 'I'm sorry, lads. Forgive me.'

His hands were quickly bound. There was no ceremony. The two hobelars hauled on the rope and the kicking, choking boy was dragged into the air.

Sir Gilbert turned away. 'Get the horses!'

Blackstone could not look at the bulging face. Nightingale's swollen tongue turned purple, blood seeped from his eyes, his legs kicked violently, but less so than a moment before.

By the time the men rode past him a few minutes later, the first crow had settled.

No prayers for the dead were said, or needed. The army's priests could pray for departed souls because that was their role. Professional soldiers would spit and curse the devil, swear vengeance against their enemies and say a private prayer of their own in thanks that they still lived – and then share their dead comrade's plunder among themselves. It took the morning to track down the villagers. They ran across the skyline between the saddle of ground that connected two corners of a forest, their silhouetted figures visible from miles away.

The horsemen gave chase and encircled them. One man who carried Nightingale's bow and arrow bag attempted to draw it but managed only to pull it back halfway and the arrow loosed was easily avoided. Fear and panic gripped the peasants. They babbled in French, tears came to their eyes. Sir Gilbert and two of his men-at-arms dismounted and drew their swords. No one spoke. Anger and revenge raised the men's swords and Blackstone watched as the knight and his men clove the Frenchmen's bodies with their war swords.

One man remained. He knelt in supplication before Sir Gilbert. Blackstone watched as his captain indicated the coat of arms on his jupon, and told the man his name. Then he ordered the man to run. At first he hesitated, but when Sir Gilbert raised his sword, he did as commanded.

The warning would race like the barn fire.

The English were coming and Sir Gilbert Killbere would lead the slaughter.

CHAPTER FOUR

Sir Gilbert and his men returned to the vanguard as Edward's army moved relentlessly down the Cotentin peninsula, cutting a swathe seven miles wide across the countryside. Blackstone watched the tide approach across the hills. Like a voracious caterpillar it devoured everything in its path.

Once the vanguard had camped for the night, Sir Gilbert reported to Godfrey de Harcourt and Sir Reginald Cobham. The old knight, with his close-cropped grey hair, was a soldier who would sleep in his armour and share the privations of the common man. When battle commenced Cobham would lead the assault, and the marshal of the army, the pugnacious William de Bohun, Earl of Northampton, would be shouting encouragement to the knight who had fought for years at his side. It was such relish for engaging and defeating the enemy that drove men like these and Sir Gilbert Killbere.

'There'll be no resistance,' Sir Gilbert reported. 'Sporadic attacks like the ambush is all we can expect.'

'We're beyond the peninsula now. We should strike eastwards and attack Caen,' Sir Reginald said. 'The city is like a boil on your arse. It needs lancing.'

The Earl of Northampton scratched two lines in the dirt with his dagger. 'It's the major obstacle in our path towards Paris; the King knows that. Battle has to be joined there before we can move on. We need to cross the Seine and then the Somme, and the devil will task us on that. We can't leave Bertrand's thousands at our backs. On to Caen before he fortifies the place further.'

'St Lô first,' de Harcourt told them.

'Godfrey, there's no point. We all know of your enmity for Bertrand, but he has enough sense to know he can't defend that against us,' Northampton told him.

'If he's there I want the bastard's head on a pole. Three of my friends were butchered there. Their skulls are on the gateway. They were Norman knights who swore fealty to Edward. He'll want his revenge as much as I. St Lô, I say, and then Caen,' de Harcourt insisted.

Sir Reginald looked to the earl. 'Well, it's a rich city. There's wine and cloth for the taking.'

'But it slows the advance!' Northampton argued. 'It's what Bertrand wants. To slow us down. God's teeth! There's a French army coming from the south-west and Philip is moving to cut us off at Rouen. This diversion will cost us more than it's worth.'

'When the King learns of its riches, and the fate of the men loyal to him, he will want St Lô plundered and burned,' the baron replied.

Sir Gilbert stayed silent. He had no definite proof that the French harassing force had gone to defend the rich city. The Earl of Northampton looked to his knight. 'Not much to argue there, Gilbert, but you have an opinion, no doubt. You always have.'

'If I were Bertrand I would abandon St Lô. Sir Reginald is right, it's rich and it's a temptation that's hard to resist, but Bertrand will run like the fox he's proving to be. He won't leave troops there; he'll already be fortifying Caen. St Lô is the bait to keep us wriggling a while longer.'

'But it's a fat worm,' the Earl of Northampton conceded.

The men turned away, but Godfrey de Harcourt caught Sir Gilbert's arm.

'If we are to attack St Lô, there is another matter for you and your men,' he said.

Except for Blackstone, the archers replenished their weapons from the wagonloads of white-painted staves. They tested and drew the hemp cords, discarded one stave in favour of another, until each man was satisfied he had the bow that best suited him. They were made mostly of English ash and elm, fine weapons for any archer, but inferior to Blackstone's yew bow.

The men each took another two dozen arrows in an arrow bag, and readied themselves to ride out again with men chosen by Elfred, who had been made centenar by Sir Gilbert. There was a solemn mood among the survivors of the fire. Comrades had been lost in the barn and Blackstone's friend was a rotting corpse hanging from a broad-leafed chestnut tree. Combat at least offered men the chance to die fighting their enemy, but dying trapped like rats and burned alive was a perverse act of the devil, defying God's will. So God would not help any villagers who found themselves at the archers' mercy – there would be none.

Blackstone was sitting with his brother and Elfred, as Will Longdon cursed the bastard French cowards to the dead men's replacements.

'Blackstone!' Sir Gilbert bellowed.

He got to his feet, gestured for his brother to stay, and walked quickly to his captain, who turned on his heel towards their commanders' banners. The lame de Harcourt watched the young archer as he bowed, but Blackstone's eyes had gone past the Norman. Twenty paces away, talking to Sir Richard Cobham and the Earl of Northampton, was the young Prince of Wales. His pavilion had been pitched and servants scurried, as cooks prepared food. Blackstone's mouth watered, he could not remember when he had last tasted meat. A dozen knights stayed a respectful distance from the Prince, but it was clear they were there to protect the heir to the throne. Now that he was closer than in the church Blackstone could see the boy's fine features more clearly.

'Your captain tells me you have skills; that your father was an archer who married a French woman, and that she was not a whore, and you speak French. And that you have a head on your shoulders,' de Harcourt said.

Blackstone could not help but wonder what accident of birth determined their fate. Perhaps God had his favourites. The boy looked strong, but could he wield a sword for hours on end as Blackstone could swing a mason's hammer? Perhaps too much was being asked of such a young Prince who had yet to prove himself in battle. Perhaps...

Sir Gilbert cuffed him across the back of the head.

'Wake up! My lord speaks to you.' Sir Gilbert grimaced at de Harcourt. 'Apologies, my lord, perhaps I chose badly. His dumb ox of a brother might have been a better choice. His is only a dumb insolence.'

Godfrey de Harcourt ignored him, and stared at Blackstone, who went down on one knee in penance. 'Forgive me, lord.'

'Common men seldom get so close to the King's son. Stand up,' de Harcourt commanded. Blackstone obeyed but kept his eyes averted for fear of appearing impertinent.

'You would serve your Prince?' de Harcourt asked Blackstone. 'Look at me, boy.'

Blackstone looked into the deep brown eyes of a man who was considered by most in France, except for other feudal lords in Normandy, as a traitor.

'I would, lord. With all that I have.'

'And what you have, according to Sir Gilbert, is the ability to use what lies between your ears. And the knowledge of how a fortress is built.'

Blackstone had never cut stone for more than Lord Marldon's manor, but he could read a plan and understand geometric designs. Did that qualify him? Sir Gilbert obviously thought so and to deny it would surely place Sir Gilbert in a poor light.

'I have, my lord.'

'Then you know where a weakness may lie. And how to breach such a place.'

Blackstone was uncertain whether it was a statement or a question, so he simply nodded.

'Then you will ride with Sir Gilbert to Caen. We will scourge St Lô tomorrow, but Bertrand has four thousand men-at-arms with Genoese crossbowmen waiting for us, and a citizenry ready to fight at Caen. If they decide to defend the city then we cannot afford to be held there. I have not seen it since before I was exiled to England. We need your eyes to find the weakest defences. The Prince leads the attack. We must seize the city, but the fortress is impregnable. You will see what is for the taking.'

'I will, Sir Godfrey.'

De Harcourt studied him a moment longer and took a silver shilling from his purse. 'Today is St Christopher's Day. A saint who was strong, simple, kind, and dedicated to one thing – serving his Lord by serving his fellow men. You saved lives in the ambush and at the barn, young Blackstone, because you used your instincts. Or was it your intelligence? We shall see. You have a reward.' He flipped the coin, and Blackstone caught it.

He nodded to Sir Gilbert and turned away.

'Sweet suffering Jesus, you get rewarded for not scratching your arse. Go back to Elfred, tell him to secure food and fresh horses. We've thirty miles ahead of us,' said Sir Gilbert irritably, cursing quietly that he was to be denied a chance of plunder. St Lô was indeed a rich prize. Less deserving men, even common soldiers, would load the baggage wagons with cloth and its citizens' wealth.

'Thank you, Sir Gilbert.'

The knight scowled. 'For what?'

'You must have told the marshal about the ambush.' Blackstone's brother sat with four other men whom Blackstone had not seen before, replacements for the dead archers. They played dice and one of them, a man with a ravaged face from a life of womanizing and drink, and bearing scars from tavern brawls and warfare, grinned his blackened stumps and slapped Blackstone's brother on the shoulder.

'You win again, donkey,' he said, dropping the dice into the leather cup and shaking it in front of the boy's face. 'Can you hear that, you dumb bastard, them's dice waiting for you. Come on, lad.' He rubbed finger and thumb together, wanting Richard to bet.

Blackstone stepped up to the group and touched his brother's head. The boy looked up and grinned, making a grunting noise that indicated excitement and pleasure of being with the men, and of having two silver coins in front of him.

'Let's go,' Blackstone said quietly, gesturing to his brother.

Richard made another unintelligible sound, and picked up the two silver pieces. He was winning, why should he leave?

'We must,' Blackstone insisted, and tugged gently on his brother's sleeve. But the boy pulled away defiantly.

The new men looked up at Blackstone. The one with the black stumped teeth didn't smile when he spoke. 'He's got our money. We want a chance to get it back.'

'You know he can neither hear nor speak. You've let him win, he has nothing to give you other than that.'

'Leave him be. Everyone's been looting. He's got something,' the man snarled.

'No, he hasn't.' Blackstone bent down, grabbed the coins, and tossed them back into the man's lap. Before the man could get to his feet, Richard snatched Blackstone's arm, and catching him off-balance, threw him to the ground. Men scattered, anticipating a fight, and formed a circle around the two archers.

Blackstone was taken by surprise. Richard's weight on his chest winded him. His brother had seldom shown petulance. When he was much younger his father had spent hours calming the boy's rage and frustration. Richard had never attacked him before.

There was no doubt that Richard was the stronger. And for the first time Blackstone saw something in his brother's eyes that frightened him. Anger clouded the boy's thoughts. The caged restraint had been released. Blackstone couldn't shift the weight from his chest and shoulders. His brother nodded and grinned. The spittle dribbled from his malformed jaw. He was the strongest. Perhaps he was the best. The boy looked at those around him and from his silent prison saw men mouthing and shouting, faces twisted, fists clenched, urging him to beat the man beneath him.

Blackstone hadn't moved, deliberately not resisting. His brother's eyes changed as realization cleared the rage. He rolled free, sweeping an arm against the jeering men, as a chained dog lunges at its tormentors. The archers backed away. Blackstone got to his feet. His brother faced him and Blackstone eased him gently away.

'Take your money. Leave him be,' he said to the men.

As the brothers moved towards the horses tethered in the tree-line, Elfred approached the replacements. He had witnessed the confrontation.

'You men ready yourself. Draw salted cod from the supply wagon. Two days' worth. Your name?' he said, pointing at the ravaged man.

'Skinner of Leicester.'

'You'd do well to leave the deaf mute. The boys are brothers. They're Sir Gilbert's sworn men.'

Skinner gathered up his arrow bag and put the coins in a pouch, then spat. 'So what?' he said.

The tears that welled in Richard's eyes were blinked away. Blackstone kept his distance, staying back a few paces as his brother sheathed his new bow, and checked his haversack, then attended to the saddle. How many times had Blackstone wanted to hear words chatter from his brother's throat, like John Nightingale who could tell tales and laugh without a care? No cares now for him, though. He walked to where Richard waited in the shade of the tree. Blackstone reached out and placed his hand on his brother's heart. In a few simple gestures he mimicked a mother cradling a child. He opened the palm of his hand three times. Three times five fingers. He took the shilling from his pouch and gave it to him. It was Richard Blackstone's fifteenth birthday. Blackstone bent forward and kissed his brother on the lips. No greater sign of affection could be offered. His brother was now of the legal age to go to war.

Elfred rode at the head of the archers. Roger Oakley served as ventenar – a sergeant for twenty of the men – and Blackstone and

Richard fell into his company. Sir Gilbert led the hobelars. The small reconnaissance group was the King's eyes. Sir Gilbert would rather have been the King's sword arm. There was little pleasure to be had from burning the abandoned hamlets and villages they came upon. Once the war had passed by, these cob and thatch hovels could be easily replaced and the villagers would return to their miserable existence. The peasants had driven their livestock away from the approaching army, making it more difficult for the horde of men to feed off the land. Where wheat and barley had been gathered, and hay for the livestock, it had been either carted away or burned before the soldiers could take it. Another village was destroyed. There was a surge of horsemen. Skinner came alongside Richard, twirling a burning torch, laughing, encouraging the boy to throw his own. It was only a moment, but Blackstone caught the man's eye before Skinner yanked the horse's head around and galloped away past the burning houses. He knew that the gambler's attempted friendship was a pretence; he was trying to encourage Richard to join him for no other purpose than entertainment. Blackstone had promised his father that Richard would always be at his side, that he would be responsible for him. He was keeping that promise. Warfare brought differing kinds and conditions of men together, and many of those from his own county were dead. These new archers did not share laughter. They were different – like wolves.

A pig squealed, breaking cover. One of the hobelars lowered his lance and pierced its squirming body and although it was only a small pig, it was a prize, and it would feed the hobelars when the others had only salted fish.

Blackstone threw a burning torch into the thatch of one hovel. It was no different from his own village. His sense of regret turned to one of bewilderment. Was it the confidence of being an archer or something more? he wondered. Whatever it was, he knew that if this were his village his bow would be strung and by now half of these twenty men would be dead. He would have fought for his home. And his pig.

* * *

Plumes of smoke blackened the horizon. Every building that lay before the advancing army was burned. The English King wanted his enemies to know that nothing would be spared that stood in his way. The countryside was being stripped bare, the people forced into the cities, to give the French defenders bigger problems to deal with. The Prince's vanguard division had swept through St Lô, and would reach Caen soon after dawn the next day. Sir Gilbert wanted his men fed and ready to fight. No fires would be permitted that night to give away their position. The hobelars may have had pork, but a broadhead arrow the archers used for killing horses in battle brought down a sheep, which Skinner butchered, that being his trade. Fresh mutton instead of the salted fish would do a better job of filling a belly for the fight ahead.

Sir Gilbert took Blackstone forward to within a mile or so of the city on the high ground to the south-east in order to observe where the main resistance from the defenders would be.

'We don't have an army big enough,' Blackstone said when he saw the city walls rising up like cliffs from the marshy ground, bordered by the Orne and with the Odon winding through it. Buttressed walls and towers bristled with armed men; conical-roofed bastions would allow the French to pour crossfire into the English ranks. The English were going to be slaughtered. Those archers who knew had told him that Caen was Normandy's largest city after Rouen; ten thousand people lived there and with Bertrand's army and Genoese crossbowmen it could be a deathtrap for an invading English army. Banners flew from the towers and steeples and from William the Conqueror's fortress, which stood in the northern part of the city. Several of the rivers' channels and adjacent marshland offered defence for the city and its southern suburbs, which, by the look of the houses and gardens, Blackstone took to be the wealthiest area of the city. His eyes searched the city walls for weaknesses, but wherever one existed defenders had dug trenches and erected palisades. The massive castle at the northern end of the city held his eye. He knew that generations of masons would have laboured on it.

'That fortress could not be taken without siege machines,' he said to Sir Gilbert without taking his eyes from the vastness of the city.

'The King won't lay siege – he hasn't the time – but he can't leave a French force to his rear. We have to move north and get across the Seine for Paris. You can be sure the French will have every bridge defended or destroyed. This is where they want to slow us so Philip's army can come from the south.' He flicked a piece of meat from his teeth. 'Then, young Blackstone, we are as skewered as that pig we roasted.'

Blackstone nodded and let his eyes follow the contours of the city's old walls, across the marshlands and the river, to the road that led directly to the bridge that was being heavily fortified.

'It's been a dry summer, the marshland will be low, it should be firm underfoot, and the riverbeds won't carry much water. I don't think you could use horses down there, but men could run across.'

Sir Gilbert followed Blackstone's gaze.

'And hard fighting it'll be as well. But you're right; we could assault them across there. That's the Ile St Jean.' He pointed to the merchant's suburb completely surrounded by the river. 'That's the city's soft underbelly and there's plunder to be had, but that bridge...' He let his words trail away. The bridge that connected the suburb to the city was heavily fortified and barges had been moored and manned by crossbowmen.

For an hour they sat in the shade of a tree and watched the people moving through the streets. Soldiers and men-at-arms had crossed over the bridge and built barriers of overturned wagons, palisades, stacked doors ripped from their hinges and furniture taken from houses. The barbican towers manned by crossbowmen at one end of the stone bridge and the barricade at the other made it impassable. Sir Gilbert made a tutting sound. 'The fools,' was all he said. And then a moment later, 'Tell me what you see.'

Blackstone gazed at the scurrying people below. Soldiers and citizens alike were still barricading the bridge, crossbowmen were clambering aboard barges moored against the riverbank, others had climbed to the upper floors of the houses and lifted the window shutters that allowed them to fire down into the streets.

'They're defending the main bridge to the city and the walls to the east.'

'When you fight a war you choose your ground. Where you fight is as important as how you fight. Look again,' Sir Gilbert told him.

What Blackstone could see was that the biggest obstacle would be to fight through the densely built-up streets. Even though one of the rivers looped around the southern part of the city, and another bisected it, the merchant's houses on the Ile St Jean, with their own strips of land, were definitely the weakest point on the south. If men could get through those streets and across the bridge into the old town in sufficient numbers the city could be taken. But not now. Not with the new defences being put in place. Sir Gilbert picked his teeth, his eyes staying on the sprawling city.

And then Blackstone realized what Sir Gilbert had already seen.

'They're defending the Ile St Jean and the city rather than the fortress. Most of their defences are on that south bridge. If our men get inside the city and attack from behind them they'd be trapped by their own making.' He pointed along the western wall. 'There. A gate in the wall. Do you see it? It's old, the masonry will be crumbling and the gates will splinter. And it's poorly defended. That's the weakest spot in the wall.'

Sir Gilbert stepped further back into the dappled shade where their horses were tethered.

'We'll make a soldier out of a stonescraper yet,' he said.

Blackstone spent the night huddled on the hillside watching thousands of flickering torches, fireflies in the darkness, as the people below prepared to defend their city. He didn't know if they were as frightened as he felt, because the time was coming when he would be face-to-face with the enemy and not killing from a distance. When Sir Gilbert told the men where he thought their attack would be, Blackstone watched their faces. They wanted to kill. Caen was going to give them wealth and women.

The English army had risen and moved before dawn. Three divisions of four thousand men apiece came across the hillsides. Blackstone saw the pennons and banners emerge over the dull grey horizon, the breeze catching the cloth like fluttering birds of prey. The Prince of Wales's vanguard moved towards the northern outskirts, and behind them a swarm of non-combatants swelled the English ranks – wagon drivers, cooks, grooms, blacksmiths and carpenters. They halted well behind the vanguard as if they were another battle division, a deception to make the French think the advancing army was bigger than they had expected. The King's division moved directly in from the west. Thomas Hatfield, soldier and clergyman – he was also the Bishop of Durham – commanded the rear.

Elfred kept Richard at his side as Blackstone rode off with Sir Gilbert to report to Godfrey de Harcourt.

Blackstone felt the trepidation beating in his chest. He was riding directly towards the Prince of Wales and the marshals of the army. Knights in armour, shields and banners bearing coats of arms, their jupons with the cross of St George on their sleeves, a bristling forest of lances held by esquires, thousands of footsoldiers, archers and Welsh spearmen tramped forwards. Blackstone's view was a confusion of gold, scarlet and blue – woven images on surcoats, snorting destriers eager to gallop, scenting the excitement of the warriors – and he wondered how anyone could not fear the approaching horde. The trumpets blared so loudly it seemed they could crumble the city's walls.

'Why do *I* have to speak to Sir Godfrey?' Blackstone asked as they rode closer to the approaching vanguard.

'Because it's not every day a common man from the ranks has the chance to report to a marshal of the English army. He wanted your opinion, he expects you to give it. It'll do you no harm to be noticed. He's a Norman, for Christ's sake, he's as common as you are. Only difference is, he had someone important fornicate with his mother,' Sir Gilbert answered.

'But you saw their defences before I did,' said Blackstone.

'If I've a choice I prefer not to talk to traitors, no matter whose side they fight on,' Sir Gilbert said. He pulled up and waited. A troop of horsemen galloped forward bearing Godfrey de Harcourt's colours of gold and red.

'Well?' the lame baron scowled at the archer. 'Have you found a way to spend my shilling on French whores?'

CHAPTER FIVE

Blackstone ran hard and fast, gulping lungfuls of air, his cheeks smeared with tears of exertion, his grip on his bow so tight that his knuckles ached. He and the other archers had waited for the command to attack, coiled and cursing, desperate to unleash the strength that they held in check – a witch's brew of fear and exultation – as they yearned to surge ahead and strike.

'Hold... hold...' A command had been given from some arse-scratching commander in the background. 'Wait for the trumpets. Wait...'

Better if he had been in the baggage train tethering horses than standing here with men watching their chance to get into the city being denied every moment they waited, while it was being reinforced. You had to be blind not to see the chance that was being lost.

'Hold...'

And then the archers broke free of the command, no longer able to ignore the opportunity. Sir Gilbert's handful of men-at-arms ran with him, chain mail hissing, armour clanking and breath heaving. Welsh spearmen yelled an incoherent cry of defiance and raced them to the gate. Elfred's archers led the way, but after a hundred long strides the centenar raised his arm and stopped their charge, letting the heavier armed men carry through their lines. The archers, following his lead, nocked their arrows, drew cords and sent a withering hail of fire that landed twenty yards ahead of the charging men, slaying defenders, buying Sir Gilbert time to get closer. Then they ran towards the screams and the first clash of steel against shield and spear. Another thirty yards and they fired again. English archers and Welsh spearmen fell as crossbow bolts thudded into their unarmoured bodies. The defence was hard fought and the grunting, heaving sounds of hand-to-hand combat blurred into the vision that Blackstone saw before him. The lightly armoured troops fought savagely against the French men-at-arms. The ferocity of the English and Welsh attack pummelled the defenders back. Men clambered across barricades, Welshmen jabbed their long spears down into the defenders as Sir Gilbert's men wielded sword and axe. They were breaking through. Blackstone recognized men wearing the same surcoats as those who had ambushed them. They leaned across the walls, using every piece of rock and stone as cover, as they cranked their crossbows, loosing the bolts into the attacking men.

Once again Elfred stopped the advance. Blackstone watched him jab a handful of bodkin-pointed shafts into the ground before him. Archers followed his example. A path needed to be cleared. The trajectory was low; the fire had to be rapid.

Through the roar of blood in his ears, Blackstone heard Elfred's command: 'Nock! Mark! Draw! Loose!'

Every archer's hands and body followed the rhythm of the command. Richard was a half-pace behind him and followed Blackstone's actions to the second. Half a dozen more times Elfred called the rate of fire and bodies fell in the path of the men-at-arms.

Then they charged again. Elfred had drawn his long knife and slashed at a man as he clambered across the trenches and barricades. A crossbowman aimed and loosed and the bolt struck a spearman at Elfred's shoulder. Blackstone had drawn, but his brother's arrow loosed first and the Italian defender fell with the shaft through his throat. Blackstone was almost at the barricade. Smoke began to funnel through the narrow streets as soldiers fought their way along the slender passageways, burning the tightly packed houses as they went. And then it was hand-to-hand. Blackstone panicked, forgot he even carried a sword, and struck a French defender in the eye with the horned nock at the tip of his bow. Jabbed, and jabbed again as the man's hands scrabbled for the stave, crying out in agony, but Blackstone was yelling something. A voice within his head echoed others shouting their battle cry: *Saint George! Saint George for King Edward! SAINT GEORGE!* The force bellowing from his lungs powered Blackstone's panic across the writhing man. A surge of bodies carried him forward. His brother was no longer with him. He turned, saw him drawing and releasing an arrow, killing a Frenchman wielding a halberd, and then the fighting and the press of men heaved him out of sight.

A glancing blow caught Blackstone on the side of his head. He tasted blood, faltered, saw the Frenchman bring his sword down from the high guard position, ready to cleave the archer from collarbone to hip. A bloody sword slashed past his face. Someone behind him had lunged a blade into the man's armpit, piercing chain mail and heart. It was an English man-at-arms, his wounded arm lame at his side but his striking arm still swinging his sword. Blackstone looked at the man's visor, could see nothing, but laughed anyway. Laughed at the ferocity, laughed because he was still alive. At the heightened fear.

'Fight on!' the man-at-arms shouted, turning away, slashing left and right, leaving the archer he had just saved.

Alleyways seethed as men-at-arms mingled with spearmen. The French fought with desperate courage; none would yield. Blackstone clambered over another barricade, French fighters still slashing at their attackers. Elfred was already thirty paces ahead; Skinner, Pedloe, Richard Whet, Henry Torpoleye and the others were separated as the defenders drew them into side streets and there stood their ground. Blackstone's scabbard caught in a wicker fortification and he fell headlong just as a sliver of steel slashed past his face. Forgetting Sir Gilbert's advice had saved him. The French man-at-arms had half a dozen men dead at his feet. His helm visor was closed, his armour smeared with English and Welsh blood. His arcing blows kept men dying from his striking rhythm, a smothering close-quarter battle where the man seemed tireless in his killing. He swung his war sword with a relentless efficiency. His splattered surcoat showed a bear in profile against an azure field with a fleur-de-lys in each corner. He was a knight of high standing and he could not yield to anyone of lesser rank. And it was known that archers neither gave nor expected mercy in a fight. Blackstone regained his balance, stepped across savaged bodies, levelled his bow, and drew back. All he needed was a clear shot for one second, a brief moment when the attacking men either fell at the knight's feet or swarmed past him to fight others. The bodkin arrowhead would take the man through his plate armour. No matter how brave his heart, it would not survive a strike from this distance.

A spearman behind Blackstone gasped as a crossbow bolt shattered his face. Gurgling terror spluttered blood across Blackstone's neck as the man's body slumped against him, knocking him off his feet. The arrow flew harmlessly into the side of a smouldering house as flames sought its lath walls. Blackstone regained his foothold and saw the French knight give ground before the press of English footsoldiers, who now fought with axes, knives and maces taken from the dead French. Forced against a wall, he could retreat no further and the Englishmen began to overpower him, like hounds tearing down a stag. Knives and swords stabbed and swung; spears jabbed until they cut his legs from beneath him. Then he went to his knees and they hacked him to death. It was over within seconds. Blackstone spat blood from his mouth and felt an unaccountable despair over the courageous knight's death.

'Richard!' Blackstone shouted, desperate to be heard above the clash of fighting, knowing his brother would never hear his cry, but hoping others would know where the fight had taken him.

Sweat sluiced down his spine; the leather jerkin worn beneath the padded gambeson for added protection felt as clammy as a second skin. He fell into a doorway, tripping over a body. The momentary stillness of the dimly lit passage gave a brief respite from the clamour. The stench of stale urine stung his nostrils. Blackstone steadied himself, trying to cage his fear. A hand reached out and touched his ankle. He twisted around, slamming his back against the wall, knife in hand, ready to strike.

A ruptured cough came from the dying man on the floor. His hose were stained with dark blood from a stomach wound, his vital organs pierced, his death inevitable. A sucking wound in his chest bubbled with frothy blood. The grey-whiskered man was old enough to be his grandfather. His balding head was plastered with wisps of sweat-caked hair and his cap long since discarded or lost. His stave lay broken, hacked by sword blows, his arrow bag, from which fletchings of grey goose feathers protruded, was half-full. The man said something in a language Blackstone could not understand and then he realized he was a Welsh archer, one of those who had attacked with the spearmen. The dying man's grip was fierce and Blackstone yielded to it. He wiped the older man's face, smearing away blood and sweat from his eyes.

'Archer?' the old man whispered in English.

Blackstone nodded.

'The best of men...' the old man smiled, then faltered. 'Kill... the bastards, boy...' He pushed his arrow bag into Blackstone's hands. In that moment his eyes locked onto the young archer's face, read the fear that had still not left him.

'It's nothing ... dying... Don't be afraid. You're an archer... eh?'

'I am,' Blackstone whispered.

'Well then... they're more scared... of you.'

The veteran's bloody teeth were bared in a grin. He tugged a small medallion from around his neck, pressed it to his lips and put it in Blackstone's hand, gripping his own gnarled fist around it. Then his grip slackened and a final bubble of air escaped from his chest wound.

Blackstone looked at the talisman, a simple figure in silver of a woman, captured in a wheel of silver, whose curved arms met above her head. He curled the cord and pushed it into the folds of his jacket, then forced himself back into the street. Infantry and archers fought side by side with spearmen as men-at-arms hacked their way through the retreating pockets of French defenders. Not a yard was given without fierce resistance. Blackstone caught sight of Richard Whet, shielded by a drunken-leaning house's wooden supports as he fired steadily at Genoese crossbowmen in the upper windows. French troops had barricaded the next corner in an attempt to funnel their attackers into the narrow confines of the alleys, where citizens threw tiles and stones down onto them. Bodies littered the street; streams of blood congealed on the cobbles. Half a dozen archers sheltered in whatever cover they could find and brought down defenders, while the infantry and men-at-arms fought pitched battles along the stone-strewn streets. A surge took Blackstone closer to the Earl of Warwick's men as they crashed into the barricade while another group of men pushed along a side street. Every corner was being fought for.

'My brother?' he shouted as Whet took the last arrow from his bag.

'With Skinner and Pedloe. They followed Sir Gilbert.' He pointed down an alleyway, deeply shadowed by the tightly packed buildings. Citizens mixed with soldiers as they defended their homes. A woman shouted abuse as she used a window shutter for a shield while her companion attacked a wounded man on the bloodied cobblestones. Whet's arrow shattered the makeshift shield and the woman fell back, her hands clutching the wound, eyes wild with pain, testament to the shock and power of the shaft's impact.

'I need more arrows, Thomas!'

Blackstone pushed the Welshman's bag into Whet's hands and ran into the alley, an arrow nocked, held by finger and thumb, ready to be drawn and loosed. The narrowness of the street made it difficult to move quickly. He made his way past bodies slumped in doorways and sprawled across the ground, their injuries bearing witness to the brutality of the fighting that had gone before him. The alleyway widened. Smoke swept across the next junction, where knights from the Prince's division fought on foot, shoulder to shoulder with their own infantry – common and noble killing their King's enemies together. Blackstone fired into the defenders, then moved forward, finding deeper shadows to conceal him and thus make less of a target for the crossbowmen who still sent their lethal quarrels down into the street fighting. Whenever a crossbow edged across a rooftop's skyline Blackstone sent an arrow three inches above its crescent, and an Italian mercenary would fall back. Several Genoese had tumbled into the street pierced through the head or throat as he moved position, instinctively seeking cover, denying the crossbowmen a standing target. His desperation to find his brother propelled him through the fighting and his fear.

Men whimpered in pain from hacked flesh, torn sinew and broken bone; the shock of brutal injuries sent them into unconsciousness from which they would never awake. He saw an injured archer, little more than a boy, crawling to safety – his face familiar, his name lost in the mayhem of conflict. A French infantryman lowered his spear to ram it into the injured boy's ribs. Blackstone yelled a warning; the distracted Frenchman turned and Blackstone's arrow took him through his chest. He ran across the street and dragged the archer into a doorway. His screams of pain lessened as Blackstone laid him as gently as he could against the wall.

'Thomas! Thank God! My leg, bind my leg,' the young archer begged. Blackstone tore the red-stained shirt from a dead man and bound the broken leg, using an arrow as a splint. The archer screamed again, forcing his arm into his face, biting into his jacket. Blackstone could do little for him. The archer gulped air. 'Do you have water? God, I'm parched. D'you have any?'

Blackstone was suddenly aware how thirsty he was. 'No. Nothing. Have you seen my brother? He's with Skinner and Pedloe. And Sir Gilbert.'

The archer shook his head, then rested back against the wall. 'Sweet Jesus, this hurts. Find me wine, Thomas – find me something, for God's sake!'

Blackstone glanced back towards the square. The French were retreating. He remembered the boy's name, Alan of Marsh. He was from the next village to his own. His mother was a bondswoman to Lord Marldon. Blackstone fought for her name in his mind in order to offer the boy some comfort, but it eluded him.

'Alan, I'll find us something,' he said and shouldered the half-open door into a darkened room. No one had ransacked it, the fighting having bypassed the small rooms that made up the ground floor of the townhouse. He kicked aside a pallet with its grimy straw mattress, and turned the reed flooring in case there were any hidden cavities in the floorboards that might yield hidden supplies. All he could find were carrots and onions soaking in a bowl of water and a few of last season's apples still mouldering on a rack. He found a small cask, its cork reddened by the contents, but there was no sign of fresh water and the communal well could be anywhere.

Blackstone unplugged the barrel, then slumped in the doorway with the injured boy. The wine would revive him, and the raw onion tasted almost as good as the soggy apple. For a few moments neither archer spoke, exhaustion of battle and the scourge of fear depleting them. Blackstone got to his feet, feeling his leg muscles complain. He had rested too long. He wished he could crawl back inside the darkened room and sleep on the lice-infested mattress, leaving the battle to end when it must.

'I'll come back for you when it's finished,' he said, touching the boy on the shoulder. He unhooked his scabbard and drew the blade for the boy so he might have a weapon. He would be unable to use his bow to defend himself propped against the wall. The wine had eased the boy's pain and thirst, though Blackstone knew that unless a physician could be found his chances of survival would be slender.

'Tell my father and mother, Thomas. When you go home. Tell them I killed more than the others. And give them some plate, there's plunder in every house. Send them something for me, I beg you.'

The boy's parents were peasants – ignorant, superstitious and untrustworthy – and would as soon steal your firewood as kill for a pig. Consumed by superstition, they prayed to spirits of the woods and fields, and the death of their son would prove a curse because he was no longer able to bring in the harvest. But to the wounded archer it was home. Blackstone hesitated. How far adrift must a man be to lose hope?

'I'll come back for you – then you can tell them yourself,' he said.
Hope was everything.

Thousands of men crammed the streets, defenders and their attackers
milled back and forth as informal fighting groups gathered and
attacked each strongpoint that they encountered. Blackstone ran,
searching for his brother, praying not to find his body among the
many that lay in huddled groups. Wherever he found a dead archer
he took his unused arrows, though there were few; the archers had
sold their lives at great cost to the French. Blackstone saw a dozen
Welsh spearmen and as many archers – the Earl of Oxford's; others
showing Cobham's colours. There were none of Blackstone's own
men. Few had more than two or three arrows left.

Blackstone ran among them, seeking out anyone he might
know. By the time he got to their head screams and shouts came
from the other side of the barricade. Men were streaming across
the marshes; Welsh spearmen waded into the river in a suicidal
attack against the barges and the Genoese bowmen. To their rear
English and Welsh archers covered them as best they could, but
the spearmen were being slaughtered. Those on Blackstone's side
of the barricade had no choice – they had to throw themselves at
the French men-at-arms.

Smoke swept across the barbican towers that stood sentinel by
the city gates and the defended bridge. The spearmen gathered at
the edge of a tower's walls. An older man, shoulder-length white
hair tied back with cord, commanded respect, others nodding in
agreement at what he said. There was no choice, they had to attack
the heavily defended barricade at once. Their countrymen on the
other side were going down under the hail of crossbow bolts. The
man looked at Blackstone.

'Can you and your men cover us?' he said.

Blackstone realized that of the archers present his surcoat was
the most bloody and that the head wound sustained at the barricade
had encrusted his hair. He looked as though he had fought through
the worst of it. He nodded.

'As best we can. There's no more than two volleys.'

'Ready yourself,' the Welshman said.

Blackstone turned to the archers without thought that there were veterans in the group. Elfred had shown him the way earlier and these men would follow the regimen of command.

'Nock!' No one questioned.

'Mark!' All obeyed.

'Draw!' The disciplined English killing machine was ready. The stretch of hemp cord and bent yew and ash staves sounded as one.

'Loose!' he cried.

The Welshmen charged.

The French heard their battle cry and turned. A dozen went down from the archers' volley, but others stepped forward and hacked five or six of the men down. Blackstone saw the white-haired soldier thrust at a man-at-arms and then disappear from view as men around him fell beneath savage, hacking blows.

He called the order again and the last of the arrows arched and fell into the armoured men. The Welshmen had killed as many as their own fallen, but wooden-shafted spears could not withstand the cut of axe and sword. The attack might fail. Blackstone secured the bow across his back, feeling the stave press against his spine. A backbone of yew was no bad thing at that moment. He reached for his sword but the scabbard had gone. Then he remembered that he had left it with the wounded archer. All he had was his long knife. He unsheathed it and released the cry that exploded from his chest – and charged into madness.

None of the archers would survive. Except for their knives they were defenceless, and their padded jackets would split like skin once the French men-at-arms struck with sword and axe. The bodies of the dead and dying Welshmen littered the ground, French dead lay beside them, pierced by lance or arrow, and within another twenty paces Blackstone saw the wall of armoured men raise their swords, readying themselves for the easiest killing they would have that day.

Ten paces.

A violent storm of bloodcurdling howls blew at his back.

The black smoke shifted and from the defenders' flank English knights stormed into attack with a ferocity that slowed Blackstone and the archers' charge as the English set about killing their enemy. Steel clashed, shields thudded from blows. One shield took the brunt of an axe blow, its coat of arms declaring the knight's reputation.

'Sir Gilbert!' Blackstone yelled, but the knight was cutting his way through the French with methodical sword strokes as blood spewed and shattered bone pierced muscle. It was a slaughterhouse. One of Warwick's archers overtook Blackstone and leapt on a French man-at-arms hammered to the ground by a mace-wielding Englishman. He threw his weight on the fallen man and with all his strength jabbed his knife through his visor, twisting the blade as blood spurted and the man's legs kicked in agony.

The English were clambering across the barricade from the opposite end of the bridge's defences and suddenly Frenchmen were yielding, down on one knee, offering their swords to their English equals.

English knights blocked the archers from killing more men-at-arms; some of Oxford's men were pulled away moments before ramming their knife blades beneath the knights' helms into their throats.

For a moment the smoke wrapped itself around a dream-like vision as English knights encircled their French hostages, protecting them against their own men.

Caen had fallen.

Sporadic fighting continued all day, and as dusk settled houses still burned. Pockets of resistance remained – citizens and some of Sir Robert Bertrand's soldiers who had survived the main attacks. Bertrand and a couple of hundred men were in the castle and posed no threat to the King's forces. A company of soldiers was placed to ensure the French did not try a counter-attack in the night. By the end of the battle more than a hundred

French knights and men-at-arms, and that number again of esquires, had surrendered to men of equal rank, but the streets were littered with thousands of French dead. The English had proved their courage, especially the archers and infantry, who had fought hand-to-hand against the armoured French. But the wolves tore through the city. No one was safe. No man, woman or child dare contest the rape and plunder. With a ferocity the like of which the citizens of Caen could not even have imagined, English and Welsh soldiers eviscerated their city.

Sir Gilbert had accepted the surrender of a local knight who was taken, along with other captured noblemen, aboard English ships that had sailed up the River Orne on the tide. They would be returned to England and held until their ransoms were paid. The King had issued another proclamation forbidding violence to women and children and the pillaging of churches, but the marshals and captains could not enforce it. There was no protection from looting for the rich merchant houses and the marketplaces. The soldiers needed their spoils of war, and it would serve as a lesson to citizens in other towns not to resist in the future.

Elfred had survived the battle, so too Will Longdon, both bloodied with wounds but remaining steadfast with Sir Gilbert throughout the fighting. Blackstone's brother had been with them most of the way, but Skinner and others had come under fire from crossbowmen and had attacked a street barricade. The fighting had been intense, but it was a rolling battle and the men were separated. Archers were missing from the company and Sir Gilbert sent his men into the streets to find the dead and recall those who were plundering or caught up in the final skirmishes.

Blackstone trudged back through the streets searching for his brother, ignoring the pockets of resistance that still held an alleyway or square. Grime was etched into his skin with blood and dried sweat, and the stench of his own body made him yearn for water to scrape away the day's filth. Every muscle ached and his bow arm felt as though it had been beaten with a mace. Soldiers slept in doorways, others dragged bodies into the streets, stripping them of coin or jewellery. Small groups of men sat drinking looted wine or gorging on bread, eggs and cheese, ravenous after the day's efforts. Whatever meat was found in larders or smokehouses was ignored. It was Wednesday, a fast day when no meat could be consumed, even when men and women could be slaughtered.

Blackstone retraced his steps trying to find the alleyways and streets to take him back to the barricade where he last saw his brother. He came across Alan of Marsh, who still lay in the doorway but whose body had been mutilated, most probably by the town's citizens. The sword was missing, but it was no great loss, it was, after all, a poor knight's sword. A mass grave awaited the boy, but at least he would lie with the other archers. The grim cost of the fighting settled like curdled milk in Blackstone's stomach. It made no difference where a man was buried. Dead was dead and putrid meat would wriggle with maggots once the flies settled.

Charred buildings altered the shape of the streets and his memory faltered. He had taken a wrong turn somewhere and came across a man-at-arms commanding a group of infantrymen piling bodies of French dead in the street, readying them for burial. Blackstone was ordered to help and for the next two hours dragged and stripped corpses, laying them in a row the length of the street. As the soldiers slowed, giving way to their exhaustion, Blackstone slipped down a darkened passageway and made his way to the streets where he had fought. He asked every Englishman he met if they had seen his brother during the fighting. A weary group of Welsh spearmen said they saw the boy's hulk smashing his way down the street behind his captain. The archer was using a polehammer like a scythe. Then another spearman added that he had seen the knight whom he knew to be Sir Gilbert Killbere attack a barricade and swore he had been killed in the fighting. Blackstone said he had survived. The white-haired man who had asked Blackstone for help at the bridge barricade came into the group. He was haggard from battle. The others made room for him. He looked sharply at Blackstone and then extended his hand.

'I am Gruffydd ap Madoc.'

'Thomas Blackstone.'

They talked of the fighting and Blackstone gratefully shared the bread and cheese they offered. He told them about the Welsh archer who had given him courage. He was nameless and the spearmen did not know him either. But from what Blackstone described of the man's wounds they agreed he had fought well. He showed them the medallion the dying man had pressed into his hand.

Gruffydd examined it and laid it back in Blackstone's hand. 'Keep it. The old man wanted you to have it. She's a protector of men in this life and she will carry your soul across to the other side when it's time. She is called Arianrhod, Goddess of the Silver Wheel. It doesn't matter whether you believe it or not. She is with you.'

As the men curled into sleep where they lay, Blackstone went further into the ravaged city. Fires still burned and cries and moans still echoed through the labyrinth of streets. A proclamation was not enough to stop women being raped and their husbands slaughtered. He ignored the rampaging groups of drunken soldiers; they were too dangerous to approach. Blood-lust and rape drove them through house after house. He allowed only a glance at small, frightened children, half naked and snot-nosed, wandering helplessly near their homes, waiting for a mother to return, bewildered by the stench of gutted bodies and howls of anguish from women being ravished.

Rape was a hanging offence – but not that night.

Firelight showed the three-storey house leaning at its threatening angle. This was where crossbowmen had held the streets, and more than a dozen of their bodies littered the cobblestones, all killed by one archer. Blackstone retraced his steps and found Richard Whet twisted in a doorway. The wood was splintered, three crossbow bolts embedded in the hardwood planking. Whet must have come under attack and attempted to retreat and this was where he fought his last. No arrows remained in his bag and the spare arrow bag

Blackstone had given him was also empty. Blackstone saw the bolt in Whet's shoulder that would have disabled him, leaving him barely able to defend himself. What chance of survival did his brother have when so many other archers had been slain?

Blackstone made his way through the shadows, ducking into doorways and stepping over bodies as small marauding gangs of English soldiers ripped their way through the townhouses. Slowly but surely he began to identify the area where he had fought. The surge of emotion from the battle had blurred the streets and buildings, but now his mind focused and he recognized a corner house here, a craftsman's sign there. As he moved towards one of the burning houses hasty footsteps rapidly approached down one of the side alleys. Men were shouting, but they were French voices. From the end of the darkened passage a priest ran as if the devil himself were after him, then tripped over a body that lay sprawled across the cobblestones. The cowled figure tumbled, arms outstretched, falling full-length, hard and painfully, to the ground. Half-stunned by the impact he tried to raise himself, but the three men pursuing him were already upon him. They were armed townsmen and had obviously been part of the city's defence against the English attack, but now they were intent on killing the priest. One of them struck the black-cloaked figure with a pole, the other kicked the huddled body and the third readied himself with a billhook to hack the man to death.

Almost without thought Blackstone pulled an arrow from a body lying less than two paces away. The loosed arrow took the Frenchman down as he was about to decapitate the priest. The other men faltered from the shock of the arrow hissing from the darkness and striking their companion. Blackstone came at them knife in hand. In what seemed an effort to save himself one man shouted something and pointed at the priest. The words came thick and fast but Blackstone recognized only some of them; an accusation that the priest was stealing from the dead. But with less than fifteen paces before he reached them the Frenchmen turned and ran back down the alleyway.

The injured priest groaned, blood on his face, knuckles and hands skinned from the rough cobbles. Blackstone looked quickly around him; if men still fought and killed on the streets he didn't want a sudden attack from the encroaching shadows. He dragged the injured man to the corner of a house.

'All right, Father, you're safe for now. King Edward has offered his protection to the clergy,' he said in faltering French. He bent down and pulled the cowl back from the priest's face, revealing a gaunt man in his twenties. For a moment Blackstone felt a shock of uncertainty, the man's eyes were like dark pools in his skull. Strands of long hair, matted with blood and dank street water, clung to the sides of his face like a cat's claw. The rescued man gave a snort of derision, then pushed himself back against the wall, clasping a clergyman's crucifix around his neck.

'You're English, but you speak French,' he said, wiping blood away from his mouth. He snorted blood and spat. 'I never imagined I would owe my life to a bastard Englishman.'

Being a priest did not necessarily imbue a man with gentleness or gratitude. A benefice could be bought or given. This man's words stank of ill-concealed hatred despite his life being spared. Blackstone pushed a foot into his chest and held him there.

'What's in the sack, priest?' he said.

'A feast,' he answered. *'Benedic nos Domine et haec tua dona.'* His insolent smile suggesting a common archer would not understand, but Blackstone had heard the blessing before and cut the tied bag, spilling its contents into the half-light. Rings and trinkets, stuck together with black, congealed blood, fell onto the cobblestones. Some of the rings were embedded in the skin of engorged fingers hacked from victims' hands. In the moment of uncertainty at what Blackstone saw at his feet, the priest twisted and kicked, freeing himself. Blackstone swung with his knife and caught the man's outstretched palm, severing his little finger, which hung from a shred of skin. Blackstone would have struck again, but the priest was agile and danced away like a soldier avoiding a sword strike. And then he ran without another word or curse.

Blackstone gave chase, slamming into the side of a building, rolling free and propelling himself after the looter. As he jumped across fallen bodies, he snatched another arrow, never taking his eyes from the fleeing shadow as he ran through the twisting darkness. As the cloaked figure reached the heavy studded door of a church he turned and looked back towards his pursuer. Sanctuary was a step away. Blackstone's arrow would have pinned him to that holy place, but it seemed as if the man had a sixth sense. He stepped away as the shaft thudded into the door where he had stood a moment before. Then the door was slammed shut and a bolt thrown. Blackstone put his shoulder to it, but the wood was solid and unyielding. There would be other doors into other passageways. The man was gone. Mutilation of the dead was nothing unusual, but the guise of a priest was cunning. And yet, the man wore a clerical crucifix around his neck and had spoken in Latin, which was a schooled language reserved for the nobility or the clergy. Blackstone decided that it obviously made no difference who you were when there was killing to be done.

Tiredness gnawed at him; he cared little for the body looter, but as he turned back towards the streets a window shattered amidst a woman's screams as men's voices jeered and laughed. It would be another alleyway assault, except for one sound that carried louder than the others and started Blackstone running towards the commotion. The diminishing light from the burning buildings crept far enough towards the end of an alley, fading into darkness ten paces from a house where the glow from torchlight threw grotesque shadows into the street. Blackstone unsheathed his knife and edged into the doorway. In the flickering light three drunken men, half-naked ghosts of pale skin, dried bloodstains and soot grime on face and arms, held a naked woman across a table. One of the men fell spluttering against the wall as he poured red wine from a jug into his mouth and across his face; the second held the woman's arms behind her head as the third slavered over her breasts, pouring wine across them, then slathering his face and tongue as his naked arse plunged back and forth. The man with the wine jug was Pedloe, the one holding the woman's arms was Skinner and the rapist was Richard Blackstone, grunting and baying like a rutting animal. The sound Blackstone had heard.

Blackstone moved quickly out of the darkness and yanked his brother's shoulder. Caught by surprise Richard swept around, his extended arm smashing into Blackstone, the force of the blow sending his knife skittering away. The sudden shock of the attack stunned Skinner and Pedloe, but Blackstone's brother had already turned and leapt upon the intruder, his hands smothering Blackstone's face in the gloom, grappling for his throat. Blackstone could barely see Richard's glazed, drunken eyes, and crying out would have no effect. Blackstone bucked and kicked under his brother's weight as the other men held the woman and peered drunkenly into the shadows trying to identify their assailant.

Blackstone pulled aside his brother's grip and in that instant Richard focused and recognized who it was he was close to killing. Blackstone grabbed his shirtfront, yanked his head down and butted him across the nose. Recognition and sudden pain rocked Richard back. He sprawled, staring at the blood on his hand from his shattered nose. Blackstone was already on his feet as Skinner snarled, threw the woman aside and came at him, his knife held low in a knife-fighter's stance then slashed upwards – a disembowelling stroke. With his stonemason's strength Blackstone grabbed his wrist, defeating even the veteran archer's power. He held him, held him still, forcing him down onto his knees and reached out with his free hand, grasping for a weapon, for anything to stop the writhing man. Skinner's drunkenness gave him the added force to twist free and slash across Blackstone's chest. His padded jacket was slit like a wineskin, only the leather undershirt stopping the blade from reaching his flesh.

Blackstone stumbled backwards, blindly reaching out again, keeping his eyes on the killer as Skinner attacked. His hand found an arrow bag and, as Skinner lunged forward for the kill, Blackstone extended his arm and a bodkin-pointed shaft pierced his attacker's gullet. Skinner gasped and tried to speak, but choked on his blood. He went slowly to his knees, his hands grasping the shaft, his eyes wide with incomprehension, unable to do anything but die. Pedloe, sobered by the fight, reached for his own knife; in two strides he would be at Blackstone's blind side. The shadow that fell across him twisted his head in one violent motion. Blackstone heard the grinding snap from his brother's grip on the man's neck. Pedloe was dead before his body touched the floor. The two archers lay in the pooling blood.

After a moment's silence Blackstone dragged his gaze away from the dead men. 'Get dressed,' he said quietly. His brother stared back. Blackstone gestured and the boy understood. Blackstone knelt next to the woman, who cowered away from him, muttering for mercy. He found her clothes and gently draped them across her nakedness. She flinched as the cloth touched her skin, but then clung to it. Blackstone attempted to wipe the sweat and dirt from her face but she recoiled. He showed her the palm of his hand, to calm her.

'I'm sorry,' he said. She stayed frozen in fear. Blackstone reached for his brother's belt on the floor and opened the pouch. 'I have money,' he said, 'I have money,' he repeated, letting his voice soothe her. His fingers searched for the silver shilling, as his voice and eyes kept trying to calm the terrified woman. He held the coin between finger and thumb and offered it to her. She shook her head. Perhaps she thought that despite the rape he was trying to pay for more sex. He placed it next to her on a stool and stepped back. There was nothing more he could do.

He turned to his brother, who was now dressed, and threw him his belt. As he buckled it around his jacket and gathered his weapons Blackstone saw a looped cord with a small drawstring leather pouch on the floor. He must have snatched it from beneath his brother's shirt in the struggle. He picked it up. He had seen it before. His fingers trembled. He knew this purse. He knew what he would find inside. If there was a God he had to perform a miracle now. He had to make Blackstone be wrong. He had to make the two beads and the three periwinkle shells in the purse disappear. The drawstring purse would never have been parted with freely. It held small treasures given to a village girl by her runaway brother. Gifts that smelled of the sea and beads from a lady's broken bracelet. The promise of another life across a different horizon from her own. A more distant horizon than the corn and rye fields where she lay with men and dreamed of buying her freedom from servitude as a bondswoman.

Blackstone had touched that purse when he lay across her milk-white breasts and caressed their aroused nipples. Sarah Flaxley had been a young man's joy, a girl of easy virtue who cared only that she was loved with a passion that helped ease her loveless life. Drayman had been hanged for the girl's murder. His approval against Richard Blackstone had been thought an act of revenge. He had pleaded innocence of the girl's murder, but had attempted to indict the killer.

Shadows flickered as the tallow lamp burned low. Blackstone looked to his unmoving brother who gazed at the purse with a silent, sickening guilt. He touched his heart, pointed lamely at the purse and touched his lips. He loved her, he said.

Blackstone let the pouch fall to the floor and the shells cracked under his feet as he walked into the night. God had not heard his prayer.

Thousands of other souls needed Him that night.

CHAPTER SIX

The mist was rising slowly from the river when Blackstone found Sir Gilbert sitting beneath the low branches of a tree on the riverbank. The morning light reflected dully on his chain mail draped across a fallen tree trunk, next to his washed undershirt drying on a branch. His sword lay on the ground within arm's reach. Using a piece of linen he swabbed his arms and shoulder, marked by welts and bruises from battle. A slash across the back of his left shoulder and ribs was held by a dozen crude stitches, smeared with a greasy-looking salve. Blackstone held back; he had approached quietly and stood for a moment staring at the man's wounds. Sir Gilbert wrung the linen and spoke without turning.

'You stink like a hog's groin, Blackstone. Either move down-wind or wash yourself.'

Blackstone stepped forward but kept his distance. He squatted at the water's edge, staying silent, embarrassed by his clumsiness at being seen.

'I'm not a goddamn magician. I saw you climb the town walls. If I was a French bowman I could have had a crossbow bolt between your eyes. What do you want? I'm tired.'

'You're wounded,' said Blackstone lamely.

'It barely cut the skin. There's a monastery on the other side of the forest. I had the monks use their dark arts. They have herbs and potions. I don't want any of our bloodletters near me.'

'Elfred told me you were here,' Blackstone said, and scooped water onto his face. He looked across at the ships being loaded with the wealth from Caen. 'We lost a lot of men.'

'You're still alive, that's all you have to be concerned about. Your brother?'

Blackstone nodded.

'He fought well. I saw him. Did you find plunder? There was plenty of gold coin in those houses.'

Blackstone shook his head.

'How do you expect to raise your status if you don't loot? Take what you can and increase your wealth. One day, if you survive the fighting, and when you're older and rheumatism seizes your bow arm, you buy your own men. Then you contract them to the King. His servants have stripped the merchants' houses. What do you think is being loaded onto those ships? How do you think the King makes money?'

'You don't take part in the looting, Sir Gilbert.'

'I don't care for it. Besides, I have a prisoner.'

Blackstone nodded. 'I'll take what I can find.'

Sir Gilbert laughed. 'There's nothing left. The ships will sail back to England, we'll bury the dead and then we'll march on to Paris. We haven't yet fought the battle to win this war.' He wiped his sword's blade, waiting for Blackstone to tell him whatever it was that was clearly bothering him. 'Where's your sword?'

'I gave it to a wounded archer, Alan of Marsh. He needed a weapon. I went back for him but he was dead. They took his bow and the sword.'

'It was yours to give, but a man-at-arms would never gift a sword won in battle – though he might sell it.'

Sir Gilbert's mild chastisement evaporated like the river mist. 'Richard Whet's dead, Torpoleye, Skinner, Pedloe...' said Blackstone quickly, recounting the losses, creeping closer to confession.

'Archers always pay a heavy price when they fight an armoured enemy. We won because we were reckless, stupid bastards who clawed our enemy to death. The King knows that. That's why he loves us. It's why we fight for him.'

'I killed Skinner,' Blackstone said quickly.

Sir Gilbert barely hesitated as he cleaned the blade. 'That must have been some fight. He was a vicious bastard who'd have killed his own mother if there was a coin to be had.'

'He raped a woman,' Blackstone said.

'It's what soldiers do. Was she a whore?'

'No.'

'Then you saved him from the rope,' Sir Gilbert told him. 'Did you kill Pedloe as well?' he asked. 'Nothing kept those two apart.'

Blackstone shook his head.

'Why are you telling me this? What do you expect me to do? Flog you? Have you hanged? Dear Christ, Blackstone, it's goddamn war. Some men deserve to die more than others. I don't give a dog's turd for the likes of Skinner and Pedloe. The army's got plenty of their kind. Go away. I'm not your Father Confessor and I don't want you snivelling about a tavern fight.'

Blackstone tried to keep the secret bottled. 'Sir Gilbert, would you have my brother serve with the baggage train? He'll be safe there.'

'Lose an archer like him? No. And he fights like a lion with a spear up its arse. He stays with the company.'

'I don't want him near me!' Blackstone shouted, and then fell silent, sickened by his outburst.

Sir Gilbert forced the blade into the ground. It stood like a cross. For a few moments he said nothing and then he began to dress, easing the mail onto his battered body over the linen shirt.

'War is a trade, and trade feeds war. Blame the damned sheep if you like,' he said. 'Jesus, Thomas, take that stupid look off your face. Wool from a sheep's back pays for war. We guarantee it to the Flemish for their weavers and they give us loyalty and troops to keep Philip contained in the north. We guarantee it to the Italians who lend your King the money he needs to wage war. We pay for the privilege of fighting. They are agreements.'

'I don't understand what any of that has to do with me or my brother,' Blackstone said.

'Loyalty binds men, Thomas, and Lord Marldon's loyalty to your father ensnares me as well. His lordship promised his friend, your father, that you and your brother would be protected for as long as Lord Marldon lived.'

'By sending us to war?'

'By saving your brother's life. There was a witness.'

Sir Gilbert's words froze the moment. The overhanging branches framed a tapestry of ships' sails unfurling to catch the rising breeze, and a moorhen dipping its head for insects as it padded through shallow reed beds.

'So now you know what he did,' said Sir Gilbert.

'A witness?' The question was unnecessary, but it escaped Blackstone's lips. He shook his head, not comprehending that others knew what had happened. 'Chandler. Lord Marldon's reeve. He saw your brother that day. You worked at the manor, Richard was at the quarry, but not all day. He went to Sarah Flaxley, saw Drayman leave her. He killed her, whether he intended to or not, and Chandler traded his silence for your land. Lord Marldon would have slain him, but he's his reeve and is as sly as a stoat. Who was to say he had not secured that information elsewhere? In time Lord Marldon will discover whether he did or not, and Chandler will be found with his throat slit outside an alehouse.'

Sir Gilbert buckled his sword and picked up his bascinet. 'A man's loyalty and honour determine who he is in this godforsaken world. And your lord honoured his promise to your father. It was a trade. A piss-poor one in my opinion, but a trade it was.'

He stepped away from Blackstone.

'Your brother stays in the company of archers. And Thomas, never relinquish a sword if it's won in battle.'

It seemed to Blackstone that his father's action all those years ago in saving Lord Marldon's life had bound them all together. He was obliged to care for his brother and had he not also given his word to Lord Marldon? For Blackstone to break that chain of promise and honour would mean the end of – what? He didn't know and it was something that gnawed away at him. Honour had become too tenuous, an ideal that had seemed binding, but was lost when the slaughter began. Was not the honour broken when his brother strangled Sarah Flaxley? The image of it still sickened him. His mind imagined the scene, and despite the carnage of the battle at Caen, his brother's act of violent passion was the one that haunted his dreams. He banished Richard to walk as far behind him as possible. No longer did he want him at his shoulder. A part of him wished his brother had perished in the battle, then Blackstone would not have known of his crime and he would have died innocent.

The army lingered five days in Caen. A vast communal grave was dug in the churchyard of Ile St-Jean, and they buried five hundred Frenchmen, but there were so many bodies in the city they could not be counted – some said it was as many as five thousand. For days the rivers carried bodies out to sea on the tide. Of the English knights or men-at-arms only one had died, but the infantry and the archers who led the assault, and whose courage won the day, lost many of their number. The King sent orders to England to raise another twelve hundred archers and supply six thousand sheaves of arrows. The fortress, as Blackstone had predicted, proved impregnable and a contingent of men was left to contain Sir Godfrey's old enemy, Bertrand, and the few hundred who remained behind its walls. Time, and the French force from the south, was closing in on the English King. If the spies' reports were to be believed, King Philip rallied his army in Rouen. The English were being squeezed between river and coast. If this war was to be won Edward had to outrun the French and choose his ground. When the King attended to his prayers before each daybreak he, like his common archer Thomas Blackstone, needed a simple miracle – a bridge left intact across the Seine.

And once again God had other prayers to answer.

The army moved eastwards, scorching the land as it went. Towns-folk, villagers and villeins, knowing that the great city of Caen had fallen, fled before it. They took their livestock and food, leaving nothing for the English army. Skirmishes along the way slowed the army's advance, but the vanguard division pushed on relentlessly, desperate to find a way of crossing the Seine. King Edward's small army had been depleted by death and injury, disease and desertion; he now had fewer than thirteen thousand men to fight the French army, which had at least twice as many. Slowed by the baggage wagons, the English made only thirty miles in three days. Keeping the carts and wagons moving across the marshland and difficult, undulating terrain made huge demands on muscle and stamina. The commanders knew that they could not increase the pace without diminishing the army's fighting capabilities. Horses and men were tiring. A knight's mount carried its rider, his armour and weapons – up to three hundred pounds of weight – day in and day out. Fodder and water were crucial. The troops scavenged what little remained from the countryside, but the bread was exhausted and foraged mutton gave insufficient strength to a fighting man. Soldiers needed that and their diet of pease, grain porridge and bread to give them the stamina for battle.

The great looping bends of the lower Seine curled across a broad valley, but no crossing had been found. Paris taunted the English King. He was within twenty miles of the capital, and from the high ground Edward could look across the five bends of the Seine and see the city's towers. The French King had bottled up his enemy on the opposite bank. Outnumbered and outflanked, Edward's army could soon die with their backs to the sea and leave the gates of England open for the invasion the French had always desired and planned.

Now not only the King's survival but also that of his nation were at stake.

Godfrey de Harcourt rode south with archers and men-at-arms, following the course of the Seine. This was countryside familiar to de Harcourt, since the territory belonged to his brother, the count, and their ancestral home, the Castle de Harcourt, lay a few miles to the south-east. No bridge across the river remained intact and by now his scouting party was close to the great city of Rouen where, if the rumours were to be believed, the King of France had gathered his army in readiness to stop Edward's advance. Marshals of the English army had been charged with finding either a bridge that could be attacked and taken, or a crossing that the French had left intact. No crossing had yet been found. Those bridges that remained were heavily defended from towers on the enemy's side of the river. Skirmishes against them ended in failure. The French King had anticipated Edward's advance and, by denying him access across the Seine, also denied him the chance to attack Paris. The French would drive the English northwards and trap them between river and coast.

As the sun climbed higher the tireless de Harcourt drove the men onward through wooded valleys and over gentle hills until they reached a wide track cut through the forest. It led to a clearing and a stone-built castle, whose rounded towers and battlements occupied a dominant position. Its wide, deep outer moat would make a direct attack difficult and its second one, crescent shaped that hugged the inner walls, would probably drown any attackers who survived the other defences. However, to attack was not the purpose for which Godfrey de Harcourt had swung away from the Seine. Sir Gilbert and his men waited in the trees for orders. The Norman rode with half a dozen of his knights around the perimeter. There were no defenders on the walls and the narrow wooden bridge across its fosse, broad enough for a wagon to pass through the wall's iron-studded gates, was intact.

'Thing is, with a place like this, it can be very tricky to get inside, if that's what Sir Godfrey's planning,' muttered John Weston, examining dust-clogged snot on the end of his finger. 'No scaling ladders, no siege engines. Just thee and me and a few cracked-arsed hobelars. And if he's a mind to ride across yonder bridge and knock on the door he'll either get a cauldron of boiling oil or a piss pot tipped on his noble head. So if anyone asks for volunteers I'll be taking a shit behind that tree.'

'Shut up,' Sir Gilbert told him. 'And you'll take a shit when I tell you, you goddamned boil on the backside of humanity.'

Elfred and the others smiled at Weston who, by way of revenge, shifted in his saddle and farted. 'That could crumble some of them fine stone walls,' he muttered. 'Oh, hello, he's sent a poor sod to knock on the door.'

The men watched as a squire rode forward from the gathered knights. The hollow thud of hooves on wood echoed up to the men waiting in the coolness of the trees.

Weston kept a murmured commentary going. 'Anyone home? We were just passing and wondered if you had any virgins who might need some attention. Not that anyone has the energy right now, not after grinding our arses on swayback nags for thirty miles.'

The herald called for the gates to be opened, citing de Harcourt's name. There was silence. Even from where they sat in the trees Blackstone could see de Harcourt's irritation, which was not contained for long. He bellowed, 'In the name of Christ! Open the gates or I will burn them through.'

'Those are iron-clad gates. We'll be here for some time,' Blackstone said quietly. 'Whoever built that castle knew what they were doing. Conical towers each side of the entrance. Half a dozen side towers on the outer wall. Good field of fire from those loopholes. See how the cut stone supports the archway? The iron hinges are concealed. Windows to the side are a weak spot, but you'd need to get across the fosse. Good builders.'

'They should surrender,' Elfred agreed.

'They must know the rules of war,' Will Longdon said.

'Cling-shit peasants,' John Weston said, spitting in disgust.

'Do I have to sit and listen to your babble?' Sir Gilbert said, turning in the saddle. 'You damned washerwomen could wear a threshing stone down with your talk.' He spurred his horse forward. 'With me!'

The four men followed Sir Gilbert down to where de Harcourt waited for a response from those inside the castle.

'My lord, there's an old boat tied at the bank. We could put three or four men across and let them try that lower window.'

Longdon and Weston looked sourly at Blackstone.

'There's no defence. Whoever's inside has no stomach for a fight,' Sir Gilbert said finally.

De Harcourt nodded. 'Choose your men. Make it plain; no harm to those inside. My nephew's wife is in there. Perhaps with some of his men. Kill only in self-defence.' He turned his horse away and rode to the sheltering trees.

Sir Gilbert looked at Blackstone and the men around him – Blackstone's brother, Longdon and Weston. 'You heard his lordship. Get inside and open the gates. And don't take all day.'

The men crawled through the forest until they could slip down the bank unseen and release the boat's painter. The moat was sixty feet wide and probably as deep. Will Longdon rowed and John Weston moaned. Once they eased along the wall Blackstone palmed the wall until they were below the window, twelve feet or so above them.

'Can you hold it steady? I don't want to end up in the fosse. There's a depth to it and the banks are steep.'

'We'll hold it,' Weston said. 'Just don't tip us over. I can't swim. I'd go down like a stone.'

He and Longdon steadied the boat as Blackstone showed his brother what he wanted. How many times had they reached up into a tree for a wild beehive and scooped out the combs? Speed was the key, and the stings would be few. Blackstone hoped no crossbowmen's bites awaited him inside. His brother braced his feet and leaned onto the wall. Blackstone climbed from his thigh to his shoulder and balanced. The boat rocked.

'Steady, you dumb ox,' Weston muttered as Richard's weight shifted. Blackstone stretched as high as he could, his fingertips found the mullion, and then his brother took his feet and lifted him higher. The boy's strength held as Blackstone clambered through the opening.

He tipped into a big room with chestnut beams. The smooth walls were three feet thick, and as he crawled through he saw de

Harcourt's coat of arms, once painted onto damp plaster, but now faded. A cut-stone surround boxed in a soot-laden fireplace. There was a table and chairs turned over, and a worn carpet that lay across the flagstone floor had been pulled back. This had to be a room where the nobility had sat and eaten, but where someone had scavenged. A wooden chest lay on its side, its contents looted, probably silver plate, Blackstone thought as he went to the door and eased it open. Stone steps went up one way to the next storey and on the other turned down into a shadowed passage. He went back to the window and beckoned Longdon and Weston. They tried to climb as Blackstone had done, but it needed two men to hold the boat steady. They came close to tipping.

'We can't,' Will Longdon told him. 'Come back down, Thomas, we can't get men inside.'

Blackstone leaned over the sill. He gestured to Richard.

'I'll see what I can find out,' he called down. 'Wait for me.'

'Wait?' John Weston asked. 'Wait how long? There could be Genoese bastards in there as we speak, hiding in the damned shadows.'

'If I don't come back by the time you've imagined fashioning a bodkin onto a shaft and fletched it, then tell Sir Gilbert we need more men.' He ducked out of sight.

'Now he thinks I'm a damned bowyer and fletcher as well as boatman. Hey, hey...' he tugged at Richard's sleeve. 'Sit down. Down.' He gestured. 'And whatever you do, don't move.' He smiled at the scowling boy. 'If you please,' he added.

Blackstone had already gone from the window. He nocked an arrow and stepped onto the half-landing outside the doors. He decided to climb higher; that way he might have the advantage if armed men waited in ambush below in the castle's bailey.

Light streamed down from an upper terrace. He tried to remember Lord Marldon's fortified manor. It did not have the grandeur or scale of this castle but he guessed French nobles would live like their English cousins, who had, after all, inherited much of the results of Norman castle building. He stepped warily, knowing the rising steps would impede his drawing the bow fully.

The steps opened out into a broad walkway with rectangular-cut windows that allowed him to look down across the horseshoe-shaped bailey, which was big enough to hold all of Sir Godfrey's raiding party twice over and still have room for horses and livestock. But now it held shadows pressed tight against the rough stone walls. The darkened shapes were armed men.

Blackstone stepped back quickly. He edged to the corner and looked down on the men. They were unmoving. He reasoned they were disciplined but were not de Harcourt's nephew's men. They were deserters or mercenaries who wore no collective surcoats or garb. Around to one side he could see a dozen or more bodies. Bloodied, they had been thrown into the corner of the yard. By the look of their dress they were servants. Blackstone calculated that he could kill at least a dozen of the thirty or so men, and then what? He would still be unable to reach the gate and open it and the men would soon co-ordinate an attack and kill him. Best to slip away and report to Sir Godfrey. He pressed against the wall and ran quickly back the way he had come. As he turned in at the door he saw a movement at the turn of the stairs. A hand had moved in the shadow. Blackstone ran down the remaining steps until he reached the join between the walls. It was a narrow chasm in the rough-hewn stone, barely wide enough for a slender child to enter.

'Help me,' a girl's voice whispered.

Blackstone overcame his uncertainty and reached into the gap. His arm felt that of the girl and he pulled her gently towards him. She was scraped and bruised, her cloak covered in lime dust from the walls. She was small, with delicate features, and as she came closer to him he saw that her eyes were green and her hair the colour of a broadleaf in autumn. As she eased into the stairwell, her weakness made her stagger against the wall. But she raised a hand to ward off Blackstone's help.

'English?' she asked quietly, glancing down the stairs, afraid the intruders might hear even a gentle whisper.

Blackstone nodded.

'I heard Sir Godfrey's voice. You are with him?'

'Yes.'

'Can you take me to him?'

Again she glanced down the stairs and Blackstone extended his arm to her.

'Let me help you.'

She hesitated, the sight of the dishevelled archer a barrier to overcome. His hand had not wavered but she refused to take it. She shook her head. 'Show me,' was all she said.

Blackstone turned away. It was up to her whether she decided to follow him. As he reached the window he sensed she was only a few steps away. She stood in the middle of the room, caught between that which she knew to be fatal behind her and the chance of escape with men who could cause her as much harm.

Blackstone leaned across the sill. The boat was still there.

'Will,' he called softly, raising a hand to warn of the danger. Will Longdon and Weston looked up, uncertainty creasing their faces. Richard followed their gaze, a lopsided grin when he saw his brother. 'Armed men inside,' Blackstone said. 'Servants are butchered. There's a girl. Wait.' He ducked back from the opening.

Weston wobbled the boat in his anxiety. 'A girl!' he hissed. 'Christ! Tom, leave her!' But Blackstone had gone from view.

The girl looked at him. She had not moved, deciding which action might be the less fearful. Blackstone once again extended his arm. She shook her head. 'I cannot swim,' she said.

'You don't have to,' he assured her. Still she hesitated. 'I can't wait. If you want to see Sir Godfrey you have to trust me. And you must stay silent. My brother is in the boat. Don't let his disfigurement frighten you.'

She took his hand and in a quick movement Blackstone lifted her and swung her across the opening. She clenched her jaw, squeezing her eyes closed, and let him swing her out quickly. Her weight caused him no difficulty and he reached down, lowering her into his brother's waiting arms as Longdon and a cursing Weston steadied the boat.

The three men stared at her as she sat in the bow. None of them had been so close to a woman with such delicate features or soft-shaded hair. 'Sweet Jesus,' Weston muttered. 'My lady...' he added. For once words failed him.

'Will!'

They looked up. Blackstone was clambering down and needed his brother's shoulders. Longdon steadied Richard as Blackstone eased himself down the wall.

John Weston shipped the oars, eager to pull away. 'How many men?'

'Two dozen or more,' Blackstone said.

'I'd wager a couple more of us in there and we'd have taken them,' Longdon said, turning back to watch the empty window.

'Like killing ducks on a pond, Will. But they were too many for one man and they'd have got to me and you'd have been examining the bottom of this moat with your dying gaze,' Blackstone told him. They bumped into the bank. The men jumped clear, Blackstone's brother extended his hand to help the girl, but she turned to Blackstone and put out her hand to him.

Her name was Christiana; she was sixteen years old and served her mistress, Countess Blanche de Ponthieu, wife of John V de Harcourt, Sir Godfrey's nephew.

'Where is your mistress?' Godfrey de Harcourt asked her.

'When she heard the English were trying to cross the Seine she feared for her mother. She's gone to Noyelles, my lord,' Christiana answered.

Years of family tension gnawed away at de Harcourt. For the first time Blackstone saw him ease his lame leg. 'Courage was never her problem. My nephew married a headstrong woman, there's no denying that. And these men?'

'Villagers came and asked us for protection. It was a trick. When we opened the gates they attacked. They killed everyone. There are more bodies this young archer never saw. I have been hiding for two days.'

Sir Godfrey showed a tenderness towards the girl that no man under his command would ever experience. 'We will take you to the English. For now you are safe. What about my brother and my nephew?'

'They took their men-at-arms and joined the King's forces. More than a week ago.'

'At Rouen?'

She nodded.

'Is there a crossing?'

'How would I know, my lord? I am only in service to my lady,' Christiana answered.

'Of course,' said de Harcourt. Her unwavering voice made it clear that if she knew of such a crossing she would not betray it to the English, or those fighting with them, even though they now offered her sanctuary. He acknowledged Blackstone.

'You did well. Stay with her.'

'My lord.' Obeying Sir Godfrey he ushered Christiana into the forest where the horses were tethered as the other men were called forward by Sir Gilbert. He settled her on dry bracken and found her wine and bread with salted cod. She had not eaten since hiding from the killers, but she ate carefully and without haste. Blackstone knew that he would have been like a ravening wolf. He sat in the dappled shade, watching her whenever she looked away. This was one fight he was happy to miss. Minutes later Elfred and the archers filtered back into the trees.

'You lucky bastard,' Will Longdon said as he unsheathed his bow. 'We've to be awake in the treeline and kill these scum while you snuggle up to the princess here.'

'You make sure your bow stays sheathed,' John Weston said, with a toothless grin.

Elfred walked through the trees. 'Thomas, you're to stay with the girl. Shall I leave Richard with you?'

Blackstone hesitated, then shook his head. 'Keep him at your shoulder, Elfred. He trusts you.'

'He don't want his baby brother hanging around here tonight, do you, my lad?' Weston said, leering at the girl who was facing the other way.

'John, I hope your eyes stop watering before you have to draw your bow. I'll think of you sitting cramped with your arse in nettles while I'm tucked up here, protecting the lady,' Blackstone told him with a grin.

'Sod me if he isn't going to do exactly what I said he was,' Weston muttered.

The men moved away. Blackstone took his blanket and gave it to Christiana. 'The forest gets chilled at night,' he said. 'Don't worry about the men. You're under Sir Godfrey's protection.'

'And yours?' she asked, taking the blanket and tucking it around her.

'And mine,' he answered, feeling suddenly awkward and foolish.

Godfrey de Harcourt and his handful of men-at-arms rode once again to the end of the bridge. Dusk was falling and the grey light crept across the silent castle.

'Madame!' de Harcourt shouted. 'I apologize for my earlier threat. I know you must be fearful because the English are close, but I implore you once again to open the gates. I am here, as I promised, to give you the gold for my brother's ransom!'

He turned to Sir Gilbert who rode at his side.

'You think they'll know I fight with Edward?'

'I think, my lord, they are arse-sucking scum who would be as confused as many others about your family entanglements,' Sir Gilbert answered. 'I am orphan born and orphan I shall die.'

De Harcourt grunted. 'Count yourself fortunate.'

He raised himself in the stirrups as if to add volume to his bellowing.

'Good lady! I have only six men-at-arms as escort. It is dangerous for me to linger, but we will camp here, where you can see us, until the morning. But then I leave and I take my gold with me. He is your husband, for pity's sake, and a fine knight. Let us give the English that which they demand.'

He turned his horse. 'Flies would be less likely to settle on a dung heap than for them to ignore the chance of gold.'

Sir Godfrey and the men-at-arms tethered their horses, built a fire in full view and settled beneath their cloaks for the night. Huddled around the flames, they offered themselves as bait. Within the forest edge Elfred and the archers waited while Blackstone sat a few feet from the sleeping girl. Moonlight came and went beneath scattering clouds, and when the soft light filtered through the branches he could see her sleeping like a child, hair against her face, her lips slightly parted. He felt that, if he were sleeping, this would be a dream of finding a beautiful forest child, abandoned by Mother Nature.

He pulled back from the illusion. She served a countess. There was no point yielding to the feelings that confused and bedevilled him. He returned his gaze to the shadows and the faint movement of the branches where the archers stayed out of sight. If he were the men inside he would wait until first light, when the fire had sunk to embers and the morning chill kept men, aching in their armour, curled for a few moments more of warmth beneath their cloaks.

And that is what the killers did.

CHAPTER SEVEN

One of the gates eased open to let twenty men creep as quietly as they could across the wooden bridge. In the clearing, less than fifty paces beyond the bridge, the sleeping men-at-arms had not stirred. Wisps of smoke from dying embers curled in the dawn's still air. A horse snuffled, another whinnied, but still the sleeping men did not move. The killers' confidence increased. They raced forward, unconcerned about the sound of their footfalls. The men on the ground would be dead in seconds.

In the grey light one of the attackers faltered. He had seen something inexplicable. The treeline, a hundred paces away, shivered. The forest moved. Before the first sword strike could be delivered, a hum, as bowstrings released, resonated from the trees and a hissing wind swept the sky.

Blackstone sat crouched from his vantage point and watched as the attackers fell under the archers' volley. They died to a man twenty paces from Sir Godfrey and his men, who threw back their cloaks and ran onto the bridge. No words were uttered, no battle cry shouted; all that could be heard was the pounding of hooves as the lone figure of Sir Gilbert charged from the trees to secure the gate's opening. As the defenders shouldered the iron-clad doors his sword swept down and blood sprayed the gates. He hacked his way past the desperate men who shouted their warnings to others inside, but the ferocity of the attack and the sudden rush of the men-at-arms caught them off-guard. They were expecting half their number to return with a knight's ransom; instead they were cut down where they stood.

Blackstone watched the efficient killing. It was only when the screams of men being slaughtered reached the forest that Christiana jerked awake.

'It's all right,' he told her.

She gathered her cloak about her and went to where he stood watching the attack. Elfred's archers moved from the treeline down the gentle slope towards the clearing to recover whatever arrows could be reused and to slit the throats of the wounded.

Christiana flinched but did not turn away.

Within an hour the dead had been dragged to a ditch filled with dry kindling and branches ready to be burned. Four of the mercenaries were wounded and knelt before Sir Godfrey, their arms tied behind their backs. They whimpered in pain and begged for mercy. The lame knight had not been as quick to reach the castle gates as his more able-bodied men, but he had done his share of killing. He beckoned Christiana forward. Blackstone stayed with the archers who stood idly waiting for the executions to be done with.

'These men killed my family's servants and villagers who sought my brother's protection. What shall we do with these who live? I leave their fate to you.'

A couple of the men raised their heads and implored Christiana for their lives. They were as young as Blackstone. Christiana had tears in her eyes as she looked down on the men. Blackstone quietly cursed de Harcourt for making her face those who had wreaked havoc.

One of them smiled up at her.

'My lady, your tears are well spent. I went with these men because I was afraid of the battle. Save me, I beg you, and I will serve you for the rest of my life.'

Christiana wiped her tears and turned to Sir Godfrey.

'I weep for those loyal in my lady's house and the atrocity these men committed on them. Do what justice demands, my lord.'

She walked away. The archers parted to let her through. Any thoughts of a vulnerable girl subdued by her emotions were as defeated as the kneeling men. Swords swung down and heads thudded onto the ground. A final scream and cry for mercy was cut short. The bodies were dragged from the blood-soaked ground and thrown onto the pyre.

Godfrey de Harcourt's men dug a communal grave and laid the dead servants and villagers to rest. He spoke a prayer in Latin and then turned his men towards their mission at the river. Christiana rode behind Blackstone with no choice but to wrap her arms around him. The gibes and taunts from the men would be saved for later, when Blackstone was alone.

Behind them the deserted Castle de Harcourt was protected by the dead. A dozen heads stuck on poles served as a warning to any other marauding bands.

Godfrey de Harcourt's relentless search for a river crossing took his force back north to a curl of the Seine. As the baron sat on a crested rise, hunched across his saddle's pommel, Blackstone and the others waited fifty paces behind.

'Holy God,' Will Longdon muttered when he saw the host gathered in the city. 'I thought there were only twice as many as us.'

'My money says that's not even their whole army,' Elfred said.

The battlements and suburbs of Rouen confirmed King Edward's information that the French army had called its *arrière ban*, the conscription of every able-bodied man and knight. The banners and pennons of French noble pride fluttered across the skyline. Smoke rose from thousands of fires. And Elfred was correct. The King and the main force defended Paris. King Edward's army was going to be crushed between the hammer and anvil of French might.

'We won't be going across the river here, that's for certain,' Blackstone said. He scanned the flock of banners. Amidst the royalty and honour of France, the gold and red colours of the de Harcourt family drew the eye to the bloodline of the Norman who sat on this side of the river having sworn loyalty to the English King. Godfrey de Harcourt, his thoughts his own, turned his horse. His men followed.

Blackstone looked across the wide river. The division between himself and Richard was as great as that between de Harcourt and his brother.

As de Harcourt and other knights led their scouting parties searching for a crossing, the King and the army reached Poissy, twelve miles from Paris, and found the town undefended. Fear had made the wealthy citizens abandon the town favoured by French royalty for its beauty and where the King of France had his mansion next to the Dominican nuns' priory. The unwalled town lay deserted on a bend of the Seine, less than twenty miles from Paris. God whispered in Edward's ear that He would give him a chance, a slim chance, to cross the river. The retreating French had destroyed the bridge but had left the stanchions. The carpenters began to cut wood.

By the time de Harcourt and his men returned to the main force, Edward's carpenters had managed to lay a single sixty-foot beam across the stanchions at Poissy. There was no opposition on the far bank; the French, believing that they had destroyed the bridge, had retreated to Paris.

Roger Oakley beckoned Blackstone forward from the company. 'Thomas, there's not many can please the lame baron, but you must have done some good in rescuing this girl. He wants you. Take yourself to him.'

As Blackstone eased the horse past Elfred he asked a favour.

'Elfred, will you keep Richard with you? I don't know what it is Sir Godfrey wants with me.'

'I will. I'll have food kept for you,' the centenar answered.

Blackstone approached de Harcourt and Sir Gilbert. Sir Godfrey spoke to Christiana. 'This man will take you to the King's baggage train. You're a courageous young woman. Your mistress will be proud,' de Harcourt said. 'Sir Gilbert! We'll report to the King.' He spurred the horse forward.

Sir Gilbert sidled alongside Blackstone and Christiana. 'I want you back here, not supping delicate foods stolen from the King's kitchen. Speak to one of the King's captains. Tell him Sir Godfrey wishes her safe.' He looked at the girl. 'You're fortunate Thomas Blackstone found you. He's my sworn man.' He paused, as if considering what he said next. 'I would trust him with my life.'

He urged the horse forward, following Sir Godfrey towards the King's banner flying outside the new palace Philip had built for himself.

'Sir Gilbert honours you,' she said.

'I don't know why,' Blackstone said modestly. But his captain's compliment meant more than anyone would ever know.

Her arms tightened around his waist as he turned the horse. 'I wasn't brave,' Christiana said quietly. 'I was frightened. More frightened than I have ever been in my life.'

Not, Blackstone thought, as frightened as he felt with her body pressed tightly against his.

Sir Gilbert stood at the water's edge, anxious to remove the burden of his plate armour after the days of riding, but while Godfrey de Harcourt still spoke to the King, he had been summoned by William de Bohun, Earl of Northampton. The rebuilding of the bridge could never be fast enough for the marshal's liking.

'Get your arses moving, or by Christ I'll cut off your ears and have you sent out as treasonable bastards who are deliberately slowing your King's progress.' He turned to Sir Gilbert. 'From what you and Godfrey said, we're caught between the millstones of Philip's armies.'

'We are if we don't get across the river.'

'Aye, and there's another ninety miles north if we're to meet up with Hastings and his Flemish whoresons. We can catch Philip by surprise if we're quick enough. We're a spit away from Paris. The King believes this is God's gift.'

'And what do you think?'

'That we've ended in the buttery on our arses. Once your lads are fed I need a company of archers ready to get across this damned ditch and defend the other side. If we're to feint to Paris and—'

'My lord!'

Northampton and Sir Gilbert looked to where the carpenter pointed. Beyond the far bank a line of French horsemen appeared, with infantry running at their flanks.

'The butter's just curdled,' Northampton said and grabbed his helm.

Even Sir Gilbert's experience of war did not prepare him for what Northampton did next. The pugnacious earl pulled on his helm, drew his sword and began to move across the foot-wide plank towards the enemy. Encased in eighty pounds of armour and chain mail, on a slippery footing across a swirling river, the mad bastard was going to attack.

'Sound the alarm!' Sir Gilbert called.

Blackstone had ridden to the rear of the column with Christiana. Camp followers and whores were kept furthest from the milling activity of this community of non-combatants. The baggage train carried all the King's personal effects, the royal kitchen and its cooks. There were carpenters, masons and horsemasters. Blacksmiths and farriers unloaded portable forges and the charcoal to heat them. Two-pence-a-day grooms cared for the beasts of burden and war. Wagons stacked with bushels of corn, peas and beans as fodder for the war horses, which needed more than grass as their diet, were drawn up to one side of the town. Sacks of oats were carried for the heavy carthorses. More food for the beasts than the men, Blackstone thought as he guided the horse through the coming and going of servants.

Surgeons had their own retinues, clerks kept records, the hier-archy of officials and attendants seemed a natural state of affairs to those involved, but Blackstone was used to the uncomplicated structure and discipline of an archers' company and the milling of these people confused him.

As wagoners unbridled their large carthorses, armourers stood watch over two wagons that carried saltpetre and sulphur for the three bombards strapped below. These cannons would fire stone shot, though Sir Gilbert had told him that such bombards caused more noise – like a clap of thunder – than killing: that was left to the King's archers.

Blackstone eased the horse forward to a robed official who was directing others to their duties.

'Sir, I'm charged by Sir Godfrey de Harcourt to deliver this lady into safekeeping.'

The man looked up at the weather-scoured archer whose matted hair clung to his dirt-streaked face, and whose jupon was so faded that its coat of arms was unrecognizable. He looked little better than a vagabond. Archers were thieves and killers. The King favoured their strength, which was why half his army consisted of these scum from the shires. Was this a rescued lady from one of the ransacked towns or a noble's whore needing protecting? One could never tell and discretion could make the difference between demotion and a flogging or a favourable mention from the marshal's woman.

The official looked the girl over. Her face showed no sign of the pox and her delicate hands bore no raw redness from lime soap. She was too slight for heavy work and her cloak was of good quality. She was no whore or working woman, the official determined.

'The lady shall be safe here. Assure Sir Godfrey I shall arrange as much comfort as is possible under the circumstances.'

Blackstone quickly dismounted and reached up to Christiana. As she allowed him to ease her down a small crucifix swung clear from her neck. Blackstone held her a moment longer than he could have hoped for.

'Thank you. I can feel the ground beneath my feet. I don't think I shall stumble now,' she said.

He released his hands from her waist. She came to no higher than his chest but she kept her gaze on his. 'I owe you a kindness,' she said.

The thoughts of a kiss rushed through his mind. He bent his head but she smiled and raised the crucifix.

'Rather let your lips touch the cross of Christ and then I can pray you will be blessed and kept safe.' She held the small gold crucifix to his lips but her eyes stayed on his. 'Kiss the cross of Christ if you believe in His... love.' The whispered final word seemed carefully chosen to Blackstone's ears.

He had no thoughts of whether God even existed. The Church said so, as did the whoring village priest at home – a landowner's son who had taken the cloth instead of the sword. But if it meant Blackstone could spend another moment with this girl whose dark green eyes still looked into his, he would have joined the priesthood himself.

He put his face close to hers and smelled the fragrance of her hair as he kissed the crucifix.

'Bless you, Thomas Blackstone. I shall pray for your safety.'

The moment passed. She turned and walked quickly away to where the official waited, glaring in the archer's direction.

Blackstone was about to call after her when he heard a trumpet sounding the alarm from the river.

Armoured men in single file balanced their way across the narrow plank. Blackstone looked down from the hillside and watched as the first of them, Northampton and others, including Sir Gilbert, gained the other bank. By the time the French reached the slope twenty or so English banners were raised. It was too slender a force to hold the shore and there was no time to find and load boats with infantry. A thousand Frenchmen, for that was about the number that Blackstone gauged was swarming towards the river, would crush the courageous Northampton and his knights. Despite the unquestionable courage of the men following, Blackstone knew that if this bridge could not be repaired, or if the French gained sufficient strength to hold the shore, then they would all be trapped like rats. And Christiana was part of the English camp.

He spurred the horse forward. Archers were running into position. Elfred's men were still at the rear being fed after their arduous time in the saddle, but there were a dozen or more archers, guards for the carpenters, running for the bank and levelling their bows. Blackstone dismounted and unslung his bow. It was obvious that these next few minutes would be vital.

'Downriver!' he cried to the men and was already running along the riverbank beyond the stanchions. They were Warwick's men, but they responded to the command because archers needed a clear target and the mêlée on the other shore already consumed English and French men-at-arms. They realized Lord Marldon's man must have seen something they had not. Two hundred yards along the bank showed the approaching infantry. Northampton and the others had their backs to the river, the spearmen's numbers would overwhelm them.

One of the older men in Warwick's contingent shouted, 'Right, lad. We see the bastards.'

There was no need for a command. The archers hauled back their bowcords and, despite how few they were, began a steady killing fire. The infantry faltered but came on. Blackstone saw Sir Gilbert turn with a dozen men-at-arms to face the attack.

As more men got across the river the French began to fall back. It could not have been a main force from the French army, Blackstone reasoned, but a flying column sent to secure a crossing they thought already destroyed. They were dying too quickly to succeed. More archers joined Blackstone, others got across the river. They had to keep the slender foothold that was the army's escape.

Elfred ran into view with Richard Blackstone at his shoulder. Weston, Longdon and all the others took up position on the opposite end of the riverbank and began firing steadily. Blackstone saw his brother at Elfred's shoulder. A pang of uncertainty gripped him. Had the boy found a new guardian? Elfred was a kinder, older man who could easily have been their father. A thought shot through his mind like a bodkin piercing armour: was he happy to see responsibility for his brother gone from his life? He gripped his father's war bow, his hand the breadth of his father's. The man's spirit lived on – so too the demands he had placed on his eldest son.

Men-at-arms were pushing the French back, but Blackstone had stopped firing. He wanted to fight with the comrades he knew.

'That's my company,' he told the Warwick man. And then, knowing the answer to his own uncertainty, 'My brother's there.'

'Aye. Off you go then, son. You did well bringing us here. We'll hold the flank. Northampton and his men have the day, I reckon. He's a lunatic bastard, thank God. You have to love him for it.'

Blackstone ran the few hundred yards to his friends. Richard saw him and his braying made John Weston turn as he nocked another arrow.

'You took your time! Barely got your breeches back on, did you? Don't mind us, we can win this fight without you.'

'Thought you'd run off with her!' Will Longdon said as he loosed another shaft.

Blackstone took his place with the others and drew back. 'No, that's later,' he answered.

By the end of the day several hundred French lay dead; others were hunted down as they ran. Some managed to retreat towards Paris and deliver the news the French King would despair at hearing: English infantry with men-at-arms, flanked by Welsh spearmen and archers, held the crossing at Poissy. Edward had lost many men in the bitter fighting, but he had his bridge. Now he could escape the tightening noose – that sent a message of fear to the French King. No foreign invader had ever sacked the capital. He was not about to let Edward's savage, mongrel army be the first. Philip prepared his army to do battle on the outskirts of the city.

The exertion of the fighting had reopened Sir Gilbert's wound sustained at Caen. He sat on a log without chest armour and chain mail as a surgeon inserted stitches to the sides of the raw gash.

'I wouldn't let you wipe my arse with silk, you damned butcher, if it weren't for my lord's grace in sending you,' he said as Godfrey de Harcourt looked on.

'The Prince's surgeon should be accorded some respect, Gilbert,' de Harcourt chided him gently.

'So too should this damned wound on my back. You'd think the man was stitching a pig for roasting.' Sir Gilbert swigged from a flask. 'The brandy helps – to a point. I hope you'll thank him in case I don't survive his cripple-fingered administration.'

'I've done all I can, Sir Gilbert,' said the surgeon.

Sir Gilbert held up the pot of salve. 'Then smear this on and dress it with a clean piece of linen, and your duties will be discharged.'

The surgeon sniffed the pot. His nose wrinkled.

'It's not a brothel salve; it's honey and lavender from the monks at Caen. Do it and be gone and make sure the linen is clean. Then bind me.' The surgeon did as he was told.

'Can you ride?' de Harcourt asked.

'What is it you want, Sir Godfrey?' he answered. The Norman's question seemed to him tantamount to an insult.

'I'm to lay waste as close to Paris as I can get – it's a diversion. Edward has to get the army north and across the Somme to meet up with Hastings and the Flemish. He'll be running like a stag with the French hunt on his scent.'

Sir Gilbert let the brandy catch the back of his throat, its warmth easing the pain in his body. 'He was never going to attack Paris. I knew that. We would be caught in a thousand streets and alleys. It'd be a hundred times worse than Caen. How much time does the King need?'

'Nine days at the most.'

'And what do you want of me and my men?'

'Find a crossing on the Somme.'

'Dear God, haven't we done with trying to cross rivers? That's the devil's gate of a ditch. Worse than this place. Let's do battle now and finish it.'

'Edward's ordered more archers and supplies. There's a port north of the river at Le Crotoy, and to reach there we need to cross the Somme. There's no victory unless we meet Hastings then turn and fight Philip. Supplies and men. That's what we need.'

'And a miracle.'

'We'll meet north of Amiens.' De Harcourt turned his horse away.

Sir Gilbert grunted as the last binding was tied off. Six weeks of fighting sucked more than energy out of man and horse. They needed rest and food and care for their injuries. The army marched on worn-out shoes, and horses travelled on a meagre diet. Wounds festered and men died, desertion was not uncommon and soldiers had been hanged for looting monasteries. Yet still the warrior King asked more of his men. It was remarkable that they held him in such esteem that they bound up their feet, ignored their suffering and pushed onwards. And now there was to be a seventy-mile dash to get across another major river. Exhaustion was claiming them all.

The army crossed the Seine at Poissy and made certain the bridge was destroyed completely. Philip would not be able to attack from their rear, for now the race was on to march north. De Harcourt's raiding party had burned their way to the outskirts of Paris itself, but the French army was on the move, and once he had done all that could be done the tireless baron rode hard to join the reconnaissance parties that were trying to find a crossing. The army had left the difficult terrain of the hedgerows and *bocage* of Normandy and, fuelled by desperation, cut across the plain of Picardy in a straight line for seventy miles with barely a mile's divergence either side of the column. The sea to the north-west was close, the Somme's salt marshlands and estuary to the west – and a determined French King, knowing his English cousin's bedraggled army was making a last great effort to reach his Flemish allies, pursued him from the south. The English had slipped the noose once, he would tighten it again. And kick away the stool.

Sir Gilbert's men-at-arms and archers, like every other reconnaissance group, burned every village and hovel they found. Smoke clung to the land as if the whole of France was a funeral pyre. But no bridge had been found and, as Philip's men had stopped the crossing of the Seine, so too he stopped the English at the Somme.

Edward's strategy had failed and the cost of trying to attack the fortified bridges on the river had cost too many lives. Time was running out as fast as the river's tide, and Edward, King of England, would soon be stranded and forced to face an overwhelming army and fight them at a place not of his choosing.

The day before St Bartholomew's Day was a fast day. Not that the men had a choice. There was neither meat nor fowl to eat. John Weston tethered his horse and, grinning like a monkey, scurried to where his own company of archers camped after their day's fruitless search for a crossing. He dragged a dead swan behind him, its silk-like feathers saturated with its own blood. He dumped it on the ground in front of the others.

'All right then, lads, got us a morsel here that'd grace the King's table.'

'Sweet Jesus, don't let Sir Godfrey see it or he'll have it himself,' Roger Oakley said, as he dragged the heavy carcass out of sight. Two of the men began cleaning the bird.

'Get some more wood on that fire. We'll need a few rocks as well,' Blackstone told Will Longdon, 'and dig the pit deeper. We'll cook it slow.'

'Right y'are, your highness, sire, my lord,' Longdon teased. A swan was a fine meal and this was no time to worry about a younger man organizing the fire pit. 'Bull's balls, lad! You'd make a fine nobleman,' Elfred said.

'If he weren't a guttersnipe archer,' Weston told him.

'And you would know,' Blackstone answered with a smile. The men were in good cheer now that there was to be a succulent bird for their next day's breakfast.

Sir Gilbert walked across to them. 'There'll be a fight on your hands in the morning when the others smell those juices. I daresay I can keep things under control for the price of a drumstick.'

'That's exactly what we were saying a minute ago, Sir Gilbert,' said Elfred, 'weren't we, lads?' There was good-humoured agreement from the archers.

'Is one bird all you could manage, John Weston?'

'There were two pairs, Sir Gilbert, but I had to wade in to grab this one before the tide took him out to sea,' John Weston told him, as he slit the neck free from the body. 'The others weren't about to paddle around and wait on another arrow coming their way. Just as well, mind you, damned near drowned m'self in that current.'

Blackstone threw more wood on the fire. What John Weston said reminded him of the river at home where he and Richard would set fish traps. The swans there were for Lord Marldon's table, but they were usually taken at low tide when they were feeding.

'Were they feeding?' Blackstone asked.

'That they were. Head down, arse up. I couldn't miss, not that I ever do. Mind you, the bloody tide nearly took my legs away and I can't swim, so thank the good Lord, he brought me back with you wretches' breakfast.'

Blackstone turned to Sir Gilbert. 'If there is a low tide on the estuary, shallow enough for the swans to feed, and John got himself out into the stream, then perhaps that's where we can cross, Sir Gilbert.'

'John?' Sir Gilbert asked the forager.

'Aye, it could be done, I suppose. Risky as tickling the devil's arse with a wet fletching, though.'

'Show me.'

'Right you are, Sir Gilbert. But your authority would go some way to saving the bird from being thieved by the time we're back.'

'The bird stays in the pit. Cook it slow, lads. It'll be ready for the morning,' Sir Gilbert told the men. 'Elfred, Thomas, John, with me.'

They rode under moonlight until they crested a hill and saw the Somme's estuary widen across the tidal marshland, its water a glistening ribbon that stretched towards the sea. A breeze rippled the broad reach of water whose eddies testified to the truth of Weston's assertion of a strong tidal current. Sir Gilbert followed the archer's route down through the edge of the marshes and then dismounted.

'I went in about here. Had about a hundred-odd paces to where the nearest bird was feeding. The others were midstream. Didn't see no point in risking the loss of an arrow.'

The squelching marsh gave under their weight, but they walked further towards the river.

'Tide's on the turn, Sir Gilbert,' Blackstone said. 'You remember the river at home? It'll be a death trap if men are out there when the flood starts.'

Sir Gilbert ignored him and waded out further into the stream. Blackstone gathered the horses' reins and gave them to his brother. No further instruction was needed. The disgraced boy was to stay behind.

The archers followed their captain into the deeper water that tugged at their thighs. The men spread out a hundred paces across, each testing his own foothold in the silt. After a while Elfred raised his arm.

'It's here,' he called. 'It's firm underfoot.'

The others waded towards him and felt the riverbed harden. Elfred stared across the moonlit water to the far bank. 'Has to be a mile if it's a cloth-yard,' he said.

'Mile and a half,' Blackstone said quietly. 'At least.' The frightening prospect of wading that distance if there were Genoese crossbows waiting for them was more chilling than the cold water lapping his groin.

'Mile and a half it is, then,' Sir Gilbert acknowledged. 'At least.'

The swan was left in the fire pit, abandoned when Godfrey de Harcourt's scouting party returned to the main force with news of the crossing. They needed sleep and food, but neither was given once the King was told of the chance that his army could cross the Somme. Trumpets blared, the army roused and each captain told his men what was expected.

'If we don't ford the river we'll be trapped. The French vanguard is less than seven miles to our rear. We've only the sea ahead of us. It's as simple as that,' said Sir Gilbert. 'And we haven't come

seven hundred miles to be slain like rats in a pit by a rabid terrier.'
He walked along the line, making sure that every archer and man-
at-arms could hear. 'We march tonight through the marshes.'

There was a shuffle of worn boots and a murmur of uncertainty
among the gathered men. Moving across marshland at night was
exhausting and dangerous. 'There's nothing for it, lads. We have
to get across. There are Frenchmen to be killed and a crown to
be gained. We'll be at the river by dawn. Sir Reginald leads and
I follow.'

He turned and faced the bowmen. By now he knew every name
under his command. 'Archers will go across first,' he said solemnly.

Blackstone's exhausted gaze followed the water's current.

'It's still too high.'

'We wait,' Sir Gilbert said. 'And pray the French are still yawn-
ing and scratching their balls.'

The army slowly gathered behind them, men and animals packed
tight on the riverbank, their ranks lying in depth, jostling back
into the trees, across pastureland and cornfields. Twelve thousand
men to ford a river estuary two thousand yards broad on a firm
footing so narrow as to permit only ten men to stand shoulder to
shoulder. If the French approaching from the south caught up with
them now there would be no chance to form battle lines. They'd
be slaughtered mid-river.

They waited for the tide and watched as a French contingent
from the main army at Abbeville secured the far bank.

'How long to get across, d'you think?' Will Longdon said.

'Sun'll be quartered, up near them clouds,' Elfred answered. It
would be nearly an hour before their feet touched the distant shore.

'Aye, that's what I thought,' Longdon confirmed. 'Was hoping
I was wrong. I go down, someone'd better drag me up.'

Elfred turned to Blackstone. 'Thomas, you get Richard on hand
to haul his soggy arse up. I need him for killing them bastards.'

Blackstone nodded. 'Might be better if we all took a swim,' he
said pointing to the far shore.

The horizon changed shape as pennons and banners cluttered

the skyline along the hundred-and-fifty-foot-high embankment on the far shore. The French defenders drew up in three lines along the water's edge.

'They must have known this was the only ford,' Sir Gilbert said. He looked at the French banners, some of which he recognized. 'Godemar du Fay. He's a Burgundian knight. He'll be the one laying that defence across the shoreline.'

'Beloved Christ, don't ask Thomas how many there are or he'll tell us,' said John Weston as he gazed at the swarming infantry and men-at-arms.

'We've not seen the worst of it yet, lads,' Blackstone said, his eyes fixed on the embankment where five hundred crossbowmen swarmed into position, keeping to the heights, giving themselves additional range.

'I was just about to say I were glad there weren't no bloody crossbowmen with 'em,' Will Longdon said.

'You think their eyesight's as good as ours?' John Weston asked.

'You'll know when a quarrel takes your head off,' Sir Gilbert answered.

'Hey! French bastards!' Weston shouted and walked to the shallows, untied his hose and pissed in the river. 'Can you see this?'

The men laughed and roared derision at the Frenchmen and their hired mercenaries.

'God help us, Weston, we've to wade in there. Your piss could rot armour,' Sir Gilbert told him.

'It's chilly in there, Sir Gilbert, I was just warming it up for you.'

Fear slipped behind their bravado; a healthy disdain for the enemy could drive a soldier to face a hellish attack. Blackstone's brother edged towards him, and tugged his sleeve. He uttered a muted sound and gestured. He wanted to be at Blackstone's shoulder. Blackstone saw the longing in his face. He had tried to forgive, had tried not to think of the boy killing the girl he professed to love. There was no forgiveness. But there was duty. Blackstone nodded. The boy made no sign of joy but tears welled momentarily and then he stood a pace behind Blackstone's shoulder.

The Earl of Northampton stood in front of the company.

'The French think we're coarse, ignorant ruffians! And they'd be right!'

The men shouted their approval. The earl raised his sword.

'Their knights will ride down their own infantry in order to kill us. You archers are going to make them bleed and then we will slaughter them until this damned river runs red. Kill them, and keep killing them until they weep for mercy and then kill them some more! Go to it!'

A wave of battle cries carried across the broad expanse of water like a threatening summer storm about to strike.

Sir Gilbert tied a leather loop around his sword grip and wrist. He smiled. 'My blood knot. I'm not losing hold of my damned sword because a squirming Frenchman spews blood all over me. Good luck to you, Thomas.'

'You too, Sir Gilbert.'

Three hours after prime, the eighth hour from midnight, on St Bartholomew's Day, Sir Reginald Cobham with the Earl of Northampton and Sir Gilbert Killbere formed a column of one hundred men-at-arms. To their front Elfred's hundred archers formed an extended line, ten men wide and ten men deep, across the breadth of the ford.

With their bows raised to keep their cords dry they waded into the water.

CHAPTER EIGHT

The tide sucked at their legs; the taller men were knee deep, for the others the water was waist high. They cursed and grumbled, but they kept their formation as best they could. Three hundred yards from the shore the first crossbow bolts struck. Blackstone and the other archers could not yet level their bows in the deep water and the undefended men were the first to die. The added height of the embankment gave the Genoese bowmen extra distance and the bolts cut down twenty or thirty men in the first volley. Their bodies fell against others carrying them, floundering, into the current. Men cried out, others cursed.

'Keep going! Keep going!' someone shouted.

As men fell others took their place, surging forward to take the fallen men's position, less through bravery than to get themselves to the far shore as quickly as they could. They were dying out here, exposed and helpless.

Iron-clad bolts whirred through the air, Blackstone ducked instinctively, heard them strike wooden shields of the men-at-arms behind them, tapping like a score of drunken woodpeckers.

'Faster, for Christ's sake, faster,' Blackstone urged himself. *Dear God, don't let me die... don't let me die... not here... not like this.*

The man next to Blackstone suddenly tumbled backward as a bolt smacked into his forehead with a sickening crunch. Too many archers were dying. Roger Oakley pushed forward. 'Come on, lads, come on!'

His surge carried thirty-odd men with him, forcing their leg muscles to fight the water. Archers gasped for air, exertion and fear driving them onwards. More men fell. The splash of their bodies sounding as rapid as the terrible, unrelenting whirring wind that shuddered past the survivors. *Too many down! We'll never get there! Sweet Mother of God, forgive me.* Blackstone's mind taunted him with the prospect of dying in the river. What was being asked was impossible.

But they kept going.

Roger Oakley turned and looked at his men. 'They'll be crying for their mothers. Another two hundred yards, boys. That's all! Push on, lads, push on!' His constant encouragement was a beacon for the floundering archers to follow. 'You're my archers! And we'll be first to take the bastards down and—'

The double strike tore through Oakley's cap, shattering his face and jaw, the second bolt ripped through his throat. A gurgle of blood, and his twisting body was taken by the current. The line of men faltered.

A voice carried from behind. 'Keep going, for Christ's sake, or we're dead!' It was Sir Gilbert with his men-at-arms. If the archers failed the attack was doomed.

Blackstone saw Oakley's death throes as he swirled in the water, a hand feebly trying to grasp air for a few seconds, but the shattered head and throat told them all he was already dead. Blackstone stumbled, but before he went down his brother's grip hauled him to his feet. Neither looked at the other, their eyes fixed on the figures they could see on the skyline cranking their crossbows, while the French men-at-arms waited on the shoreline to kill the survivors.

And then the water shoaled. 'Go wide!' Elfred shouted, and the men broke the ranks to spread their line and lessen the target offered to the crossbows. One hundred and fifty yards from shore Elfred levelled his bow as did every man with him, and the first storm of arrows fell like God's vengeance on the crossbowmen. In less than a minute the archers had advanced another thirty yards and delivered six more volleys until the Genoese dead lay scattered on the forward slope of the embankment or retreated to get out of the archers' range.

Elfred looked for Roger Oakley and saw only Blackstone firing steadily with what remained of the line of men. Will Longdon and John Weston were to Elfred's left.

'Thomas! Take twenty men! Flank! Flank! You hear me?' he cried as he veered left with the others, opening a gap for Sir Gilbert's men behind them to pour through. Blackstone waded to the right.

'With me! Take position!' he called. 'Men-at-arms! Kill the men-at arms!'

Northampton, Cobham and Sir Gilbert were already splashing through the gap created as the archers loosed again. Now the arrow hail beat down on plate armour and chain mail. By the time the English knights waded ashore they had to step over the French dead. The clash of steel and shield rolled across the water. And the archers fired until their missiles were depleted. But Edward and his marshals knew that unless the bowmen could sustain their fire the English men-at-arms could not fight and clamber uphill against so many – and he had ordered pages and clerics with armfuls of bound arrow sheaves to re-supply the advance. Knives quickly cut the wrappings of the bundles, and archers fired relentlessly until more men-at-arms pushed in behind those fighting on the shore. Where five men fell, another ten took their place. It was a desperate and determined attack to gain the heavily defended shore before King Philip's army swept up from the rear and slaughtered them mid-stream.

Blackstone and the archers had sown a field of death and scrambled from the shallows to stop any attacking force outflanking the tenuous beachhead. Cobham cut and thrust, his high guard scything the men to his front and side, his steady, forward pace and skill matched only by Northampton, bloodied from head to foot, and Sir Gilbert, the three of them relentlessly killing those before them. French bravery could not be faulted; they fought for every inch of the gore-drenched sand.

Blackstone was eighty yards away from Sir Gilbert. He saw French men-at-arms bearing down on his sworn knight, who braced his stance and fought the first four men away, but the numbers would soon overwhelm him. Half a dozen of his own men around him were killed or wounded. The French attack surged.

Blackstone could run no harder towards the beleaguered knight. An arrow was already nocked, the cord drawn back. He hesitated, seeing the flight in his mind's eye – all of a second's thought, for if he was wrong the arrow could kill Sir Gilbert. Two men struck Sir Gilbert – hard, stunning blows from mace and poleaxe. It was a relentless assault; Sir Gilbert went onto one knee, shield raised. A French knight raised his sword for a double-handed strike. Blackstone was already reaching for another arrow when the first knifed through the knight's plate armour. His knees buckled and he fell backwards. Blackstone saw Sir Gilbert try to stand, still stunned from the blows.

Richard bellowed and ran forwards, past Blackstone's shoulder.

Two arrows flew in quick succession. Blackstone grabbed all that remained from his bag and stuck the six shafts into the ground at his feet. In swift succession those arrows landed two yards in front of Sir Gilbert, who struggled to get to his feet. Two vital accurate yards, the skill of a man raised by a master archer and taught to use every fibre and thought to loose a yard-long shaft exactly where its archer determined it should fly. The lethal pin-cushion slayed four more men and badly wounded another two.

And then Richard Blackstone was there with more Englishmen at his heels. The boy bent and dragged Sir Gilbert as the English soldiers surrounded him. Sir Gilbert struggled, but Richard pinned his body to the ground. The exhaustion and his wounds, aided by the mute boy's weight and strength, finally made the injured knight slip into the dark river of unconsciousness. As the Englishmen held their ground, fighting around the fallen knight, Blackstone's brother lifted Sir Gilbert across his shoulders and loped back to the safety of the trees as if he carried a slain sheep.

Blackstone had run ahead of his own men, sidestepping dead and injured. One wounded man half raised himself and swung his mace in a futile, dying gesture. It slipped from his blood-soaked gauntlet and struck Blackstone on the side of the head, reopening the wound he had suffered at Caen. His steel-rimmed leather helmet took most of the impact but he stumbled, felt the earth spin, and in that moment knew he was vulnerable to a killing blow. He had to stand and defend himself. Using his bow as a crutch he hauled himself to his feet, hand on knife, ready to kill. There was no need. His attacker lay dead and the French men-at-arms were shuffling back across their fallen men as their war horses were committed to the fray, relying on the extra momentum given by the slope to trample those Englishmen below. But Edward's men had torn a mortal wound in the French defences, and as those on foot skirted their attackers, English mounted knights cantered across the narrow ford. King Edward had taken the greatest risk of all and committed his whole army across the stretch of water – and prayed that the main French force was no closer than he suspected. The destriers' power took the fight onwards, the weight in English numbers forcing the French horsemen back from the contested ground.

Blackstone, wiping the blood from his face, saw that his brother had taken Sir Gilbert to safety and raised his war bow above his head. He roared in triumph as the French retreated before the lances and swords of the English knights and their men-at-arms.

And every man left standing, including the great Earl of North-ampton, William de Bohun, and the old warrior at his side, Sir Reginald Cobham, roared with him.

And roared again.

Against the odds a small contingent of lightly armed men of the English army had attacked a well-defended position and defeated a well-prepared enemy in a strong position – a fight they should have lost. This feat of courage crushed King Philip's plan of entrapping the English army. The Prince of Wales's retinue splashed across the ford, his dark armour muting the sunlight that glistened from the water. Godfrey de Harcourt reined his horse to where wounded men sat amidst the devastation as men-at-arms and hobelars rode after French survivors. The stench of death hung over the field like a sickly fog and the carnage that littered the beachhead testified to the savagery of the fight.

De Harcourt eased his grey destrier closer to where Blackstone sat with Sir Gilbert, who lay bareheaded but conscious, his half-crushed bascinet at his side.

'So you made it, boy,' he said, calming the highly strung horse.

'Aye, my lord. Some of us did,' Blackstone replied. He and his brother stood before de Harcourt.

'And you've a wound,' the Norman said.

The encrusted blood on Blackstone's face smeared down from his scalp. 'It's nothing,' he replied. 'A glancing blow, is all.'

The older man grunted, eyed Richard, but did not allow his gaze to linger. 'Sir Gilbert, you'll be resting after your exertions,' he said lightly.

Sir Gilbert, still recovering, raised his gauntlet, the sword dangling from its blood knot. 'For a moment, my lord; I feel as though I've been kicked by a horse.'

'Then when you feel unkicked I shall need your service, and that of your man.' He hesitated and glanced again at the blood-smeared Richard. 'And your dumb ox.'

'The mute should be our talisman. He saved me a walk from the field. I was glad of it, being weary at the time,' Sir Gilbert said. 'And once the damned sky stops spinning I shall join you, my lord.'

De Harcourt threw down a wineskin. 'Gascony red. It will replenish your strength and settle the heavens.'

The ford was choked with troops, and as they came ashore the marshals formed them up to defend the bank.

'My lord,' Blackstone asked a moment before de Harcourt turned back to the beachhead's defence. 'Is Christiana safe?'

'The King abandoned some of the baggage train, for speed's sake. The Bohemian cavalry have caught us up. They've killed some of the wagon masters. The Bishop's rearguard holds them from the river but his time is short. The tide's running fast. I gave orders that she be brought across. I've not seen her yet.'

The marshal turned his horse and trotted towards the Prince's retinue. Blackstone gazed back to the meandering line of troops and equipment choking the ford. The tail end would extend beyond the southern riverbank, through the trees. How far back did the stragglers go? There seemed to be no more wagons to cross over. He took the half-dozen arrows from his brother's bag. His look and a gesture told him to stay with Sir Gilbert. He ran to where the horsemasters and pages held the archers' mounts.

'Thomas!' Elfred called.

'She's back there,' he answered.

'God's teeth, lad. A bloody woman! The tide's coming in! You'll never make it back!'

Blackstone turned his horse into the water.

The last stragglers from the far bank were wading chest deep in places. Men floundered and he saw one or two stumble and sink below the breeze-scuffed surface. An arm raised in desperation, a cry lost beneath the sound of rustling reed beds. There were no more wagons to cross the ford. Infantrymen struggled through the marshlands, it was every man for himself. And nowhere was there a sign of Christiana. Blackstone's horse struggled against the strengthening current. He navigated it through the eddies and found shallow water.

Horsemen cantered through the trees and down the slope, forcing Blackstone aside. They were Englishmen belonging to the Bishop of Durham's rearguard. Men-at-arms, hobelars and archers.

'Did you see a woman with the wagons?' he called to one, recognizing the jupon from a man of the Earl of Arundel's division.

The man steadied his horse, waiting his turn to ease down the slope and into the water. Like the other men he kept turning in the saddle and looking back.

'A woman?'

'She's French. Cloaked, small, autumn hair.'

The man shook his head. 'There's no one alive back there.'

He spurred his horse forward into the water. They were the last of the Englishmen to cross the ford.

Blackstone eased his horse forward through the trees. If Christiana had survived she might have handed herself over to the French allies, the Bohemians, telling them she was taken against her will. But he knew that a woman of any class ran the risk of rape and murder when a soldier's blood was up. Within minutes he was skirting the village, staying out of sight, watching as Bohemian cavalrymen picked their way through the burning wagons. Whatever food and booty had been loaded now lay on the ground, allowing the men to take what they wanted. A group of thirty or so men rode towards the riverbank through the trees not fifty paces from where Blackstone waited. His russet jacket and muddied jupon smudged his profile into the branches. He leaned low across the horse's neck, laying a soothing hand on its flank. Once the first group had gone to the river he eased the horse carefully through the woodland, watching as the remaining horsemen, shouting in a language he did not understand, dragged a wagoner from the undergrowth and quickly slaughtered him.

He remembered the first ambush when he had killed the old knight, whose movement had given away his position. Blackstone needed to remain as still as possible so that, even if the Bohemians looked his way, they would see nothing but the trees and undergrowth. Easing himself from the horse he let his hand rest on its muzzle. The cavalrymen were little more than a hundred paces away and he could have killed half of them, but the others would have flushed him out. He tethered the horse and waited. The men turned their attention to the few houses, abandoned when the English camped there before the crossing. And then he saw her. As the men went into the first house she passed the hovel's small window, her dark cloak and hair caught by the mottled sunlight. Blackstone moved quickly along the treeline towards the back of the house. He unslung his bow and nocked an arrow. If she was trying to move ahead of the searching troops she would have to come out the back of the house. A man's voice called out. A warning shout. Blackstone could hear the soldiers run quickly through the room. She cried out as her cloak's cowl caught a wicker door. She twisted away, but the cavalryman had her in his grasp. The Bohemian looked up when he saw the movement of the English archer drawing back his bowcord less than thirty paces away. The shout of surprise never left his lips. He fell back into the man behind him, who yelled a warning. Christiana ran to Blackstone.

'Run straight ten paces, then right! My horse is twenty paces back in the trees!' he told her. She hesitated only for a moment; Blackstone was already drawing back another arrow. He loosed into a man who ran around the building, the arrow striking with the force of a poleaxe. The Bohemians' shouts and cries added to the men's confusion. He ran back along the treeline, shadowing Christiana, making certain that the remaining men saw him and not her. Two of the men climbed onto their horses. The first fell across his saddle, Blackstone's arrow piercing shoulder and heart; the second alerted the other Bohemians to their attacker's position. In his haste to charge down the lone English archer he had failed to lower his visor. In less than ten paces he fell back across his startled horse with Blackstone's fletching at the end of his nose. With only two arrows remaining Blackstone ran across the end of a second building and loosed into a knight trying to calm a panicked horse. Now the other men turned, uncertain as to how many were attacking them. Blackstone cut diagonally across the open space, less than forty paces from the remaining men who were now mounted. The moment he was in the trees he scoured the half-light for Christiana. His horse was being reined in as she called his name. He turned back to face the advancing Bohemians and knew the moment his last arrow flew that the leading man was as good as dead and that the three others would swerve to avoid him. Precious seconds had been bought.

He leapt up behind her and kicked the horse's flanks. Branches whipped at their faces as they bent low across the willing beast's neck. The sound of pursuit was not far behind. And then they were free of the trees, the horse sliding on its haunches down the thirty-foot embankment to the water's edge.

'Hold on!' he shouted. If either fell now they would die under the swords and hooves of the cavalrymen.

The horse plunged into the water, finding the ford's firm stone riverbed. The Bohemians reached the bank and, expert horsemen that they were, guided their horses more easily down the slope, gaining vital yards on the lumbering horse carrying two instead of one. Blackstone used his stave as a riding whip, urging the horse on, pushing him towards the deeper current, deep enough when the tide was full for a trading ship to sail through. The current pushed them. Blackstone slung his bow across his back.

'Grab hold of its mane,' he told her as he eased her into the water. The horse snorted, eyes wide, and kicked in panic, propelling it forward from the men in pursuit. Blackstone turned and saw the horsemen falter. If they fell into the tide they would surely drown under the weight of their armour.

They were halfway across and in danger of being swept out to sea or tumbled beneath the rising waves. Buffeted by the wind, the water was now above the saddle. Blackstone coughed sea water. The exhaustion of the day finally began to sap his strength. On the north shore the English army stretched out in defensive formation. He could see the banners of his King and his Prince, the fluttering pennons of the knights and the dark lines of the spearmen. 'Sweet Jesus, help me,' he whispered to himself. His grip on the horse's mane began to slip, his eyes stung from the salt water.

'Thomas! No!' Christiana cried, feeling him fall back. She turned and clutched at his sleeve. His mind raced, fragments of thought challenging each other. His father's war bow. That's what worried him. The salt water on the cord. An unimportant thought that thrust itself into his mind. He fancied he heard voices. He saw her mouth opening, calling his name but heard nothing. And then his head cleared and he heard other voices growing louder, not as one cry but rather a swinging cadence as the men on the shore urged him on.

'Swim, lad, swim!'

'Come on, boy!'

'Blackstone, Blackstone!'

'Keep going, man! Keep going!'

They were well past the halfway mark; another three or four hundred yards and they would be safe. Blackstone twisted his head behind him, and saw that one horseman had dared to challenge the fast-flowing tide. His horse, a powerful destrier, still had enough clearance in the water to pursue them. The cavalryman held his sword ready to strike. In another fifty yards he would be on them.

Blackstone's fear gripped him. He pulled himself alongside Christiana, she was failing, slipping away from him. Grabbing the horse's mane with one hand he supported her with the other. Horse and archer head-to-head focused on the shoreline. Blackstone urged the horse onwards as Christiana succumbed to the cold and fear that sapped her body of will and energy.

The Bohemian horseman was now less than thirty yards behind him and still beyond the killing range of the archers on the shore. The shoreline seemed no closer. Blackstone could hear the cavalryman shouting at him in what was obviously his battle cry. He saw the current twist yards ahead, swirling in a snake's tail carrying muddied water in a loop. If he could get into that stream he could gain another thirty yards.

'Let go of the horse,' he commanded.

Christiana looked uncertainly at him – the horse was their strength, their lifeline – but Blackstone kicked and pulled her away from the labouring beast. Her body turned and now she too could see the approaching horseman, so close that his expression under his open-faced helmet was visible. He snarled as he approached for the kill. There were less than ten yards before the sword would strike them. With enormous effort Blackstone pulled his arm back and powered them through the water. The abandoned horse drifted in the way of the attacking Bohemian, slowing him for critical seconds. And then a sudden turbulence in the current snatched them away from the man.

The horseman was still beyond the range of the English archers, but only by twenty yards or so. As Blackstone pulled Christiana higher into his shoulder, so that her body lay across his, he saw black rods fall through the sky and land between him and the courageous horseman. There could be no stronger warning that if the man continued his pursuit he would be in range and the next volley would kill him.

The Bohemian halted, fought the current for a moment, then raised his sword and shouted something. The destrier's strength allowed the rider to turn and make his way slowly back to where the other horsemen waited.

The tide swept them along the shore and now men moved right to the water's edge. Blackstone used the last of his strength to push Christiana towards the shore. Their feet found the riverbed. He dragged her onto the bank, and both slumped into the wet sand. Further down the bank the horse clambered ashore.

'Useless bastard!' a voice shouted at him. 'Bloody useless!' It was John Weston running into the shallows with Will Longdon as Elfred was easing the exhausted girl to her feet. A cheer from other soldiers washed over him as the two men dragged him onto firm ground.

'You swim like a goddamned chicken,' Will Longdon said.

Blackstone looked up to where Godfrey de Harcourt's esquire had come forward to help Christiana. She pulled herself away momentarily, looking back at Blackstone with concern.

'By St Agnes's teeth, I hope she's not going to come back and stroke you like a damned pup,' Weston said. 'Not in front of the whole damned army.'

Christiana saw he was alive and allowed the escort to help her away.

'I'll wager you'd not have come back for me if I'd been left behind,' Longdon said, hunching down next to the saturated Blackstone, who vomited salty estuary water.

'Not even if you wore a wimple and had teeth,' Blackstone told him.

Godfrey de Harcourt came forward. 'A damned stupid risk.

I can ill afford to lose a horse and even less an archer. Feed the horse and whip the boy.'

It was a fair judgement. Blackstone had taken it upon himself to go back and find the girl. But then a murmur swept along the line of men. The archers had paid dearly for getting the army across the ford. The hum of discontent quietened as a figure stepped through the ranks. Men moved aside as the young Prince of Wales and thirty of his entourage came down to the water's edge.

Blackstone, exhausted, was still on all fours when the men around him went down on one knee. Edward of Woodstock, Prince of Wales, stood before Thomas Blackstone.

'Who is this archer?'

Sir Godfrey bowed. 'His name is Thomas Blackstone,' he said.

'We feel such courage should not be rewarded with punishment,' the Prince said. 'Get up, Master Blackstone,' he gently commanded.

Blackstone got to his feet. For a moment he kept his head bowed, not wishing to force the heir to the throne of England to look up at one of his humble subjects. Blackstone was taller. Then he realized that the Prince stood a few feet away on the higher ground. He raised his head and looked into the face of a boy the same age as he.

'Who is the girl?' the Prince asked de Harcourt.

'She is a lady who serves my nephew's wife, Blanche, Countess de Harcourt, sire,' Sir Godfrey answered. The Prince had kept his eyes on Blackstone, observing the boy's features and the strength in his shoulders and arms. This was one of his archers who served in his division. He turned to the lame knight.

'And her husband and your brother serve with King Philip.'

'Yes, sire. My nephew and brother are sworn men to him. They could not be persuaded otherwise. The girl was trying to rejoin her mistress at Noyelles.'

The Prince nodded. The de Harcourts were a divided family. He looked back at Blackstone who lowered his eyes.

'Why did you go back for the girl?'

'I had given her my word that I would see her safely returned to the service of her lady, sire.'

'A pledge kept is honour gained. What reward would you have, Thomas Blackstone?'

'None, sire.'

'Well answered. We are pleased. But it is also our pleasure that you be rewarded. What shall it be?'

Blackstone dared to look up. The young Prince had a kindly face, but his eyes were unflinching as they studied him.

'Some food for the company of archers that led the way across the river, sire.'

'There is little food left, but we shall see it is given. They have earned that and more.' The Prince turned to de Harcourt. 'We are now in the county of Ponthieu, my father's inheritance from my grandmother. Your family is here. Take the girl to them and assure the lady countess and her mother that we wish them no harm. Sir Godfrey, we acknowledge your fealty. See them safe.'

'I will, sire.'

The Prince nodded. 'And see my archers fed.'

He made his way back through the ranks, offering words of encouragement and thanks to his fighting men, who cheered him.

'There'll be food and wine,' said Sir Godfrey, 'but you'd best re-arm yourself, Blackstone. Noyelles will be burning by nightfall.'

CHAPTER NINE

Chaos surged through the town's streets. The English soldiers, still charged with blood-lust from the bitter fighting at the ford, slaughtered the survivors from the beachhead and looted and burned the houses. King Edward expected his supplies from England to be waiting at Le Crotoy, a few miles up the coast. Noyelles was in the way of his raiding force.

Sir Gilbert led the way towards the town's castle. Choking, acrid smoke carried across rooftops, drifting into back alleys, forcing the citizens to flee. Behind Sir Gilbert the archers and men-at-arms shielded Christiana and Sir Godfrey from any final desperate act by townsmen or surviving levies. The flames of their hatred for the English had been fanned by despair at their King's failure to stop the invaders. Godfrey de Harcourt sent a herald forward with an armed escort to declare his identity at the castle and then issued orders for Sir Gilbert to secure the town from further destruction, placing it under his protection.

The castle gates were opened reluctantly by servants once de Harcourt's promise of safety had been relayed to the countess. Sir Godfrey and his men dismounted in the courtyard as the massive doors swung closed behind them. Blackstone looked at the high walls and parapets. A marshal of the English army and a company of archers with ten men-at-arms would have a hard time fighting their way out should this be an ambush. And why would it not be? Godfrey de Harcourt was a traitor and the women who waited for him in the keep might well be prepared to exact revenge. Blackstone checked himself, his thoughts now concentrated on preparing for the worst. He gave his reins to Richard and waited, hovering near

Christiana, hoping he might be instructed to help her dismount.

'Bring her,' de Harcourt ordered.

Before Blackstone could reach up and help her from the saddle, Christiana dismounted without aid. She gave Blackstone barely a glance, but pressed a piece of embroidered linen into the fold of his jacket and then turned away quickly to follow Sir Godfrey towards the four-storey tower. The lame man climbed the steps to the great hall without effort. Blackstone followed three men behind Christiana who had not looked back at him once. Uncertainty gnawed at him. Her warmth and sentiments seemed to have been swept away as if by the tide. Was she now a lady delivered safely, unconcerned about a common archer's feelings? Was the piece of linen only a token of gratitude?

'String your bows,' Elfred ordered the archers. He pointed at four of the men. 'Two here, two at those windows.' The archers moved into position. Blackstone knew that Elfred's natural inclination was the same as his own. Had the gates been opened too easily? Godfrey de Harcourt was a tenacious fighter who could ride a man half his age into the ground, but inbred arrogance could blind the most far-sighted man.

'Thomas, take your brother. Cover Sir Godfrey and his men inside.'

Elfred sent other men onto the walls. This bear pit of a place needed archers in good firing positions.

'Tom, Henry, search those stables. Matthew – top of those stairs!'

Blackstone looked at the archers as he followed de Harcourt, whose men-at-arms fell back, taking up posts at doorways and passage entrances.

Tom Brock and Matthew Hampton were old hands, Warwick's men like Will Longdon.

'Find a loophole, Thomas, we'll need some cover from up there,' Matthew said as he took up position. 'And don't get separated from the others. It's easy done in twisting corridors. Have your knife ready if you do.'

Blackstone nodded and went into the castle's gloom and chilled air. Men moved hurriedly, and the scraping of armour on stone walls along narrow passageways heralded de Harcourt's approach. One of the men cursed as his couter, an elbow guard, caught a protruding piece of badly mortared stone. If Blackstone had laid a wall in such a manner his master stonemason would have beaten him. The memory of that past life, abandoned only weeks ago, seemed so distant now. So too the times he shared with Richard, who, despite his affliction, could express laughter and joy. That had all been murdered and swept away like the bodies cast into the river at Caen.

Blackstone put his brother at a stairwell and had him watch through the arrow loops into the courtyard. Blackstone stayed ten paces behind Christiana and Sir Godfrey, who pushed open the doors into the great hall. He held his place and watched the girl rush forward, out of sight. Women's voices uttered cries of delight as Christiana was welcomed. And then one of the women stepped into view. Blackstone thought her to be about ten years older than himself. Her raven hair was curled into a knot at her shoulder, framing the beauty of her face. She was slightly taller than Christiana, who now stood by her side. However, the woman's fine features could not distract from the armour she wore, nor the sword in her hand. Blackstone edged closer to the half-opened door.

'My lady, we will cause no harm here,' de Harcourt told her.

'Your Englishmen do not share your sentiments,' she replied, but laid the sword down across an oak table in a gesture of acceptance. 'But you brought Christiana to us. I thank you for that.'

'Sir Godfrey and his Englishmen rescued me, my lady,' Christiana said. She looked towards de Harcourt who had his back to the door. Her eyes caught Blackstone. She pointed. 'He's the one who saved my life.'

Blackstone quickly stepped back as de Harcourt turned. Before he could admonish Blackstone for being so close, the armoured woman called, 'Let me see you!'

Christiana came forward and opened the door fully. Blackstone felt a flush of blood colouring his neck and face as he stood in the doorway under de Harcourt's glare. He stepped forward as ordered by de Harcourt's gesture.

'An archer.' She crossed herself. 'Dear sweet mother of God! I don't want these murderers in my sight. Get him out of this place,' she said.

Blackstone faltered. Christiana looked wounded. The older of the three women, dressed in the clothes of a noblewoman and with a bearing that commanded respect, stepped into view. 'Blanche, that will do,' she said quietly, but firmly.

In that moment Blanche de Harcourt looked as if she could snatch up the sword and attack Blackstone. 'Mother, you know what these men have done. You know their reputation.'

'I also know that my brother was a Norman, that the French King took his land and that four years ago he died fighting in alliance with the English.' She spoke directly to Blackstone. 'And he spoke of rough, crude men, English archers, and said he wished we had such men fighting for us. I am Countess d'Aumale and this lady who would strike at you is my daughter, Countess Blanche de Ponthieu, wife of Sir Godfrey's nephew. Your enemy.'

Blackstone tried to find words through his confusion and embarrassment, but none came. He went down on one knee.

'You have some manners, young English archer. Perhaps not all of you are as savage as your reputation suggests. Get up,' she told him.

Blackstone glanced at Christiana, who lowered her eyes. The girl had thought that the pride of showing her rescuer might have been a cause for gratitude.

'Christiana is dear to us all.' She glanced at the humbled girl. 'How might we reward you?'

Before Blackstone could reply, de Harcourt, irritated by the women's interest in a common archer, spoke for him. 'He's already refused the heir to the throne of England's offer of reward. He wants nothing.'

'If the Prince of Wales has been refused then we cannot suggest anything more, other than to offer our thanks.'

'My lady...' Blackstone stuttered.

'Get out,' Godfrey de Harcourt ordered.

Blackstone turned away, but not before seeing Christiana smile briefly at him, and a look in her eyes that he could not comprehend, but which made him feel flushed again. He stepped into the passage. Sir Godfrey slammed the door. The voices from the room were dulled by the heavy chestnut panels.

Blackstone waited a moment longer. He heard Sir Godfrey tell the women that he had seen his brother's banner at Rouen, also his nephew's. There was no doubt the French and English armies would soon clash.

'Surrender to me and you shall be protected,' Sir Godfrey said.

Blanche de Ponthieu's voice was still bitter. 'You go to fight your own family!'

De Harcourt was a man who would yield to no one, and no woman would have the better of him. His voice thundered around the hall. 'Their loyalty to King Philip is misplaced! You have no love for him! You tried to convince your husband, as I attempted to convince my brother, to side with me! You know the English will win.'

Blackstone moved away from the raised voices, needing to distract himself from the girl who was now with his enemy's family. Men-at-arms stood at their posts; his brother's back was towards him as he peered out of the arrow loop to the courtyard below where Elfred's men remained vigilant. Blackstone almost reached out to touch his shoulder. What care or love was left within his own family? He turned away and tugged out Christiana's small token of gratitude. On the square of cloth was embroidered a small bird – sharp-beaked, black-eyed, with blue plumage. It seemed familiar somehow, but he wasn't sure why. Little else of beauty had come his way in this war; he would keep it as a memento. All he could do now was to wait for Sir Godfrey.

Her presence startled him. She had slipped out of the hall and moved silently behind him. His hand had gone quickly to the knife at his belt. He muttered an apology and took a step back until he bumped into the wall. Damn, he was acting like a country oaf. She smiled. Her voice barely rose above a whisper, preventing her words from echoing through the stone corridors.

'I wish I could ask Sir Godfrey to leave you here, but my Lady de Harcourt would object,' she said.

'Why would you ask that?' he answered, forcing his voice to remain low, finding the words catching in his throat, as if they were two lovers meeting secretly.

'To protect us,' she said, and tentatively took a step closer to him. He could smell the sweet oils from her hair.

'And...' she continued, placing her hand on his, 'to keep you safe.'

Blackstone glanced nervously past her, hoping to God that none of the others happened to wander from their posts and catch sight of them. 'I'm a soldier. And I have to care for my brother. I couldn't stay, even if your lady did permit it.'

She nodded. She knew that. 'Will I see you again, Thomas Blackstone?'

'Would you wish to?' he answered, feeling the blood warm his face.

She smiled, her tenderness reaching out to him. 'Yes. I owe you my life. And you're the only one who cared enough to save it.'

Voices were raised again in the great hall. Christiana glanced anxiously over her shoulder. 'I must go.' She gripped his big, work-roughened hand that still held her embroidered cloth. 'Think of me,' she said.

Other than when her hand had rested on his they had hardly touched, and more than anything he wanted to pull her to him. But he didn't. It was too late. She had stepped away.

Men were moving somewhere along the corridors. She hesitated before going back towards the great hall, then glanced over her shoulder to him. 'I'll pray for your safe return,' she said. And was gone.

Elfred's voice carried, berating one of the men. Blackstone turned down an unguarded passage, distancing himself from the hall and the patrolling men-at-arms. It took a few moments for his head to clear. The castle's chill seeped into his hand from where he leaned against the stone wall. The rubble that had been used was smoother here; the mason had taken greater care to lay the lime mortar flush between the stone contours. Blackstone ran his palm against the castle's skin. This had been a better mason. A man who, more than a century earlier, had taken pride in his workmanship. Perhaps the cut base stone would yield the man's mark or initials. His eyes followed the line of mortar and saw the gouge in its dry curve. Someone had stumbled against it. To cut the surface they must have been wearing armour. The scar was at shoulder height and the dull stain was fresh. Blackstone looked down onto the floor. The granite slabs hid the colour of the blood but could not disguise its sheen.

Blackstone's heart thumped. This passage was no place to draw his bow. He slung it across his back and unsheathed his long archer's knife. Stepping slowly, placing his feet carefully on the cold floor, he followed where the light glinted on the bloodstains. They led to a side chamber, its entrance covered with heavy, embroidered drapes hung from a pole. He slowed his breathing, listening for any sound that might indicate immediate danger. Standing in front of where the drapes met he took out an arrow and slowly pushed it between the two hangings. He eased aside the one and took a half-step back, his grip tightening on the knife handle, ready to meet any attack.

What he saw was a boy, probably no more than nine or ten years old, who sat on the floor, his back against the bare chamber's wall. The child sweated, hair matted to his forehead, dried blood and mud covered his hose and jupon that bore the coat of arms of the knight who defended the river crossing, Godemar du Fay. The boy's breathing shuddered in fear and the dagger he held at arm's length, pointing at Blackstone, shook noticeably. The child was defending a bare-headed knight who lay next to him. He'd taken a savage beating and was barely conscious. An arrow shaft had punched through his shoulder plates. The bones would be shattered, the pain excruciating. A wound in his side seeped dark blood below his breastplate. Blackstone realized his liver must have been punctured. The man, who looked to be in his early twenties, was in du Fay's service, and the brave, shivering boy must have been his page. They were obviously survivors who had sought sanctuary with the countess. And they would be killed if Godfrey de Harcourt or his men saw them. De Harcourt had no need to ransom a wounded knight.

Blackstone glanced quickly behind him. One of the men-at-arms had passed by the end of the passage. Blackstone hesitated and then stepped into the chamber, closing the embroidered cloth behind him. The boy whimpered, tears welled in his eyes and the knife trembled even more violently. The knight whispered something, his eyes locked onto the English archer who approached, still holding the gutting knife. Blackstone stopped. If the boy lunged he might get in a lucky hit. Again the man whispered and this time Blackstone understood what he said.

'Spare the boy,' the wounded man asked.

Blackstone raised a hand and spoke gently to the terrified page. 'I shall look at your lord's wound,' he said quietly, anxious not to be heard by anyone down the passage. Then he turned to the wounded man, saying, 'I will not harm either of you. You have my word.'

He faced the boy and put a finger to his lips, then sheathed his knife. Open-handed he went down on one knee three feet from the boy. Blackstone kept his eyes on the boy's, then eased forward, allowing him the chance to attack. The dagger was only inches from his face.

The French knight sighed a command and the boy reluctantly lowered the pointed blade. Blackstone dared not ease the man's breastplate for fear that he would cry out, but the wound still seeped. There was nothing he could do about the arrow, its white fletching now saturated to a dark, sticky mass. The page had obviously tried to staunch the stomach wound, for a piece of fine linen was packed below the armour's edge – the kind of fine linen a countess would have on her person. This wounded knight must have arrived only moments before de Harcourt and his men.

Blackstone tugged the linen further. It was soaked. He unslung his bow and loosened his own jupon, then rolled it and with great care eased it beneath the plate. The man grimaced but bore the pain in silence. The pressure from the rolled cloth would hold the wound a while longer.

The man nodded in thanks.

'My lord,' Blackstone said, barely above a whisper, 'you are dying. I cannot help you. I cannot find you a priest and I cannot offer you any comfort. I will leave you now and hope the good lady of this place will soon be at your side.'

The knight nodded, reached out and touched Blackstone's sleeve. Blackstone took his hand away with a gentle pressure, then placed it into those of his page. 'Stay quietly with your brave master until we are gone. The lady will come for you,' Blackstone said. He stood and picked up his bow. Godfrey de Harcourt had summoned his men to leave. The knight's hushed voice was barely audible. 'I shall ask God when I see Him to give you His blessing and pray someone will show mercy to you in your hour of need.'

'No one will ever show me mercy,' Blackstone said. 'I'm an English archer.'

He checked that the passage was clear and stepped out, leaving the man to die.

The French army had stood impotently across the ford, the river being too high to contemplate a crossing. They waited for two tides to come and go before deciding that the English-held shore could not be assaulted. They had no choice but to retreat as far as Abbeville, cross the river and gain the northern bank to pursue Edward. What was obvious to everyone on the English side, from noble lord to common stable lad, was that the French army, recognized as the finest fighting force in Europe, was at least twice as large as Edward's.

The English reinforcements and supplies that should have been on ships from England, and waiting at Le Crotoy, had not even left their home port. The raiding party ransacked the town and surrounding countryside. At least the army would eat, but they would do battle with the weapons and men they had. A messenger brought news from Sir Hugh Hastings and the Flemish army. They had pushed south from France's northern border, but their attacks on the French fortified towns had failed and they had retreated into Flanders. The two armies could not join up; Edward was on his own. He marched his army eastwards through the county of Ponthieu, moving into the oak and beech trees of the vast forest of Crécy-en-Ponthieu, slipping out of sight of King Philip's army, which, with de Harcourt's brother and nephew, was less than ten miles away.

There would soon be no choice. The English would have to stand and fight.

'Thomas. Sir Gilbert wants you,' Will Longdon said as he picked his way through the trees. The army had camped in the forest for the night along the ridge between Crécy and the hamlet of Wadicourt. The dawn's chill crept into the aching muscles of the battle-weary men. Blackstone rolled out of his blanket, hunched his shoulders against the damp forest air, yawned and stretched out the stiffness. Richard still slept as he always had done, resting his cheek on his hands like a child.

'Where?'

'Hundred yards. That way. Edge of the forest.'

Blackstone nodded. 'D'you have food?'

'A piece of mutton from what Despenser's men foraged yesterday.'

'Will you stay with Richard until I'm back? Give him something to eat. We got little from the supplies.'

'Course I will. Here.' He offered a palm-sized piece of wrapped meat. Blackstone took a small bite and swilled it down with a mouthful of wine. He rubbed his eyes and scrubbed his fingers through his hair. He slung his bow and fastened his belt. The bristles on his face itched. The two men nodded at each other in farewell.

'Thomas.'

Blackstone turned.

'Say yes,' Longdon said and without further explanation settled himself into his friend's still-warm blanket.

Blackstone picked his way through the forest past hundreds of huddled men, the smell of their stale sweat mingling with the horses' musky odour, and caught sight of a horseman through the trees. He sighted from tree to tree, working his vision deeper into the forest. It was the King and his nobles edging their horses through the forest. Was the King leaving his troops? Perhaps at last he had decided to call a truce. Blackstone felt a flutter of panic: God knows the men were worn down with fatigue, but they were in good spirits. They had beaten the French twice when outnumbered. If Edward called a truce they would be going home; to return to the hamlet and the life he had had with his brother. The memory of that place followed him as he made his way down the slope. Could he ever return home, even if given the choice? His father's war bow had been the archer's inheritance that poured strength into his arm every time he drew it. The warrior's spirit, his father had once told him, lives on in his deeds and the weapons he cherished. But what of his duty towards Richard that had been bequeathed him? The boy had fought at his shoulder, even carrying Sir Gilbert to safety. Perhaps Richard was the better soldier after all. If there was a truce could he stay? Would a common man ever be allowed to see such a girl as Christiana again? She wasn't nobility, unlike the family she served. If she was ever to be more than a simple desire, what would happen to his brother? There was something else his father had told him: A man's duty only ended in death.

He found Sir Gilbert with Elfred, the knight's horse already saddled.

'You sleep like the dead,' Sir Gilbert said. 'Dreaming of the girl, were you?'

'I was too tired to dream of anything,' Blackstone answered.

'Tiredness is a soldier's pay. Elfred said you fought well at the river.'

'We all did,' Blackstone answered.

'Aye, but you served me at Poissy with that shooting of yours. And you've a good eye for what's what. I always thought you had.'

Blackstone didn't know what he was supposed to say. 'I see the King and the earls are riding out, Sir Gilbert. Are we moving on?'

Sir Gilbert climbed awkwardly into the saddle, barely able to hide the grimace of pain from his wounds. 'Shall I tell the King his archer Thomas Blackstone is concerned?'

'It was just a thought, Sir Gilbert.'

'That's what you do, Thomas, you think. I told Lord Marldon as much, but I didn't know you had the courage to overcome it. Too much thinking can get in the way of a soldier's life. I've tried to avoid it wherever I can. Roger Oakley died at the crossing.'

Blackstone nodded. 'I saw him fall. He led us well.'

'And he's probably leading the devil a merry dance now. The King's waiting. I'm late. Elfred, tell him.' He urged the horse away to join the retinue whose rich colours moved through the forest until they disappeared from view among the trees.

'Our lads are mostly farmers' boys and craftsmen, but they've not shied away from what's been asked of them. They're as good a company of archers as I've seen,' Elfred said.

'They've got their tails up now. Even John Weston's saying we've fought their best and won,' Blackstone said.

'He's right, but it's not over yet, Thomas. We're not running no more. The King's picked his spot, the French scouts were on that hill at first light.'

'We're to fight here?'

Elfred nodded. 'Centenars are bringing their archers out of the woods, soon as the captains tell us where the marshals want us. They've gone with the King to see the ground.'

Blackstone let the information sink in. He gazed across the hillside. The woods would form a good defence at their rear. A series of long-abandoned *radaillons* – steep, contoured cultivation terraces – offered protection to the army's left. The undulating ground would funnel the enemy around and into the centre. Pick your ground, is what Sir Gilbert had told him: choosing where you fight can make the difference between winning and losing. The French would be forced to attack uphill through the gap that the forest and hillside presented.

'It's a good place, Elfred.'

'I'll be sure to let the King know you approve.'

Blackstone smiled. 'I want my breakfast, what do you want with me?'

'There's to be no reinforcements. Hastings has lost the north. A messenger came after the crossing. It's us and the King; we're what's got to stop the French, and Thomas, none of these lads, except for some of the older hands like John and Will, have ever seen a heavy cavalry charge. It's something that can crack the strongest man's courage,' Elfred told him, biting into a stale oatcake. He passed the other half to Blackstone, who took it gratefully.

'They'll stand their ground. They won't let their fear grip them. They haven't so far,' Blackstone said.

'I've spoken to the men and they agree with me that you should be my ventenar. The twenty men you'll command have all spoken in your favour, except your brother who'll go where you go. Sir Gilbert's given the decision his blessing.'

Blackstone swallowed the dry biscuit.

'Following someone like you and Master Oakley was what I did. That's all,' he said.

'Up to you, lad. If you don't want the responsibility, you say so now.'

'What about Will Longdon, or John or any of the others?'

'Lot of the old hands don't want other men's lives depending on their decisions. We fight for each other, but commanding men is a different thing altogether.'

'I've a lot to learn still,' Blackstone said, the weight of the decision lying heavily on him.

'And there's them around who'll still show you what's necessary. You think of Nicholas Bray, Roger and Sir Gilbert – you learnt from them and I hope from me since you've been here.'

'I have, Elfred.'

'Well, then. What do I tell Sir Gilbert?'

Blackstone led his company of archers down the centre of the battle lines as the English banners and pennons were raised. The marshals placed a thousand archers at either flank, forming them up into a triangular wedge that shielded each side of the men-at-arms and knights. The archers would have first contact with the French, their arrows killing and driving the attackers into the centre – the killing ground. Blackstone and his company joined the hundred archers sent between the ranks to loose their arrows directly into the faces of the heavy cavalry when they charged.

Blackstone and his men dug pits a foot square and a foot deep to make the great destriers stumble.

'I saw you boys do that at Morlaix in 'forty-two,' a Welsh spearman said as he sat sharpening his spearhead. 'Crippled the horses, brought them down lovely it did. Had them French bastards falling arse over tit. You could hear their bones breaking like corn being ground in milling stones. Lovely sound. Meant they didn't struggle much when we stuck them like flailing pigs.' The Welshman spat and went back to his sharpening, the men with him nodding in agreement.

'Aye, well, I was at Morlaix and you're the same lazy Welsh bastards now that you were then. Instead of sitting on your arse you could lend a hand,' Will Longdon told them as he dug another pit-trap, cutting turf and scraping the hole with his long knife.

'No, no, we wouldn't want to stop a skilled man like yourself from doing what he does best. And when you've done that you could dig us fighting men a shit pit,' the spearman said. The Welshmen laughed but the humour did not touch the archers.

'We're digging them just deep enough so we can bury you bastard bog rats after the horses trample you into the ground, 'cause that'll be as much as there is left of you,' John Weston said, and spat a globule that landed dangerously close to the Welshman's feet.

The spear flicked quickly and Weston found the killing end of the spear shaft hovering close to his throat.

'You have to be careful in a battle. Easy to get taken down by your own side,' the Welshman said, his voice low with intent. 'We *bog rats* have seen that happen before.'

John Weston didn't give a damn and stayed where he was, with the spear point quivering close to his neck, as the others watched the standoff. 'Then count yourself lucky that the back of your skull's too thick for a bodkin-tipped arrow to pierce.'

One of the other Welshmen joined in. 'Lad's got a point there, Daffyd. Take more than an Englishman's arrow to get between your ears.'

The spear leveller drew it back, the rumble of agreement and laughter among the Welshmen easing the tension.

The archers went back to digging but the surly Welshman had kept his eye on Weston, a look that Blackstone realized might turn to something more when the mayhem of close-quarter battle engulfed them all. He wiped the dirt from his hands across his jacket.

'My father was a bowman, he said he'd learnt how to pull his war bow from a Welsh archer. So, when the French come, we'll bring them down and you finish them. That seems a fair bargain,' he said, looking at the Welshman.

The act of conciliation was not lost on the Welshman and the belligerent spearman nodded but then his eyes locked onto the medallion that had come free from Blackstone's jacket and the truce melted away.

'You stole that?' he said.

Blackstone took it in his fingers and tucked it away. 'A Welsh archer gave it to me at Caen.'

The other Welshmen had heard and now took an interest in Blackstone himself.

'A Welshman wouldn't give that away. Not to a bastard Englishman and Christian. Not that,' one of the others said. 'He'd have to be a dead man for you to have it.'

Blackstone looked at them; his company of archers had stopped digging and stood behind him. If there was trouble to be had they were willing to finish it.

'He was dying. I helped him. If any of you know a Welshman by the name Gruffydd ap Madoc he'll tell you. If you don't, then I don't care what you think.'

'Gruffydd ap Madoc? He'll vouch for you?'

Conciliation had passed. It was time to stand his ground. 'Repeat his name often enough and perhaps you'll remember it. Ask him,' Blackstone said. 'I've work to do.' He turned his back on the scowling Welshman and looked at his men. *His* men. Their loyalty was already being tested. Richard stood full square, knife in hand, understanding the belligerent looks. Will Longdon, John Weston, the others, none of them took their eyes from the Welshmen.

'Pick up your bows. We're done here,' Blackstone said.

'What would an Englishman know of a pagan talisman?' the spearman asked, and as Blackstone turned, the spearhead pressed against his chest.

He half raised an arm, stopping the archers from making any aggressive moves. Soldiers, when they fought each other, be the grievance perceived or real, would not stop until someone lay dead. And soon after someone else would swing from the end of a rope.

He stared down the Welshman. 'It's Arianrhod. Goddess of the Silver Wheel. She protects you in this life and then carries you across to the next. He gave it to me with his blessing. And you're as close as you're going to be to seeing if she can help you.'

Before the man could do or say anything, there was a flurry in the ranks as men were pushed aside. A figure, obscured by the others, cuffed the Welshman to the ground. Blackstone recognized the white-haired fighter from the battle for Caen.

'He's pig-shit ignorant, Thomas Blackstone. He fell from his sow-mother's belly into a ditch and has been trying to crawl out of it ever since. Are these your men?'

'They are, Gruffydd ap Madoc.'

He scowled. 'I'm not surprised. They look rougher than a thistle-eating hog's arse.'

The Welshmen laughed and a moment later so did the archers. Gruffydd enveloped Blackstone in a bearhug, and then punched him on the arm. Blackstone managed not to grimace in pain.

'Are we to have your archers in our ranks?'

'Between you and the men-at-arms.'

Gruffydd turned to his wild-looking men. 'Treat these boys with courtesy if you want them to leave you some French to kill.' He kicked the fallen man who had stayed down. 'And you would do well to remember that Arianrhod has her arms around this fellow. I will see you again, young Thomas Blackstone.'

'And I you.'

Gruffydd nodded at Blackstone and turned back to deploying his men. For a moment Blackstone felt a pang of fear, though less for himself, it seemed, than for those French who were yet to die at the hands of fierce Welsh spearmen, battle-hungry knights and the most lethal of killers on the battlefield, the archers.

CHAPTER TEN

By midday the English army had formed up on the hill slope with the woods of Crécy at their back and the town nearby to the south-east. The windmill on top of the ridge served as the King's headquarters and he settled his division there, a place where his standard would be flown for all to see. On the forward slope were two battalions, comprising a mixture of infantry and dismounted cavalry. The battles across northern France had depleted the King's army. There were only about four thousand surviving archers – a thousand to be deployed on each flank and two thousand at the rear in reserve with the King. The forward and most dangerous edge of the battleground was held by the vanguard under the Prince, and with him stood the great names of English nobility, their surcoats, shields, banners and pennons declaring to the enemy that they were the prize for any ambitious French knight. Warwick, Northampton, Cobham, Audley, Stafford and Holland – men who had led by example and fought with a tireless zeal to engage and kill their enemy and who were fired with the knowledge that they would be pursued no longer. They knew no quarter would be given and that knowledge only strengthened their determination to be the ones doing the killing. The marshals of the army, Warwick and de Harcourt, gave captains their orders. War horses were removed to the rear as knights prepared to fight on foot. Hobelars and Welsh spearmen held the centre ground with the men-at-arms, and Blackstone's archers were among them, less than one hundred paces from the Prince himself. They were the added force in place to keep any surge of Frenchmen from reaching the boy Prince. When the French swung from the south through the folding land the vanguard would be the first to take the full attack. Northampton's division was to the Prince's left and slightly back: added protection should the French be foolish enough to try to attack from the marshier ground at the bottom of the hill. The preparations were made. The King ordered his men to rest and eat whatever food was left to them. He wanted them strong when the enemy came at them. There was nothing more to do but wait.

The men sat on the ground. Richard Blackstone lay on his back watching a cloud change shape, tracing its contortions with his finger. Men ate whatever food they had been given. The muggy August heat threatened rain, and sweat trickled down their backs. Blackstone was pleased he wore no armour.

'They won't come now. Too late in the day,' Will Longdon said as he checked the fletchings, fingering each arrow, and then, like the others, pressing its point into the ground, making a small forest of ash and goose feather. Each archer had been given two sheaves and each sheaf was twenty-four arrows. These men could loose a dozen arrows and more every minute. Thirty thousand arrows would fall from the clouding sky in the first two minutes of the attack. The carnage would be terrifying and no matter how Blackstone tried to imagine it, he could not. He had never seen an army stand and fight.

'They'll be wanting food and a bed for the night and then the Kings'll parlay and decide on a time tomorrow, which suits me, because I could eat a donkey,' Weston grumbled and smoothed a hand along the bend of his bow stave, seeming to derive comfort from it.

'They'll come,' one of the Welshmen said. 'They can't wait to finish us off. Then they'll bedroll and eat.'

'Aye, they like a good slaughter, do the French,' said Matthew Hampton.

And a murmur ran along the line. There was no doubt who were the underdogs. Blackstone felt for his talisman and the rough length of linen with the embroidered bird. Two women guarded his life – Arianrhod and Christiana. He looked at Richard, who

still gazed with childish wonder at the sky; a boy who could kill
as well as any man and barely a year younger than the Prince of
Wales, who stood in the van of battle. Richard seemed not to
understand the meaning of fear. He had proved his daring and
courage often enough.

Blackstone was afraid but did not show it.

Of which son would the father have been most proud?

A roar, like a battle cry, broke Blackstone's reverie. The men
were on their feet. Above them on the ridge the King's banner – the
lions of England and the lilies of France – unfurled in the humid
air and beside it the red-painted dragon battle standard.

'Drago! Drago!' the men roared.

The cheers settled as the King rode down on a palfrey, his
great war horse already tethered with the thousands of others.
The marshals Warwick and de Harcourt with the constable of
the army, the battle-hardened Northampton, rode among the
troops. The King, bareheaded, had not yet put on his armour
and wore a green and gold pourpoint, the heavy, padded linen
undershirt worn to make the armour a more comfortable fit.
As he moved along the line of men, he pointed with a white
baton to those he recognized. Then he would stop and address
them, each of the three divisions. Blackstone and those around
him could not yet hear the King's words, but laughter and then
cheers marked his passage. By the time the King drew rein in
front of the men-at-arms and archers where Blackstone stood,
the anticipation of being so close to their King ran through them
like a shiver down a horse's back.

'Have we rested enough from our walk across Normandy, lads?'

'We have!'

'Aye!'

Men yelled out their answer.

'And with a lesson or two in swimming, sire!' one called. The
King smiled and the men laughed.

'Then we think it's time to fight this King who lays claim to
these lands and who believes that once he has beaten us this day

156

he will settle in our kingdom and let his men become acquainted with those we call our own.'

The roar of disapproval brought another smile to the King's face, but then his brow furrowed and his voice lost its cheerfulness. 'We urge you all to stand your ground, never yield, do not break ranks, because we have the better of this King, my cousin. We know him and his army. They do not lack courage; they have a ferocity that is well known and this *furor franciscus* will spew its rage onto us all. But they cannot win this battle. They cannot, I swear to you. English and Welsh blood alike will be shed, that is a promise we can make and keep, but the day is already won, that is a promise we make in the eyes of God. Our own son will stand with you, he will live or die at your side. There is no ransom to be had from the capture of a noble knight or lord, and there is to be no robbing of the dead. This is our day of glory. Their destruction will be spoken of for ages to come. They do not know what fury it is *we* possess. Keep my words close to you. We take no prisoners. We give no mercy. Kill them. Kill them all,' he commanded.

The blood-lust roar reverberated across the hills.

Richard Blackstone had not taken his eyes from his King. The silent world he inhabited was something he had understood since childhood. The scent of the wind and the change in weather comforted his senses as much as the colours of field and sky. This man chosen by God had looked at him and the air had vibrated with a hum as those around him bared their teeth and bellowed at the sky. They were angels on earth who would slay anyone who offered a threat. His brother had not looked his way and the warmth in his chest he once felt had deserted him. The fighting had been easy. It required strength and the ability to kill without feeling. He had both. Life in his caged world channelled his emotions elsewhere. The girl at home had once given him that warmth and he had tried to tell her through clumsy gestures and incoherent sounds. She would smile and stroke his head and reach down for his manhood and bring him to her. The soft moistness of her brought tears to his eyes. Nothing in the world was as tender as the rhythmic movement of that girl who laid her hands on his broken face and eased his lips onto her breasts. When her eyes closed and she smiled, he followed her into the same darkness to try to share that moment. He had not meant to kill her. The act was something he had buried within himself. When his brother had found out his secret it was as if a knife had cut into him. Now nothing could bring his brother back.

The long-haired men with spears, some with strange markings painted on their faces, avoided his gaze. The men who pulled their war bows, just as his father had taught him, were closer now than his own brother. They would jig and dance and some would fall down from drink, but all were simple savages who could kill to stay alive. There was no regret in slaying others to keep your own breath from bubbling through your chest from a sword thrust.

He looked down the line. Men in chain mail and armour stood ready, the spearmen leaned on their weapons and the men with bows had taken their places between the ranks. He could see a young man kneel before the King and the King kissed him on the lips as his brother once did to him. The King loved that boy just as his father had loved him. The boy was surrounded by the men who wore armour and coloured cloth, there were flags held around him. And then the father left the son and the boy pulled on his helm. He looked around him. Men were not bellowing now. Their jaws were set tight and their eyes squinted into the late afternoon light. He turned to look to his front and saw the green hills making a startling contrast with the colours of a multitude of men and horses.

The French had arrived.

Sir Gilbert ordered his men to their positions.

'This is where we stand or die, lads. When the honour of France comes around that hill they'll have their Oriflamme fluttering against the sky. It's not blood-red without reason. It's their sacred battle flag, blessed by every whoremongering priest in Christendom, and it means they'll not be taking prisoners either. Any of us. King,

Prince, earl or common man, they'll mean to kill us all unless we kill them first. God bless you, lads. I'll not leave this field until I am dead or our King's enemy is defeated.'

Sir Gilbert took up his position in the front rank.

Elfred went to join his archers on the extreme flank and touched Blackstone on the shoulder as he passed by.

'Till later, Thomas. Aim true. They mustn't break the line.'

Blackstone nodded; the fear was already gnawing at his bowels, but he would not let his men see it. The sound of trumpets and kettledrums rolled across the hillside.

The French were coming to slaughter them.

Five thousand Genoese crossbowmen had been hurried along the road from Abbeville. Behind them the French mounted men-at-arms and knights could barely restrain their war horses. The way to fight a war was to charge, lances cut down to six feet to kill the third line of defenders once the first had been skewered by crossbow quarrels and the second smashed by iron-shod hooves. Sword, mace, mallet and axe would scythe or cripple the rest. The world knew that the French army was the most powerful and efficient fighting force and, on this day at Crécy-en-Ponthieu, thirty thousand of them would crush an upstart King with fewer than ten thousand fighting men under his command. They who dared to confront King Philip VI of France were going to die.

As they rode towards the battlefield knights tilted their heads back with open visors, grateful for the rain that offered a respite from the humid air and dusty roads. At this pace they would soon be at the English lines. A long August twilight would give them time enough to end the day in victory.

The veil of rain that swept across the landscape swirled towards the men on the hill awaiting the onslaught. Without need of command the archers unstrung their bows and tucked the cords inside jackets and beneath leather caps. They were taking no chances of the damp stretching them and reducing the arrows' flight. The downpour passed, the clouds blew further inland and sunlight spread a warm light that turned the wet grassland to gold and glistened off wet French armour and shields.

Blackstone glanced behind him and squinted at the low sun. The King and the marshals had chosen this place more carefully than he had realized. Not only would the attacking French be clambering uphill but they would be facing into the westering sun.

'Here they come,' someone said calmly as the archers restrung their bows.

The tramping of thousands of feet and hooves vibrated through the ground. Richard Blackstone could feel it more keenly than most, the trembling land speaking to him. He breathed in the damp air and held it for a moment in his nostrils and lungs. The grass smelled sweet and the air carried a fragrance from meadows and forest. He moaned a sound of contentment. Blackstone turned and looked at his grinning face. The sadness he felt at the loss of the mute boy's innocence could not be concealed. He reached out and touched the boy's shoulder. He would give anything not to have known about the girl's death. Richard read the pain in his brother's eyes. Blackstone touched his heart and lips and then reached out his hand. A final gesture of love before the uncertainty of battle. The crooked-jawed boy took it and pressed his wet mouth against the rough palm.

Genoese crossbowmen and marines, whose numbers equalled more than half of the English army, roared insults at the stoic English. They were the first of three divisions wide, three deep, the huge Oriflamme battle flag carried by the rear division for all the English to see. The crossbowmen were soaked, and they were tired and hungry. The French treated them with disdain and had hurried them to the battlefield. When crossbowmen loosed their bolts it took time to crank their weapons' mechanisms to fire again. In a set battle they would normally be protected by large shields big enough to hide behind as they reloaded, but today their French paymasters had left these *paviseurs* with the baggage train. It was expected that the crossbowmen would cut down the English front ranks and then the armoured destriers and knights would do the rest. French impatience and a cloudburst would prove the downfall of the Genoese.

The English faced the bellowing ranks now within crossbow range and watched as several thousand steel-sprung bolts were loosed. As they fluttered earthwards the second rank had moved through them and fired. Massed trumpets and drums picked up their tempo, a cacophony of bravado. But the English and Welsh ranks did not flinch. If those bolts had fallen into them it would have been lethal, but they fell short, striking the ground in front of the English men-at-arms. Facing the sun and shooting uphill, they had misjudged their distance and the twisted rawhide cords on the crossbows had stretched from the rain.

A murmur of satisfaction rippled through English ranks.

'Poor bastards,' Will Longdon muttered. 'Is that the best they can do?'

They could hear the commands of the centenars from the right and left flanks. 'Nock! Mark! Draw! Loose!'

Blackstone and the others craned their necks as the dense hail of arrows shivered through the air. Then the thunderclaps of the ribalds, bound four-inch barrels mounted on small carts that spewed smoke and metal pieces, added their firepower. Edward had placed them each side of the archers' flanks. They were not effective killers like the bowmen, but their booming and their belching smoke and flame caused fear and confusion, ending in death when the arrows fell. It was carnage. The English went on loosing and the iron-tipped arrows plummeted into flesh and bone. The Genoese broke and ran.

'Look at that!' Blackstone said as he saw hundreds of French knights ride forward, trampling the Genoese and then killing those survivors that sword and lance could find. Sir Gilbert turned where he stood on the front rank, shield raised, sword held in the loop of his belt because every man-at-arms and knight held a lance, ready to jam into the muscles of the French stallions – those that had escaped being crippled by the pits – when they reached the lines.

'All right, lads, that's the French King's brother doing that. He's an impatient bastard, is the Duke of Alençon, and he wants to get at us. He's getting a few obstacles out of the way first. If they close on us cry out for Saint George. Shout loud. Not everyone has surcoat or shield to identify themselves. Here they come. Archers!'

The pounding charge surged across the dead Genoese, a line of knights so broad and deep that Blackstone could not see the divisions behind them. War horses, snorting nostrils blood-red, carried the armoured men forward at the charge. The destriers, heads and chests encased in arrow-deflecting plate, galloped shoulder to shoulder, battle-trained into a ruthless, crushing mass of unstoppable power. 'Broadheads!' Blackstone shouted and the archers nocked the ragged-edged hunting arrows. The triangular barbed heads would rip muscle and tear vital organs. The archers on the flanks loosed another cloud of arrows, and moments before they arced out of the sky Blackstone aimed at the horses' legs, pushing aside the long cloth coverings, the rich hues of the trappers rustling like the knights' banners.

'Draw!' His left leg went a stride forward, the bow came up, the rough hemp cord pulled back to his ear. A magnificent animal barely controlled by the knight on its back was his target. 'Loose!'

The fatal, hurtling arrowstorm struck the French from above just as their horses screamed in agony from Blackstone's lower trajectory. A tumbling, broken mass staggered on the wet grass sluiced with blood, desperate for a foothold.

'Sweet Christ,' a pagan Welshman blasphemed, unheard by the archers who had already loosed three more arrows into the flailing hooves and crippled knights. Arrows pierced the terrified horses' chests and flanks, making deep wounds that bled the vitality and life from them and inflicted more pain than any animal could endure. Legs snapped as they went down under the weight of their riders and the horsemen ploughing on from behind. Mud-spattered knights raked their spurs into their stallions' flanks, kneeing them to manoeuvre around crippled and crazed horses.

'Keep it steady!' Blackstone shouted, as he bent and loosed, creating a rhythm of fire that was unrelenting. 'Don't waste your arrows. Aim and shoot. Aim and shoot!'

The French kept coming.

And dying.

A massive heartbeat of French kettledrums thumped louder, urging the knights forward. Trumpets blew a varying pitch as if their power could knock down the English. Packed men herded closer, lances down, shields raised. Some bore wounds but rode on, and those whose wealth afforded quality armour that deflected the archers' attempts to slaughter them cried *Montjoie!* and came at the English in all their pride and savagery. Horses went nose-down at the pit-traps, others carried horrific wounds, but their courageous hearts pumped blood to muscle and sinew and kept their momentum going, urged on by vicious spurs from men who now gave no thought for the beasts they had once cherished.

Sir Gilbert's men-at-arms stepped into the fray and cut the surviv-ors down. No man died easily and the heavy clang of sword against armour echoed up and down the lines. It was hard, brutal work that demanded strength and stamina. Men wearing seventy pounds of armour had no chance of regaining their feet if they went down. To slip or be stunned meant death. Thousands of crossbowmen were dead, hundreds of knights lay mortally wounded and not one defender had died. The French men-at-arms fell back to regroup out of the archers' range. The horses' screams were pitiful.

'We should go and finish the wretched creatures,' Will Longdon said. 'It'd be a mercy.'

'You know what the King said, Will: no mercy today,' said Blackstone as he counted the arrows he had left. 'Arrows?' he called to the men.

'Three,' Will Longdon said.

'I've five,' John Weston moaned. 'Couple of the fletchings look as though they'd throw the flight.'

'It'll be close range, John. Aim and loose,' Blackstone told him. Others in the company were low on arrows. Each man called what he had: two, three, one, four, none. He could see boys and clerics running from the rear carrying tied sheaves to replenish the archers.

Sir Gilbert turned. 'They'll get closer next time. There's so many of them they'll get through eventually. You archers be ready to move back, you've no defence against men like these.'

'We'll stand our ground, Sir Gilbert. Once we have arrows we can take them head on.'

Sir Gilbert nodded, too tired to offer either admonition or praise. Boys ran with waterskins and buckets from the baggage train. Fighting men scooped handfuls, tipped the skins, sucked the life-giving moisture into their parched mouths.

The lull in the battle gave men a few moments to lean on their swords, slump onto the grass and loosen their helmets. Blackstone, sweat-soaked and hurting, considered that these armoured men could take no more battering. The fallen horses and pit-traps had slowed the French advance; they were no longer a disciplined attacking line. The ground had forced them to manoeuvre into fighting pockets of men, which left them vulnerable to infantry attack from the sides. Swarming soldiers, knights and spearmen were bringing down horsemen unable to defend themselves on all sides.

Then back came the French. Sweat-slathered horses, white flecks of foam splashing their bridles and legs, charged at full gallop; their sheer weight of numbers would bring them into the English lines. The English watched as another storm of harrowing pain fell from the sky into the determined attackers. Knights held fast in their high-pommelled saddles swayed and slumped, dead or mortally wounded as their brave horses carried them forward. Less than fifty yards from the front line the first of the horses stepped into the foot-deep pits. Men could hear the crack of bone from where they stood.

Despite the leather guard Blackstone felt the skin of his fingers tear from the constant pressure of releasing the bowcord. His strength was not diminishing; if anything, his arms found a strength he never knew existed. He was beyond pain. This butchery was a slaughter that no man had witnessed before. *That's as much glory as you'll see in a battle*, Sir Gilbert had told him when he was vomiting at the crossroads in Normandy after he had killed his first man. There could not be enough vomit in the world to puke on this field.

Richard Blackstone was firing at a greater rate than any of the men. Blackstone could almost see his arrow strikes. Whereas some archers would miss because of the swirling mêlée of men and horse, Richard's arrows struck home every time.

And the French came on. Over their dead comrades, past the white-eyed, terrified horses, flailing in agony, through the rain-storm of high-angled arrows that fell with such velocity that plate armour was no defence. Knights were shot through with a yard of ash, skewered to their saddles.

But still they came, their fury unabated, their lust to kill unquenched. Even battle-hardened English knights could do little more than admire such awesome courage. And kill them. And still the French had not breached the English lines. The knights urged their horses away from the archers' flanks, aiming themselves squarely at the Prince of Wales. His banner, and those of the nobles, was the beacon the French sought. The Prince's surcoat, quartered with the lions of England and lilies of France, was plain for all to see and he had fought this, his first engagement, with the wildness of youth abetting his strength. All the times his tutors had knocked him to the ground, with the King's permission, in order to teach him the strike and parry blows of swordsmanship were now put to good use. But the moment would come when those in the French vanguard of the attacking force would fall on the front line and the weight of those following horsemen would thrust them into the flimsy ranks of defence that still held.

Blackstone could see only the powerful horses relentlessly coming on. The ground shuddered, clods of mud flew from their hooves; lances tilted, sword arms were held high, shields were feathered with arrows. How could men see through the narrow slits of the dog-faced bascinets? he wondered as he levelled a shaft at a knight wearing a surcoat of a red cross on a dark green background. They were shooting on a flatter trajectory now and the bodkins slammed through plate armour with a punch that knocked men out of their high-pommelled saddles. Somewhere in a place of safety, clerks would record the battle and they would write that in the minute it took the Duke of Alençon and his knights to charge up the hill, more than sixteen thousand arrows fell on them. The French King's brother did not survive to the summit.

Yet, still they did not falter.

Was this the courage and glory Sir Gilbert spoke of?

Blackstone watched as the survivors turned back to gather at the base of the hill. Behind them more French horsemen gathered. The survivors re-armed themselves, determined to return and seek the victory they confidently expected. Blackstone hawked and spat to try to rid his throat of the foul taste from the stench of disembowelled horses and men. He looked to his company of haggard men, the fear and strain of battle etched into their faces as if by a stonemason's hand.

'We bought the King this piece of France today, lads. Let's keep it for him a while longer,' he told them. He unstrung his bow and fitted another, not wanting to risk a loss of power from a weakened cord.

John Weston cupped a handful of water from the bucket before the boy ran down the line. 'All I want is one rich-bastard knight to beg for surrender and his ransom'd buy the King as much bloody land as he wants. Then I wouldn't have to be losing skin off my draw fingers. Look at that,' he said, showing everyone his hand, 'even skinned off the calluses.'

'That's 'cause you've spent half the fight scratching your arse,' Will Longdon gibed.

The men laughed, glad of the distraction. Weston posed a pained expression. 'Were it you what had a saddle-cracked arse like mine you'd soon moan,' he said.

From across the valley evening mist crept slowly across the belly of the land. This late in August, nights brought a dampness and a chill that the soldiers would welcome from the day's exertions and heat. Those who lived.

Blackstone looked to his brother. The boy lay on the wet ground sucking a piece of grass as if he were at home in the hay fields watching a rising meadow lark. Blackstone knelt by him.

'What do you see?' Blackstone asked gently, as he looked into the pink-streaked clouds. Soon it would be dark and then the fighting would make it even more difficult to separate friend from foe in close-quarter battle.

Richard looked back at him, unable to grasp what had been said, as Blackstone knew he wouldn't. He shook his head when Richard grunted his lack of understanding. Blackstone knew he would never find that place again in his heart where his brother had once resided. He patted Richard's shoulder and gestured him to his feet.

There was no time for further respite. An exultant fanfare floated across the valley. The kettledrums started their rousing tattoo once more.

Blackstone gazed across the broken bodies of men and horses, a pauper's graveyard with bristling arrows for headstones. The English beheld a sight that caught their breath. Massed ranks of knights gathered. King Edward's defence, four lines deep across nearly a thousand yards of hillside, was puny compared to the body of horsemen that now started their slow, determined walk. New blood had joined those who had already thrown themselves against the English. Banners fluttered, lifted by the evening's breeze, and the colourful blaze of surcoats, shields and flags put the setting sun to shame.

'Dear Christ,' Will Longdon said and crossed himself.

'We need more than arrows, Thomas,' John Weston said. 'We need a bloody miracle, and the Church and me have been strangers for as long as I can remember.'

Blackstone scanned the pennons. Over the weeks he had learnt to recognize some of the heraldic devices of the noble French houses. But he did not need to be an expert to notice de Harcourt's coat of arms. Sir Godfrey's brother and nephew were riding in the third wave. Blackstone glanced down the line to where the Prince's retinue made themselves ready. The Prince pulled back a handful of his fair hair and settled the dark metalled helm on his head. He swung his sword arm, left and right, stretching out the muscles again from the momentary stiffness. As he turned to say something to the others his smile was plain to see for those watching. He was enjoying himself.

A few paces back from Richard FitzSimon, who held the Prince's banner firmly with both hands, Godfrey de Harcourt stood stoically in a bloodstained surcoat next to Sir Reginald Cobham. The old fighter pressed a finger to his nostril and blew grimy snot onto the ground, then waited patiently for those who survived the impending hail of arrows. Killing was not something that tugged at his emotions. Feelings such as those he would leave to women. He knew that members of de Harcourt's family were approaching to do battle. He felt no sympathy on behalf of the army's marshal. The enemy needed to be killed as efficiently as possible – family or not.

'All right, lads, form up,' Blackstone told them, placing himself at the centre of his company. He put his arm on Richard's shoulder and had him stand at his side. The boy smiled and then turned away. Blackstone almost called his name, but instead reached out with his bow and touched the boy's back. 'Here,' he said, pointing at the ground next to his shoulder.

Richard shook his head. The guttural response and the gestures told Blackstone that his brother now thought himself a man and that he would fight with other men. Blackstone could have stopped him. Should have stopped him. But perhaps this was the time he had to let him go. Had not the King placed his son in harm's way and expected him to do his duty?

Blackstone nodded, and the boy turned away to join the end of the archers' defensive line. The others each raised an arm to touch his shoulder as he passed. It was a gesture of comradeship – or perhaps they did, after all, think him their talisman. As Blackstone turned his attention to the rising tide of French horsemen moving ever closer up the hill, he realized Sir Gilbert had been watching.

'That's the way it has to be, Thomas,' he said. He tightened the blood knot on his sword and raised it above his head, then stepped in front of the army and faced the enemy. 'Saint George!' he bellowed.

The ranks roared, 'Saint George!' Then the cry flew along the lines and Blackstone saw the Prince and his nobles raise their swords. *Saint George! Saint George!* The mighty war cry swelled English hearts.

The front rank took a pace forward to stand level with Sir Gilbert.

There was no clearer message for the French King.

The English would not retreat.

There was no hot-blooded charge from the French knights this time, no death or glory gallop. Rows of horsemen gripped shields and lances, their knees touching those of the men next to them. A woman's veil could not flutter through these formations without being impaled.

When they coolly urged their horses into the archers' range, they lifted their shields to absorb the splattering hail. It was not enough. Arrows found their way through armour and horses' flanks. Raised shields presented soft underarm targets. Plate armour could deflect an arrow but chain mail was pierced as if it were bare flesh. Rank upon rank kept coming, and once again the King's beloved archers, the common men of England, slaughtered the great and good of European nobility. As man and horse fell, another from the following ranks took their place. This time the French could not be stopped. When the pain and heat for revenge took hold this time they pressed ahead with a surge of horse and armour.

And when they closed the front ranks it was Blackstone's company's turn to halt them. He yelled his commands. 'Fifty paces! Thirty! Steady... nock... draw...' He waited for another ten yards: 'Loose!'

The whisper of sound fluttered the air followed by the crash of metal beating metal. Momentum carried the wounded war horses forward, as knights slumped, some trying to wrench the bodkin-pointed arrows from their armour. But ripped muscle, ligaments and shattered bone caused them to topple in agony. Within paces of the English line, the spearmen and men-at-arms stepped forward and began their killing. Hamstrung horses crumpled, their riders defenceless. Destriers rolled and crushed men, and the English did as their King had commanded. They gave no mercy.

And then, feet away from Blackstone, they almost broke through. The line caved in on itself, but, bolstered by men bravely pushing themselves forward, it held again. The few yards gained were seized back. Grunting men flung themselves at each other, trading blows until one gave way from fatigue or injury. They fought to the death. There was no question of yielding. The French knew they would live or die in this place because they could not retreat across the open ground and suffer again the archers' lethal skill.

'Stand your ground!' Blackstone yelled to his men who had scurried back into the shelter of the Welsh spearmen who advanced into the mêlée. 'Find a target! No matter how close!' He loosed two arrows in quick succession, one taking a knight in the throat as Gruffydd ap Madoc speared the man's horse. The falling creature's weight yanked the spear from his hands and in the moment before he could pick up another, a second arrow had whispered past his ear into a knight swinging a two-handed battleaxe. The wild-eyed Welshman turned over his shoulder enough to see that it was Blackstone who had done the killing, then he lurched back into the fury. Polehammers smashed at the mounted knights, catching them across the shoulders or back of their heads, forcing their bodies forward in the saddle, exposing the unarmoured parts of thighs and buttocks. Then halberd spikes and spearheads were rammed into soft tissue, crippling the rider, leaving him to die beneath the sword strokes.

Knights and men-at-arms stood shoulder to shoulder. The shield wall for defence had changed little since Roman times.

Edward, who had studied the battle lore of the fourth-century military author Vegetius, had used it often. But every wall can be broken, and now the sheer weight of those horsemen who survived the pit-traps and the arrows hammered at those who crouched below them.

'Sword and spear! Together!' Sir Gilbert's command was heard down the line. His tireless fighting ability, despite old wounds, drew men to him, eager to fight at his side, knowing that they were next to a great soldier. As the knights came onto the line spearmen jabbed and probed at the stallions' padded trappers, searching for the weak spots on the animals' chests and flanks, pushing blades through the trappings until flesh gave and the beast reared in terror and pain. Then the swordsmen hacked and probed the Frenchmen's armour. Crushing, piercing, blinding. Great men of power lay on the torn-up grass, squirming like stuck boars at a hunt.

The Prince was under heavy and bloody attack. Knights and infantrymen were down, men-at-arms hacked a pocket of resistance around him and the Prince wielded his sword with a dogged persistence that slaughtered those who threatened him. The Prince took the fight to his father's enemies. Step by bloody step he moved a yard and then another as he wielded his sword against his attackers. Like most of the English knights he fought with his face-piece open, wanting to see the enemy clearly and to gasp the air so desperately needed. The threat from the crossbowmen had long been trampled beneath iron hooves. The dragon banner of the Prince's own principality fluttered next to him as his standard bearer FitzSimon held fast against the surging attack. His was the more dangerous position. Next to the Prince he was unable to defend himself. The Welsh dragon must be kept aloft. The Prince was the prize and the French knew it. A surge of French knights on foot, tightly packed, fighting as a disciplined unit, cut their way closer to him.

Sir Gilbert saw it and led a flanking attack, taking a dozen men with him, fighting across crazed horses and slashing swords.

The French nobles' lives of privilege were being redeemed on that bloodied hill. Howling men fought with animal savagery. Cries of *Montjoie! Saint Denis!* rallied the French.

The line broke, re-formed and then broke again. Archers were down. In the mayhem Blackstone saw John Weston grappling with a French man-at-arms. Despite the man's strength and the weight of his armour he struggled against the broad-shouldered archer, but Weston had nothing to grasp. His hands slithered on armour slippery with blood. He heard Weston scream as he went down.

'Help me! Dear Christ! No!'

Blackstone had two arrows left and he fired into the attacking man without needing to aim. The arrow punched beneath the man's raised sword arm. Weston rolled clear and scrambled on all fours trying to escape, but a second man rammed his sword into his back. John Weston spasmed, choking blood gushed, his arms twitched like a pinned insect. Blackstone had no chance to save him. There had been no clear shot. His men were dying. *Dear God help us!* he cried to himself.

'Archers! Form up! Form up! Back! Back!' He wanted them further up the hill so they could fire down into the French. Some heard his voice, turned, saw him signal them away from the marauding French, but it was too late. The unarmoured archers were already fighting. Arrows spent, it was knives and swords against plate armour.

Blackstone's final arrow was nocked when he saw a moment of bewildering beauty. A swallow on the wing flew above the blood-sluiced men, lifting itself into the twilight's haze to feed on insects, swooping across the pain and misery in its own uncaring beauty. In that moment Blackstone knew where he had seen such a bird before. It was not only embroidered on Christiana's keepsake; it had been the emblem on the surcoat of the knight he had killed at the crossroads all those weeks ago. He had slain someone belonging to Christiana.

The realization was swept away as the bedlam of fighting rang in his ears. He loosed the arrow, which could not fail to find a target, but his men were scattered. Sir Gilbert was still fighting forward. Confusion swirled about him – but then Blackstone saw Richard.

His brother's bow had been cast aside and he hammered a knight with a discarded poleaxe. The man's visor collapsed under the bone-shattering blow. The hulking boy was thirty paces away. Blackstone jumped over two men in armour rolling on the hillside, each trying to get the better of the other. The mud and detritus of battle smeared their surcoats. The one shouted for St George, so Blackstone slashed at the other's neck with his long knife. The man rolled free and, still calling on the English saint as if chanting a prayer, the Englishman finished the killing. Richard and a handful of men were hacking and smashing their way towards the beleaguered Prince, at whose side de Harcourt and others still fought tirelessly. Unknown to the lame baron his family's banner lay trampled a hundred yards away, lying beneath his dead brother, killed by Elfred's archers on the flank.

Blackstone felt every moment to be his last. His gasping lungs drove him through the turmoil as he raced towards his brother who, like the other men in the company, had no arrows left. Blackstone's vision blurred. The edges of the battle were smears of colour and movement. His every sense was focused on his part of the fight, an area of less than a hundred paces. Welshmen thrust this way and that with halberds and knives, hamstringing and disembowelling horses and leaving their riders for the men-at-arms to dispatch.

And still the French came.

Will Longdon fought with his sword and a discarded shield. Tom, Matthew, all of them, they stood their ground as their King had asked.

But Thomas Blackstone ran.

The fear of God gripped him; squeezed his gasping lungs in terror; punished him for his cowardice in casting aside his love for his brother. God was going to take the mute boy back to His sacred heart.

Richard was about to die.

And that was why Thomas Blackstone ran.

CHAPTER ELEVEN

The *running wolf* sword blade glistened with blood, its hardened steel burnished golden orange by the rays of the setting sun. Over the centuries that blade mark had become synonymous with the finest swords forged in the Bavarian town of Passau. Two hundred years earlier the swordmakers' ancestors had gone to the Holy Land during the Crusades to learn the secrets of the Saracen swordmakers from Damascus. Thereafter German temperers and grinders, polishers and swordsmiths crafted the finest blades in Europe.

The knight's father had commissioned the sword three years earlier to commemorate his firstborn's ennoblement and sent him to serve in the court of King John of Bohemia. Its razor-sharp edge could cut through chain mail. Now the twenty-three-year-old Franz von Lienhard pushed his destrier through the jumbled bodies of fallen horses and men. The horse's massive strength had carried him across the ford's current at Blanchetaque when he gave chase to a dirt-poor English archer but had been stopped by the curtain of arrows that fell before him. He had not been prepared to risk injury to such a magnificent horse, but now for the greatest prize of all he was prepared to risk everything. The Prince of Wales was less than twenty paces away and the weight of French knights against him and those nobles at his side was punishing the English defence. Men-at-arms swarmed at Lienhard, but his strength beat them off. Leaning down from the saddle with the razor-edged blade he clove his attackers' arms and heads. A spearman thrust at his neck, but he hacked the shaft, kneed the horse into position, swung his arm in a mighty arc and felt the blade cut the man's skull in two like a turnip in a jousting competition. Splattered

brain added to the sprayed blood across his legs and the horse's
caparison. He saw a heaving mass of French knights bring their
energy down on the beleaguered Prince, whose banner fell. Now
he would kill the heir to the English throne.

Franz von Lienhard raised his sword, dragged his spurs against
the sweat-streaked horse's flanks and charged.

Blackstone saw his brother run into the press of fighting knights
wielding the polehammer. Most were on foot, others jostled their
horses closer. English men-at-arms were dying. He saw Sir Gilbert
attack a horseman, jab and cut, then rake his sword across the gaps
in the man's armour. The Frenchman swung a ball and chain and
Sir Gilbert went down. The dying Frenchman yanked the reins
and the horse fell, rolling onto Sir Gilbert, crushing him.

Men fell like harvested wheat as Richard scythed the polehammer's shaft back and forth. His strength alone was enough to
maim and kill, but the lethal weapon wielded with such violence
had brought half a dozen men down with mortal wounds. He was
ten paces in front of the Prince, who fell from a Frenchman's blow
to his helmet. FitzSimon threw the banner across his lord to hide
and protect him, then attacked, both hands gripping his sword,
rallying the nobles to him and screaming curses at the French.

Blackstone leapt across a disembowelled horse. A knight swung
at him, but he turned quickly, moving much faster than the heavily
armoured man. Using his bow stave as a spear he jabbed the horn
tip up beneath the man's helm. The leather strap that held it was
soggy from sweat and the helm gave an inch, enough for the bow's
horn to pierce the man's throat. The man went down, drowning
in his own blood and unable to cry out from the ripped wound.

The Prince was on his knees, the blow he had taken on his
helm causing blood to trickle down his temple. Richard had gone
down, sucked into a maelstrom of whirring swords and mace-
wielding knights.

Blackstone screamed his brother's name.

He could see the boy's head twisting as three or four men

stabbed and slashed at his body. The boy stared at the sky and bellowed an incoherent cry, then he disappeared beneath the mass of men, like a drowning child taken by a river god, yielding to an overpowering force.

The animal sound that forced its way from Blackstone's chest was loud enough for the Prince and de Harcourt, who was now at his side, to turn, pausing a moment in their own defence. Swords and maces fell on the English line, broken lances probed and struck as Blackstone threw himself at the Frenchmen. A knight swung his sword and all Blackstone could do was try to parry with his bow stave. The blade severed it like a dry twig. And part of Blackstone broke with it. His father's great war bow was destroyed. Before the man could sweep back with a second blow, Blackstone threw himself on him, his weight carrying him to the ground on top of other bodies. His fingers clawed for the man's throat but could not get past the armour. He reached out blindly and his hand found a flanged mace, its killing head resembling an arrow's fletching but cast in iron. He brought the six-pound war-hammer down harder than a blacksmith striking an anvil; again and again he beat at the man's visor until it crumpled and he heard bone break and felt the man spasm beneath him.

A knight slashed at him, Blackstone felt his jerkin cut, and warm blood seeping from his side. He backhanded his attacker with the mace. Another sword slash cut his leg. He flailed blindly, feeling the mace smash armour. The Prince was a few feet away, being helped to his feet, but he was of no concern as Blackstone hammered his way through the dozen or more men who stood between him and the fallen Richard. Dog-faced helmets glared grotesquely in the dying light as he swung the mace with such power as only a stonemason possessed. Men fell, but still he could not reach his brother. The Prince was fighting again, with knights and men-at-arms as bodyguards, but Blackstone was to his front and heard one last agonizing cry like a beast being slaughtered from within the mass of French knights. It was his brother's death cry.

Blackstone's sob carried him onwards. Others were at his back fighting off men from the side when a horseman came forward, trampling whoever was on the ground. He was a Bohemian knight holding high a sword that caught the dying sun like a blade forged in hell. In a brief, clear moment, a hulking figure tried to stand. The boy was wounded in a dozen places or more, and by now blind from cuts to his eyes. The momentum of the knight's killing arm swung his sword down with grace and skill. Blackstone screamed. Other men blocked his view, saving him from the sight of the blow that severed Richard's head from his body.

The destrier nearly knocked Blackstone down, but he snatched at its reins and heaved. The animal's eyes rolled in terror but the knight had no angle to cut down at his attacker. Blackstone leapt at the man to drive the mace against his visor as the horse skidded on the bloodied grass. The knight was agile, as fast as Blackstone, who had trouble getting his leg to do as his brain commanded. It dragged. He looked down and saw blood pouring from a vicious cut down to the bone. His violence had pushed pain to the dark recess of his rage. The knight wasted no time in attack. From the high guard he slashed downwards, a blow to cut a man from shoulder to hip, but Blackstone's injured leg saved him – it gave under the weight of his effort to avoid the blow and the blade whispered above his head. Blackstone lurched, grabbed the man's gauntleted wrist, beat the mace against his helm, but fell when the knight hit him full in the face with his shield. As he went down, head ringing from the blow, he dropped the mace and snatched at the shield, pulling the knight down with him. The weight of the man's armour and the slippery slope unbalanced him, but he did not release his sword. Blackstone felt his cheekbone break and blood fill his mouth as the man beat him with the sword's pommel in a crushing backhand.

Blackstone spat the blood from his mouth, clambered to his feet at the same time as the knight. He knew then that his adversary was as fit and strong as he was, despite wearing eighty pounds of armour, and as determined to kill. The sword arced; Blackstone blocked the lethal blow with a fallen spear's staff. So close was the blade to his face that he saw an etched mark of a wolf below the curved crossguard. The stave splintered but had softened the blow, turning the blade's edge away as it struck his left arm. The force of it sent shock waves of pain through his shoulder. The muscle tore and the bone shattered. In that instant he knew that should he survive he would never draw a war bow again. He spat vomit from the agony, fell to his knees, right hand grasping for any weapon he could find, shaking away the swirling darkness that threatened to swallow him. As the blade swept down he instinctively drew back his head, but the tip of the blade cut through the metal bands that stiffened his leather cap. Had he not slumped when he did it would have cleft his head in two. The blade's continued downward arc cut into his forehead and nose, sliced his cheek and then snapped his left collarbone.

The fight was done. The knight's skill would take him a few more paces and, with the Frenchmen who now clambered across the bodies to join him, he would kill the Prince of Wales.

Blackstone had no thought for Edward of Woodstock, Godfrey de Harcourt, Warwick, Northampton, flags and banners or glory. He was dying. Twilight gave way to night. Lienhard knew the archer was finished. He would waste no more time on him. Blackstone could barely see as the knight took a stride to pass him, but he jerked his good arm up in a final act of defiance.

The knight screamed and fell. Blackstone's fist gripped the broken end of a spear, and twelve inches of forged, razor-sharp metal plunged between the knight's legs. Blood spurted as his hands went instinctively to his groin. Screaming into the claustrophobia of his bascinet he went to his knees. Somehow Blackstone got to his feet, grasping the man's sword by its handle, digging its blade into the ground as a crutch. The knight held his groin with one hand, pushed his visor back with the other, gulping air to drown the pain. Blackstone held the sword like a dagger and plunged it down through the open visor, feeling the metal grate against bone, then wrenched it free. His stonemason's strength held the sword in a vice-like grip. He had to find Richard. The sword would kill a hundred more Frenchmen if necessary. His brother was out there. In the darkness. Alone. But he could not take another step. The mist rose from the valley, wrapping the dead in its shroud.

Thomas Blackstone sank down and finally yielded to its cool embrace.

Fifteen charges were made against the English lines. They all failed but one, when the enemy reached the Prince of Wales. The French knights' rage and pride, their jealousy of another claiming greater glory, had made them rake their spurs and charge into a disciplined English army that never yielded ground. The French fought for themselves, the English for their King.

By the time Philip arrived at the battlefield with his final divisions it was obvious that the greatest army in Christendom had been defeated. The carnage that lay before him was staggering. Five thousand Genoese, thousands of horses and more than fifteen hundred knights lay dead in front of the English lines. Thousands more infantry lay across the hillside. Bombards still boomed, their smoke mingling with the rising mist. Horses whinnied and men screamed in agony as trumpets and drums defied a dying man's last hope for silence. It was a tapestry of hell. Honour-bound, the King ignored his nobles' pleas and spurred his horse forward. His ally, the blind warrior-king John of Bohemia, determined to strike his enemy, rode on his flank, his reins looped through their own by Henri le Moine and Heinrich von Klingenberg, loyal knights who knew that they would die before they even reached the English front line.

Philip's entourage smothered their lord with shields, but Elfred and thousands of other English archers wanted to claim his death. In a day of legend his horse was killed beneath him. He remounted, his face slashed by a bodkin point, his life spared only by the quality of his plate armour, the poor light and the rising mist.

French cavalry wheeled and charged again, but were beaten back. It was a futile assault. Edward's trumpets rallied his knights and men-at-arms and the war horses were brought from the rear. When the English rode into the field thousands of French infantry fled for their lives. It would not serve France if their King died in a battle already lost, his advisors insisted. Reluctantly he turned away, leaving the hundreds of French knights who still fought on in small groups, men bound by family ties and the comradeship of past campaigns.

The sun set as valley mist crept over that field of tears. English archers had mercilessly shot through the sacred war banner of France.

The Oriflamme lay in tatters.

King Edward, wearing full armour and helmet, rode along the lines of the Prince's division. He praised them all and urged them to thank God for their deliverance. He asked that there should be no pride or boasting for their great victory and ordered the English to stay in position in case of a counter-attack. Elfred counted the cost his archers had paid. Only he, Will Longdon and Matthew Hampton had survived, along with twenty other men from those archers who had stood with the Welshmen. Sir Gilbert lay somewhere on the battlefield. Richard Blackstone was dead; of Thomas they knew nothing other than that his attack had been witnessed before he went down. They all agreed it was a vile price to pay. The men lit fires that burned across the hillside and tended to their exhaustion and wounds. The King instructed that the windmill be filled with brushwood and set alight as a beacon for all the English to see.

Its great sails flared into a burning crucifix.

Firelight and torches illuminated the Prince and the nobles. The King removed his bascinet and kissed Prince Edward, and moved into the torchlight that lit Blackstone's body lying amidst the group of knights. A priest knelt at his side whispering the final sacrament.

'When the priest was summoned we feared it was for our son,' the King said, looking at the blood-soaked body bathed in firelight.

'Were it not for this boy it might well have been. He fought for me when I fell. FitzSimon covered me in my greatest danger that was averted by this boy. No scribe will ever be able to write of his courage that we witnessed,' said the Prince.

The King looked to the marshals of the army, Warwick and de Harcourt. They nodded. None of those gathered knew that Blackstone had fought only for his brother.

'He'll not last the hour, sire,' Northampton added. 'My God, I'll admit we were hard-pressed. He cleaved a path and bought us time.'

'He reminded me of myself when I was young,' the old knight Reginald Cobham said quietly, the evidence of his own fighting slathered across his surcoat and armour.

The King put a hand on his friend's shoulder. 'If he fought half as hard as you, Cobham, we were blessed indeed.'

Blackstone heard nothing but the vague whisper of prayer in his ear. Pain creased every nerve. Thick blood from his smashed face clogged his throat and nose. His breath rattled as he tried to see Christiana. She was there, her dark cloak close to his face. Her face was obscured in shadow. And she held a crucifix in front of his mouth, telling him to kiss the cross of Christ.

'Sire,' Northampton said as he saw the priest ease back in surprise as Blackstone raised himself towards the crucifix held by the cleric.

'He'll die on his own terms,' Warwick said, admiring the strength the boy still possessed.

Blackstone heard the words *confess*, *sins* and *forgiveness*. His right eye focused on a distant light, a fiery burning crucifix. God was showing his anger; damning him for failing Richard.

'Forgive me,' he muttered.

The priest traced the sign of the cross with his finger on Blackstone's forehead then tried to release the hand that still gripped the dead knight's sword. But Blackstone's fist would not unclench, keeping it pressed to his chest.

'Bless this boy, sire. Look at him, he will not relinquish the sword,' Cobham said gently, knowing a warrior when he saw one.

The King watched. 'We will give our thanks and take communion and take com- munion and pray for this man's soul. Is his name known?' he said quietly.

'His name is Thomas Blackstone,' de Harcourt said. 'He's an archer, sire. One of Sir Gilbert Killbere's men.'

'We were with him at Blanchetaque where he also showed honour and courage protecting a member of Godfrey's household,' the Prince said.

Sir Godfrey nodded in acknowledgement.

Blackstone heard his name. He stared at the blurred colours of the surcoats shimmering in the half-light. Were they warrior angels? He needed them to take him to Richard. Blackstone called on every fibre in his body to get up and meet the angels.

'Sweet Jesus,' Northampton said quietly without blasphemy as they watched Blackstone's shattered body force itself up from the ground. De Harcourt stepped forward to help him. The King barely raised his hand to stop him.

'No,' the King whispered. 'Let him be. It is his desire. He is defiant unto death.'

Blackstone got to his knees, the sword point in the dirt to help steady him. He could get no further. The blurred angels waited. One, with a burning torch held behind him, reflecting holy light glinting from armour, stood closer. God had sent this archangel for him. Stinging tears blurred his vision.

'Lord...' Blackstone whispered, 'take me to him...'

The King and the nobles looked uncertain for a moment. Then the King turned to his son. 'He calls for you. Honour, him, Edward. It is your right. And his.'

The now battle-hardened sixteen-year-old Prince of Wales understood his royal duty. He stepped to Blackstone, still kneeling with the sword placed squarely to his chest, helping to keep a balance that threatened to desert him at any moment and let him fall into darkness. The Prince laid his hands on Blackstone's head.

'You have behaved with honour and courage, and we are grateful. You are a loyal servant to your liege lord. Accept this charge placed upon your life and may God bless you, Sir Thomas Blackstone.'

The Prince stepped back and the King gestured for men from his retinue to ease Blackstone's body to the ground. As they laid him gently back into the Crécy mud, the King turned to de Harcourt.

'This young knight will not die if it is in our power. Our surgeon and physician will attend him. Godfrey, we charge you to accept responsibility for his safekeeping until such time as all efforts prove fruitless.'

'I gladly accept the privilege, sire,' de Harcourt answered.

'Good,' the King said, 'we need brave Englishmen in France.'

The burning windmill threw long shadows across the battlefield. A cowled priest went among the dead and dying. He seemed to be offering comfort as he went to each fallen nobleman. Weary soldiers thought nothing of it. They did not see the sack at his waist or the binding on his hand that covered a missing finger.

Twisted bodies of men and horses haunted the hillside in a macabre embrace. The fog clung to the battlefield for another day as the English waited for further attacks. None came. The French armies were beaten, their lances impaling Crécy mud instead of English and Welsh muscle. King Edward sent heralds into the stench of the battlefield to retrieve the surcoats of the fallen knights and noblemen so they might be identified and given a Christian burial with all due honour and respect paid. Peasants from the surrounding villages were rounded up and made to dig mass graves, into which the dead from both sides were tumbled and buried. Richard Blackstone's dismembered body was only one of thousands.

Godfrey de Harcourt had Blackstone carried on a bier back to the castle at Noyelles, several miles to the army's rear. Countess Blanche's indignation at having the English archer brought into her mother's home once again was softened by the evidence that

Thomas Blackstone had tried to help the wounded French knight to whom she had given refuge. The pageboy's testimony and the blood-soaked jupon that Blackstone had used to staunch the knight's wound proved his compassion.

Christiana almost fell faint with grief when she saw his shattered body. He was unrecognizable. Her mistress turned her away from the sight as they carried him to one of the rooms.

'Christiana,' she said softly, 'you're a woman in the house of de Harcourt. If you cannot attend to him then we will find you duties elsewhere.'

Christiana shook her head. 'I'll care for him,' she said, 'just as you care for your husband.'

The countess's husband, Jean, had already been brought from Crécy with wounds far less severe than those suffered by Blackstone but, like many battle injuries, they were life-threatening. Hours earlier the two men had fought on opposing sides without knowing of the other's existence; now they were to be nursed beneath the same roof. The women took control and ushered Sir Godfrey out, to return to his army's march towards Calais. The castle gates of Noyelles were barred. The young Englishman was safe in the house of his enemy's family until he either recovered or died.

War had dealt the young archer a hand that was to change his destiny.

PART TWO

WOLF SWORD

CHAPTER TWELVE

Death hovered in the shadows, like a raven waiting to pluck the soul of the wounded Blackstone.

In that timeless place of misery he fought the rearing demons that swirled from the battlefield in his mind. His haunting screams reverberated through the corridors of Noyelles until, finally, he fell silent and they thought him dead.

Christiana could feel no pulse in his body. She called for a servant to rouse the sleeping physician, shouting to hurry the fool along until her threats carried him away into the darkness with a flickering torch to guide back the only man who could save the wounded archer. Her cries of alarm echoed down the passageways and roused servants from where they lay next to the kitchen hearth, or in doorways close to their mistress. Torches flared, doors slammed open as feet scuffed their way across stone floors. Blanche de Harcourt gathered her gown about her and urged the servant who walked a step ahead with the spluttering flame to move more quickly.

Master Jordan of Canterbury, roused by his attendants, berated them loudly for interrupting his sleep. He recanted, keeping his curses to himself, when told of the urgency and the young archer's lack of breath in his body. Why his great King had suffered him to attend to this broken boy was beyond his comprehension. In the name of God, he was Edward of England's personal physician who attended him in the splendour of Windsor Castle, where gold-spun tapestries hung next to the paintings of great Italian artists. The privies had running water, there was warmth and comfort, and even on a war expedition the

King of England dined as a monarch should. Not so here. Not so the simple platters of meat and rough-grain bread – not a decent piece of well-milled white loaf to be had. But now he, Jordan of Canterbury, who, lest anyone forget, also attended the King's mother, Isabella, at Hertford Castle – so great was his standing within the royal family – was now obliged to stay in a Norman castle. These bare timber and stone walls held the cold like a corpse fished from the river in winter. These surroundings mocked the concept of noble luxury. He shivered in his misery and yearned for King Edward's hearth. When he arrived, breathless from the steps that led up to Blackstone's room, he was forced to wait a moment before lowering his face to that of his patient. His own heart needed to ease its pounding before he could determine if Blackstone's had been taken by the Almighty. He felt the archer's cold skin for any sign of fever or warmth that might indicate life. There was none.

'A bowl and water! Here!' he commanded one of his attendants.

The room's confinement seemed doubly crowded as the shadows of those present jostled one another. He turned to Christiana, who stood in the doorway, gaunt with despair, as Blanche de Harcourt comforted her with an arm around her shoulder. The countess's feelings about the common archer were well known.

'My lady, it might be that God has released both the de Harcourt family and me from our onerous duty,' he said.

His smile of feigned sympathy and shared aggrievement was met with her snapping response. 'My lord and husband lies in his bed, still sleeping from the draught that eases the pain of his own wounds. I serve him and his commands as you serve your King, Master Jordan. Is his command onerous?'

The physician bowed his head, chastised, and hoped that his remark would not filter back to the King through his attendants' gossip.

He was saved from further embarrassment by the servant returning with a half-filled bowl of water. Master Jordan took it and then balanced it carefully on Blackstone's chest. They waited in the flickering light, peering at the smooth surface for any sign of vibration from the heart. There was nothing. The physician turned away to go back to his warm bed, his duty done.

Thomas Blackstone was dead.

Deep within himself the wounded archer felt a soft embrace and comfort, a gentle warmth he had never before experienced. It was a place of safety so temptingly close. All he had to do was yield to its seductive embrace. He slid further into its comfort and the soft glow of oblivion. But the animal instinct within him clawed at his mind. To turn away from that place meant a return to the bear pit of pain. The warmth was death, the pain meant life. Like a fragment of broken spearhead, his mind thrust back into the entanglement of despair.

'My lord!' the attendant called.

There was the faintest of ripples across the water's surface.

Noyelles was safe for the time being. The English had moved north to besiege Calais, and ironically, Blackstone's presence had guaranteed the de Harcourts' safety. For three days Christiana and Master Jordan had attended to Blackstone. With the help of servants they had cut away his blood-soaked clothes and bathed his naked body until the wounds could be laid bare. Fever had gripped him and as the furnace threatened to consume him they tied his wrists and ankles to the bed's frame so that in his delirium he would not aggravate his wounds. Christiana had followed the physician's instructions, swabbing the gaping wounds with a mixture of egg yolks, rose oil and turpentine, laying a thick poultice of the mixture down the leg whose muscle lay slashed. Now the leg wound was cleansed but still malleable for closing.

The physician prepared to stitch and bind the gaping wounds. 'I cannot save his face. It will be disfigured when the muscles tighten against the stitching. 'Tis a pity, I can see he had strong features.' He eased away the poultice from the leg wound and from a bowl of wine withdrew a yard of gut, stripped from a pig's intestine. His assistant threaded it into a curved needle.

Christiana regarded it uncertainly; curved like a fisherman's awl, it looped the stitches, piercing Blackstone's leg wound. Blanche de Harcourt eased her away. 'Let Master Jordan do his work, child.'

'The leg muscle needs to be held tight,' Christiana said, 'but if they use that on his face he'll look grotesque.'

She stepped back into the room. 'Sir, if you seal his wounds will you allow me to attend to his face? I mean no disrespect to you, Master Jordan, but a smaller hand that can hem a silk gown with barely a noticeable stitch might cause less disfigurement.'

For a moment the King's physician looked uncertainly at her. No woman he had known had ever attended battlefield wounds. It was unseemly.

'This is not work for you. It is best suited to a barber-surgeon on a battlefield. I am here at my lord's request.'

Christiana bristled, but was conscious of the authority the King of England's physician held. She lowered her eyes momentarily in a small gesture to acknowledge the fact, and then faced him, determined that her reasoning should be considered.

'My sensibilities will not be harmed, sir, I have already helped bathe him and wash the congealed blood from those wounds. His body is not a mystery to me. I have attended him these past three days with barely a moment's sleep. I have never left his side. I owe this boy my life as does your Prince. It's a paltry request to try to save him from having the twisted, half-blind face of an ogre. Should King Edward and his son see the boy again, let his features not repel them. I have fine silk thread that will bind the skin tightly.'

Master Jordan looked at her and then to Blanche de Harcourt. 'This girl is in your care, my lady. Is she normally so forward?'

'I fear she is, but it can do no harm, surely?'

'Surely,' the physician was obliged to agree with a nod of his head. 'Very well, I will instruct you, and if you save his face from looking like a split, overripe plum, I shall, of course, take the credit.'

'And if I fail, sir, I will declare that I did it without your knowledge,' Christiana answered.

'Then we are in agreement. And if he lives I should hope this boy comes to realize how blessed he is – having a King and a beautiful young woman care so much for his well-being.'

As the hours wore on she watched the physician knit the wounds together as a suckling pig's belly would be threaded with cord for roasting. It was crude, but efficient work. When the King's doctor had finished she was left alone with Master Jordan's apothecary, and helped him administer a trickle of hemlock and mandrake between Blackstone's lips to ease the pain.

Christiana then carefully pulled together the slash on his face. The gall rose into her throat but she spat onto the reed floor and steadied her hands and then, slowly and with great deliberation, pressed the needle into his skin.

After attending to Blackstone's wounds Master Jordan returned to the English army besieging Calais. Sir Godfrey arranged an armed escort to take his nephew, Jean de Harcourt, along with his family and a few men of his retinue who had survived the slaughter, further south to Castle de Harcourt, where the family withdrew behind the safety of its walls. French honour and hospitality dictated that Count Jean de Harcourt, the surviving son and now head of the family, have his household treat Thomas Blackstone with respect. He was no longer a yeoman archer from a shire in England; he had been knighted by a King's son. The honour conferred by royal hand for courage on the field of battle held greater status than any other merit. Sir Godfrey, Jean's uncle, may have fought against his own family when he sided with the English, but Jean's loyalty to his own father at the battle of Crécy was simply that: honour for his father's sake.

'Why is the boy not quartered closer to us?' de Harcourt asked nearly a month later. His own wounds were healing and he now walked unaided.

His wife looked up from her needlepoint; the dogs dozing by the fire ran to their master as he entered the great hall. He ignored them and repeated the question, his irritation noticeable, before she could answer.

'He's a common man, Jean. We cannot have him in our company,' she said quickly, not wishing to risk his displeasure.

'I am master of this house, and head of this family, Blanche. I have been charged with this boy's welfare by Godfrey, and he in turn by the English King. Where is he?'

'He's in the north tower, my lord.'

De Harcourt turned his back and did not close the big doors behind him. The draught could blow through the room for all he cared. Autumn was already upon them.

Jean de Harcourt limped along the corridor that led to the unheated room where Blackstone had been quartered. The room was empty, the bed had not been slept in. He peered out of the narrow window. In the courtyard Christiana walked slowly alongside a horse, holding it by its halter. On the other side Blackstone gripped the horse's mane with one hand, to support himself as he limped painfully, forcing his injured leg to bear more weight each day. In less than a month Blackstone had fought the pain of his injuries and punished himself back almost to strength.

De Harcourt noticed the sword that had accompanied the wounded archer leaning against the wall and picked it up, feeling its fine balance against his palm, its delicate weight tipping slightly. It was the work of a master swordmaker and in the right hands would kill and maim with an efficiency that any man-at-arms would admire. He wielded it quickly left and right, the cutting edge rippling the air. It was one of the finest swords he had seen, and despite the fact that it was a weapon that only a wealthy and accomplished knight could afford Sir Godfrey had told him that Blackstone had taken it from such a knight and then slaughtered him with it – a brutal, unforgiving act, when a ransom could have been claimed despite no quarter being offered by either side at Crécy. A chance of wealth denied no matter the circumstances. And yet he knew that before the great battle, when Sir Godfrey had visited the castle at Noyelles, Blackstone had saved the life of a young page, and tried to help the boy's wounded master. A bewildering contradiction: compassion and brutality were seldom brothers-in-arms. And now this barbarian archer was in the care of his family. He replaced the sword and looked down to where Christiana turned the horse. Now he could see Blackstone more clearly; there was grim determination set upon the boy's battered features, the wound's livid welt discolouring half his face into a blackened and yellowing mass. Blackstone's hair was matted with sweat from the effort of hauling himself along. He wore only a long undershirt, the bandaging on his wounded leg not yet allowing breeches or hose. He heard Christiana's voice echo across the courtyard.

'That's enough for today, Thomas. You must rest now and let me attend to your leg.'

Blackstone shook his head. 'Once more. There and back. Across the yard,' he told her. Despite her protestations Blackstone urged the horse to walk on, and despite his pain stayed silent, forcing the leg muscles to challenge the wound.

De Harcourt gazed at the boy, one of the thousands who had faced him at Crécy; the English archers who had rained death on him and the cream of French chivalry. Their savage killing of wounded knights thrown down in that hailstorm was renowned and the thought of their brutal tactics made his gorge rise. His own wounds were nothing compared to Blackstone's, but they had confined him to his rooms for weeks, until he now felt strong enough to appear before his family and retainers again.

It was time to meet his enemy.

Blackstone sat on a small barrel in the stables as Christiana unwound the sticky bandage from his leg. From a linen bag she pulled out a roll of narrow cloth and a pot of salve. The long slice of wound that ran down his thigh was puckered and oozing pus from where the stitches held it. Using a small-bladed knife she began to pick at the wound, suddenly alarmed when she felt his leg wince.

'I'm sorry,' she whispered, reaching up for his hand.

He smiled. 'It's nothing – it's tender where the flesh is still raw, that's all. It's healing and that's good.'

A shadow filled the doorway and Christiana quickly got to her feet as de Harcourt stood in the entrance.

'My lord,' she said.

Blackstone did not move for a moment but then hauled himself to his feet, not once taking his eyes off the man who might well control his life or death.

'Christiana, there are servants who can attend to that,' de Harcourt said.

'It's delicate, my lord, I would prefer to do it myself. I have to pluck the maggots from the wound.'

De Harcourt knew of using maggots to eat away the poisoned flesh, but had never taken such action himself. 'You do this each day?'

Christiana nodded. 'The servants bring in rabbits and crows; they gut them and when they are infested we take the maggots and put them into Thomas's wound. That and the salve that Master Jordan's apothecary left with us.'

De Harcourt nodded, but all the while in his questioning of her he held Blackstone's gaze. Blackstone saw a man of about thirty years, wiry with a taut, knotted body. He was shorter than Blackstone by five or six inches and wisps of grey were evident in his beard; his hair grew long into the nape of his neck. His hands showed criss-crossed white lines, old scars from fighting. Now he limped, leaning on a gnarled hand-cut stick, but despite that, Blackstone realized, he was undiminished in stature.

'Do that later,' he said to Christiana.

For a moment she hesitated, the two men opposite each other, de Harcourt the stronger of the two, with the lesser wounds and a knife at his belt. Christiana turned away with barely a glance at Blackstone. De Harcourt waited a moment and then eased himself onto an upright sack of grain.

'I am Jean, fifth count of Harcourt and head of this family.'

Being in the presence of a noble family demanded common courtesy, and although Blackstone had been knighted by no less a personage than the Prince of Wales on the field of battle, with the blessing of Edward, King of England, Jean de Harcourt was his superior. Blackstone's broken arm was still bound and splinted, and the wounded leg that Christiana had exposed, de Harcourt silently acknowledged to himself, would cause pain at every movement. Blackstone reached out with his good arm and steadied himself against the barrel. And then slowly forced his body to obey his will. He lowered his uninjured knee towards the ground.

De Harcourt watched the sacrifice to pain, and when Blackstone's knee was almost halfway to the ground, he raised a hand, unable to allow needless suffering from a brave fighter.

'Enough. There is no need,' he said.

Blackstone ignored him, fought the agony of the wound and rested his knee into the dirt, and then raised his head to look directly at de Harcourt.

'Lord,' Blackstone said, and pulled himself up, the wound now leaking blood through the yellow pus.

De Harcourt nodded acknowledgement, realizing that Sir Godfrey's description of the defiant archer had been accurate – Blackstone would not yield. He indicated that Blackstone should sit on the barrel.

He gazed down through the layers of society, to a level with which he had had little contact other than to have beaten, forgiven or killed. Little of the middle option. It was necessary to keep such low-life in its place. But there were men who fought and secured favour and fortune, and these men earned respect. And Blackstone was somewhere along that road to securing a place in the telling.

'King Edward still lays siege to Calais. The war goes on,' he said.

'Without us, my lord,' Blackstone answered.

'Without us,' de Harcourt agreed. 'I'm told you can read.'

'I can.'

'How so?'

'My mother was French. She taught my father, he taught me.'

'Her name?'

'Annie.'

'That's not French.'

'It's what my father called her. It was Anelet.'

'Is she alive?'

'No.'

'And your father?'

'Dead.'

'An archer?'

'The best. I carried his war bow.'

'He died in battle?'

'In a stone quarry, where I served my apprenticeship as a stone-mason and freeman.'

'And can you write?'

'A little.'

'Not quite the barbarian, then.'

'Enough to do my sworn lord's bidding and kill my King's enemies,' Blackstone said, unable to keep a disrespectful tone from his answer.

De Harcourt ignored it. 'Yes. I have experience of English warmongering. Who is your sworn lord?'

'Sir Gilbert Killbere.'

'Does he live?'

'Dead beneath a war horse at Crécy.'

'I don't know of him.'

'Had you faced him in war you would.'

'You're impertinent.'

'So I have been told, my lord.'

De Harcourt could see that Blackstone showed no sign of fear, and his size and strength defied his age.

'What am I to do with you, young Thomas Blackstone?'

'I don't know, my lord, but my wounds are healing and in another month I'll be strong enough to go back to the army.'

'You will only leave when I tell you to leave,' de Harcourt said. 'Has Christiana told you why you are here? Why the English King commanded the marshal of the army, my uncle, who fought for him against his own family, to have you brought here?'

'I can only think my King wished to irritate Sir Godfrey,' Blackstone said.

De Harcourt suddenly laughed. 'Yes, that's a distinct possibility.' He flicked at a pile of horse dung with the stick. How friendly should he be with this hulking archer? His own uncertainty surprised him. The man who stood before him had a difference to him that he had not come across before in a peasant. Perhaps his upbringing had been influenced by the mother.

'The truth of the matter is that the Harcourt family have long been divided in their loyalty. Some of my ancestors went to England with William of Normandy. They still hold estates there. Distant cousins, probably best kept that way. We Normans do not take kindly to authority we do not respect. Perhaps you and I share common ground in that matter. My father died at Crécy because of his loyalty to King Philip. I served out of loyalty to my father, but now that he is dead and I am head of the family, I will choose where my fealty lies. The English King will claim the throne of France and my family will be part of his success. That's why you're here, because Sir Godfrey was charged by our future King to save you. Otherwise he'd have left you on the side of the road to rot in a ditch and die of your wounds. No matter how well you fought in defence of your Prince.' De Harcourt eased himself up. 'And he'd have taken that fine sword for himself.' He reached the stable door and turned back, adding, 'Had he been able to prise it from your fist.'

He hobbled away, leaving Blackstone still uncertain of his immediate fate.

Christiana waited until she saw her guardian's lord and husband limp back towards the great hall. She didn't ask Blackstone what had been said, he would tell her in his own time, as he usually did, offering brief glimpses of the guilt that lay in his heart at his brother's death and his sense of urgency to return to those men he had fought beside. Little by little she learnt more of Thomas Blackstone. She spent nights watching him as each nightmare unveiled a few more of his demons and each day cast them back into their cage. She dressed his wound and helped him back to the north tower, where a servant awaited them.

The man hunched and bowed his shoulders. 'My lady, I have been instructed by my lord to take Sir Thomas to his new quarters.'

It was the first time Blackstone had heard himself referred to in honoured terms.

'What's your name?' Blackstone asked.

'Marcel, Sir Thomas.'

Blackstone looked at the now empty room. The sword was missing.

'Who took my sword?'

'Lord de Harcourt took it away,' the servant answered.

It was pointless to question him further. Blackstone allowed the servant to help him along the passageways. As they passed each window overlooking the castle's walled yards to the forests beyond, the moat's glistening water became a mirror to his memory, reflecting back events that had brought him here, to the place where he had first saved Christiana. That fate should twist his life into a knot with this family was beyond his reasoning, but the girl was still at his side and his enemy had not yet cut his throat. He would take what comfort he could from that, and then build his strength to determine his own destiny. And hoped she would be a part of it.

The room, compared to the cell-like quarters in the north tower, was bright and spacious. A fire burned in the grate, logs and kindling were stacked in its hearth and there was a privy a few paces along the corridor. There was a bowl and a jug of water on a table with a linen cloth so he might wash. A bench stood beneath a window that looked south into the warmth of the autumn sun. Animal skins, stitched into a bed cover, lay across the mattress, which had been made up with blankets. The room had been prepared as if for an invited guest, with the addition of clean clothes, a long, loose shirt to accommodate Blackstone's bound-up arm and injured leg. And the sword lay on the deep sill, sunlight glinting from its burnished steel. Christiana slid beneath his arm as he pulled her to him and kissed her hair.

He was safe.

For now.

Over the following weeks Jean de Harcourt extended his own training to regain his strength so that each day he could assess Blackstone's progress. As he watched him break through the challenging pain it became a competition in de Harcourt's mind to gain the upper hand over the young archer.

Each man sweated from his efforts, and de Harcourt knew that youth and a lifetime of hard labour gave the young knight the advantage. As every day passed he learnt a little more about his charge. Blackstone would soon be strong enough to learn to fight as a man of honour would conduct himself, sword in hand, not by slaying an opponent from a distance with a war bow. Each man extended himself because each was determined to outdo the other.

Little was said between nobleman and peasant until de Harcourt felt ready to extend his courtesy. Then, slowly but surely, he drew the yeoman archer into his world. As each day's exercise session ended de Harcourt had wine, bread and cheese brought down to the courtyard. He and Blackstone sluiced the sweat from their bodies in a trough of cold water and then Christiana would be summoned to minister to Blackstone's wounds. De Harcourt realized that Blackstone had been right; another month had gone by more rapidly than anticipated – and he could see that Blackstone would soon be able to leave of his own free will – if he permitted it.

That would not be allowed to happen. Not yet. Not until his uncle, Godfrey de Harcourt, sanctioned it. He needed to reach this rough-hewn boy, to find a means of gaining his trust, and hope that the lad had sense enough to know that the honour conferred on him was more than a reflection of the King's will, it was God's blessing. There was no common ground between them, other than the conflict they had both experienced. That might serve the purpose.

'I was in the third division with my family and troops,' de Harcourt said as he pulled off his shirt and turned his back for a servant to wipe dry. Another retainer went to help Blackstone tug free his soaked shirt, but was denied. Blackstone preferred to struggle with the arm that was still bent, held by strips of wood and cut leather that had been soaked and had dried into a tight binding, bracing the broken bones.

'I saw no such division,' Blackstone told him. 'All I saw were thousands of armoured men coming at us as if they were riding out of hell. The ground shook beneath our feet and all we could think of was to slay you before you reached us, for then we would have been at your mercy, and there was none to be had that day.'

De Harcourt nodded as the servant poured two tumblers of wine, gave one to his master and was about to hand the second to Blackstone when de Harcourt personally handed his own to Blackstone. Blackstone acknowledged the small gesture of – what? Friendship? In these past weeks the men had spoken briefly, neither admitting their pain, neither accusing the other of slaughter on the battlefield. The servant stepped away.

The older man sipped his wine. 'Your arrows put the fear of Christ into us. You felled us like trees. I took one of your shafts in my side, deflected by my armour; another in my leg that pinned me to the saddle. Our charge pounded the horses against each other and broke the shaft. My squire pulled me free from the horse when I fell. He died as he got me to safety. I can still hear the screams of the horses and the men. I prayed that God would send a fireball from the heavens and sweep you archers from the face of the earth. I hated your slaughter. I hated you all. You destroyed all that I knew.' He spoke without anger or recrimination, but out of an experience that would be impossible to recount to anyone who had not endured that massacre. Of all in the confines of the castle only he and Blackstone shared the memory of the battle. 'You will never pull a war bow again, not with that arm,' said de Harcourt. 'You have to learn to fight as a man-at-arms. And I have yet to see you touch that sword.'

The truth of what de Harcourt said about his injury caused more pain than the broken arm itself. Those final moments of the battle were as vivid as a sunset across the fog-laden fields of his homeland, conjuring ghosts and demons alike from the magical shroud. 'That sword killed my brother,' Blackstone said and swallowed a mouthful of wine. 'I killed the man who did it. If I take hold of its grip I cannot stop the violence that tries to explode out of me.'

'Then you have the advantage over many. All you have to do is learn the skill to use it properly. When you're ready, I'll teach you.'

'Why?' Blackstone asked.

'Because it is my duty,' de Harcourt answered. 'Something you must learn to understand and honour.'

'You question my courage, my lord?' Blackstone asked, the flush of anger creeping up his neck.

'No. But you are no longer what you were, Thomas. You are of no use to anyone unless you can be trained. Do you think the English army would take back an archer who cannot pull a bowcord, a man who has no fighting skills? You'd be lucky if they let you pack the supply mules. You're not stupid, Thomas, you're a fighter. Learn to fight.'

De Harcourt rinsed his mouth and spat out the wine. The servant gathered his shirt and draped a cloak about his master's shoulders against the creeping damp and cold of the autumn dusk.

Blackstone watched them a moment longer and then took a knife to the leather bindings that held the splints. He rubbed the blood into the muscles, which had wasted these past months, and tested the length of his arm. He squeezed his fingers into a fist, and looked down the line of sight of his bow arm. Once the stiffness had eased he tried to turn his wrist as if holding a bow. The bones had knitted badly and the forearm resisted his efforts. There was a permanent bend in the arm. De Harcourt was right, he would never be an archer again, but perhaps God had given him a crooked limb so he could carry a shield.

The fingers of the night air tickled his skin as he walked, unaided, and with only a slight limp, back to his room and Christiana, waiting at the window.

* * *

Countess Blanche de Harcourt sat at the linen-draped table and washed her hands in the silver bowl offered by a servant while another cut and placed food on her platter. She towelled her hands dry, concentrating on the act, debating in her mind how to answer the question that her husband had asked only moments earlier.

'Is she sleeping in his bed?' de Harcourt asked again.

'Jean, how am I to know?' she answered.

'She's our ward and she's in your charge. Is she?'

'I think,' she said carefully, 'there is some affection between them.'

'Beneath the covers?'

Blanche lowered the piece of meat from her eating knife onto her plate, and delicately wiped her mouth before sipping from the goblet of wine. 'He doesn't sleep in the bed. She tells me that he pulls a blanket and a covering onto the floor. He doesn't desire comfort. Besides, I suspect his wounds prohibit him from…' She let her thoughts remain unspoken, and put another piece of meat into her mouth. Chewing was a convenient escape from her husband's cross-examination.

'His wounds wouldn't stop him. I've seen that much for myself.' He pushed the plate to one side and reached for his wine. 'Speak to her. I'll not have a bastard child from an English barbarian conceived in this house. Do I make myself clear? They'll do it soon enough, no doubt; she's a headstrong woman who should have been married off by now. If her father survives the war he can take back his responsibility. Until then it's our burden.'

'She's no burden. She has shown spirit and courage,' Blanche answered in Christiana's defence.

'And drawn to an Englishman like an arrow to his bow. He must be educated, Blanche. I can teach him to fight, but you and Christiana have to teach him some manners. He should be able to sit at a table in a civilized fashion.'

'He's a common man. I never wanted him here in the first place,' she told him, abandoning her food, her appetite spoiled.

'No matter. We have him. Speak to Christiana and decide how you're going to do it. He's your responsibility.' De Harcourt pushed away from the table, tossed the meat from his plate to the dogs, and left his wife to deal with her growing anger and frustration in her own way. How she did so was up to her. He had no understanding of the process.

The rotting skulls were still impaled on the poles beyond the gates of Castle de Harcourt, slack-jawed, gaping at the scatter of clouds flitting across the face of the moon. Their flesh had rotted and the bones were picked clean, but still they served as a warning to any deserter or marauding band who thought of attacking the stronghold. Each day, as the dawn crept through the woodland, Blackstone could see them from his window, with their lifeless gaze, guardians of the forest road that could lead to his freedom. The days had worn on and his sense of confinement grew ever stronger. Christiana had gently refused his clumsy advances. She had not done so in anger, but no matter how gentle her rejection had been it added to a confusing sense of loss and loneliness. The silence and darkness of these nights that followed began to suffocate Blackstone's thoughts. The French countryside showed no lights from nearby villages, and once the Angelus Bell rang the Harcourt household retreated to their private chapel to recite prayers in honour of the Lord's Incarnation; and then until the curfew bell rang, they would retire to the great hall and private rooms. Blackstone was in conflict with his feelings for the God that had saved him and destroyed his brother. The silver token around his neck gave more comfort, and Arianrhod's cool touch to his lips was all the blessing he could offer by way of gratitude.

In the hours between the ringing of the bells Blackstone walked the walls, ignoring the sentries and their muttered greetings to the enemy who now lived in their midst. The freedom of the night wind chilled him but he welcomed its reminder of another life spent in the wild forests and open pastures with his brother before the act of murder that had sent them to war.

As each day passed his body grew stronger, but his mind began its own torment. Those skulls were his gaolers. He missed the friendship of the archers with their coarse jokes and laughter, men who had gathered him and his brother into their fold. There was a desperation in him to hear an English voice call out in greeting or insult, to challenge him to a drunken brawl having spent his last coin on an alehouse whore and drink. He yearned to hear the rambling dialect of a fletcher or bowyer, a blacksmith's cursing, or the scolding commands of his sworn lord, Sir Gilbert Killbere. They were as lost to him as surely as the morning mist was ripped from the treetops. There was only one way he could defeat these poisonous torments – sweat them out.

Blackstone bent from the waist and picked up a broken piece of rock that lay tumbled from the damaged wall. He eased the weight upwards, testing his injured leg, demanding his crooked arm play its part. He felt the pinch in his leg, but it was little more than the wound objecting to his effort. The leg would hold and if he was careful he would not tear the lesion apart. The blackened stitches kept the slash closed like the sewn lips of a heretic. His left arm was weak compared to its power before the German's sword had smashed down across the bones. But the crooked arm was only slightly out of true and would let him use a knife or hold a shield in close-quarter fighting. That is, if he stayed entrapped in the walls of Castle de Harcourt and learnt the skills. Jean de Harcourt had spoken the truth; Blackstone would be of no use to the English army unless he could fight. He had to ignore the temptation that tugged at him like a bird returning to its roost, and make his way back to discover who had survived the great battle.

And Christiana? For the past weeks he had felt her hands on his body as she tended to his wounds, like a servant to a master, except she had servants of her own, and could easily have given her nursing duties to one of them. But she had not. She had tended to him out of something that was more than duty or kindness, and the fragrance of her closeness tormented him in a manner he could not describe. His own base instincts had been tempered by his father's prohibition on ever bringing shame on his allegiance to Lord Marldon, who had granted him his freedom and friendship. But that family pledge had been broken and the bitter taste of the shame still lingered. His memory goaded him more insistently than the pain in his wounded leg. It was impossible to smother the truth of what his brother Richard had done. If only the memory could be buried as would shovelling dirt into a deep grave bury his mutilated body – now little more than a carcass lying undiscovered among the thousands on the battlefield at Crécy. Blackstone made a silent vow: he would not let these dark harbingers of recrimination torture him further. The truth was simple: Thomas Blackstone had survived, his wounds were healing, his strength returning. His capacity to inflict violence on an enemy was diminished, but not for much longer. A man who was once an adversary, and who, secretly, might still be, had extended his hand as mentor to serve the command of the English King. As the clouded waters of his mind began to clear he realized a plan was emerging that showed him the way to his future. Everything that had happened up to this time would become a source of strength, a stone-built fortress that would never be breached again by contrition or regret. He would learn how to fight as a man-at-arms and earn the honour bestowed on him.

Blackstone wielded the stonemason's hammer and began to build the wall.

The late autumn months saw the English King's army still besieging Calais in Edward's dogged determination to secure the port that gave him the gateway to France. Neap tides swept in across the marshland around the walled city and the English were constantly forced to move their tents and wagons back and forth, and little progress was made despite the King's efforts. The siege was to be a long, miserable affair.

Crops failed that year due to the unseasonably wet weather

and the harsh winter added to French misery as the English army foraged far and wide to feed itself. News was slow to reach the castle deep in the Norman countryside, but retreating knights, abandoning the French King, would pass by and share what news they had as they returned to their estates to try to protect their families from elements of the English army who controlled almost all of south-western France. Only the road from Bordeaux northwards to Paris remained in French hands. If Edward could close the northern and southern jaws and take Paris, the crown would be his. But not this year. There were still French lords who sided with Edward and took his payment for their loyalty even as the bodies of nobles and princes who fell at Crécy were disinterred from the burial ground at the Cistercian abbey of Valloires, where Edward had first buried them after the great battle. King Philip held state funerals for them and honoured their families – but theirs were estates without their lords, and disorder and discontent swept through many of the French nobility with the bitterness of the north wind.

Jean de Harcourt slashed the sword in an upward sweeping arc. Pain seared through Blackstone's body as he stumbled backwards.

'You're an archer, you're trained to stand bracing your left leg and if you do that I'll take it off with one sword stroke. Protect your legs with a low parry. A ten-year-old boy training to be a squire could kill you. You don't have to be a damned wall of resistance; use your feet! Pass and evade! Block high, strike down, step back. How many times do you need telling? Again!' de Harcourt shouted.

Blackstone shook his head in an attempt to clear the agony from the flat-bladed blow that Jean de Harcourt had just delivered against his wounded leg. He regained his stance, holding his bent left arm forward, extending the small buckler, his only means of defence. His tutor was using wooden training swords, the kind that pageboys and squires would be given to learn their skills. But in two swift strikes de Harcourt had nearly crippled Blackstone. He felt blood oozing behind his bandaged leg and knew it would already be seeping through the breeches he had managed to fit into that morning. Neither man wore protection from the sleet that stiffened his limbs other than a linen shirt and sleeveless leather jerkin. The cold gripped his leg, slowing his agility, making him vulnerable to de Harcourt's expert strikes. The Frenchman had not even broken into a sweat after demonstrating all the attacking and defensive guards to Blackstone for the tenth time that morning. Now the lesson was being applied in its most basic and brutal manner short of causing serious injury. The day already seemed long and arduous, and Blackstone wondered if his injured leg would hold out.

It was Blackstone's anger that kept him on his feet. He raised the sword and struck out at de Harcourt who barely moved. He was on the balls of his feet, then slightly sidestepped and struck Blackstone across his ear with the flat of the sword. The stinging blow made him swing back wildly in a crosscutting arc and this time the swiftness of his movement and the weight of his body behind the sword caught de Harcourt across his arm and he could see he had scored a painful point in retaliation against his tutor.

The two men stood a few feet apart, each waiting to see who would make the next move. De Harcourt lowered his guard.

'You made three mistakes. First was to lead with your left leg without covering yourself properly with your sword. Second to lunge and throw yourself off-balance. Your reactions were good and a crosscutting strike was lucky. But I will keep on hurting you until you learn.'

'You said three mistakes,' Blackstone said, eyes blinking against the cold rain.

No sooner had he spoken than de Harcourt was suddenly upon him, his left arm fully extended, the buckler's face turned outwards ready to receive any striking blow Blackstone might have delivered, which he did not. There was no time. The sword blade whirred left and right, top to bottom like a spinning sycamore seed. The force of the attack pushed Blackstone off-balance and he fell heavily into the dirt. De Harcourt stood over him as Blackstone lay looking up at the point of the sword and realized that had this been real combat it would not be a wooden training sword at his throat, but sharpened steel that would plunge through his gullet.

'Three. I've told you before, Thomas: never stand and wait for your opponent to make the decisive move. Always attack.'

Blackstone realized that de Harcourt had lunged at him with a ruthless efficiency that came from years of training. His heart sank: what chance did he have even to get close to those skills?

'That's enough for today,' de Harcourt said. 'See to that leg.'

He turned away without offering to help Blackstone to his feet. He would struggle, and de Harcourt knew he would have it no other way. This Englishman owned a stubborn pride the likes of which had defeated the greatest army in Christendom.

Blanche de Harcourt watched as her lord and husband stripped the wet clothes from his body. His scars were healing well and the weight he had lost during his convalescence was beginning to return. When she gazed on his nakedness it showed a tapestry of hurts from battles fought. By now she could touch almost every blemish and scar and know which conflict had given them. And if she felt that about her husband why should not Christiana feel the same about Thomas Blackstone? She had watched the girl and had the servants report to her if she had gone to Blackstone's room at night. Servants slept in corridors in whatever nook or doorwell they could find and she ensured that one of her most trusted would strip the linen from Blackstone's bed each week and check for signs of a virgin's blood. Time and again the servant had reported that Blackstone still slept on the floor and the linen did not bear even the creases from his body. Blanche wondered if Christiana had realized that she was being watched whenever she was out of her company. Each stable-hand, servant and scullion was told to report what they saw of what went on between Christiana and Blackstone. But so far there had been no indication of intimacy.

Blanche waited as Jean eased himself into the steaming water of the wooden bathtub. Her lust for her husband was something she always handled with care, not wishing to offend him with her desire. She slipped the gown from her body as she walked in front of him, the light from the window behind her, softening her shape, making her even more desirable. She could tell from his expression that the sensuous image she had offered would not be rejected. She slipped into the warm water and straddled him. Lust needed to be controlled to allow the full pleasure of its fulfilment.

As she felt him enter her, his hands and mouth unable to resist her breasts, she knew that sooner rather than later Christiana would lie with Blackstone. Women had little control over their lives but a man's bed could alter such poverty of influence. And she, Countess Blanche de Harcourt et Ponthieu, a woman of rank in her own right, had made sure that her ward was versed in these ways that could bring such influence into her own life.

The straw man was stitched into old sackcloth, and hung suspended like a common thief, his legs splayed, tied by rope to stakes in the ground. Blackstone scuffed the dirt beneath his feet to aid his footing, and focused on his helpless victim. The first flurries of snow had fallen but the full force of winter had yet to settle itself upon them. Day after day, time and again, de Harcourt had repeated the several positions a swordsman could take when preparing to engage his enemy. Blackstone's bruises and welts were testament to these lessons that were being beaten into him. Now he stood alone in the training yard while those in the castle went about their business, their heightened activity heralding the anticipated arrival of visitors.

The scarecrow gazed blindly at the figure before him who moved his feet and arms in a tightly configured dance of death. Blackstone's right leg held his balance, arms bent forward against any high strike down across his legs. His left arm covered his chest with the buckler while with the other he rested the weapon flat-bladed on his crooked arm, like a fiddler about to scrape a tune. It was a guard to protect legs and vital organs. The voice in his head commanded obedience – *balance and movement, sidestep*

and strike – the balls of his feet turned him a stride as if stepping
around an opponent, and then he slashed the sword down and
the straw man flinched.

Once again he repeated the attack and then extended his arm,
bringing the small buckler shield to his front, the sword now resting
on his right shoulder, cutting edge to the sky, his thumb pressing
against the crossguard above the grip to give added strength and
impetus to a strike. His left leg shuffled forward, the angry welt
still fringed by the black piercing of its stitches, still painful at the
stretch, but stronger now in its support of his upper body, with its
additional strength of archer's muscles across back and shoulder.
He had not told de Harcourt of his own regime of constant exercises
using a length of iron, heavier and more cumbersome than any
sword, which he lifted and swung, day in, day out.

Wolf Sword still kept its place by his bed – the blade sharp
and bright, the corded grip darkened by old blood. It waited like
a sentinel, needing a worthy hand to heft its deadly edge against
an opponent. Blackstone knew he was not yet worthy.

Nock, mark, draw and loose! The rhythm that had given him
his skill as an archer now gave way to another lethal combination
of movement. His wounded leg protested as he pushed it forward
in a sudden change of stance, bringing his sword arm to the front
of his face, the honed edge uppermost. This head-guard strike
enabled a powerful downward cut from right to left that severed
the straw man's leg at the thigh. The wooden sword's edge must
have found weak stitching.

The discipline of the fighting sequence flooded him with energy
and bolstered his confidence, but in that moment, as he struck,
a clamouring vision of the final moments at Crécy leapt at him
from a subdued memory. That attacking blow had been the very
one that the German knight had used against him, but somehow
Blackstone's instincts had turned him out of the blade's killing
range, exchanging a severed limb for the wound that he now carried.

The memory of the hulking knight who had slain his brother
and then scythed his way towards the English Prince was shrouded

in the evening's gloom. It had all happened so quickly. His mind's eye held the mute vision. Blackstone stood unmoving, sword arm lowered, body turned at the hips, the butchered torso leaking straw in the wind. He had been so close to being cleft by that knight that only now as he learnt the killing techniques did he sense the blessing that a few vital seconds had afforded him.

Out of the turmoil of the memory an insistent voice called his name.

He turned. Christiana stood ten feet behind him wrapped in a cloak, looking concerned, as if she had been too scared to approach any closer.

'I've been calling you,' she said against the buffeting wind. Then smiled, hoping it would penetrate the glazed look of incomprehension on his face. 'Thomas?'

He nodded and stepped towards her, pulling her small body into his own, then brushed a snowflake from her nose.

'I'm sorry,' he told her. 'I was being attacked by a scarecrow.'

She laughed as he tossed the wooden sword aside and led her away from the memory.

The straw man surrendered to the wind and scattered across the darkening sky.

CHAPTER THIRTEEN

Blackstone eased in the last piece of cut stone on St Nicholas's Day, as the darkening sky threatened a heavy snowfall. His wall now stood at the height of his shoulder and would serve as a defensive redoubt should intruders scale the walls, as had happened before when lawless scum had slaughtered de Harcourt's soldiers and servants. It was no great feat of stonemasonry, nor would a lord of the manor see it as vital, but de Harcourt had indulged the Englishman and silently admired the boy's skill. He would find a use for it, perhaps it would serve as an enclosure for his serfs to let loose a pig then chase it to see who could be first to club the animal to death. It would be good sport, a gift of their lord's Christmastime generosity.

Blackstone washed the dirt from his arms and watched the fevered activity going on around him. It was no surprise for him to learn that a half-dozen Norman lords and their entourages would soon be arriving to celebrate Christmas. The horses would need to be cared for with almost as much hospitality as the guests themselves. The air carried the smell of roasted and boiled meat, as Jean de Harcourt's household made final preparations for the feast that would follow the days of fasting.

Fresh straw and extra sacks of oats had been brought into the castle over the previous week from the surrounding villages. Farriers' apprentices worked tirelessly at their bellows, as hammer met steel, forging new shoes for de Harcourt's horses. De Harcourt had returned before midday from an early morning hunt with half a dozen retainers. The falcon on his arm was now hooded but the raptor's victims, heron, swan and crane, were tied across the pack-saddles, as were several deer carcasses, bloodied by the spear points that had pierced hearts and lungs.

Since arriving at the castle Blackstone had seen servants scuttling about darkened corridors but now more of them seemed to have crept into sight, as if from the wall's cracked lime mortar. Barked commands echoed across courtyard and halls as servants dressed in de Harcourt's livery scurried about their duties with a tangible air of excitement. They prepared rooms, linen was aired, dried herbs were scattered through the halls and chambers to offer the guests sweet fragrance underfoot. Corridors and privies were swept and cleaned; ornaments of silver were laid out as silk-embroidered cloths were draped on tables and benches. A steady procession of peasants carried bushels of kindling and firewood on their backs from nearby villages, cursing as they were shouldered off the narrow paths by grooms leading pack horses laden with victuals. The thought of more French knights arriving at the castle worried Blackstone. They would be men who had fought the English and probably, like their host, survived the slaughter of Crécy. How could de Harcourt have him under the same roof without causing dissent? Now that his strength was returning he felt even more the need to go beyond the walls, and perhaps if these men turned out to be bitter enemies he would be forced to escape their anger. Jean de Harcourt's hospitality would not be dishonoured, of that he was certain, but an assassin could be bought cheaply these days.

The candlelight flickered as Blackstone peered at the manuscript that lay open on the table before him. The neat copied text was smudged in places, evidence that sweat from a monk's skilful hand had caught the trailing words at the edge of the page. As much as Blackstone's eyesight struggled in the gloom his mind fought the lesson being given by Christiana.

'Why don't you try again?' she said, and went back to rubbing the soothing olive oil and lavender into his slashed face.

'I'll smell like a woman if you keep putting that on me,' he said.

'Do you know how expensive this oil is? It's healing the wound. Shall we read that poem again?'

'I don't have any interest in this, why are you trying to get me to learn it?' he said, frustrated with her insistence that he spend each night reading the cantering words across the page. 'It's boring. There are better things to be doing than sitting here.'

He pushed his thigh against hers and for a moment she did not resist, but then edged an inch or two away from him and put her finger back onto the page at the place where he had stopped reciting the poem.

'You must appreciate beauty, Thomas, and poets spend years of their lives finding a way to share such things with us,' she answered.

'I know all about beauty,' he told her. 'Every day on my way to the quarry I used to pass the brook and see the fish glide through the weed like a silver comb through a woman's hair. You don't see beauty in scratchings on a page. Whoever wrote this has never spent months on horseback through forests and fields of wildflowers. I don't want to do this any more,' he said and placed his hand on her thigh. 'I have enough beauty right here. I don't need a poet's imagination to tell me about such things.'

The half-light disguised the livid wound and allowed her to ease forward and gently kiss his unmarked cheek in an almost dismissive manner. But she hesitated too long before pushing herself away from him as he snatched her back and kissed her lips, his hand reaching for her breast. Once again her resistance was momentary but as his other hand moved further up her thigh she pulled away and stood up from the bench they shared at the table.

Even in the candlelight he could see the flush creep up her neck into her face and saw her nipples harden through the weave of her dress. Unlike her guardian the countess, and despite the chilled air, she never wore a mantle. The cleft between her breasts was just visible and he watched as she placed a hand across them, as if calming her heartbeat.

She poured a half glass of wine, its red juice colouring her lips. 'You're expected to be aware of more tender things than going to war. A knight should be able to recite poetry for his friends and family to show the gentle side of his nature.'

'I don't have friends or family and the gentle side of my nature lies beyond these walls in the countryside where I grew up. Don't try and make me something I am not,' he said, feeling the annoyance of rejection and his faltering place in the world of courtly manners.

Her anger flared, but she held a tight rein on it. 'The de Harcourt family are your friends and family now! These are the people in your life who have offered you shelter and the chance to better yourself.'

'I'm still an English archer to them! In their hearts they still hate me, there's no friendship, there's no family; what they do they do out of duty,' he answered sharply.

'And that duty serves you well. Everything you're being taught is to make you behave in a civilized manner. This is the challenge you have been given, to improve yourself, to meet a standard of behaviour that is acceptable in a house such as this.'

'I have the respect of the English King, that's enough for any man. I'll learn to fight because then I can be of some use to him so don't expect me to stand up and sing for my supper like a minstrel. I shall wash my arse after I shit and wipe my mouth after drinking from one of your fancy glasses, but who I am is who I am!'

'You're deliberately being crude and unpleasant. You're talking like a peasant,' she said.

'Because that's what I am to you and the people here. I'm a peasant archer, I'm crude and I'm brutal, and no matter how many fine clothes you give me, or dainty cuts of meat on a silver platter, I prefer my life to be simple and rough-edged.'

She moved quickly to the door, avoiding his quickly outstretched hand. 'Then you'll never have me in your bed, Thomas Blackstone, because I see greater things in you than you can see yourself. And if you cannot meet the challenge to be a better man, then I am wasting my time trying to help you,' she said, and closed the heavy door behind her, causing the candle flames to lean away from her anger.

His leg slowed him, but Blackstone yanked open the door and yelled down the corridor after her. 'I'll not be a damned pet monkey to the French! And I won't be held prisoner here! And when I take you to my bed you'll wish you'd have done it sooner!' He threw the bound manuscript after her, hitting one of the terrified servants curled in a doorway. He slammed the oak door, and cursed the pain that stretched from his leg wound. He needed time to finish his training and then he would be gone from this place and make his way back to England. He pulled aside the shutter from the window; the candles faltered and then died from the cold blast of air. Blackstone let the sleet gust into the room and watched it swirl into the blackness outside. A nagging question bothered him: was Christiana worth more to him than his freedom? Could he leave this place without her? Perhaps his defiance was so deep-rooted that he could never learn the subtle manners demanded by any house of nobility.

He closed out the storm and relit the candles – if there was reading to be done the subject would be of his own choosing. Jean de Harcourt had manuscripts in his library, bound parchments that documented ancient battles, drawings that showed the construction of the castle, something that would make sense to a common stonemason and archer.

Poets be damned. They were scribes trying to capture the glow of a candle; Blackstone preferred to feel the flame's heat between finger and thumb when he extinguished that light.

Jean de Harcourt made a relentless attack on Blackstone, who not only took the blows but used every guard taught him to parry and return the attack. Both men were drenched in sweat despite the cold north wind. De Harcourt, though, still had the edge of experience and pressed closely upon Blackstone, despite the younger man being bigger and stronger.

'Strike from over the right shoulder! No wide or useless positions. Keep your fighting stance! Break my attack! Break it, man!' The litany of commands hammered down on Blackstone as rapidly as the blows.

Blackstone's feet were planted firmly but he moved onto the

balls of his feet and altered his balance, blocking de Harcourt's blows, which in an instant allowed him to counter-attack. Blade met blade and Blackstone remembered the lesson: *Feel the pressure of your opponent's blade and react!* He struck at de Harcourt left and right, but could not unbalance the wily swordsman. Sweat stung his eyes, and he was beginning to lose focus. And then de Harcourt came at him hard and fast. Blackstone confronted him without altering his stance, solid in defence – ready to deliver a killing blow. He was only two sword strokes away from finally beating his tutor. De Harcourt's face snarled with effort, his eyes locked on his opponent's. And then, just as Blackstone blocked the attack and brought his sword down towards the man's exposed neck, he was suddenly flung backwards into the mud. And yet again de Harcourt had the sword at his throat.

De Harcourt stepped back. 'You've done well, Thomas. I'm pleased. You learn quickly and your strength serves you well. Once your wounds finally heal you'll have learnt as much in months as it takes a young squire to learn in years.'

Blackstone crawled up from the mud, shaking it from his hands and regripping the wooden sword.

'What happened? I blocked and counter-attacked, my balance was good, and still you put me down.'

De Harcourt waited for him to get onto his feet and prepare for another attack. 'You close with a man, you come under his guard; he's waiting for the strike. Wrap, grip and pull. Press yourself against him, seize his belt and yank and he'll go down.' De Harcourt smiled. 'It doesn't matter how big your opponent is.'

The two men were preparing to fight again when a cry came down from the sentry. 'Horsemen approaching!' And then after a moment, when the riders' armorial banner became clearer, 'It's Sir Guy de Ruymont!'

The gates opened and horses clattered into the yard as de Harcourt abandoned Blackstone and walked quickly to where grooms ran to hold the nobleman's bridle. A page and a squire rode behind a woman accompanying de Ruymont, who climbed quickly down from his horse and embraced de Harcourt, each kissing the other's cheek.

'Jean, your wounds! Look at you! My God, they're healed! How are you, dear friend? How are you?'

'I'm well, and as you can see, I'm fit again. The wounds were nothing,' de Harcourt said, dismissing his old injuries, and then stepped towards the woman. 'Joanna, if you'll allow me,' he said and reached up to help her down.

'It's been too long, Jean,' she said.

Servants ran from the house, escorting Blanche de Harcourt down the steps and across the wooden bridge that spanned the inner moat and into the outer bailey to greet her guests.

Blackstone watched as the old friends exchanged their pleasantries and the knight's page and squire took control of the horses, following the grooms towards the stables.

'Who's this?' de Ruymont asked, looking towards Blackstone. 'He's got a face like a cow's arse. Are you teaching the servants to fight now? Sweet Christ, Jean, is France that hard up for recruits?'

'I'll tell you later,' de Harcourt said, and in as much of a flurry as they had arrived the guests were ushered through the castle doors. Moments later the squire came out of the stables and ran after them, carrying his lord's sword and scabbard.

A devil wind of activity caught up everyone except Blackstone, who stood alone, the sweat chilling on his body. One of the soldiers went past him and picked up the discarded wooden sword and offered it to Blackstone without hiding the sneer on his face.

'You might need this if the King of France finds out you're here,' he said.

Blackstone took it from him. There would be another training session soon. But the way the soldier spoke made Blackstone realize that other nobles, like the one who had just ridden in, might not be so protective towards an English bowman.

Blackstone had finished washing and was dabbing the puckered face wound with a clean piece of linen when there was a tap on his door, and a voice beckoned him from the corridor. 'My lord, Countess Blanche has requested you join her in the great hall.'

Blackstone pulled on his tunic and opened the door to where Marcel waited.

'The great hall?' Blackstone asked. He had never been invited into the heart of Castle de Harcourt before; it was a place where the family lived and where invited guests would gather.

The servant bowed his head again and replied. 'Yes, Sir Thomas.'

'Do you know why?' Blackstone asked.

'No, Sir Thomas,' Marcel answered.

'And if you did, it is not your place to tell me.'

'Quite so, my lord.'

'Are all those who serve in this household as discreet as you?'

'I am an old man and my life is as comfortable as I could wish it to be, thanks to Countess Blanche. How could I jeopardize that, Sir Thomas?'

'Then, Marcel, I won't embarrass you further, or test your loyalty to your mistress.'

Blackstone guessed the man was already more than forty years old and was most likely right; his life was the best he could hope for. He carried himself stooped from a lifetime of subservience and the effect on his bones of the penetrating damp from the cold stone walls.

'Thank you, Master Blackstone,' he said, but hesitated as he led Blackstone down the corridor. 'We have all heard of your bravery, my lord, and that you are here under the protection of this family, but there are some things that they will not discuss with you, and it is for someone base, like myself, to explain these in a crude manner.'

'I don't know what you're talking about,' Blackstone said.

'They have prepared a table in the great hall. There's food and wine. And...'

'And?'

'I would remind you not to pick your teeth with a knife or wipe your mouth on your sleeve, they'll give you a napkin for that.' Marcel increased his pace, his suggestions tumbling quickly as they got closer to the great hall where once again he hesitated.

'And, Master Blackstone, don't spit, belch or fart.'

Blackstone waited outside the huge doors as Marcel stepped through and announced his presence. He was ushered inside. There was a blazing fire in the hearth, big enough for ten men to stand shoulder to shoulder, with logs stacked to one side and bushels of kindling at the other. Fresh reeds covered the floor and there was the scent of lavender drifting into the room from the flames. There were neither dogs nor their master in sight; instead Countess Blanche de Harcourt and Christiana stood waiting for him in the middle of the room. Behind them was a long trestle table covered in linen and laid with platters of cut meats with small silver bowls filled with salt and sauces. Three or four servants stood against the wall, strategically placed for their stations at the table.

Blackstone quickly calculated the size of the room. It was similar to Lord Marldon's, but this one seemed to offer more warmth. De Harcourt could probably have fitted a hundred or more men in this hall, with no man's shoulder touching another's. The vaulted ceiling towered sixty feet above Blackstone, with arched timber trusses and woven tapestries hanging from cast-iron bars. Light streamed in from the half-wall of leaded windows with stone sills big enough for a grown man to sit in and covered in brightly coloured cushions. De Harcourt had employed painters to decorate the walls in whitewash, with an earth-coloured border rising two feet above the stone floor. One wall looked as though it were a massive window looking out through the painted branches of a flowering tree in a flower-filled meadow. It was the kind of decoration that was, perhaps, under the control of the countess, who now stood before him.

'My lord and husband is with his friend Guy de Ruymont, and so Christiana and I thought this an opportune moment to introduce you to certain...' she hesitated, searching for the right word, 'customs, when we are gathered to dine here.'

Christiana smiled at him and move forward in an attempt to ease his awkwardness.

'Thomas, my lady and I are going to explain how best to behave when in the company of honoured guests.'

Blackstone bristled. 'I doubt someone like me is ever going to share a table with *honoured* guests. What would I be? A figure for discussion? A curiosity to see how my callused hands daintily put pieces of meat into my mouth?'

Christiana blushed with embarrassment and Blackstone immediately regretted his words, which confirmed his lack of good manners and coarseness of character. Blanche de Harcourt showed no such sign of intemperance.

'Your wounds are healing, Thomas. Are you being well looked after?' she said, ignoring his unpleasantness.

'I am, my lady, thank you,' Blackstone said, immediately humbled by her kindness, knowing her good manners were like the paint covering the walls, a smothering of what lay beneath.

She moved closer to him, making him even more uncertain of what to do next. He bowed – and kept his head down.

'Thomas,' she said more gently than he deserved, 'lift up your head.'

He averted his eyes, but she reached out her hand and turned his chin so that she could examine his face more carefully. The Englishman towered over her, but he remembered her fierceness when he'd first seen her at Noyelles, wearing a breastplate of armour and gripping a sword she had been prepared to wield. Women like her confused him.

'It's still an ugly wound, the skin looks inflamed, but I suspect the scar will be a good one. Better than I expected.'

'I owe that to Christiana's skill, my lady.'

'So you do, and much else. She's been your constant companion at her own request, and with my permission.'

Blackstone sensed an opening, a moment when she might allow him some leeway.

'I won't be kept here forever, will I, countess? I wonder why you're taking so much trouble to teach me courtly manners. I have no interest in poetry or dance, and I eat when I am hungry, as quickly and as simply as I can. I'm never going to be admitted to your high table, am I?'

She did not move her gaze from his face. 'I doubt you ever will. No.'

'Then why play this game, my lady?'

'Because one day, if you live long enough, you might be asked to sit at a nobleman's table, and when that happens I do not want them knowing that you were in our care and remained in your half-civilized state. The shame would be ours, not yours.'

Blackstone knew that, had the same proposal been put to his once sworn lord, Sir Gilbert Killbere, he'd have turned on his heel and left these trumped-up lords who were more concerned with table manners than with loyalty to their King.

But something stopped him. Sir Gilbert's words, once uttered at the invasion beach when an inexperienced Blackstone had boasted of his skills with his war bow echoed from the past. *You're a free man; behave like one*, Killbere had berated him. No matter how good the men around him had been, the knight had told him that they stood in his father's shadow. *You're better than they are. Start thinking and behaving like him*. Blackstone had learnt the ways of battle and if the de Harcourt family saw him as little more than an efficient and brutal killer, then so be it. He owned his dignity and he would not let them get the better of him, even if they *had* helped save his life. All he had to do was keep his wits about him and he would soon walk away from this place – and take the girl with him.

Blackstone bowed his head, only slightly this time. 'My lady, I would prefer the shame was mine alone, for being such a worthless pupil.'

Her eyes widened. 'My word, Thomas, you learn quickly,' she said and turned to Christiana, who made no attempt to hide her smile at his cleverness. 'Let us show our guest to the table.'

CHAPTER FOURTEEN

Over the following days more of de Harcourt's friends arrived to celebrate Christmas. Some of the Norman lords brought their wives, two did not. They were all unknown to him until he was tutored by the Countess's servant Marcel. Blackstone made a point of remembering their names and their coats of arms. Louis de Vitry, Jacques Brienne, Henri Livay, Bernard Aubriet. Every one of them was still at war with England, each had answered King Philip's call, and all of them had now gathered at the castle of one of the most loyal French families. Jean de Harcourt's father, killed at Crécy, lay dead in the family crypt, honoured by the King of France and remembered by the court. So, Blackstone wondered as he watched these men return with their bloodied spoils from the day's hunt, why were they gathering here when he was living under the same roof? Who was in the most danger, he or the Frenchman who sheltered him?

The weather turned colder, blustering winds came and went, as indecisive as Blackstone's feelings about the presence of so many nobles. There were some who were similar in age to de Harcourt himself; others had ten years or more on him. These older men must, Blackstone thought, have more influence on events than those who were younger. Blackstone kept himself in the training yard out of sight, left alone by Jean de Harcourt, who now spent his time with his guests. When they didn't hunt they stayed in the library behind closed doors. It seemed to be less of a festive celebration than a council of powerful lords. If the women did not join their men riding out to hunt they gathered in Blanche's rooms or were entertained in the great hall by minstrels, summoned by de Harcourt from Paris to entertain his guests and to pass on the news or gossip gleaned from the capital.

Lord de Graville, grey twists in his beard, sat hunched in his cloak. His page and squire, in charge of two pack horses loaded with their lord's personal weapons and gifts, were smoothly practised at their duties. They knew the castle, asked no directions, and ordered de Harcourt's servants and grooms with an ease borne of long-standing superiority. De Graville was a voice of authority in Normandy, as was the man who rode through the gates with him that day – the Lord de Mainemares – whose face seemed to be set in a permanent scowl, even when greeted by de Harcourt. The men embraced and kissed, and it was obvious that the guests were trusted friends and both believed in the divine will of God. Blackstone would see them go to pray in the chapel three times a day, more on a holy day. Blackstone knew these devout nobles were about the same age as Sir Godfrey, the renegade of the de Harcourt family.

Each nobleman's arrival would be marked by another feast with music, and so it went on over the course of a week. Christiana spoke with more candour than Marcel ever could, and warned him that these Normans swore allegiance to those who would benefit them the most.

'You sound bitter,' he told her as they watched another group arrive.

'My father is an impoverished knight. He holds no land and serves his lord in the west, and his allegiance was to the King of France. These men who come here can be bought. He could not.'

Blackstone felt a shiver of uncertainty whenever she mentioned her father. The English had swept down the Cotentin peninsula and beaten French forces back at every turn and Sir Godfrey, his benefactor's uncle, had been in the vanguard, pursuing and destroying those loyal to the French crown using Killbere and the mounted archers.

'I still don't know what's happened to him,' she said. 'I'm hoping one of these lords can tell me.' She touched his arm. 'Be careful of that man, Thomas,' she said fearfully, pointing out one of the nobles, a man no more than twenty or twenty-one years old.

'Who is he?'

'William de Fossat. He rode at the side of the Count of Alençon at Crécy.' Her voice was tinged with dislike. 'They slaughtered the Genoese bowmen so they could charge at your Prince.' She smiled. 'Perhaps it's just as well – otherwise you might not be here today.'

'They were helpless anyway. We'd killed so many of them it made no difference,' he said, aware as soon as he'd spoken that his words were emotionless and matter-of-fact. The English were exhausted when Alençon made his charge, but they had stopped him anyway. And killed him. Blackstone watched de Fossat pull off his riding gloves and take Blanche de Harcourt's outstretched hand, his lips hovering above her fair skin. His face reminded Blackstone of Jean de Harcourt's falcon – a sharp, beaked nose and eyes that never settled. William de Fossat, she told him, had fallen foul of John, Duke of Normandy, the King's son, and lost most of his estates.

'He's been known to commit murder,' she added.

'Soldiers die in battle.'

'No. He killed his cousin for refusing to meet a challenge and then killed the man who made that challenge. Most of these men in their own way are dangerous, Thomas. Stay away from them.'

Blackstone had done his best to do just that. Whenever de Harcourt and the lords rode forth or returned he kept out of sight. He had become invisible to everyone except Christiana, who now spent more time with the other women, all revelling in the opportunity to gossip, since they so often lived alone in their husband's manor houses or castles, with no other women of equal rank for company, save perhaps a daughter. It was an ideal time for Blackstone to take advantage of the men's absence and the women's gathering in order to use the library. The servants barely had time to notice him being there, but piles of warm ash in the fireplace told him that de Harcourt and the nobles were spending hours locked in the room.

The room was not large – big enough for a bolstered chair, stools and a table beneath the window. The fireplace dominated the room, candle holders the main source of light. There were rolled documents tied with ribbon, layered like firewood on shelves, and cut sheets of parchment, stitched and bound, laid like a stonemason's dry wall. A woven rug covered the tiled floor instead of cut reeds. The room suggested a sanctuary for the lord of the manor.

On an age-polished slab of chestnut that served as a table was a rolled parchment. Blackstone made sure that there was no activity in the yard that might herald de Harcourt's return, and then unfurled what turned out to be a crude, hand-drawn map of France, an uneven line sketched down one quarter of the country, splitting the kingdom. Blackstone traced his finger down from Paris and located Castle de Harcourt. There were dozens of marks made on the map, speckling the parchment – small red crosses, black dots and circles spread like the pox down from Normandy, across to Brittany and south into Bordeaux.

They were locations marking something of importance, and if Castle de Harcourt had been identified then perhaps, Blackstone thought, these were other castles scattered across the countryside. He worked out where the English army had landed and the route he must have taken as he fought his way across Normandy. There was no mark for Crécy, and he had no idea where it might lie. Only the cities of Caen, Rouen, Paris and Bordeaux were shown and in his mind's eye he tried to imagine what lay beneath his fingertips. He had never seen a map like this before and his imagination took him like an eagle soaring across the route they had marched.

He rolled the map and went back to the shelves, running his fingers lightly over the parchments and bindings. How could one man read so many books? On a lower shelf he found sheets of drawings embellished with Latin text, bound with an illuminated cover showing a monk wielding a sword. Blackstone eased it from its resting place and moved to the window for better light, and to watch for de Harcourt's return. As he turned each sheet he saw that the images were drawings showing the guard positions that Jean de Harcourt had taught him. It was a book on swordsmanship. Blackstone slipped the manuscript beneath his jacket. He had found a book that interested him.

It seemed to Blackstone that the guests would be staying for some time. Christmas seemed an on-going feast, one to which he had not been invited. He took his meals in his room, brought by a servant, sometimes joined by Christiana, who gently continued to coax his table manners. It was a far cry from the Holy Day's rest in his village, when the local priest would give them a serving of Christmas ale, and they would rest for a day, and be brought together in prayer in the church that was as cold as a grave. They were good memories of hard work and brotherly love, such as the Christmas when Richard Blackstone had bent that malformed face of his into an idiot's grin and bellowed with joy as he skinned and gutted a snared rabbit for the Christmas pot.

Dear Lord and all Your angels, Blackstone's thought went out in prayer, look after my brother as I could not.

'Thomas?' Christiana asked, breaking his reverie.

'What?'

'Where were you?'

'Remembering another time.'

She moved closer to him, her fingers touched her lips and then laid them on his scar.

'It's healing well. When summer comes and you get some warmth on your face there'll only be a white line.'

He held her to him and lowered his lips to hers. 'How long must I wait?'

'Until it's time,' she said, her voice almost a whisper, but she did not turn away.

He pressed her against him, her lips softened with balm, and he felt them part as the tip of her tongue gently teased his own.

And then she eased back.

'Too tight. You crush me,' she said softly.

He hadn't realized how hard he held her, and once again his clumsiness embarrassed him. 'I'm sorry.'

'You'll learn. I'm not as frail as I sound, it's just that you're stronger than you realize. Now, we must go.'

'I've no place to go.'

'You've been invited to the great hall.'

He pulled away from her as if she had slapped him across his wounded face.

'Don't be alarmed. You know how to behave,' she said.

'With you and Countess Blanche perhaps, but not with all those noblemen and their wives. Why?'

'You know why. You're a curiosity. You're a common man blessed by a King. They want to take the measure of you.'

'They can go to hell.'

'They'll pay a priest to save them from that,' she said, soothing his fear as best she could. 'Listen, my love, these are some of the most powerful men in Normandy and you are under Count Jean's protection.'

Blackstone turned away from her.

'Thomas, don't act like a child,' she said carefully.

He spun around, anger ready to explode, but she stood her ground and smiled, waiting patiently for the man she loved to appear before her. Her demeanour stopped him.

'I can't go down there,' he said, already defeated before he had stepped beyond his own room.

'When you served Sir Gilbert and your centenar that you told me about...'

'Elfred.'

'Yes, Elfred. What did they teach you when you fought?'

'How to kill my enemy.'

'In anger?'

'No, for each other and the love of my King.' He paused and then understood. 'In a disciplined and determined way.'

'Then that is all you have to do tonight. If you lose your temper you confirm why they despise you.'

'Do they?'

'They despise the brutal archer you were, but they're intrigued to see the man-at-arms you're being trained to become. Find that place inside you that is disciplined and determined and you'll have beaten them.' She kissed him tenderly. 'Again,' she added.

Shadows danced across the great hall's walls from two huge iron chandeliers, ten feet across, their metal rims hoisted by pulleys to the ceiling, each holding forty or more candles. Around the hall spiked iron stands impaled candles the thickness of a man's arm and the fireplace crackled and roared from blazing oak and ash logs.

At the high table Jean de Harcourt and Blanche sat with the nobles and their wives. As Blackstone walked past the cloth-covered trestle table near the entrance, the half-dozen squires, most of them older than Blackstone, stared at the Englishman who had already gained knighthood and honour without their years of service and training. Blackstone barely saw them from the corner of his eye, his attention fixed on the far table and the nobles who displayed their wealth and power with fur-edged, richly embroidered clothing and jewellery. He stopped, knowing he was expected to kneel. These men were his superiors. Instead, he stood defiantly and looked at each face in turn, noting with some satisfaction the glare of annoyance from each of the Normans and the ripple of discomfort at his ill-mannered and contemptuous behaviour. *I am a humble English archer in this great Norman hall and I've faced you and your kind before – and beaten you.* His thoughts resonated as though they had painstakingly been chiselled in stone. Only when his eyes moved back to Jean de Harcourt did he bow his head and then kneel before him.

Jean de Harcourt made him stay on his knee longer than was usual. The wound would soon complain but Thomas Blackstone needed to be taught a lesson.

'Join us,' de Harcourt said at last.

It still took effort for him to rise but he disguised his discomfort as best he could. There would be little satisfaction given to the Frenchmen. The usher guided Blackstone to the furthest seat at the end of the table and placed Christiana at his side. The gathered nobles and their wives could not take their eyes from him; he was physically bigger than any grown man at the table, which made the petite girl at his side look more frail than she was.

'I have never had a man of such low status sit at my table,' said one of the nobles with apparent disgust. He was a barrel-chested man, with a full beard and jet black hair, thick as a horse's mane, brushed back onto his shoulders. Blackstone could see the dark eyes glaring, but also noticed the man's strength. Without doubt he was a fighter.

'Then we are both at a disadvantage, my Lord de Fossat,' said Blackstone, pleased to see the man react to the fact that he knew his name, 'because I have never dined in such distinguished company.'

His response caused a ripple of amusement.

'And with the greatest respect, this is my lord, the Count de Harcourt's table.' There was a murmur of intrigue at the Englishman's impertinence, which Blackstone quickly turned to his advantage, adding, 'Unless, of course, he's sold it to you.'

Jean de Harcourt laughed, and the others followed, even de Fossat smiled.

'I told you he had a mind of his own,' de Harcourt said, and then urged his guests to eat, but as they did so their eyes kept glancing to the far end of the table.

A servant placed a large loaf of bread in front of Blackstone. He instinctively reached out to tear a chunk from it, but as his hands went forward he felt, rather than heard, Christiana's intake of breath. Blackstone corrected himself and carefully sliced a piece of bread.

Christiana's knee pressed against his beneath the tablecloth.

He had learnt some manners.

All he had to do now, Blackstone thought, was to learn to stay alive among these powerful men.

* * *

Blackstone managed to get through the meal without causing offence from any lack of table manners, though it was not without help. When he was about to stab a piece of meat Christiana quite casually mentioned that she always thought he preferred a less tender cut. Blackstone gratefully followed her prompt and passed the finer cuts of meat to others. Her influence was so natural it went unnoticed, except by Blanche de Harcourt whose smile of encouragement settled Christiana's own nervousness. No one spoke to Blackstone, no one included him in their conversation, and he was glad of it. Being ignored allowed him to keep his eyes down and his ears open. Snippets of conversation filtered through the chatter; gossip about the King and his anger that his son John, Duke of Normandy, had not marched quickly enough from the south to fight in the great battle of Crécy; that the King's wife was too young; that widows from the war left with great estates now looked for younger men to wed so their inheritance might be defended and then passed on when their children came of age. The war had torn France apart. Perhaps those who chattered didn't care what he heard. To them Blackstone was still little more than a servant whose blindness and deafness were guaranteed if he wished to continue to be fed with a roof over his head. But when Blackstone did raise his eyes he caught some of those around the table glancing in his direction; nervous looks, penetrating stares that darted away quickly when he looked back. The dinner seemed to go on forever as course after course arrived. Blackstone had never washed his hands so often and the rich food churned his stomach. A hunk of bread and cheese and a bubbling pot of pottage was all he wanted – that and a mighty thrust of Wolf Sword to burst this bubble of chivalric behaviour that seemed more important than anything else.

Blackstone's own charade was nearly exposed when the musicians were commanded to play dance music and the nobles took their wives to where the reeds had been swept aside, exposing the tiled floor. Guy de Ruymont's wife, long-faced, her wimple bound so tightly on her forehead that Blackstone wondered if the blood had been cut off from her pale face, leaned across to him and said, 'Will you be asking any of the ladies other than Christiana to dance, Master Thomas? I suspect we all are rather frightened of you, but something as gentle as a dance might soothe those fears.'

Blackstone could barely hide his panic. Guy de Ruymont saw it and knew that his wife was playing devil's advocate. Dancing, or the lack of it, was one element of Blackstone's tutoring that would expose his common character.

'My dear lady, you expect too much of Master Blackstone, you must remember he still bears his wounds.'

'Of course, forgive me, how could I forget that you fought at Crécy?' she said, but this time there was a chill in her voice and a frown on her thin-lipped face as she brushed past him.

'I'm grateful, my lord,' Blackstone said to de Ruymont as he passed by.

'I've seen fear in men's eyes before,' de Ruymont said. 'We are all soldiers in the field of battle, and dancing doesn't come easily to many of us, as you might observe when I accompany my wife.' He took a pace away but then, almost as an afterthought, and to explain his wife's jibe, he said, 'She lost her brother and four kinsmen at Crécy. Time has not yet healed *her* wounds.'

In that brief moment Blackstone felt an enormous gratitude to the French nobleman whose gentle manner and quick thinking had saved him from the embarrassment they had all been waiting for. He was also under no illusion that he was seen as the butcher who sat at their table, and who had slaughtered their loved ones. How far could their civility be stretched before someone drank from the poisoned chalice and betrayed his presence to the French court? Jean de Harcourt was seen as a loyal subject to King Philip but harbouring an Englishman, and an archer at that, could easily lead to a charge of treason. De Harcourt risked a great deal to fulfil his uncle's wishes, and Sir Godfrey himself would be beheaded if he were ever captured by French forces. Why,

Blackstone wondered, had Jean de Harcourt exposed himself to such a risk by inviting these influential men to his home for Christmas and allowing them to see him? Whatever the reason, it would unfold in its own time.

And once again Blackstone's instincts told him not to wait too long to find out. Sooner or later he must seize his own destiny.

The minstrels' music lilted across the hall as Blackstone fidgeted, squirming inside as he remembered Christiana trying to teach him the courtliness of the dance: men and women facing each other, three steps back, a bow, forward, take the lady's hand, three more lightly taken steps, a pause, a faltering stutter of a walk in Blackstone's case, clumsy and uncoordinated, leading the lady by the hand, *keep going, keep going, now pause again, turn in the opposite direction, walk, turn, face your partner! Thomas! You're like a wandering cow!* Enough had been enough.

While Christiana danced Blackstone quietly eased away into the night air. One of de Harcourt's dogs followed him, perhaps as tired of the music as was Blackstone. He looked across the glittering sky and the frost that settled across the landscape. Sentries stood at their posts and the world seemed to have eased into silence. Moonlight illuminated the silhouettes of the forests but their darkness soon absorbed what light there was. If he were to defend this castle, he decided, he would cut back the trees another hundred yards from the north gate and use the timber to build another palisade beyond the outer moat. Defence was everything when facing an enemy, and King Edward had proved that when he chose his ground to fight. All the lessons Blackstone had learnt this past year were clear in his mind and he knew instinctively that he would use them again when he eventually left this place. The dog sat at his side as Blackstone stroked its velvety ears, but he felt it tense, its muscles shivering in anticipation. Blackstone looked along the passageways; the shadows showed no sign of movement, yet he knew the darkness held someone.

'Who's there?' he called.

The dog uttered a low rumbling growl as Blackstone braced himself for any sudden attack.

'If you please, sir, hold the dog. I don't wish you any harm,' a young voice answered from somewhere ahead.

Blackstone comforted the dog, and took hold of its broad leather collar. 'Then come forward and show yourself,' he replied.

A small figure stepped from the darkness into a shaft of moonlight; it was a boy.

'The dog could pull me down,' the boy said.

'I have him, you come forward and give him your scent.'

The boy came closer, his arm extended towards the dog's nose. It was a pageboy who, despite his fear of the dog, had stepped forward confidently on Blackstone's command. The dog whined, strained at the collar and then, tail wagging, licked the boy's hand.

The pale light kept the boy's features indistinct. 'Who are you?' Blackstone asked.

'My name is Guillaume Bourdin,' the boy answered, and gazed up at Blackstone's scarred face, made to look even more vicious by the shadows.

'And who do you serve?' Blackstone asked.

'Countess de Harcourt had me placed with Lord Henri Livay,' the boy answered.

Blackstone gazed at him, there was something about him that seemed familiar, but he had no idea what it was.

'All right, Master Bourdin, why aren't you with the other pages in the stable? Isn't that where you're supposed to be while the squires dine with their masters?'

'I saw you training, Sir Thomas, but I could not approach you without being seen, and so I waited for a moment when I might thank you and tell you how pleased I am that you have recovered so well from your terrible wounds.'

'I don't know you, boy, so why would you need to thank me? And what do you know of my wounds?'

'I was at the castle at Noyelles when you were brought there after the battle. And before that you tried to help my master and spared my life. And so I will always be in your debt, Sir Thomas.'

Blackstone realized it was the boy who had guarded the wounded knight concealed behind the curtain. The incident seemed so long ago.

'Surely your master couldn't have survived those wounds?' said Blackstone, already knowing the answer.

'No, Sir Thomas, he died less than an hour after you left the castle.'

'How long did you serve him as a page?'

'Nearly four years. I'm almost eleven now.'

'And so Countess Blanche placed you with a new lord. Who did you say?'

'My Lord Henri Livay,' the boy said, his smile telling Blackstone that Blanche de Harcourt had been careful in the boy's placement.

'Is he a good master?'

'He is, Sir Thomas. He is kind and I'm learning quickly.'

'Does his squire beat you?'

'Only when I fail in my duty.'

'Is that often?'

'No, Sir Thomas, I am determined to serve well and with courage.'

'You have courage already,' Blackstone said. 'I saw that for myself back at Noyelles. I'm pleased that you've been placed under such good care as that of Lord Livay and that you will learn all the skills to become a good squire,' Blackstone said, feeling a satisfied warmth that out of all the slaughter and pain, this boy had survived and been given the chance to serve an honourable master.

'All right, get back to the others before the squires return and check on you. Obey them and learn, young Master Guillaume. It seems we have both been given a second chance to change our lives.'

The boy bowed and turned away, disappearing quickly into the shadows, using the darkness to mask his return. The boy's instincts serve him well, Blackstone thought, and then stepped back himself into the darkness offered by a pillar as a servant opened the door, spilling a yellow glow from inside the great hall. The musicians had fallen silent as the servant looked left and right. Blackstone stepped forward, allowing the man to see him.

'Sir Thomas, the ladies have retired and my lord commands me to take you to the library.'

Blackstone followed the man and was ushered into the candlelit room. The fire's blaze threw its warmth into the small room and cast the men's shadows behind them onto the walls, making them appear even more threatening than Blackstone felt them to be.

'You continue to show bad manners, Thomas,' de Harcourt said. 'A social inferior does not leave his host's table until given permission to do so. I'll not be embarrassed in front of my friends again, you understand?'

Blackstone bowed his head. 'Please accept my apologies, lord. I thought my presence at your table had outstayed its welcome.'

'He has an answer for everything,' said William de Fossat. 'Were he not knighted by a Prince I'd have the impertinence beaten out of him.'

No one else spoke, but they held glasses of wine in their hands and gazed towards the Englishman in their midst. Most seemed less concerned about Blackstone's presence than their aggressive companion, de Fossat.

'But a Prince *has* honoured him,' said de Harcourt, 'and that is why we have agreed to allow him among us. Sit down, Thomas; we want to talk to you. And you'll speak freely, understood?'

Blackstone nodded and sat on a bench to face his inquisitors.

'You're being taught swordsmanship,' one of the men asked.

'I am, lord.'

'And the lance?'

'No, lord. No lance. I see no purpose.'

The murmur of disapproval made it obvious that Blackstone had no understanding of how a man-at-arms should fight.

Henri Livay smiled indulgently. 'You see no purpose? A knight is often measured by his prowess with a lance when he rides in the lists.'

'I've never seen a tournament, though I've heard noblemen and men-at-arms have died from their injuries when they joust. It seems a waste of a good fighting man – dying just to wear pride on your sleeve.' Blackstone's comments made the men look at each other in disbelief, but he knew his antagonism was justified. 'A lance is a useless weapon on horseback. You never reached us with your lances. We killed your horses. We dug pits and we pulled you down. My lords, the day of the lance is finished unless it is held on the ground by two or three men and used to kill charging horses.'

'I'll not have a bastard archer sit there and talk of damned tactics and tell me how he slaughtered us!' shouted de Fossat.

'Shame! Shame on you, Jean! You bring this butcher into our circle of friendship?' another challenged de Harcourt.

De Harcourt raised a hand to pacify their anger. 'Does he not speak the truth?' he said calmly. 'How many of us reached their lines? And those who did, what weapons did we use? Eh? Sword, mace and axe.'

'And it wasn't enough,' added another. The men began arguing until one of them stood and strode towards Blackstone. He wore a dark blue cloak, edged in gold braid with an ermine collar. He had wealth and authority and was used to showing both. Like most of the men in the room he was shorter than Blackstone by nearly six inches, but his bulk was muscle and his stocky appearance carried the menace of a man used to close-quarter battle. *That's a powerful man, Thomas*, Christiana had told him when she had pointed him out earlier. *Lord de Graville is a close friend of Sir Godfrey's, but he didn't go over to the English.*

'Listen to me, boy. There's a code of chivalry that we hold as dear to us as the lance. A knight will always carry both into battle,' he said, the spittle from his disgust clinging to his beard.

Blackstone let the others mutter their agreement, but de Harcourt stayed silent. He had given his pupil free rein. If Blackstone was cowed by these men then he was little more than a worthless yeoman who could no longer draw a war bow. If he had the making of a fighting man he would defend himself using his brain and his tongue as his weapons. So far, Jean de Harcourt noted, Blackstone had defied his enemies in the room.

'I believe I understand honour, my lords. My own sworn lord told me that a man is measured by his honour and loyalty. But chivalry?'

'Aye!' Louis de Vitry shouted. 'A knight's chivalry is his birthright and duty.'

Blackstone allowed a moment to pass. There was no point in jumping into the angry fray, he knew that choosing his words was as important as choosing his ground for a fight. 'I'm a coarse man from a plain background, taught by my father to use a war bow. But what I see of chivalry is like a cloak that hides a leper's body. What kind of chivalry was it that caused you to trample down your own peasant infantry and put your own bowmen to the sword? If that's chivalry I've no use for it. I'll fight to the death for my King and my friends around me. I'll kill because I want my enemy dead, and that can't be disguised as anything else.'

For a moment there was little more than the sound of the men's laboured breathing. It was incomprehensible that a base English archer had made such impertinent comments. Blackstone didn't flinch under their glare.

De Vitry got up from his chair. 'Jean, I'll not stay in the same room as this vile creature. Perhaps we have overestimated the King of England for allowing this low fellow to be honoured.'

De Harcourt stood quickly and blocked his friend from reaching the door.

'Louis, we must let him speak. He's not one of us, he never can be. But what he did was an act of great courage. He has suffered his own loss in battle and he's endured wounds that would have many of us still lying in our beds. He's no fool and he has the making of a swordsman. Killing the English is not enough. We need to understand them.'

Louis de Vitry, barely six years older than Blackstone, but, like de Harcourt, a son and heir of one of Normandy's greatest families, allowed his friend's words to calm him. He returned to his seat by the fire, but kept his gaze on the flames.

De Harcourt faced Blackstone. 'Impertinence such as yours is something we have little experience of, Thomas.'

'I apologize, lord. I don't mean to offend. I can only speak plainly.'

'The thing is, Thomas, you never sound as though you mean it when you apologize,' said de Harcourt without anger.

One of the older men refilled his glass, but did not offer Blackstone a drink. 'We fought with a ferocity that should have swept your English King and his army back into the ditch that separates our two countries. Our humiliation is more painful than the wounds we endured,' he said.

The silence indicated that Blackstone should answer. 'Our King warned us of your ferocity, my Lord de Mainemares. He said you were the greatest army in Christendom and that you would crush us if we faltered.'

'The question still remains: why did you not falter against such overwhelming odds?' Guy de Ruymont asked.

Blackstone could find no obvious reason for being questioned but knew that his answers would be important to these touchy and violent men. 'We had a great advantage over you.'

'Yes, you had archers that slaughtered from a distance. There's no honour in that,' said one of the other men.

'If you had broken through our lines, as you did in places, then you would have slaughtered us archers because we carried no means of defence against you. And that's why we killed you as quickly as we could and without mercy, just as your King raised the Oriflamme against us. Would you have stopped killing us had we surrendered? I don't think so. And our knights were better suited for the fight than you,' Blackstone said.

'You bastard!' de Fossat spat and made a move towards Blackstone, who stood quickly to defend himself.

'William!' de Harcourt commanded, making the impetuous knight hold back.

No one spoke for a moment. Blackstone knew he had gone too

far. 'Not that they were braver. But their courage had been tested many times. They were experienced from the Scottish wars and they were committed to their King.'

'And we were not?' said Henri Livay.

'You were not, my lord, not in the same way.'

'Christ's suffering, Jean. Why do we have this murdering butcher here at all?' said another nobleman.

'Because,' de Graville interrupted, 'he was there, facing our might. He could see the battle and how it went. And he's an Englishman who thinks differently than us. Explain yourself.'

'I don't have the wisdom of a King or a Prince, or any of the men-at-arms who fought you. I can tell you what I heard and what I saw, lord. My King chose his ground. You gave your bowmen no protection. You were impatient to kill us.'

'What in God's name does that mean? You taunt us with insults now, Blackstone?' de Fossat yelled.

'I mean that you did not serve your King as we served ours.'

This time it was the elder Lord de Mainemares who snatched at de Fossat's arm to hold back his lunge. 'Control yourself, damn you! Or go and sit with the women and their tittle-tattle. This man and those with him caused us great slaughter. Our nobles are held to ransom, our King licks his wounds behind the walls of Paris. We can learn from this humble archer.'

'Who, as Jean said, has proved his bravery as much as any man here,' Henri Livay acknowledged.

'And is no longer a bowman,' Guy de Ruymont said. 'Tell us what you mean, Master Blackstone.'

Blackstone controlled his breathing, steadying the panic that threatened to take hold of him as he faced the Norman war lords.

'My lords, from what I understand, you fight for your honour, and your honour alone. You fight together as families, as men who are kin to each other and who compete with others to see who can kill us English first. You won't be denied your day of battle – and it was this impatience that killed you.'

The men stared at Blackstone, as if chastised by him.

Blackstone didn't wait for any further question or challenge. He needed to tell these mighty Frenchmen how their own arrogance had caused them to lose. 'We were rallied by my sovereign lord. He spoke to us all. He held us close and we fought for him and for him alone.' They were silent. Not one man turned his eyes from Blackstone. What he said smothered their pride. 'Our King was the greater King,' he said, and waited for another outburst. And it came immediately.

'You will not insult the King of France!' said Louis de Vitry harshly.

The men's voices rose in anger again, each shouting over the other, but Blackstone had faced down men like these thundering towards him riding their great war horses. Their angry words were harmless. Only Jean de Harcourt and Lord de Graville stayed silent, a glance between them that Blackstone noticed. A glance that told they knew the young knight's words were the truth.

Blackstone stood, and for some reason he did not understand, the men fell silent.

'A great King does not lose a great battle,' he said quietly.

He paused and then bowed to Jean de Harcourt, who nodded, giving permission for Blackstone to leave. There was nothing more the young archer could say that night.

As the doors closed behind him the cold night air chilled the sweat-drenched shirt that clung to his body. He finally let the coiled tension seep away and steadied himself against the wall, took a deep, slow breath and for a moment tried to understand what had just happened in that room. He had challenged and probably insulted men of rank who knew his identity, who were probably still his enemies. But no one had struck him, no one demanded of Jean de Harcourt that he be cast out from these walls. Blackstone had stood his ground and given no quarter. Strength surged through him.

A change had taken place within him.

And the taste of it made him smile.

CHAPTER FIFTEEN

Jean de Harcourt stood at the window and looked down to where grooms and pages prepared mounts for the day's hunt. To one side, almost out of sight of the early morning activity, he saw Blackstone going through his training ritual. The Englishman was there every day and he had secretly watched him since his guests had arrived. The sense of loss from not training with Blackstone was something he had not anticipated. A master—pupil camaraderie had been forged between the two men, who were obliged to live within the same castle walls. He had given Thomas Blackstone freedom of speech at the previous night's meeting in the library and the Englishman had stripped bare his guests' emotions. Now he wondered whether those men would rebel against the long-term plans that he and de Graville had considered for Thomas Blackstone. There was still much to discuss with the barons, but they needed to tread carefully, for the betrayal of even their conversations meant certain death at the hands of King Philip. The English King had promised much, but still the war had not ended and the Normans needed to control their own destiny. De Harcourt's plans were little more than a will-o'-the-wisp, a restive spirit that could not be captured – so too his ideas for Blackstone. They were as yet unformed, but carried the hope that they might prove feasible. Having a young, trained man-at-arms in the heart of Normandy who carried the favour of the English King might well, in good time, serve King Edward's interests and the French who sided with him. But not yet. To think of using Blackstone now as an instrument of their ambition was premature.

On these cold winter mornings, de Harcourt would stand at the window wrapped in his cloak against the freezing air and watch his pupil practise time and again. Secretly observing Blackstone gave him mixed feelings of both satisfaction and envy. Blackstone still lacked the capability of fighting effectively toe to toe, but his skills were sufficient for de Harcourt to think that he could pit him against any of the squires who had accompanied their masters over the past weeks. In truth, he could pit him against some of the knights themselves, because Blackstone's ferocity was something only the most skilled swordsman would be able to parry and turn to his advantage. There was still a fundamental flaw in the way Blackstone attacked an opponent, but de Harcourt could not yet see how to change the archer's faults. The twinge of envy came from the knowledge that someone from a humble beginning had the quick intelligence to learn and to speak plainly about the meaning of honour. There was no doubt in de Harcourt's mind that the knight who had been Blackstone's sworn lord, Sir Gilbert Killbere, had played a profound role in the boy's maturity.

De Harcourt had another concern. There were those among his guests who had taken Blackstone's comments as personal insults. If they could not rise above their feelings and see that what the Englishman had said was true, then there might be one among them who would try to exact revenge. The older men had taken Blackstone's words at face value, for, like de Harcourt himself, they knew that the impetuousness and poor decision-making of the French King still underlay his poor leadership. It was the younger men who bridled at the hurtful truth. It would most likely be William de Fossat who would make some kind of challenge against Blackstone. And his violence would be difficult to temper and almost impossible for de Harcourt to stop once his hospitality ended. If emotions ran high enough then a collective anger from the younger men could result in a direct assault against the archer. And if that happened de Harcourt would have no choice but to defend him and that would drive a wedge as sharp as any blade between him and the others.

He was about to turn back into the room when he saw one of the barons making his way towards Blackstone in the training yard.

He couldn't see the man's face but he knew it wasn't de Fossat. Then he realized that it was instead Louis de Vitry, who had been inflamed by Blackstone's comments about the French monarch.

'Blackstone!' de Vitry called.

Blackstone turned and saw the young nobleman, flushed with anger and determination.

'You want me, my lord?' Blackstone said, feeling his own belligerence rise. He was already warmed up from his sword practice and if this Norman wanted a fight Blackstone would not back down. The wooden sword in his hand would be useless against the blade that de Vitry carried and he quickly looked around for another weapon. There was a pitchfork near the feed store but it would take half a dozen strides to reach it by which time de Vitry could have his sword clear of its scabbard and deliver a fatal blow. No sooner had he dismissed the thought than de Vitry unbuckled the scabbard and picked up a training sword.

'You need to be taught some manners. I'm a guest here, but beating a servant means nothing.'

'I serve no one in this house, so that's your first mistake,' Blackstone answered, watching the man's eyes, reading his intentions. 'And your second is that you're not used to fighting a common man.' Blackstone taunted him with a smile. 'You could get hurt.'

It was enough to ignite the man's injured pride and with a yell he lunged. Blackstone sidestepped, positioned his guard, blocked the strikes, found his footing and attacked with a flurry of blows. De Vitry's initial ill-tempered attack was soon brought under disciplined control and Blackstone knew that he was fighting a man who had as much skill as de Harcourt. But Blackstone's demanding training and his tutor's painful lessons now served him well. His opponent made an error in his stance, Blackstone struck him with a mighty blow and he staggered back. Blackstone's focus saw nothing but the man's face and, fearless of impending blows in retaliation, he took control of the encounter and pressed home his advantage. Instinctively he felt he could break the man's defence, but then de Vitry counter-attacked with such skill that

Blackstone was taken by surprise. Stinging blows from the wooden sword struck his thigh, chest and neck. The pain told him that he would have been dead in a real fight. He recovered quickly, held his guard, and pressed de Vitry back again, landing blows on arms and legs that would also have proved fatal in combat. For a moment neither man had the advantage and then, moving on the balls of his feet, Blackstone feinted left, drew in his opponent and struck with such force that de Vitry's wooden sword broke in two. He stumbled back against the wall but Blackstone's violence was such that he saw nothing more than beating the nobleman to his knees.

De Vitry snatched up the pitchfork and lunged. The fight was now deadly. Blackstone parried, but like a pikeman in the front line of battle his opponent had the advantage. Blackstone twisted away from the deadly tines, but his leg failed him and he fell. De Vitry's eyes were wide and a shout of victory left him as he lunged downwards. Blackstone half-turned, kicked, and caught the man's legs. De Vitry lost his footing, the pitchfork slipping free from his muddied hands.

Blackstone's vision blurred. The violent concentration was no different from when he had cut and thrust his way towards his dying brother. He grappled forward, snatching at the man's clothing, going for his throat, ready to strangle him. They closed and Blackstone grabbed de Vitry's belt and head-butted him, barely missing his nose but slamming his forehead between his eyes. The nobleman howled in pain but held onto Blackstone. Their combined weight was too much for his weakened leg and they fell, giving de Vitry the chance he needed. The dagger from his belt was suddenly in his hand and raised back to strike down into Blackstone's exposed throat.

The moment before the blade fell another man suddenly blocked Blackstone's vision. The bear of a man wrapped an arm around de Vitry's chest and held him as if he were little more than a child. De Vitry struggled, almost smothered by the embrace, but kept there until the intruder's words pierced his blind anger.

'Louis! LOUIS! Enough! That's enough! Listen to me! Do you hear? It's enough now!'

De Vitry back-pedalled in the dirt as William de Fossat loosened his grip. The most aggressive of Blackstone's critics stood between the two men, calming the young Norman baron. 'You cannot kill him, Louis. He's done nothing to warrant that. Do you hear me now?' he demanded of de Vitry, who gathered his senses and looked blankly up at the man who stood over him. He spat the phlegm and dirt from his mouth and nodded. 'I hear you, William,' he acknowledged and accepted the extended hand to pull him up.

Blackstone was already on his feet, still alert for another attack. For all he knew de Fossat could take over from where he had stopped his friend and continue the assault.

De Fossat looked at Blackstone. 'You fight like a bear-baiting dog, Master Thomas.'

'I'm a mongrel born and bred, my lord,' Blackstone answered.

Before any more could be said Jean de Harcourt stood at the entrance. 'What is this? Do you assault my guests, Blackstone?' he said, knowing full well what had happened, having seen everything from his vantage point.

'I apologize, lord,' Blackstone answered. 'The count was keen to give me instruction and I caught him by surprise with my common brawling. I was trying to show him how we fight in an alehouse.'

De Harcourt looked at de Vitry. 'Is that how it was, Louis?'

The young count's anger had been quenched by the fight but he still hesitated in answering. 'He does not explain things with the clarity that he did last night, Jean.'

'Are you saying he's lying?'

De Vitry shook his head. 'It was my intention to thrash him for his insulting remarks. It seems you've taught him a great deal in the months he's been here. Had he been armed I believe he could have killed me. The fault of this is mine and mine alone. Blackstone suffocates the truth in order to spare me humiliation.' He bowed his head towards Blackstone in acknowledgement. 'My humiliation is nothing compared to what my country endures,

Master Blackstone, but I don't need the likes of you to spare my feelings.' He turned away, brushing the mud from his tunic, and then turned back. 'Oh, and should we fight again, I'll kill you before you have the opportunity to inflict injury upon me. Now, Jean, excuse me as I must change my clothes if we're to hunt.'

William de Fossat waited until the nobleman was out of ear-shot. His smile broke the darkness of his beard. 'You're a violent bastard, Thomas Blackstone. You get that leg of yours stronger and I'd think twice about challenging you myself.' He snorted the cold morning moisture from his nose and spat. 'Count de Vitry is a good swordsman and you need more practice, lad,' he said and then turned to de Harcourt. 'Jean, we're all running a risk being here with this self-proclaimed mongrel. Pray that Louis doesn't leak word to the King's men. It'd be a pity to hand him over now he's come this far.' He laid a hand on de Harcourt's shoulder. 'Now, my balls are already freezing, can we get on with this damned hunt and kill ourselves a boar?'

Wire-haired hounds and two mastiffs peered out from their wooden cages on the back of a cart that rumbled away down the forest track. Their wet noses sniffed the air but none whined, having not yet scented the boar. These hounds were trained to hunt the wild boar and corner it and they were mature, seasoned trackers that had survived many an encounter with that most dangerous of forest animals. Many a foolish young dog had tried to attack a boar, whose tusks could disembowel a horse. Once the hounds had run down the boar and the beast was cornered the mastiffs would be loosed. Their huge weight could hold down a boar's muscled strength and then their jaws would clamp over its ears and neck. Only then when the creature had been subdued would a spear be thrust into its heart. There were exceptions to killing it from the safety of a spear's length, for if the boar was not too big a bold hunter could go forward on foot and plunge a knife into its throat. But de Harcourt expected to lose dogs this day if they came across the particular boar he sought. He was an old survivor that carried scars from spear and arrow, and in all the years he had been rooting through these forests no one had dared go into the thickets after him. De Harcourt's father had come close to killing him once, but this boar's tusks were long and razor-sharp and projected a dozen inches from its lower jaw. De Harcourt had seen this huge boar rip dog and man when he charged from a thicket. Jean's father had lost three dogs and a servant that day, when the cornered beast made his stand. This boar was a legend and when he was last seen de Harcourt's forest workers had run for their lives. There was no necessity to exaggerate the beast's size and weight. It would take more than one man to kill it and they would have to spear it quickly and pray no horses went down. It was this sense of anticipation, of facing down a worthy opponent, that sent the men impatiently ahead of the women and their escorts.

The women rode astride their horses, accompanied by the knights' pages as the squires rode ahead with their spear-carrying masters. Although the morning fog clung stubbornly to the treetops it would melt away within the next hour or so, and once they were deep inside the forest those shafts of sunlight would allow them to follow the dogs and their handlers. De Harcourt's villeins had been watching for signs for months and reported that the furrows ploughed by the great boar's snout were concentrated in one area. Everyone's spirits were high. The women laughed and chattered.

'It will be the perfect Christmas,' Blanche de Harcourt shouted as the horses broke into a canter. 'What better feast than a wild boar on a spit and its head on the table!'

After his conflict with de Vitry, Jean de Harcourt had chastised his pupil. 'You let him break your guard. You were thinking too much. Killing with a sword has to be as instinctive as using your war bow. Your eye and brain told you when to release a shaft. Neither is separate from the other. Each is attuned – heart, mind and eye. Instinctive – every damned part of you. I'll not have you fail me, boy. I'll take the sword to you myself and thrash you with it.'

Blackstone had stood silently and taken his admonition. Jean de Harcourt seemed to be thinking something through, almost as if he struggled with himself to make a decision. His gaze followed the muddied figure of Louis de Vitry as he went back into the castle to change his clothes.

'All right, let's see if we can get your brain to work as well as that right arm of yours. Come with me.'

Jean de Harcourt strode into his library, his dogs trotting at his heels. Their master clicked his fingers and pointed and they quickly settled themselves in front of the fire, their eyes still following his movements. The library had been his father's, but his own upbringing of study and learning meant that he had spent many hours under the strict tutelage of a monk whose broken, dirt-engrained nails and stinking cassock were forever imprinted in his memory, as much as the lessons learnt and the beatings permitted by his father. His father had insisted on an education beyond that given a squire before he took on the years of service to become a knight.

His was a great family whose ancestors reached back to Bernard the Dane, who was granted the territory that became Normandy. One of his forefathers, the Sire de Harcourt, commanded the archers who fought with William the Conqueror, the bastard Duke of Normandy, when he claimed the English throne. Another, Robert II, rode with Richard the Lionheart in crusade and served as a loyal and valued retainer. That both his father and his uncle, Sir Godfrey, had split the family over their diverse loyalties was a wound that would need longer healing than the young Englishman's injuries. And more painful. His father was old-fashioned, proud and arrogant, dismissive of a weak French King but who would never waiver in his allegiance to the crown. He was Captain of Rouen, the greatest city in Normandy. The son had begged the father to support Sir Godfrey. The English King had a legitimate right to the French throne. But his father's deep-seated pride caught him by surprise. Jean de Harcourt was thirty years old, strong and lean, with strength to fight for hours on end, but the old man's blow came so fast it put Jean on his knees. A Norman's honour was his own, not for sale at a whorehouse, his father had spat at him. Jean would have gone with Sir Godfrey, but his duty lay with his father. And so it was that the family faced each other across that killing field. The battle's savagery was beyond description and when his father went down, Jean helplessly watched him die, sword slaked in blood, visor up, blood spilling between his teeth as the arrows struck him. He went down with his charger, the churned ground holding him like a pagan spirit, refusing to release his dying body until the armoured horses in the following rank swept him up beneath their hooves, rolling and pounding his body into a battered mass of bone and blood.

Jean's hand found the document he sought. He turned to face the soaking wet Blackstone, who stood well back from the warmth of the fire, waiting for permission to move closer. There was arrogance and defiance in that act alone, de Harcourt realized. Blackstone would not give anyone the satisfaction of seeing his need. Well, that suited de Harcourt. He felt no compulsion to allow him such comfort. There were moments when his memory made him want to punish the English archer, not help him, and having Blackstone under his roof was causing a rift between him and his friends, nobles he needed to have on his side. It took a few moments for de Harcourt to subdue his nagging anger, but he reminded himself that fighting a war was a gamble. Good fortune had deserted them at Crécy and one young Englishman, placed in his care, could not be the whipping boy for a nation's humiliation. Besides, he grudgingly admitted to himself, Blackstone's character and courage demanded respect.

He tossed the scroll to Blackstone. 'You don't need to be able to read to understand that,' he said and then joined the dogs at the fireside as Blackstone unfurled the scroll.

'My ancestors brought that back when they fought the Saracens. They understood the human body in a way we do not. Our physicians are ignorant peasants compared to them. You can read a builder's plan, so you should be able to comprehend that,' he said and waited while what he hoped might be the missing keystone to Blackstone's fighting skills was given to him. What he held was a faded drawing of a naked man, arms outstretched to touch the circle around him. Another line bisected the torso across his waist, and two matching lines in the form of a cross cut the man's body from each shoulder down through his hip. Within each segment vital organs were shown – heart, lungs, liver, stomach – it was a drawing of God's perfect cathedral.

'You understand it?' de Harcourt asked.

'It's geometry,' he answered.

'It's heresy. The Holy Church bans dissection, but that was done by a Muslim physician before my father was born. Now when you fight a man you think of that and strike accordingly. Keep it to yourself.' He turned his face away; he had now given the young archer everything he needed to kill effectively.

'Is that leg ready yet to straddle a horse?' de Harcourt asked.

'I believe so, lord,' said Blackstone hopefully.

'Then it needs to be tested. It's time you got out from behind these walls. I'll have a groom pick out a horse that won't throw you.'

Blackstone could barely believe his luck. At last he was being allowed freedom from the castle; not only that but it was to be with the hunt.

'All right, Thomas, go and clean off that filth and change. Take the drawing to your room to study later.'

'Thank you,' Blackstone said, unable to find any other words to express his gratitude for the Saracen's drawing and the chance to ride out. 'But I've never used a spear against wild boar – or anything, come to that.'

'You won't have to. Personal protection is all you'll need. Bring that sword of yours. You ride with the women and the pageboys.'

Blackstone's heart sank. 'The women? Can't I hunt with the men?'

'Don't test my generosity, Thomas. The women need protecting at the rear. You and the pageboys should be able to manage that, don't you think?'

* * *

And so Blackstone had sluiced the stench of sweat from his body and changed his clothes, but rode behind the ladies as they followed their knights. De Harcourt had found a scabbard for Wolf Sword that now hung from the horse's pommel. It was the first time he had taken the sword from his quarters and he felt a strange mixture of pride and self-consciousness. Before he slid the pointed blade into its covering he felt a twinge of uncertainty. Sir Gilbert had taught him to keep his sword ready, but this was not combat and to parade the fine weapon was unnecessary. For a few spellbound moments he held its perfect balance, the weight positioned below the crossguard allowing the blade the freedom to do its work. It seemed a shame to hide its beauty, but he slid it into the scabbard.

Food and drink was carried by the pages and the oldest of them, including the ten-year-old Guillaume, were given the task of laying out the blankets and coverings for the midday refreshment of which the hunters would partake. The day would be short and the light gone within a few hours, but wood was gathered and fires lit for the winter picnic beneath a sapphire-clear sky. A cry went up as a roe deer was flushed from a coppice into an open meadow and the women spurred their horses to surge after their men. The startled creature darted left and right, zigzagging away from the yelling men. The dogs howled but were restrained by their handlers. A deer was an easy kill. The women shouted their encouragement.

'Louis! It's yours!' Henri Livay called to de Vitry as the deer gracefully evaded his efforts to spear it.

Once again the terrified animal veered left and right, skittishly unsettling the horses' strides. Blackstone kept pace with the women whose gowns and headdresses fluttered behind them. Like angel wings, Blackstone thought as he guided the horse closer to Christiana's. The look on her face, though, was anything but angelic. Eyes wide, gasping for breath with the excitement of the impending kill, she and Blanche de Harcourt rode side by side, laughing with lust for the deer's death. Her passion for the hunt caught him unawares and in that moment his own longing for her deepened. A wild thought ran through his head: if he could separate Christiana from the others he'd take her to a glade and lay down a blanket where he would undress her slowly and smother her shivering body with his own. Could there be a better time to slake their lust? he wondered.

Those thoughts took his attention off the hunt for a few scant seconds, long enough for his horse to veer sharply from a tufted clump of grass for no apparent reason. As the shouts of victory and the baying cry of the speared and dying animal travelled across the field, Blackstone's foot came free of the stirrup, his balance shifted and his wild grab at the horse's mane could not save him from tumbling into space. It seemed a long time before he hit the ground that rushed up to greet him, but when he did it felt like a mighty hammer blow that knocked the wind out of him.

He could hear the hoof beats pounding away, their vibration trembling through the ground into his spine. Richard Blackstone had been able to feel the sound of trumpet and drum, perhaps this was what it was like when his brother died in his silent world, Blackstone thought, as he lay unmoving in silence, his ears flooded with the pulsing of his own blood. He groaned and eased himself up.

The dogs could barely be restrained by their handlers as the deer's throat was cut by one of the runners, its blood spurting from its dying heartbeat. De Vitry's spear was yanked from the carcass and the servants set about gutting the animal before its eyes had even glazed in death. They would be given the heart and liver as a special Christmas treat and the lungs would go to the dogs when the hunt returned home. By the time Blackstone noted all of this his horse had been caught by one of the men, and the group's attention turned back to where he staggered to his feet. The laughter that greeted his hobbling stance felt like a barrage of arrow shafts flying across the meadow.

He saw one of the squires holding his horse and then de Harcourt's gestures indicated that Christiana was to take the horse back to Blackstone. Clearly the men thought Blackstone deserved the additional humiliation of having his mount returned by a woman. He smiled foolishly as she got closer, and then laughed as she pulled the horse up sharply. She was scowling so much that plumes of breath funnelled from her nostrils.

'You think this is funny?' she said angrily.

'You look so ferocious, Christiana, like a snorting devil,' he said. 'What's wrong? Didn't you join everyone else to laugh at my misfortune?'

She threw down his reins. 'Can my embarrassment get any worse? You were thrashed this morning by Count de Vitry and now you fall from a docile palfrey? These people *are* laughing at you, Thomas. You're not an English peasant any longer; you're in the company of men of rank. Riding a horse is the least skill demanded of you.'

Blackstone took the reins and steadied the horse and spoke to her as if he were already her lord and husband. 'Don't act like a child. I had the better of de Vitry. Those barons are masters of hypocrisy, Christiana. They play a game of divided loyalties and one day either my King or yours will make them pay. They're a squirming nest of adders and I wouldn't trust any of them. Are they your kind of people?'

'I'm my father's only child and he served his lord faithfully and sent me here for safekeeping!'

'That doesn't make you one of them! Are you embarrassed or ashamed? There's a difference.'

His challenge confused her, which made her angrier still. She wheeled her horse and rode back to where the hunting party waited for her. Blackstone pulled himself into the saddle, wishing more than anything that he was back with his own kind. How far was it to Calais? he wondered.

The day grew shorter, with only a few hours remaining before the sun dipped below the treetops. The clear sky would have made a glorious day for falconry, but none had been taken out, the sole purpose of today's hunt being to provide meat from the forest, especially boar, for the Christmas table. Blackstone had meandered with the women, some of whom were beginning to complain about the cold as the shafts of light narrowed, taking what little warmth remained with them. Now that they moved through the forest Blackstone's senses sharpened and he stayed vigilant. He quietly guided the horse through saplings and mature trees, remembering another forest across the river at Blanchetaque when he pulled Christiana to freedom away from the Bohemian soldiers. It was easy to hide in woodland; if a man stayed still it was almost impossible for him to be seen. Even slow movement was masked by the trees and now he feared outlaws who might run from a thicket and pull him from his horse. Then those he protected would be vulnerable and he would have failed in his duty. Turning the horse in and out between the trees he kept the splashes of colour from the women's garments and the shadows of the pages who diligently followed them in sight. The women's chatter still carried so that when his eyes looked through the forest, tree to tree, yard by yard, penetrating the woodland, his ears placed their whereabouts.

The men's distant voices were muffled by the trees as they called to each other. They had obviously split up and their shouts told others where each man was, or thought they were. Henri Livay was lost, and as he called Blackstone heard a distant shout that sounded like Guy de Ruymont telling him where to ride. Then silence fell again, leaving only the crunch of horse's hooves on the forest floor and the calls of birds going to roost.

They passed through clearings, treeless islands where foresters had once camped. Luxuriant ferns blanketed the ground where deer had not grazed. Bramble thickets crept into these places, as did the failing sun, but Blackstone saw no sign of habitation, no cold embers of fires long past, and if men still used this part of the forest they would have camped here for the warmth the sunlight offered and a soft bed of ferns. As he turned the horse into the clearing a scream shattered the quiet as dogs yelped and barked, then fell silent. The women quickly reined in their startled horses, their own cries of alarm stifled as the man's scream intensified. Men's distant voices cried out, desperately seeking the location of the terrifying sounds.

'Into the clearing! Now!' Blackstone yelled, driving the horse forward, forcing the women into the open space. Blanche de Harcourt's spirited courser veered away violently from the mêlée as the women whipped and reined their horses into the middle of the open ground. Blackstone's injured leg crushed against its flank, but he ignored the pain and grabbed her bridle, his strength forcing the horse to behave.

'Encircle! Arm yourselves!' he shouted to the pages who, despite their youth, showed no sign of panic as they obeyed his command. The screaming became louder and then suddenly stopped. In that chilling moment of silence, barely a heartbeat passed before the disparate voices, closer than before, called again, and were muffled as a horse's anguished whinnying screeched from the depth of the forest. Blackstone had heard those death throes on the battlefield when the English lanced and disembowelled the French war horses.

'Help me! Here!' a man's voice begged. And again: 'Here!'

'That's Jean!' Blanche de Harcourt cried, pulling the reins towards the cry.

'Stay here!' Blackstone shouted at her without any regard for her rank, cuffing her horse's head, forcing it back into the throng of riders as he spurred his horse forward. It was pure instinct that forced him on through the trees, bending low across the horse's withers as branches whipped at him. The old palfrey served him well, fearlessly pushing through the forest as Blackstone yanked him this way and that to avoid the trees.

Sunlight splintered the woodland where it had been coppiced and the unmistakable metallic taste of spilt blood caught at the back of his throat. His horse fought the reins as he broke through the saplings into an oasis of light, not unlike the clearing he had just left. What lay before him was a gladiatorial arena of gore-splattered ferns. A man's torso lay ripped apart, his gaunt death mask hinged on a broken neck, arms akimbo as his fists curled into the fern stems. Much of the area was trampled. The dead man was one of de Harcourt's dog handlers and two of the hounds lay dead with him. Less than fifty paces away a dense bramble thicket as high as a horse blanketed the far side of the clearing. Here and there new tree growth had pushed its way through the ferns and Jean de Harcourt lay pinned beneath a horse so badly injured it could barely raise its head.

Standing off the corpses and the entrapped man was a wild boar slaked in blood from a spear wound to its neck, its flanks heaving from exertion. When they were growing up Blackstone and his brother had run through Lord Marldon's forests, snaring rabbits and squirrels for the pot, and watched the hunt from their hiding places, but the nobles had never killed a boar bigger than a growing boy or one that stood higher than a man's knee. This creature was more frightening than any sword-wielding man. The cornered beast had defended itself and its malevolent eyes showed nothing more than an animal in fear of its life as they fastened onto the intruder. Blackstone fought the frightened horse, which pushed him against a tree, the lower branches scratching at his face. Easing himself onto the ground he let the horse run from its terror, his own mouth dry from fear, the only comfort was his hand squeezing the sword's grip so tightly that his knuckles ached. What use was a damned sword, he thought, killing it would be easy if I could draw a bow. I'd nock a broadhead arrow and the beast would be shot through. No one need get hurt. But there was no bow, no archer's arm to hold it. The day could end badly and it could end in the next couple of minutes.

The boar must have been more than twice Blackstone's weight, at least four hundred pounds, and stood higher than a cloth-yard arrow, taller than a man's hip. Judging from the sprawled remains of the dead man the boar was longer than six feet. Its tusks and snout were smothered in flesh and blood from its victims, but other than the slight movement of its head as it watched Blackstone edge closer to de Harcourt, it remained motionless. Blackstone prayed that by moving slowly he would allow the boar to escape and either turn back into the bramble thicket to hide or run through the saplings that lay behind his right shoulder.

De Harcourt lay still, face turned to watch the Englishman's wary approach.

'Is your leg broken?' Blackstone asked, in what seemed barely a whisper.

'No. Trapped. I wounded him. He went to ground in the thicket. I swear it ambushed us,' he said quietly.

All Blackstone wanted to do was to get out of the boar's way and give it a clear run past him. He had no interest in killing it and he sensed that if he moved slowly it would give them all a chance of life, but as he shuffled carefully through the ferns that snagged at his ankles, he looped the leather thong around his wrist from the sword's crossguard. If the boar charged it would take all his strength to keep hold of the sword and the blood knot would give him a second chance should it be yanked from his grip.

'Christ Jesus, Thomas... use the spear,' de Harcourt hissed. 'You'll never stop it if it charges.'

Blackstone saw the spear shaft lying a dozen feet away, half tangled in the ferns. He shook his head. 'Too far. It'll be on me as soon as I give it a chance.' Each thud of his heart pounded through his brain like the hammer on a bell. It rang out the moments before death was surely upon him. He eased further away, barely daring to look at the wounded boar. Had the spear thrust weakened it or enraged it? For an animal that grubbed roots and worms it seemed more dangerous than a carnivorous wolf.

Four more heartbeats and Blackstone thought he had moved far enough away but then the crashing sound of a horse pushing through the undergrowth changed everything. A horseman forced his way through the forest's edge and the startled boar charged straight at Blackstone, who still stood in the way of its escape. It came at him head down, tusks ready to slash. Blackstone's heart banged against his ribs so hard he could barely breathe. Thoughts flashed through his mind, telling him his leg might not allow a quick pivot to one side, and if he fell there would be no defence. There was no time even to consider what action to take. All the lessons he had endured disappeared from his mind as he instinctively raised the sword with a double-handed grip, his crooked left arm bent at the elbow, the blade held high across his shoulder.

He could smell the wild pig's laboured breath, which billowed into the chill air. Like a premonition he knew, right at that moment, that a strike from this high guard could not save him. *Choose your ground!* There was a mound pushing up the ferns, several paces ahead, and he realized it was a fallen tree, rotten, barely knee high and long consumed by the foliage. Perhaps it had even been responsible for Harcourt's horse going down. Blackstone leapt forward, straight at the charging boar. If it didn't veer away from the attack it would have to jump across the tree. He dropped to one knee, buried his fist and the sword's pommel into the ground and took the boar full on as its forelegs rose up. The speed and weight of the charge threw him backwards, and the mighty boar trampled over him. A sudden, blurred image of the vicious yellow tusks passed close to his face, as he felt his chest and arm muscles wrenched from the impact as the blood knot tightened on his wrist. Pulling himself in like a hedgehog he gathered the blade to him, hugging it as a drowning man in a violent sea cradles a lifesaving piece of wood.

The stench of foul liquid spurted over him. He rolled clear and got to one knee, telling himself he was still alive and that if the tusks had cut him he didn't yet feel the pain. The boar went on for another three yards, then crumpled, snout first into the deep ferns, its back legs kicking for purchase, a pitiful, grunting scream coming from its gaping jaws. Blackstone's sword had taken it in the chest, its momentum burying the honed steel deeper into its innards.

Blackstone stepped forward, swung down the blade in a high, sweeping arc and severed the head.

He stood over the slain beast for a moment, and then dropped a hand to his tunic and breeches. The gore and liquid were not his. His hands began to shake as he sank to his knees and wiped the blade against the foliage, staying hunched down to let the moment pass.

It had been William de Fossat who had crashed through the trees and watched helplessly as the young Englishman took the boar's charge. He had dismounted the moment Blackstone killed the boar and dispatched his friend's horse with a knife thrust, and then eased de Harcourt from under the dead animal. Others soon arrived. Louis de Vitry dismounted and saw that there was nothing more to be done, the carnage told its own story and there was no need for explanation. Blanche de Harcourt forced her unwilling horse, skittish from the smell of death, into the clearing. Thanks to God were uttered as husband and wife embraced. Blackstone got to his feet and, without thinking, raised the talisman to his lips and kissed the Celtic goddess in thanks for her protection. Perhaps, he thought, God allowed angels and goddesses to share His kingdom so they might shadow the likes of him who constantly sinned through lack of prayer and who harboured doubt about His existence. The smeared blade cleaned easily, and as he undid the blood knot and turned his wrist the mark of the running wolf below the crossguard seemed to move, as if leaping after its prey. He ran his fingers through his matted hair, which stuck to the blood on his face, and then wiped his hand.

As servants and squires gathered, and the dog handlers lifted their dead animals into their arms, Henri Livay commanded them to lay the dead man on the cart to be taken back for burial.

Blanche turned to Blackstone. 'There's an old French proverb, Thomas: "Gratitude is the heart's memory." You have my thanks.'

Jean de Harcourt eased his wife aside, and limped towards Blackstone as the others watched.

'Are you hurt, Thomas?'

'No, my lord, but I stink,' he answered, wondering why he was saying something so self-consciously stupid.

De Harcourt smiled and reached for Blackstone's shoulders, pulling his face down so he could kiss each bloodied cheek.

Blackstone could barely believe he had been honoured by a mark of friendship and affection that was never given lightly. 'You have to be alive to smell your own stench, my friend. You need a hot bath scented with dried rose petals and lavender.'

'I've never had a bath in my life, my lord,' said Blackstone.

'Then now is the time,' de Harcourt told him.

CHAPTER SIXTEEN

By the time the hunting party returned to the castle, neither the dead dogs nor their savaged handler were of any concern to the noblemen. The peasant could be replaced more easily than the dogs; more importantly, the trophy boar's head would grace the Christmas table and its carcass would be spit-roasted. Servants rejoiced in their lord's safe return, and the steward commended his master's hunting abilities. As the women retired to attend to their dressing, de Harcourt, ignoring his aching leg, bounded triumphantly up the steps as if he were an all-conquering Caesar. He turned to where Blackstone stood near the stables.

'Thomas! We'll freshen up and then we'll dine after prayers. You'll join us? Of course you will! By God, we'll have a party!'

He did not wait for a reply, and none escaped Blackstone's lips. The bustle of activity as grooms and stable-hands attended to the horses was where he wanted to be. Christiana had mocked him and then, after the kill, had tried to approach him, but he had turned away from her, a deep, unsettling dissatisfaction resting heavily in his chest. The smell of the stables and the sweat of the horses made him want to take hold of a bridle and vigorously rub a horse down with straw. The heavy scent of the beasts and the stale, metallic taste of blood mingled in his mouth. Like a fading dream, he was being disconnected from the life of a village stonemason. A slow, living death, where there was nothing to hold onto. Even de Harcourt's servants, who worked feverishly to satisfy their lord's demands, saw him as being different. They too had their own hierarchy. Older boys kicked and beat the younger ones, as the grooms' coarse language berated the stable-hands. Obey and live in fear.

He plunged Wolf Sword's grip into the horse trough and scrubbed away the dried blood. I'm lying in the land between two armies, he thought, watching the pageboys diligently cleaning their masters' weapons, the strenuous efforts of the stable-hands to get the horses cleaned, fed, and then bedded down with fresh straw forked into their stalls. He rubbed harder. Finger and thumb flecking away the dark stains. You're alone, Thomas Blackstone, and you'd better learn to accept it, nagged the voice in his head. You're neither noble nor peasant, you're a creation born out of blood and fear. And anger, don't forget anger, he told himself. He shook his head, answering his own doubt: I'll always be a stonemason and an archer. I don't care to join anyone's hunting pack. I'll do what my father and Sir Gilbert would expect of me.

Guillaume Bourdin carried Henri Livay's saddle and boots to be cleaned. He bowed his head. 'My lord Blackstone, shall I clean your sword?'

Blackstone looked at the boy's eager expression. 'Master Bourdin, what is it that makes you so eager to attend me? You've your own master's work to settle.'

'It would be an honour, Sir Thomas,' the boy said.

'Is Lord Livay all you know of family? Are you an orphan?'

'Yes, lord.'

'Have you ever known a mother's comfort?'

'Only until I was six, Sir Thomas, then she died and my uncle placed me with the good knight and gentleman whom I served when you found us at the castle at Noyelles.'

'You were at the river crossing at Blanchetaque?' Blackstone already knew the answer. How else could the terrified boy's knight be so badly wounded? But it was worth asking, to see if the boy had false bravado. Like so many others.

The boy nodded, the memory casting a shadow of fear across his eyes.

'And you were frightened?' Blackstone asked him.

He nodded again. 'I am ashamed of my fear, Sir Thomas.'

Blackstone studied the youngster for a moment longer. 'Don't be. You can use it. Turn it to your advantage. It's only a beast that hides in the bushes. You flush it out and it either dies or runs away. Never be ashamed of fear, Master Bourdin.' He offered the boy a comforting smile, which tugged at his raw, scarred face. 'I need no help today with my sword – perhaps another time.'

Guillaume bowed his head and accepted his dismissal. When he was that age, Blackstone remembered, his father was teaching him to draw his war bow, though no thoughts of war or killing entered his head back then. They were long, hard days at the quarry, with regular beatings from the master stonemason, but afterwards in those wide meadows, where oak and ash spread cool shadows from the summer's heat, there was laughter and high jinks with a brother who knew where the wild bees made their honey, and larks' eggs nestled under tufts of grass – a yearned-for life more distant now than his home village.

Blackstone walked back towards the castle and as he strode past those who laboured in the stables, they stopped what they were doing, and bowed at his presence.

That life was long gone.

Blackstone returned to his room, where the wooden tub lined with linen steamed from hot water and the unmistakable scent of rosemary and lavender. A dozen candles or more burned and fresh underclothes and a doublet were laid out on his bed, woollen socks and clean boots arranged next to them. Blackstone looked at the servant who stood, head bowed, with linen towels draped over the crook of his arm.

'Marcel, what is this?'

'It is your bath, Sir Thomas.'

'I can see that, but what are you doing here?'

'I am your attendant, Sir Thomas,' the servant replied.

'To do what?' said Blackstone, placing the sword on the window-sill, and opening the window to let cold air into the scent-laden room.

'To help you undress and bathe, lord.'

Blackstone stripped off his bloodied tunic and swirled his hand into the hot water, touching his fingertips to his lips. 'It tastes like medicine.'

'The heat and the herbs cleanse the body,' Marcel said.

'You've tried it, then?'

Marcel's shocked expression at being asked such a provocative question left no doubt that he had never immersed his body in such luxury.

Blackstone nodded. 'All right, Marcel, you can go now. I can undress myself and I daresay I can get into there without drowning.'

'With all due respect, if I do not attend to you, as my Lord de Harcourt has instructed, then I will be flogged.'

The momentary stalemate gave Blackstone no alternative. 'Stand... there,' he said, flicking a finger somewhere further back. 'I'll undress and get into the water.'

Marcel bowed his head and stepped back to the rear of the wooden tub as Blackstone dropped his clothes and eased himself slowly into the hot water. It was a sensation never before experienced, and as the water reached the top of his chest the water's embrace seeped away the stiffness from his aching muscles, and the scented steam cleared his nostrils from the stench of the kill. With a long-drawn-out sigh, he lowered his head backwards and could not erase the image of a fat sow wallowing with pleasure in mud.

He dunked his head and scratched through his long, matted hair. Marcel stood next to him and handed him a block of soap. The brief moment of uncertainty as Blackstone brought it to his nose allowed Marcel to make small gestures to his head and his crotch.

'I may be a common man, Marcel, but I know what it is and what it's for. I've washed my hair and balls before now.'

Marcel retreated again as Blackstone rubbed the block of soap through his tangled hair, then plunged his head one more beneath the water. As he bent forward, Marcel washed his back and apologized before Blackstone could reprimand him.

'I have my orders, Sir Thomas. I beg you – please allow me to do my duty. My Lord de Harcourt's hand can be heavy. When you are ready I shall dry you.'

'Marcel, if I give you my word that I will not tell our Lord de Harcourt, will you at least allow me to dry myself? I'm not a damned child.'

'As you wish, Sir Thomas. Thank you for your kindness. Now, can I finish scrubbing your back?'

Blackstone relented and bent forward, admitting to himself that the experience of bathing was not unpleasant, but he could see the disadvantage of doing it too often. Christmas was probably a good enough occasion, but any more frequently than that would sap a man's strength.

The vigorous rubbing motion scoured neck and shoulders and down onto the packed muscle that came from those years in the quarry and the pulling of a war bow. His mind drifted, thinking of what his life might be in the future. His choices were limited. If he became proficient with the sword he could approach one of the lords back home in England. Perhaps become a reeve, or a bailiff. He could read and write and could defend a lord's manorial interests. But to be the instrument of exacting another tax or levy on those who had so little would cause him to hesitate in that duty. It was obvious: there could only be a soldier's life for him once he left this place.

Marcel's ministrations softened, pressing the warmth of the cloth into his neck and shoulders, and then dragged fingers through his hair.

'Marcel, if you continue in that manner, I'll fall asleep and drown in here. Then what would your master say?'

'I don't know,' Christiana answered, as she moved around so he could see her. 'What would he say, my lord?'

Blackstone jolted so that the water splashed. Marcel was gone. Blackstone barely managed a pathetic utterance: 'Christiana.'

She closed the window, her nipples already pressing against her undershift, the only clothing she wore. She blew out some of the candles so that a deepening shadow settled from their warm yellow glow. 'Is my lord likely to drown?' she said.

He shook his head.

Blackstone could not take his eyes from the swell of her breasts. Since that day he took her across the river he'd imagined her being naked.

'Is my lord's silence still one of anger with a foolish woman?' she said gently and slipped her undershift free. Blackstone's racing heartbeat made him gasp for breath as she lowered herself into the water. He felt her legs touch him as her hands reached for his face and raised his lips to her own.

The fullness of her breasts touched his face as she leaned forward and he hungrily squeezed them, sucking a nipple like a starving man. She gasped and drew back from him. The urge that flooded through her own body was as startling as his yearning for her. He wrapped his arms around her – not too tightly, for fear of breaking the spell. Her breasts crushed against him and he felt her heart beating as rapidly as his own. His mind urged him to measure the moment, to savour it as long as possible. He cupped her breasts and teased the puckered nipples with his tongue, and then eased her legs apart so he could reach for her. Tantalizing moments passed before he stroked her sex, and then, as she gasped he enfolded her in his arms and eased them both from the water.

He covered her in a linen sheet and dried the moisture from her body as she leaned into him, her hand moving behind to touch his hardness. The logs in the fireplace sparked, and she jumped, her nervousness so acute that she spun into him. Their tension made them laugh, then Blackstone pushed her back gently onto the bed.

He caressed her with his tongue and tried to keep the scar's ugly welt from her, but she turned his head and kissed it.

'Every scar is earned, I'll not have you hide any part of you from me. Ever.'

He hesitated at her tenderness. Guilt stroked his conscience. The first man he had killed wore a surcoat bearing the same design as the embroidered cloth she had once given him. What connection was there between them? She mistook his hesitation as being that of a young lover. She drew him to her, letting her own desire guide her hands onto him. It was not fear that made her struggle against him, it was her impatience. All doubts were washed away from Blackstone's thoughts. The past did not matter. His strength held her as he teased her, and kept her legs apart until she whimpered and writhed beneath him. As he finally went into her, he released her arms. She clung to him, and gave a small cry; pain and pleasure mingling for the first time. Blackstone moved slowly, watching her eyes, their pupils flaring and her lips trembling as she pushed her hips against him, twisting her head against the bolster. She seemed to suffocate, as if it was impossible to catch her breath, and as she arched her back, their sweat mingled and ran between her breasts. She reached out for him, clinging to his neck, holding onto the surging pleasure that peaked time and again, until finally she gave a shuddering cry.

The wind rattled the shutters as a beckoning dawn struggled against the low-lying clouds. Blackstone had always risen before dawn so he could feel the chill of the night giving way to the easing warmth of the lightening sky. It had become his habit to spend the first hour going through the ritual of practising his sword stroke, by which time de Harcourt's house buzzed with activity. This morning would be no different. Blackstone rekindled the fire and slipped away quietly, easing the door closed behind him. Marcel lay hunched in the opposite door embrasure, where he always slept. Blackstone nudged him with the toe of his boot and the startled servant was quickly awake.

'You were paid?' asked Blackstone.

Marcel nodded.

'By Lady Christiana?'

'Yes, lord.'

'And now you will report to your master, I suppose.'

'Sir Thomas, I took your lady's coin, and gave my word that I would not tell Lord de Harcourt,' Marcel answered.

Marcel had still not raised his eyes to meet Blackstone's. 'Look at me,' Blackstone told him.

The old man obeyed.

'Now tell me again that you will not tell his lordship.'

'I will not,' Marcel said.

Blackstone nodded, satisfied. 'Go about your duties, there's no need for you to see Lady Christiana when she leaves my room.'

Marcel's shoulders hunched in servile obedience, as he shuffled away down the passageway – on his way to report the news that the young Englishman had taken Christiana to his bed. His promise to Blackstone was as sound as the granite walls – Lord Jean de Harcourt would have thrashed the flesh from his bones for relaying such information. However, he served Countess Blanche and it was she who had instructed him to watch Blackstone and report when he and the girl fornicated.

Blackstone sluiced the sweat away in a horse trough after breaking the sliver of ice on its surface. The colder weather would soon make itself felt, he thought, and winter behind these walls seemed unavoidable unless an opportunity to escape presented itself. But the thought of escape had now become a much more complicated matter.

His desire to stay at Christiana's side was now more compelling, but habit and necessity had forced him from the warmth of her embrace. She had barely moved as he slipped away from her. Some excuse would have to be found for not attending the previous night's dinner, and if he had broken his habit of practising each morning, perhaps Jean de Harcourt would suspect that something more enticing than sleep had held Blackstone in his bed. Christiana was de Harcourt's ward, and taking the girl's virginity while under her guardian's protection, no matter that she was willing, might prove a more dangerous prospect than facing a man-killing boar. He knew he had to continue his routine as before, and become bolder still in his requests to be allowed time away from the castle. Alone.

'Thomas!'

Blackstone turned and saw de Harcourt, wrapped in his cloak, beckoning him from an upper window. He was being summoned. Had he been discovered already? Marcel! The bastard. How could Blackstone deny what had happened? He pulled his tunic over his shirt, the goose bumps from the cold settling on his wet skin. Or was that fear? he wondered. Of what? Not violence. He could deal with that. Banishment. And losing Christiana. That was the chill that prickled his skin.

De Harcourt turned back into the room from the window. 'More wood, for Christ's sake! Get a blaze going, you useless pig!' he shouted at a servant. Blanche sat at a small table eating cold cuts, a thick winter gown, rich with fur trimming, tugged up around her neck.

'Jean. It's nearly Christmas,' she admonished him.

De Harcourt poured a glass of wine, his eyes bleary from the previous night's excess. 'And a fine time will be had by all. What?' he asked as she stared him down.

'Blasphemy, particularly now, is unforgivable.'

'What's unforgivable is that my damned English hero did not attend dinner. But there he is, before daybreak, with only torchlight to see his way, slashing away the darkness. God's blood, Blanche, the man has no joy in him.' He swallowed the wine and poured another. His pause was deliberate. 'And where was she?' he said, eyeing his wife's expression over the rim of his glass.

The servant threw bundled kindling and dry wood onto the grate and the fire flared. 'Get out,' de Harcourt told him, as Blanche moved closer to the warmth.

'I hate winter,' she said. 'We should go south. De Foix still holds Provence. You know him. We could invite ourselves. It would make a nice change. I tire of the fog and the damp. Don't you?'

'This is where we're safe, Blanche. This is where the barons control. So, where was she?'

Blanche de Harcourt sighed. 'I made her stay in her room. She behaved like a child. She insulted Thomas.'

Jean de Harcourt stared at his wife, who never blinked as she lied.

'My lord?' Blackstone said as he entered the room and went down on one knee. De Harcourt turned.

'Get up. Get up. There's a time and a place for that, Thomas, and now is neither.'

Blackstone got to his feet, glanced at the countess, who turned away to face the fire.

'Well? What do you have to say for yourself?' de Harcourt demanded.

Blackstone's mind raced. Should he try and lie his way out of the truth? He could accept the blame and say he forced himself on her.

'I don't know what to say, lord,' Blackstone answered, trying to buy time.

'You don't usually have a problem controlling your tongue,' de Harcourt said, waiting a moment longer. 'You did not grace us with your presence last night. Am I to be continually insulted? Am I expected to go on forgiving your misdemeanours?' he said, exasperated.

Perhaps, Blackstone thought, they did not know the truth, so the lie could be altered. 'I fell asleep, lord.'

'What?' de Harcourt asked, as if he had not understood the answer.

'The bathing. It lulled me into a state I had never experienced before. Its warmth took me. I daresay it was the day's events that tired me more than I knew.'

De Harcourt was close to him, then moved behind him, sniffing the air. 'You still smell of lavender, Thomas. And something else,' he said.

Blackstone did not move.

'It's the rose petals, my lord,' Blanche said. 'Their oils seep into the water.'

For a moment Blackstone thought de Harcourt did not believe her. Then he nodded. 'I'm pleased you enjoyed the experience, Thomas. I questioned Marcel this morning. He said he left you in the tub. That you commanded him to leave.'

'I did. I don't like being attended to, lord.'

'Well, I cuffed the bastard around the head for leaving you. And my wishes are not to be questioned in my house. I offered you friendship for what you did. You must tolerate me offering my thanks. I'm a proud man, Thomas. I can't change that. None of us can.'

Blackstone bowed his head in acknowledgement. 'Then may I beg a favour, lord?'

'In friendship, yes.'

'Do not invite me to dine with you and the nobles. I am uncomfortable in such exalted company. I'm a coarse man, and I can never be anything other than that, even though you and my lady teach me manners. I beg you, let me eat alone.'

De Harcourt's frustration spun him away from Blackstone. 'Have you eaten this morning? No. I thought not. I've watched you. Every day, Thomas. You think you're the only one who braves the cold? Well, you're wrong. I'm there. Every day. Every time you wield that sword arm of yours I'm watching,' de Harcourt said rapidly, answering his own questions. He placed his hand on Blackstone's shoulder, suddenly relenting. 'I'm trying to make it easier for you. If I am to fulfil my obligations to your King, then I open the doors to my home and my heart. You need the company of men who understand war. And we have to learn to tolerate someone like you in our midst. Now, don't square those shoulders of yours because you feel insulted; they're broad enough, for God's sake. We all have to learn not to be so quick to take offence. All of us. Now, what would you have me do with you?'

'Let me ride out alone. I want to see the countryside and the villages.'

'You're not a mendicant monk, Thomas, you're a fighting man.'

'Then it's even more important for me to know the lie of the land.'

De Harcourt turned to his wife. 'These English – they have an answer for everything. They are consummate liars; their nobles hide their duplicity through good manners and in battle their commoners carry a shield of disregard for nobility the likes of which I've never come across.' He nodded to Blackstone. 'Get yourself dressed, find a horse and you can go.'

'I'm grateful, lord.'

'Well, you might not be when I send an escort with you.' He sipped his wine and locked eyes with Blackstone. 'I trust you, Thomas. You saved my life. But I can't have a lone Englishman riding through my lands. If the King's men come across you we'll have to lie and tell them you're a prisoner. Understand?'

'Yes. Thank you.'

'I doubt you'll come across any more vicious boars. You've already killed a legend in these parts. Unless he has relatives. You have to be careful of families, Thomas, they can hold grudges.'

Blackstone was uncertain if that was a veiled warning. Was de Harcourt telling him that no matter what had happened between them, an act against the family honour would never be forgiven? He bowed and left the room. De Harcourt threw another log on the fire. Blanche smiled and extended her hand to him. 'You're a good man, my husband. You're generous and honourable.'

He brought her hand to his lips. 'And I'm no fool, Blanche. He's had her. I could smell it on him.'

CHAPTER SEVENTEEN

There were shouts from beyond the walls as men who had trudged from the forest, laden with firewood like beasts of burden, were held by the sentries at the far end of the bridge that spanned the moat. No one would enter the citadel until daylight made identification easier. Brigands had once talked their way into the castle, now it was obvious that Jean de Harcourt would not allow the same mistake again.

Ever since the castle had been attacked and its servants and villagers slaughtered, the household had had few replacements. A temporary steward was in command of the servants and it was obvious that everyone worked almost without rest in order to prepare for the Christmas celebrations. The war was costing the nobility money and stripping them of their resources – a level of poverty they were unused to, and which meant that some servants were not as skilled in their duties.

Blackstone had been granted the right to leave the castle provided four armed men accompanied him. That was no hardship and would not stop him from getting a better picture of the surrounding countryside should the day come when he was forced to make his escape. When King Edward had scorched across Normandy and Sir Godfrey had brought him and the others to the castle earlier, they had travelled from the north and west. Now Blackstone wanted to venture further south.

De Harcourt came into the stables as a stable-hand finished cinching a horse's saddle. The sudden look of anger that crossed de Harcourt's face made the man flinch.

'Who chose this horse?' de Harcourt demanded.

'I did,' Blackstone answered uncertainly.

De Harcourt snatched a riding whip from a rack and thrashed the hapless groom three or four times until he stepped back and went down on his knee. In the moments that Blackstone resisted the urge to lunge forward and grab his whip hand the punishment was over and de Harcourt threw the whip onto the straw-covered floor.

'Get a courser,' he commanded the servant whose welts now streaked his face and neck.

As the man scurried back into the darkness of the horse stalls Blackstone challenged de Harcourt. 'Why did you do that? Did I pick the wrong horse?'

'Don't question what I do in my house, Thomas. I have given my friendship but you have no rights here other than what I grant you.'

'If you punish a man for something that I did, then I have a right to know what I did wrong.'

'You chose a mare. All my servants know you are knighted, and a knight never rides a mare.'

'And you thrashed him for that? Have some pity.'

'I barely laid the whip on him. He should have corrected your choice. Now, let the piece of shit get your horse saddled. I'll not have you ride out from here and make me a laughing stock.'

Blackstone's instincts were to go to the beaten man who had paid for his mistake, but he resisted the temptation in case his actions brought further punishment on an innocent man. This new-found land of privilege was a foreign shore and he wished for the day when he was as far from it as possible.

Christiana had not been pleased. Why would he wish to venture beyond the forests to the far reaches of de Harcourt's land and influence? Violence lay in wait for the unwary traveller. Brigands and murderers could conjure themselves like night spirits in a dream. Why risk that now? Why not wait? Wait until he was stronger still and had the company of de Harcourt himself?

He allowed her anxiety to wear itself out. He was learning

that there were times when her emotions ran like a swollen stream and it was best to let them flood across him. It took only a few moments for her to remember that she had no right to stand in his way, but her deep, passionate kiss in farewell left him with the taste and promise of a welcome return.

Blackstone eyed the soldiers who were to accompany him. De Harcourt had chosen the biggest and strongest from his small garrison force, knowing it would take four strong men to have any chance of stopping Blackstone should he try to disobey their master's orders. All of the men wore de Harcourt's livery and were several years older than Blackstone.

'Meulon,' he said, pointing at one of the men, 'is in charge of your escort. He's a good fighter – listen to what he tells you. You'll go no further than a week's ride. My influence extends only so far and there are towns held by the King's men and routiers, and those mercenary bastards will take your skin as a trophy if they discover you're an Englishman and then sell it to the King. Butchery is their business. You're not to stray from the main tracks through the forests and if you see armed men you keep out of their way. And keep your mouth shut, your accent isn't from these parts.'

'I'm surprised you're letting me go at all,' Blackstone told him.

'If I don't you'll find your own way out sooner or later, something you can probably do already,' de Harcourt said. 'You've spent nights in my library. I suppose you know every passage and doorway by now.'

Blackstone had not realized such a close watch had been kept on his movements during the hours of darkness. 'I'm a stonemason, I like drawings of buildings, and you had them from your father's days,' said Blackstone by way of a stumbling apology.

'Understand this, once and for all, Thomas. I gave my word to my uncle that you would be under my protection and he gave his word to your King, don't ever forget that. This is a debt of honour.'

'But you haven't asked me to give you my word that I won't try and escape. You think I'm not worthy of honour?'

De Harcourt looked at him and smiled. 'I don't have to ask you. You'll come back,' he said and signalled for the gates to be opened.

'You don't know that.'

'Yes, I do. Christiana is here.'

De Harcourt turned back towards the house, his dogs loyally following. Blackstone was as free as he wished, but the Norman baron was right; the ties that bound him lay within the castle's walls.

Blackstone's wounded leg protested as he heeled the horse forward across the narrow wooden bridge, making those same clattering sounds that had echoed when Sir Gilbert Killbere had thundered to the attack only a few months earlier, in what seemed another lifetime. Now the young archer himself rode out as a knight, with four armed men as escort and Wolf Sword at his side.

Blackstone made no objection to his escort's silence as they travelled along the known roads that petered out into tracks used by villagers to and from their hamlets. The surly guards kept twenty paces behind him, but he occasionally heard them grumbling about the duty they had been given. Each night they camped it was obvious from the snippets of conversation he heard that they had no love for the Englishman, but also that Jean de Harcourt would not be disobeyed. Even if they killed him on the road and made it look as though they were ambushed by brigands, their own lives would be forfeit. Blackstone was as safe as he could be for the time being.

In the clear morning air the dusting of snow that had frozen in the night crunched underfoot, and because the day was windless the distant drifting smoke from village fires told him where each settlement lay. The landscape drew itself as a map in his mind; angled edges of forests gave way to rolling hills, a skein of geese that followed the winding river told him which direction the water took once it disappeared into the distant woods. But the further they rode from the castle, the more nervous his escort became. They drew up closer to him and two of them took it upon themselves to ride fifty paces ahead. As they reached a crossroads the countryside

opened up before them in a vast swathe of meadowland on each side
of which stood broadleaf forests, their now-bare branches writhing
starkly upwards – witches' claws beseeching the darkening sky.
Superstition was religion's bedmate. Even Blackstone felt there was
something sinister lurking just out of sight within the trees, and
when a crow glided down from the treetops across their front and
then settled in a nearby branch, its beady-eyed stare gazing down
at them, the men crossed themselves, and Blackstone kissed the
silver charm at his neck. Superstition warned them all that death
disguised itself in the devil's form and that a hooded crow was a
portent of something more sinister than bad luck.

Blackstone turned his horse away and went in the opposite
direction. There was no point in proving bravery against evil
spirits. As the horsemen followed him he heard their murmur of
agreement. It seemed the Englishman was now less of a liability.
Neither they nor the man they guarded could guess that their
misplaced confidence in playing safe would soon disappear like
their plumed breath.

They reached the edge of de Harcourt's influence on the fifth day.
Village hovels squatted like fat sows in mud. Chickens pecked the
dirt and a cur yelped from a peasant's brutal kick. As they rode
through the thoroughfare men's hollow-eyed stares gazed back at
them from fearful yet resentful eyes. The shelters tumbled back
from the opening into the forest so it was impossible for Blackstone
to know how many people lived in the village of Christophe-
la-Campagne.

The fields were empty of sheep. They'd have been slaughtered
a month ago and most likely eaten; any spare mutton would be
salted for the coming dark months. Blackstone saw little sign of
activity. Winter sowing of barley would have been done by now
and the mounds of turnips piled next to many of the hovels were
proof that their winter food had already been gathered.

There was the bitter smell from a forge in the air, so a blacksmith
was at work somewhere, though there was no tell-tale clanging of

hammer against metal. Sodden roofs still dripped from the night's frost, the houses held in the shade, too low in the landscape to get warmth from the sun's shallow arc. Smoke snagged the reed thatch like silk on a thorn bush.

This place was no different from any other that Blackstone and the mounted archers had burned to the ground on their way to Caen.

'How many people live here?' he turned and asked one of the men.

'No one knows. They breed like fleas on a dog's back,' the man answered and spat into the mud.

'Does your master safeguard them?' Blackstone said. 'Are they part of the manor?'

'I don't know, my lord, some of these places are in our juris-diction, there's no abbey close by, no other manor house. Maybe they're Lord de Harcourt's scum, maybe somebody else's. We shouldn't stay here. They hate the English and there's enough of them to cause trouble.'

'You think they'd start a hue and cry against me?'

'A mob gets going here and we'd have shit for dinner. They're like damned creatures of the night coming out of nowhere. And a peasant with a billhook can take a horseman's leg off as good as any cursed English man-at-arms, begging your pardon, sir.'

Blackstone ignored the taunt. If this were England Blackstone would know which village belonged to which manor. County fairs and feast days would bring the villeins together and news and gossip would pass between them and each hamlet would learn from the other. Here, these peasants lived in the darkness of the forest and seemed turned in on themselves, probably fornicating with their own and with a sour disposition towards any stranger.

Blackstone eased the horse towards the edge of the village. 'You should find out about these people. They need to know you and who you serve. Your lord might need them one day. Your King might need them.' And, Blackstone thought to himself, so too might he if he came this way again.

'Aye, m'lord, we saw how useful the likes of these were when they were called up on the *arrière ban*. Fodder for your arrows and trampled by our knights. Used like battering rams to break your shield wall.' He spat again. 'As much use as a nun wearing a chastity belt in a whorehouse.'

Blackstone pulled the horse up next to a farm building that was more substantial than the others.

'You smell that?'

'A shit pit.'

'No, there's food,' Blackstone said dismounting.

'Don't go there,' one of the other men warned him. 'These bastards don't like any stranger no matter where they're from.'

'It'll cause no harm,' Blackstone replied as the men turned in their saddles and confronted him.

'Even the King's men aren't safe since we lost Crécy. They think we ran from the English,' another told him.

'I saw no cowardice at Crécy. I saw none braver than those who came against us,' Blackstone answered.

'Master Thomas, try telling that to the likes of this lot.'

The soldiers were obviously in agreement about leaving this place. 'Peasants carry disease and even the air they breathe can kill a man,' another chimed in.

Meulon pulled up next to Blackstone. 'It's not wise and we can't secure a picket on a village this size. Time we were getting back. We're past halfway, I reckon,' he said.

But Blackstone had already swung down from the saddle.

'Master Thomas! If there's trouble?'

'Piss on them!' Blackstone laughed, speaking English, feeling the momentary joy of an insult in his own language and then relented into French. 'Wait for me,' he commanded, and before anyone could stop him he was already making his way through the animal pens, the oxen's body heat steaming the cold air. Despite the stench of the animals and slurry pits he could still smell cooking. As he squelched across the yard he saw smoke rising from a ventilation hole in the barn's upper floor. Pulling the cloak that Christiana had given him tighter around his shoulders, he took the wooden steps one at a time using the strength of his right leg to push himself upwards. By the time he reached the top of the stairs he felt the trickle of sweat run down his spine from the effort. He pushed open the slatted wooden door and peered into the loft's gloom. It took only a moment for the movement of those inside to alert him that half a dozen men and women sat hunched around the fire and the blackened pot that hung above its flames. It was a sight he'd seen many times in his own village in England. A shared meal above a cattle byre in the middle of winter. A place where villeins, bondmen and free, could talk about their abbot's greed, the constable's brutality and the manor's unwelcome tithes. Their narrow lives knew nothing beyond their village or shire, and what conversation there was usually turned upon a broken plough or lame oxen unable to mark a furrow or what depth they should plant this year's winter barley after its past failure. Harsh weather was either God's desire to make them pray harder or the devil's curse for someone's misdeed, drunkenness or fornication. It was a small place of sanctuary away from the eyes and ears of the reeve or manor's steward.

Blackstone's arrival startled the serfs, the men and women who collected the dung, cut the wood and swept yards. Even a household's servants were of higher standing than these people, who would have walked miles to a manor house each day for their menial labour and the hope of not being raided by brigands or stripped of what little they had by excessive tithes and taxes.

The huddled mass scrambled to their feet and lowered their eyes, as women bent a knee and men bowed, tongues licking the dribbling food from their lips. Blackstone suddenly felt the discomfort of being an intruder. But now he was inside the room and didn't know what to do. Some of them cast furtive looks at his scarred face; his disfigurement might be seen as a mark of Cain. A priest's admonition, aided by tales of retribution, to give more to the Mother Church was a villein's constant shadow. Blackstone realized that if he turned away without uttering a word it would create fear in these people's hearts that they might have been overheard murmuring disloyal comments about their masters.

'I smelt the food,' he said awkwardly, 'it's been a long time since I've eaten pottage.'

Meat was a rich man's diet, it was barley that gave strength to fight or do a hard day's work and he had craved it since recuperating in the closed world of the castle's rooms and corridors. He stepped closer to the pot. 'What is it? Peas and barley?'

One of the women stepped forward, her eyes still averted. 'It is, my lord.'

Her deference caught him unaware, adding to his discomfort of now being treated as a higher rank. It suddenly occurred to him how differently he was dressed from these villagers, who were caked in dried mud and dung, their faces lined with dirt.

'Can I taste the food?'

The question created an immediate reaction. Their fear was written on their faces.

The woman stuttered, 'My lord, there is nothing we should not have. There's humble pie from a pig's innards and only the vegetables we are permitted.'

'Don't be afraid, I'm not here to entrap you. If you've snared your lordship's conies or lured the fish from his river, it's of no concern to me,' he said. He slowly reached forward and took the wooden spoon from the woman's hand. He almost felt her shudder.

'My lord, it's not right. It's been at my own lips,' she said, resisting the tug of his fingers.

He saw the flutter of confusion on their faces as he took it from her and dipped the spoon into the simmering pot, gathering the boiled grain. 'Woman, I'm no lord of the manor, I'm a common man made good by a Prince's hand.'

As he put the spoon to his lips and blew the heat from it, one of the men dared to speak.

'Then you are no longer a common man, my lord,' he said.

Blackstone's hand faltered. Was that the truth? His brush with death had snatched him from his modest past and brought him to another world. The broth settled on his tongue. He tapped the spoon clean on the edge of the pot and handed it back to the woman. The stench of animals and man mingling with acrid smoke that stung his eyes and clung to his clothes was his past.

'The heart of a man stays what it is,' he said.

Two of the men shuffled nervously towards him, blocking the door.

'Your accent, it's not from around here, my lord. Are you from Paris? One of the King's men?'

The atmosphere had suddenly changed, a threat had emerged without Blackstone realizing it.

'No. I am a guest with Count Jean de Harcourt,' Blackstone said quickly, seeing that de Harcourt's name checked any further advance.

'A man at arms, my lord? At Crécy? Would that be where you took that wound?' another asked.

Before any of them dared question him again, one of his escorts was at the door.

'You'd better get out here and see this. There might be trouble,' he said, gripping a short-handled battleaxe. The men stepped back and let Blackstone pass. As he got outside he saw that his guards had gathered close together, forming protection around a man lying sprawled in the mud, while a gathering crowd was murmuring discontent.

'Who the hell is that?' Blackstone demanded, leading the way down the steps as his escort covered his back.

'A squire or some such thing. We can't see his livery because of the mud and bloodstains but he's no peasant, that's for sure,' his escort said. Blackstone had no time to register his surprise. 'When you get to the bottom of the steps cut through the animal pens and look to the right,' his escort told him.

Blackstone forced his way through the few startled cattle and got back into the village thoroughfare, its deep rutted tracks still crisp with morning ice. Now that he looked more carefully towards the end of the village and the light had shifted he could see that a man had been hanged and his mud-caked body was the colour of red earth, only it wasn't dirt that matted his hair and tunic but a caved-in skull and half-ripped face that had bled down onto his body.

He looked towards the man who lay motionless in the mud. 'Is he alive?'

'Just about, he's had a beating and a half,' his escort answered.

'Get him onto a horse,' Blackstone said, grabbing hold of his saddle horn and hoisting himself up, his leg still unable to bear the full weight of being bent into a stirrup.

'Take him?' the man challenged.

'Do it. Now.' Blackstone's command was forceful enough for the soldier to obey without further challenge. Those villagers who were gathering around the horsemen grew more restive, their curses more vocal and threatening. As Blackstone and two others used their horses to keep them back, the unconscious man was draped across a horse's withers and once the men were mounted, Blackstone urged them away at a canter until they had crested a meadow's knoll a mile away and could see that they were not being pursued.

They lay the man down and dribbled water onto his cracked lips.

As Blackstone tried to wipe some of the dirt from his face, his hand brushed aside the man's hair.

'Look at this,' Blackstone said. A fleur-de-lys was branded on the beaten man's forehead, still raw from the hot iron.

Meulon bent down.

'Is he French? Blackstone asked.

'I don't know. Maybe he's Gascon,' Meulon answered. The Gascons from the south-west were loyal to the English King. 'If these villagers catch anyone they think is a thief or spying for the routiers they brand them.'

Blackstone brushed some of the dirt away from the man's tunic. The wounded man's eyes fluttered and then stared like a fox dug from its earth.

'English?' he whispered desperately, barely audible.

'Yes,' Blackstone answered, already knowing that the livery was King Edward's.

The relived man smiled. 'Thank God... your face scared the shit out of me,' he whispered before slipping back into unconsciousness.

Blackstone gave up his cloak to give the man warmth as the soldiers cut down saplings and stripped their bark to weave a litter for the fallen man, so they could drag him slowly home.

'My Lord de Harcourt will have me flogged for bringing an enemy into his walls,' Meulon moaned as they got closer to home.

'No, he won't,' Blackstone said, 'he's given refuge to one already.'

They were less than a day's ride from home when the horsemen appeared. One of the escorts saw a half-dozen men ride across an open meadow before disappearing behind hedgerows.

'They'll be further down the road on a blind bend,' one of the soldiers said. 'I saw at least six of them, and they're not wearing livery. They'll be brigands. Shit, this is going badly. They outnumber us and they're vicious bastards.'

Meulon turned in the saddle and looked about for an escape route. 'We cut the litter free and make a run for it up the hill and through the forest.'

'We're not leaving him,' Blackstone said.

Meulon pushed his horse next to Blackstone. 'Listen, *Master* Thomas, this is no time to be a hero,' he said disrespectfully. 'Those savage bastards outnumber us six to four.'

'Six to five,' Blackstone answered.

'For Christ's sake, this isn't a practice session with a wooden sword, you've never fought like this. They want our weapons and horses.'

'Then we'll tell them they can't have them,' Blackstone answered.

'Oh, aye, brigands like nothing better than a bit of chat. If we had bread and cheese we could share that with them as well,' he snarled, then turned to the others. 'Cut the litter free. We make for the forest.'

'Wait!' Blackstone shouted. 'We're not leaving this man. If you run I stay – and you can explain yourself to your lord as to how I died.'

He could see his argument had struck home. The men wheeled their horses in confusion and Blackstone pushed to the front. 'I'll take two of you forward. We leave the litter here in the trees,' he said and pointed to two of the men. 'Use the other side of this hedgerow for cover. Tether your horses and go on foot. Take your crossbows and swords only, leave your shields behind. If there's six of them they're jammed between the hedgerow banks and the slope of the forest. You flank them.'

The men looked undecided for a moment and then Meulon spat, 'I'll do it. We'll stay close to the hedge. Come on,' he said to one of the men, then passed his shield to Blackstone. 'You'll need this, and if you get yourself killed at least I can say we tried to save you. You're a mad bastard, Master Thomas. I just hope you don't get us all killed.'

They tethered their horses and readied their crossbows, then clambered up the bank and pushed through the hedgerow. Blackstone gave them time to make headway and then turned his horse. He said a silent prayer that the lesson he had learnt at that first crossroads in Normandy would work here. Sir Gilbert Killbere had put his life into the hands of his archers that day and the ambush gave them victory. Now Thomas Blackstone was asking two Frenchmen to make sure he survived.

'I'll do the talking,' Blackstone said.

'And if they don't listen?' one of the men asked.

'We kill them,' said Blackstone.

Blackstone took the lead, easing the horse forward as the two remaining soldiers flanked either side, half a length back. If he had read the situation correctly the brigands would have no room to manoeuvre, so if there was a fight Blackstone could surge forward in a spearhead. That idea fled as soon as they turned the bend. The brigands had already blocked the road, jamming themselves in with no other means of passage. Steam rose from their horses; they must have been following Blackstone's group for a while and pushed their horses hard to catch up with them. Blackstone realized that they too had read the ground: there would be no surge forward from Blackstone and his men.

The unshaven men looked as though they had crawled from an alehouse's mud floor. Their leather jerkins shone through years of grease and sweat; they wore caps and open-faced bascinets and looked like any bunch of deserters who lived rough and took what they could to survive. Their horses were of poor quality, and probably stolen from villages that had the least capable of beasts, but for these men swayback horses were as good as they could get until they stole better mounts. And any garrison's horse, better fed and watered with a farrier and blacksmith to keep them well shod, was worth killing for.

Blackstone and his men held their sword blades on their right shoulders and kept their horses moving forward at the walk until they were a half-dozen horse lengths away from the brigands. The trick now was to make them manoeuvre so they would each hinder the other. Blackstone stopped his men at a slight curve in the road, a passing place for carts. If he could bring the enemy to him they had the better place to fight. He summoned the courage to find the words that might entice the men to fight. Bravado could carry the day.

'Did your mother's claws rip that face of yours when they pulled you from her belly?' one of the brigands said, and who was obviously their leader.

'It was given by a better man than you,' Blackstone said, testing the man for provocation. 'And I killed him for it.'

'A boy like you?' the man sneered.

'An English archer like me,' Blackstone answered and saw their expressions change into unconcealed hatred.

'What's this, then? You ride with a Norman lord's men?'

'I ride with those I choose. Your business lies elsewhere. Shouldn't you be clearing shit pits for a monastery or does your stench outweigh that of a monk's bowels?'

The brigand's face twisted. 'You're going no further on this road, you English scum,' the man answered.

'It's an open highway, and we carry no coin,' Blackstone said, buying as much time as he could until he thought his crossbowmen should be in position.

'No matter, this is our road now, and we take what we want, when we want it. Where are the other two men?' the man asked.

'If you know there are other men, then you know we have a wounded man with us on a litter. They're back down the road guarding him.'

The brigands' leader thought about it for a moment and then grunted, satisfied at the explanation. 'Then they'll not put up a fight once you've surrendered your horses and weapons. Then you'll be free to go.' He was an ugly man with sagging skin, pitted with blackheads, and yellowing eyes from too much drink, but the broken nose and scarred hands told Blackstone that he was a fighter at best and a cold-hearted killer at worst. No man, woman or child's death would touch him. No one spoke or moved, each man readying themselves for the fight. The brigands' horses pressed against each other, forcing their riders to pull back and jostle for position.

'You're not a man to bargain, then?' Blackstone said.

'Bargain?' The man laughed and looked to his men. 'You have something to trade?'

One of those at his side pointed his sword at his leader. 'Guescin here would rob and rape the Virgin Mary even if she bargained with the devil not to!' The men laughed, murmuring their agreement, and waited smiling, as the Englishman in front of them held his place and his nerve.

Blackstone felt his leg wound tighten and the fear creep into his stomach. His mouth dried. He would be first to strike. What he did would determine the outcome of the confrontation.

'Two of these men are better than all of your dog-shit routiers put together. Get off the damned road now before I set them on you,' Blackstone said, hoping that his men behind him had not grimaced at the thought of leading the attack.

The mercenary sniffed the air. 'Has one of you shat themselves? I can smell their fear from here. Come on, boy, let's have you on the ground and on your knees and begging for your lives.'

'I'll trade your life for the road,' Blackstone said. 'Give way or I'm going to kill you first and then your men.'

The man's face creased in uncertainty, as if working out a complex puzzle. It was the provocation Blackstone had wanted.

His thumb pressed into the sword's corded grip.

His fear was gone.

The man yelled, spurring his horse forward. Those to his side were startled and their moment of hesitation gave Blackstone the advantage. He kicked back his heels and the animal surged. The brigand's sword was halfway down its arc when Blackstone's blade swept beneath it and took him across the throat. The momentum barged his horse into the brigand to his left, his shield blocking the man's attack as the dead man's horse veered, throwing its head to one side and blocking another of the men. Blackstone twisted, felt the blade turn in the shield, yanking the man forward as one of Blackstone's escorts rammed his spear into the man's exposed ribs. Then crossbow quarrels thudded into the two brigands at the rear, and as they fell they trapped the surviving men. One managed to turn his horse, but Meulon had pushed through the hedgerow and struck at him from the top of the bank, his blade slicing across the man's skull, splitting it from ear to neck.

Blackstone was exposed on his right as a horseman pushed past his leader's panicked horse and now positioned himself to attack. The man who was supposed to protect Blackstone on that side took two hefty blows despite his efforts to block any attack on Blackstone and was struck from the horse. As the soldier fell the brigand's sword swept around ready to take Blackstone's head. He threw himself across the horse's mane, the flat edge of the blade skimming his shoulder, tearing his gambeson without cutting flesh. The man had turned with the stroke and Blackstone threw his weight forward, ramming Wolf Sword into the man's liver and lungs. The force of the lunge held the blade and, as the man fell it was yanked from Blackstone's hand and unbalanced him from the saddle. He went down among the hooves, his memory cursing him for not tying a blood knot from his sword's crossguard. He curled into a protective ball, as men's screams and cries of agony competed with the whinnying of the terrified horses. His leg felt as though molten lead had been poured into the wound, and a hoof caught his head. For a dizzying moment he felt the world swirling. Instinct forced him to push himself into the bank for protection and then someone was there between him and the horse.

'Get up!' Meulon shouted. 'They're all dead except one.'

Blackstone accepted the man's extended arm and hauled himself up. Meulon looked at him questioningly as Blackstone pulled the hair back from his face and saw the smear of blood on his hand. He'd been lucky.

'I'm all right,' Blackstone told him.

'It seems you know how to use this, Sir Thomas,' Meulon said, acknowledging Blackstone's rank for the first time as he handed back the recovered Wolf Sword.

Blackstone walked down the track to where one of the escorts guarded the surviving brigand. Another of de Harcourt's men held the horses as the soldier who had been at Blackstone's side sat, ashen-faced, against the bank.

'Gaillard. He's taken a cut through his mail, he'll bleed a bit longer and then it'll congeal. He'll survive, though he deserves no sympathy for making such a piss-poor mess of it. God's blood! He only had to ride at your side. I'll make sure he loses pay and gets a flogging because of it.' The injured man's face hardened at the thought of more pain and of losing what little he earned.

'He did well,' Blackstone lied, 'he slowed the man attacking me. Give him some wine and we'll attend to his wound before we leave this place.'

The wounded man gritted his teeth and got to his feet. 'My thanks, Sir Thomas.'

Meulon nodded. 'You're a lucky bastard, Gaillard, in more ways than one,' he said, knowing full well that it was more usual for a man-at-arms to blame a common soldier for any misfortune that befell him, and that Blackstone had almost gone down under the routier's sword.

The prisoner was on his knees in the mud, his hands tied behind his back. Greasy hair plastered his face from the sweat of the fight. Meulon yanked his head back, the man gasped, exposing the broken and blackened stumps that had once been teeth.

'Who do you fight for?' Blackstone asked him.

'We serve no one,' he answered, and then fell to Meulon's kick.

'Lying bastard. Half a dozen scum like you don't survive on your own. There's more of you. Where?' Meulon demanded.

The man shook his head in denial, and earned another kick for his resistance.

Blackstone raised a hand. 'That's enough. Listen to me,' he said, 'I'm going to set you free.'

Meulon couldn't believe what he'd heard. 'We string this piece of shit up and leave his body as a warning to others who trespass on my lord's territory!'

'No, I do this my way,' Blackstone answered. 'Get him on his knees and untie him.'

Meulon stepped in front of Blackstone, his face close to the Englishman. 'We make an example of him, as would my Lord de Harcourt.'

'He's not here,' Blackstone said and tried to step aside, but Meulon positioned himself again.

'We kill him,' Meulon hissed. The other men couldn't hide their disgust and murmured their agreement.

A fragment of memory shot into Blackstone's mind of Killbere's strength and authority, of the man who made the decisions without favour. 'Do as I say and do it now,' Blackstone told him without raising his voice. 'I know what needs to be done.'

Once again Meulon hesitated, but Blackstone had not moved and showed no sign of changing his mind. Finally, Meulon obeyed and dragged the man by his hair onto his knees and cut free the bonds.

'Now, tell me who you serve, and you're free to go,' Blackstone told him.

'You'll kill me anyway,' the man said defiantly.

'No. I will not kill you. I give you my word.'

'And what's that worth?'

'My honour has been well earned,' said Blackstone. 'It means everything.'

The man hesitated. 'I need a drink.'

'No drink, only your freedom as I promised. Now who do you ride for?'

The man thought about it for a moment. What was there to lose? 'Routiers hold Chaulion.'

Blackstone looked to Meulon to explain. 'Eighty miles or more to the south. It controls one of the crossroads,' Meulon told him.

'Who's there? How many?' Blackstone demanded as Meulon's fist was raised ready to punish.

The man flinched. 'Germans, French, Gascons – all kinds. English deserters as well. More than sixty men, sometimes more. Saquet leads them. He's their leader. Saquet, *le poigne de fer*.'

'The "Iron Fist". I've heard of him,' Meulon said, 'he's a Breton, murdering bastards every last one of them, they'd sell their mothers for a jug of wine. He's one of the worst. They call him that because he likes to kill a man on the ground by smashing his skull with his fist.'

Blackstone knew that de Harcourt's men would gut and hang the man as a warning for others not to stray into their lord's domain. They looked at him expectantly. Sometimes harsh actions were necessary. He faltered, trying to decide on what act would serve its purpose. Finding the lesser of the evils was what separated wanton torture and killing from exacting a harsh lesson on an enemy.

'Bring him over here,' he ordered.

Meulon dragged the man by his hair and beard across to a fallen tree. Blackstone raised his sword ready to strike. The man's knees sagged beneath him; spittle and snot clung to his beard as he begged for his life.

'No, no! You gave your honour!'

'I always keep my word. I'll give you your freedom. Meulon, his arm, there,' Blackstone said, pointing to the tree stump. Meulon and another of de Harcourt's men held the man down and forced his arm across the stump.

'You tell this "Iron Fist" that he will not come again into this territory and that Sir Thomas Blackstone, sworn to his sovereign lord, the English King, will seek him out and kill him, and that this is fair warning.'

Blackstone's blade severed the fingers cleanly from the man's sword hand.

Blackstone had the brigand's wound bound, but before they sent him on his way he was given another lesson: they gathered the slain men's swords and spiked their bodies to the trees as a warning. Meulon and the others stayed silent once the work was done. Whatever doubts they had harboured about the Englishman seeped away like the blood spilled on the track.

CHAPTER EIGHTEEN

Jean de Harcourt watched the blood-spattered escort return. Their arrival caused a flurry of activity in the courtyard as the injured men were helped. Blackstone briefly explained what had happened and that mercenaries held the town of Chaulion.

'We knew it had been taken, but that they were raiding this far is worrying news,' said de Harcourt.

'Is the King testing those of us he doubts?' Louis de Vitry asked.

'There's no saying they're being paid by our King,' Guy de Ruymont said, 'they are as likely to be serving their own ends as that of his.'

'My lord,' said Blackstone, 'the Englishman wears the livery of the King of England, and there was another man hanged in the village. I don't know what they were doing so far south.'

'What they were doing, young Blackstone, is telling Frenchmen that Edward would protect them if they swore allegiance,' said de Mainemares, the noblemen's elder statesman, who pushed his way through the group and tugged at the wounded man's livery as he was being carried into the castle. 'He's sending out runners and without much success. Perhaps your King's authority and influence is not what we believe it to be.' He nodded for the litter bearers to take the man inside.

'Put him next to Sir Thomas's quarters,' de Harcourt commanded. 'Thomas, stay with him and see what you can find out when he regains consciousness, you're the only one who speaks the language.'

There had been no condemnation of Blackstone's actions, but neither had there been praise for stopping the mercenaries. The

293

gathered nobles stood aside as the young knight followed the litter through the castle doors.

William de Fossat pulled his fingers through his thatch of beard.

'A good kill, Jean. It'll teach those thieving bastards to keep their distance.'

De Vitry agreed. 'If they hold Chaulion, they control the trade that passes on those roads. We should burn them out before more skinners join them.'

Jean de Harcourt remained silent. Murmurs of agreement joined de Vitry and Fossat.

'Meulon!' de Harcourt called as the soldier attended to his injured man near the stables. 'Inside. Now.'

De Harcourt turned on his heel, followed by the others. He needed to know whether Thomas Blackstone's actions had been foolish and disturbed a hornet's nest that could bring raiders onto his lands, or whether he had started a chain of events that would suit the Norman barons and their long-term plans.

The servants put the unconscious man onto a fresh litter and gathered their medicines and herbs. As they washed the grime from his face and hands he stirred and muttered something in his delirium.

'Master Blackstone,' Marcel called. 'He said something.'

Blackstone sat next to the unconscious man. 'What have you given him?'

'Comfrey for the burn on his forehead and his broken ribs. His foot is at the wrong angle so we will also use it in the binding. We have stitched the wound on his head as best we can and we'll prepare more herbs.'

'And what's this?' Blackstone asked.

'Common rue heals many things and wards off evil spirits,' Marcel said.

'Perhaps prayer might do that,' Blackstone suggested.

Marcel took back the pouch of herbs. 'We must take all pre-cautions, Sir Thomas. Lady Christiana prayed three times a day for your recovery but we also tended you with these same potions once Master Jordan returned to the English army. Evil spirits find their way into our souls when we are helpless. No one should risk being caught in the jaws of hell through the lack of a few herbs.'

Blackstone couldn't argue. Not with his own superstitions. He unconsciously touched the silver lady at his throat and saw Marcel's glimmer of a smile.

The injured man turned his head and half opened his eyes. 'Do I live?' he said in barely a whisper.

Blackstone lowered his face to hear more clearly. The man repeated his question. 'Yes,' Blackstone told him, 'and you're safe.' He beckoned for Marcel and the other servant in the room to raise the man so he could drink. They eased the liquid to his lips. He sipped and then closed his eyes. Blackstone waited, and moments later he recovered again.

'Who are you?' Blackstone asked him.

'I am a messenger for the King of England. I had a warrant of safe passage.' He sighed, closed his eyes, rested a moment and then spoke again. 'I should have used it to wipe my arse.' He wheezed, as if his lungs could not fill with air. It took a few seconds for him to recover. 'Those bloody French heathens tore us down like a pack of wolves.' He grimaced. 'I feel as though I've been kicked and trampled by a bloody war horse. I'm no fighting man, I'm a runner for the King.' He sighed again and once more closed his eyes, his ability to speak coming in fits and starts.

Blackstone brushed the man's hair from his face and looked again at the brand burned into his forehead. It was difficult to determine how old he was but he guessed he was a few years older than himself. That he was a commoner was obvious. He would have been part of the King's retinue, serving the chamberlain and used for delivering proclamations. A trickle of blood seeped from the corner of the man's mouth.

'Marcel?' Blackstone asked, indicating the blood.

'His lungs. They must be pierced by a rib. I don't know if that can be healed,' Marcel answered. 'I'll burn some coltsfoot, it is said that can help with poor breathing.' Marcel left the room in search of more herbs.

'So I said to myself...' the man said, as if carrying on from a conversation, ignorant that he had once again slipped into unconsciousness, '... I said, a dog's bollocks couldn't squeeze through the gap in this cage – did I tell you that? – that they put me in a wicker cage once they beat and branded me? I did, didn't I? After they slaughtered poor old Jeffrey, strung him up like a cat at a village fair... for the sport of it...'

He faltered again, perhaps it was the pain-killing herbs that jumbled the man's thoughts.

'What's your name?' Blackstone asked.

The man looked bewildered, as if he had to remember an obscure message that eluded him. 'It's... Harness, William Harness, and I am a runner for the King of England. Did I tell you that?'

'Yes. My name is Thomas Blackstone. I'm an Englishman. Do you know of Sir Gilbert Killbere? He was close to the Prince at Crécy.'

'Is that where they cut you?' Harness said, gazing at Blackstone's scar.

'Yes. Do you know him?'

'Am I in England? What's your name?'

'Thomas. My name is Thomas. You're in France. In Normandy. What about Sir Gilbert? Does he live?'

'Are you a prisoner?'

Blackstone held his impatience in check. 'No, I rescued you from that village.'

'That's right. I remember. I was in the cage when I saw your horsemen. I thought... Sweet Jesus, God bless my King for sending troops to find us. Then a voice that gave me hope. Piss! Piss on them! That's what I heard. Only an Englishman would say that, I thought. Piss on them. Too right, I said to myself. I broke through the cage with my last ounce of strength. I wanted to be back with my lord King, and my friends. Those... bastards... they... tore at us... Sir Gilbert Killbere. I've heard the name. I don't know. We slaughtered the French. Were you there?'

Harness was losing his grasp on reality again. It was too soon to question him.

'Yes,' Blackstone said again, 'I was there.'

His grip closed on Blackstone's arm. 'I'm frightened. Frightened. Fearful of the dark and what awaits me. Don't let them take me. Swear you won't let them take me again.'

'I swear. You're safe here. You're protected from all harm.'

The man sighed and closed his eyes, drifting into sleep.

If they were attacking and killing the English King's messengers, then there was still a core of resistance embedded in the French countryside. No matter that a great victory had been won months ago, Edward's influence was failing, and if that was the case then Blackstone knew his own life might once again be in jeopardy.

In the great hall Meulon stood to attention in front of the silent barons.

'Sir Thomas went into the village against my wishes. As he went inside one of the hovels we saw a man held in a pigpen struggling to break out. At first we thought he may have belonged to one of the local lords. We saw another man had been beaten and strung up, and Sir Thomas commanded us to take the man we'd found with us. We got about a couple of miles from the village when the Englishman came to and said something to Master Thomas, which I didn't understand. Then a few days later we saw the routiers. I did all I could to make him leave the Englishman, but he insisted we fight. It could have gone badly for us, but he positioned us on the track and sent me and another man to outflank them. He taught them a good lesson. He was right and I was wrong. I beg your forgiveness, lord, for not being able to fulfil your command and avoid danger.'

'You think the Englishman thought it through?' asked de Graville. 'Or was he trying to impress you and your men?'

'Oh yes, lord, he thought about it. We could have run from

the fight, but he knew exactly what he was doing. It was a good ambush.'

'And then?' Fossat asked.

'Then he stopped me from killing the last man alive. I wanted to gut the pig and put his head on a stake. But he wouldn't have that. No, my lords, he promised the man his life if he would give him more information. Said he would keep his word. That his word was his honour. The bastard had never heard such a promise. And once we had it, the information I mean, that's when he took the man's fingers from his hand and sent the bastard back. He never faltered. Like taking the head off a chicken. That was the message he sent. To tell Saquet that he was not to raid into my Lord de Harcourt's territory again or he, I mean Sir Thomas, would kill him.'

The questioning men fell silent, the tension was palpable. Meulon felt fear nip at his stomach, his eyes blinked with uncertainty.

'You would say he has ability?' asked de Harcourt. 'Or was it luck?'

'Lord, we all need luck in a fight, but in the time it took for us to kill those skinners, Sir Thomas led the way. He was unhorsed, but I think that was because his leg weakened. It made no difference to his courage. He has guts, sir. I didn't see a sign of fear even on his face. His hands were steady. I thought for a minute he was relishing the idea. Of getting stuck in. There's a word for it, my lords… means… he's ready to fight.'

'Belligerent,' suggested de Graville.

'I think that's the word, sir,' said Meulon. 'Sounds right. And when he took the bastard's fingers, well, we knew then he had what it takes.' Meulon licked his lips; his throat was getting dry from all the talk and a sudden fear that he may have upset his own master by praising the young Englishman.

'How did he treat you?' Jean de Harcourt asked his captain.

'Sir?'

'Did he treat you as an equal? He is a common man. The fact that he was honoured on the battlefield means nothing when he rides into a fight with other soldiers. You are my captain and you have experience of taking men forward into the fight. So how did he behave with you?'

Meulon thought about that for a moment, because his lord's question was asked with his usual authority, but its curious nature troubled the soldier. When violence took place and a man fought for his life, then he put his trust in God and his sword and the man who led them. Some men pissed and shat their breeches in battle when the terror gripped them, and there would be none who would sneer at another if they lived through it. Others created that terror.

'Sir Thomas might be a common man, lord, he carries no burden of nobility, that's for sure, and if he had tried to befriend us common soldiers then he would have raised doubts about his ability to take command. That's what he did and why we obeyed. He took command and proved his worth, my lord.'

The nobles exchanged glances as Meulon waited nervously, still standing rigidly, not daring to look at any of these powerful men for fear of being insubordinate.

It was Henri Livay who broke their silence. 'Meulon, you've fought with your master, so too the men who rode with you today.'

Meulon hesitated. Everyone knew they had served with Jean de Harcourt and his father. Was it a question he was being asked? 'I don't understand, lord. Forgive me.'

'It's simple. Would Sir Thomas be the kind of man you and your soldiers – all of you, experienced as you are – would follow? To fight?'

Meulon paused before answering. The Englishman meant nothing to him. There was no fealty. But he had saved Gaillard from a flogging, had earned his loyalty. And Meulon's. You had to believe in someone if they put you into danger.

'I think... we all would, my lord. Aye, we'd follow Master Blackstone.'

Now that Blackstone and Christiana had tasted the pleasure of each other, she would come down the narrow staircase, its rough stone damping any footfall. She would hesitate and look down the passageway to see that those who slept in the doorways had their backs to her, or were curled against the cold of the stone floor, huddled in sleep. It was then a few short paces to Blackstone's room. Their nights spiralled into a restless, indulgent passion that carried them beyond any care of discovery. Only the cold arrival of each dawn awoke them to the dangers of being found out. They could not know that Blanche de Harcourt was aware of every moment they shared and that she, in turn, played a delicate game against her husband. His tolerance could only be stretched so far, but she knew that he and the others were planning to use Blackstone. She did not yet know what scheme they were hatching, but the moment it was finalized, Thomas and Christiana would have little chance to continue their illicit lovemaking. It might only be a matter of time.

The devils' cleft tongues snaked from their jaws as the tumbling bodies of sinners were consumed, like a rabid dog would savage a child. The ladder to heaven pierced the underworld where unfortunates held on grimly with fingers torn and bleeding as they were dragged below the earth's crust. A plaintive cry for forgiveness could almost be heard as their eyes were raised to the calm beauty of God whose extended hand blessed all of those good men and angels around him.

Blackstone had no idea when the murals had been painted in de Harcourt's chapel, but the flickering candlelight made the figures look as if they chased and scorched their way across the walls. The images were faded but still clear enough to show mankind's fall from grace and the eternal damnation that awaited sinners. Repent, the angels cried, and be loved by God. Blackstone and Christiana sat huddled in the cold, damp chapel. No light yet penetrated the high, small windows; only the spluttering candles fought against this almost total darkness. He held his cape around her as she shivered, despite her own thick woollen gown, while he banished the chill from his own mind.

Christiana had convinced him that they should show themselves to God and ask for forgiveness for their lust and to make a promise before the altar that their passion was an extension of their love for each other.

It took some convincing.

She prayed, and as her whispers of confession to the Almighty recounted her base feelings, pushing her head lower in repentance, Blackstone felt himself aroused. Was it a mortal sin to fornicate in a church or would the fires of hell just singe his arse? he wondered.

She eased herself up from her knees, face flushed with the excitement of unburdening herself.

'We could never confess to the priest,' she said. 'His stipend is paid by my Lord de Harcourt.'

'I don't intend confessing anything to anyone. Lust is part of my feelings for you. I'd lie with you all day and night if I thought we wouldn't be noticed. Not that there would be much chance of that – the way you scream into the pillow could still wake the dead.'

Her eyes flared with anger as she hissed at him. 'Thomas, have some respect for where we are! Don't shame me further.'

'There's no shame to be had from pleasure, Christiana. God knows all about us and what we do.'

This had been the one morning that he had not gone out into the cold hour before dawn. And he already regretted submitting to her insistent demands to avail themselves of God's forgiveness.

'You'll attend Mass with me on Christmas Day, Thomas,' Christiana said. 'It will be expected.'

The fear of God was a tangible emotion for Christiana, but for him their desire for each other held God's wrath at bay.

'I'll not go to Mass. I'm not yet ready to forgive God.'

The candlelight bathed them in a warm glow but he saw the blood drain from her face as she crossed herself. 'That's blasphemy,' she whispered.

'I lay dying in the mud of Crécy and saw the burning cross. Warrior angels gathered around me and I begged forgiveness, but they barred my way to heaven. It's an argument I carry with the Almighty.'

'Stop that! I won't hear another word,' she said, her echoing words bright and sharp.

She tried to avoid his embrace but he held her. 'Listen to me. I see God's work everywhere. I don't have to go into a cold stone building to speak my thoughts to Him. I see the spirits in the forest and His angels in the clouds. Don't bury me in your fear, Christiana. Besides, I'm safe from any retribution because you'll pray twice as hard and save us both.'

The sound of servants moving in the corridor stopped her from arguing further. She pulled her cloak around her, checked the passageway and then stepped quickly onto the stairs, leaving Blackstone alone in the tomb of silence.

The devils danced but Blackstone turned his back on them.

Damnation was already his travelling companion.

He checked on the English messenger, who slept fitfully, slipping in and out of consciousness. The servant whose duty it was to sit with the injured man told Blackstone he had stayed silent most of the night and that the administered draught had numbed his pain. Food was being sent from the kitchen. Blackstone dismissed the servant and sat next to Harness's bed. It seemed to him that other than the obvious wounds the man's body was broken inside.

He wrung out a cloth in a bowl of water and dabbed Harness's head. The brand was livid, but might one day be borne as a badge of honour. A servant came in with a bowl of soup.

'I was told the man must be fed as often as he was able to eat,' the man said.

'I'll see to it,' Blackstone told him, taking the bowl of broth, pungent with herbs.

Harness awoke at the disturbance.

'William, I'm told you've slept through most of the night. You're on the mend. Here, let's sit you up.'

He eased Harness into a sitting position. 'Is there ale?' Harness asked, dragging his tongue from the roof of his mouth as he stared at the room. 'Where am I?'

'In Castle de Harcourt, and there's no decent ale in these parts, I can vouch for that. There's wine or water.'

'Water?'

Blackstone smiled at Harness's reaction. He was pale, his face gaunt, and his hands trembled. The dried blood from his lungs moistened again now that he was conscious and talking. Blackstone put the damp cloth onto his lips. 'This will moisten your mouth. You'll have wine after you've eaten.'

Harness sucked the moisture and nodded his thanks.

'No food. I've a thirst. All right, I'll take wine if that's all there is.'

Blackstone held a small bowl of red wine and let him drink as best he could, his ragged breath making it difficult for him to swallow. 'The Virgin Mary herself must have sent you to save me,' he gasped, the effort making him tremble even more. 'Finding another Englishman among all these bastard Frenchies, Blessed Mother of Christ be praised, I'll spend the rest of my life on my knees in any cock-arsed priest's church.' He lapsed into a quiet exhaustion again, but smiled, and rested his hand on Blackstone's arm.

'You should rest,' Blackstone told him, 'talking will weaken you.'

'Fornication weakens me but I don't get enough of that either,' he laughed, but then spluttered. Blackstone put the cloth to his lips again and noticed the speckles of blood.

Harness raised his hand, and breathed slowly. 'I woke up… sometime… don't know when. Candles were burning… thought I was in heaven… a woman came in… bloody angel, I said to myself, God's sent an angel, and all I could think about was putting my hand up her gown and my cock in her. Where did you say I was?'

'You're in a Norman baron's castle and I think you were dreaming,' Blackstone told him. None of the noblewomen would venture this far down the corridors, and Christiana lay in his arms all night. He raised the bowl of soup to Harness's mouth. He crinkled his nose.

'It's the herbs,' Blackstone told him. 'They'll nourish you.'

'A piece of salted mutton would do me good,' he said looking over the bowl's rim to Blackstone.

'Take what you can of this and I'll see what I can do,' Blackstone told him.

'She was here, y'know, I saw her clear as I see you. And a damned sight prettier than your mangled face. Who did that to you?'

'It doesn't matter. He's dead.'

Harness thought for a moment. 'They castrated my friend, Jeffrey. Do you know that? The lad they hanged in the village. No mercy shown. We offered them the King's protection and they took a knife to him and strung him up. They were saving me for something special. Can you kill them? Teach 'em a lesson?'

'It's Christmas, William. The holiest of times. Forgiveness for all.'

'Oh aye?' His face hardened and tears formed in his eyes. 'Piss on that. He was a lad, younger than you and me both. Loved his King and his horse in equal measure, I reckon. Proud to have been chosen. God, that boy could ride day and night, taking the King's word. Would've rode through hell for his sovereign lord.' He wiped the tears from his face. 'Hurt him something cruel. Pitiful to watch it was. And once they'd beaten me half to death they made me look at 'em doing it.' He shook his head. 'When I'm able, I'll borrow me a horse and I'll ride back to them vermin and I'll put a torch to them. Then they can try and kill me again.' He spluttered again as his rattling chest released more fluid. 'I'm no soldier but I'm the King's man. And I'll see them dead before I go.'

The broth remained untouched. Blackstone understood Harness's hatred. Every time he thought of his brother's death the squirming in his stomach always rose like a serpent and squeezed his heart. Perhaps that desire for vengeance could keep Harness alive as it had done for Blackstone.

'We'll burn them out together. How about that?'

'You swear?'

'I do.'

'That's a grand idea. You're a fighting man, I can see that. I'll take your lead, and we'll burn the scum out.' He sighed and closed his eyes again. 'Aye, we'll teach them. Poor lad… killing's one thing… but for what they did… they'll burn.' He stayed silent for a while until Blackstone knew he could do no more good by sitting with him. Best to let him sleep. As he stood to leave the room, Harness half opened his eyes.

'She was here. I saw her. Braided hair and blue gown. Like the Virgin Mary she was. Came to see William Harness in his hour of need.'

Blackstone did not reply as Harness fell asleep but he knew the man had not seen a vision in his delirium. It was Blanche de Harcourt who had come into the room, and if she had been this close to Blackstone's quarters then perhaps she knew of Christiana being in his bed.

Desperation crept into him. How long could he and Christiana sleep together without being discovered? The servant, Marcel, already knew, but Jean de Harcourt had made no accusation. He must know, he *must*! How could such a powerful man, who would use his authority to have any man punished most brutally, not know what went on under his roof?

Unless, of course, his interests and concerns lay only in political matters and the pursuit of power against a feeble King. Blackstone realized he had not understood the emotions that ran through the de Harcourt family. When he had rescued Christiana and they had gone to the castle at Noyelles it had been Blanche de Harcourt who held the family together while her lord and husband fought the English. Sir Godfrey de Harcourt might well have offered her protection, but Blackstone remembered the relief that Blanche showed when Christiana had been returned to her safekeeping.

And her armed aggression would have cut men down if her family were threatened. She was a force to be reckoned with. After that the family meant nothing to Blackstone and certainly, once he was wounded, he cared little about who nursed him. Christiana was a ward and it was the countess who kept her close. And so too Marcel. *Marcel!* What a fool I've been, he thought. Marcel wasn't his master's servant, his loyalty lay with Blanche de Harcourt. Christiana may have thought that she had bribed the servant to allow her to slip into his room the night of the hunt, but he would not have dared to risk disobeying the one person who controlled his life. Blanche de Harcourt. Christiana was the daughter of a knight, but, in truth, she carried no authority within the de Harcourt household. Marcel would only have let her into his room if he knew that his mistress would not be offended. Blanche de Harcourt knew they could not be kept apart much longer. She *allowed* it to happen.

Blackstone had not thought it through clearly enough. Blanche de Harcourt could never be her lord and husband's equal in this house, but she was a born noblewoman, with land and title of her own, and would influence her husband in any way she could to ensure his power. Blackstone's desperation was clearer now. It was as if he had to fight two battles at the same time. He had to discover why she would permit Christiana to become so intimate with him, and yet, as he believed, not tell her husband. Christ Jesus, he thought, I'm being pulled into something here that I have no control over. Jean de Harcourt had given friendship, and Blanche had allowed her ward to lose her virginity and fall in love with an Englishman.

It was Blanche who moved the pieces on the chessboard.

And Blackstone needed to find out what they were going to be.

CHAPTER NINETEEN

There was a buzz of excitement in the air as the servants prepared the Christmas Day feast. It was a time of the year when they would share in the joy and benevolence of their master who would grant them an audience to consider any grievance and to gift alms and food. Everyone would eat well and the pageboys would share in the festivities and help serve at the tables.

Blackstone climbed the ramparts and walked along the walls. The sentries respectfully lowered their eyes; none would dare show disrespect after what happened. Gaillard's wound was healing, and Meulon, the blacksmith's son who, all those years ago, had run away from home and gained seniority in his lordship's service, made it clear that they owed their lives to the Englishman. A French knight wouldn't save a man from a flogging and he wagered those bastard English knights wouldn't either.

Blackstone gazed across the landscape, watching the veering wind sweep the clouds along, taking his thoughts with them. Where was this place that he had been brought to? That he was south of Rouen and not that far from Paris he had discovered from snippets of conversation. Even Christiana did not know where the great cities lay, or where the powerful landowners held their estates. The world was a small place, defined only by their immediate surroundings and the tales of travellers. Men tramped to battlefields and left their blood to soak into a part of France of which they had no knowledge. To die without any understanding of a cause was a heresy, Blackstone thought. A man needs to know why his precious life is being offered into the hands of his enemy. And when had these thoughts begun? he asked himself. Thoughts and feelings that were once alien now possessed him as strongly as the anger that gave strength to his sword arm.

Had it only been a year ago that he was still leading his contented life in the village, and indulging in laughter and games at the village fair? He remembered the long run across the meadows and the swarming bees, with a ducking in the river to save himself from their stings. Times of being up to no good when the holy days kept them from working. How a man put food on his table with all those restrictions had never really occurred to him, but it all seemed so much simpler then. He was a free man blessed by the good grace of his lord and in care of a lumbering brother who could neither speak nor hear but who felt the breath of a moth's wings and sensed the hoof-fall of a newborn fawn. How had so much happened in such a short time? It had been only one Christmas past when they had taken food from the hands of Lord Marldon, and earned a cuff around the head from his reeve, for insolence. Would there be trout this far upstream again, Marldon had asked the young archer, and if there were would Blackstone and his brother leave enough for his lordship's keeper to have on his table? Blackstone could not remember his exact words in reply, but a cheeky response had made the reeve strike him. Lord Marldon had let it go at that because the boy was ignorant of the bond between his father and his lord.

Only a year ago, and now look where he was. He had been close to death, but the angels he saw that day when he lay at Crécy had sent him back to this world, to serve out his penance for not looking after his brother. There was no denying the heaviness of his doubt, for he did not know what lay in store for him. The pull he felt, like a silken thread that refused to break, was the desire to return to England. It was becoming stronger, made more tangible by the wounded William Harness. The man's despair at the loss of his companion echoed Blackstone's feelings about his brother. Both wanted retribution. Was it as simple as a need for vengeance? It seemed more complex than that. He didn't know, but whatever it was, it now steered his life. The Christmas celebrations were a time to ask for favours and if William Harness survived the next two or three days he would ask de Harcourt to release him from his patronage and let him make his way back, with the wounded herald, to the English lines at Calais. Once there he would present himself to his Prince and the King and then see where this new life would take him. Christiana would come with him because the two of them were now entwined in a passion that could only be destroyed by the Church's condemnation or the forced separation inflicted by Jean de Harcourt. Either one, Blackstone knew, he would ignore.

The boar's head occupied pride of place on the table, its eyes gazing sightlessly at the bejewelled and colourfully dressed men and women who laughed and shouted above the minstrels' music. Blackstone sat at the end of the table again but Christiana had been placed between Guy de Ruymont and his wife Joanna, with Jacques Brienne, an unmarried knight, sitting opposite her. He had already danced three times with her, and Christiana had studiously ignored Blackstone. Was he being punished for something? he wondered. Were Jean and Blanche de Harcourt making it clear that they knew of his intimacy with Christiana? Alone, and ignored, he sat and watched, a hapless spectator. None of the wives looked his way, and he had the sense of being shunned by the women, as if ordered by their husbands not to engage with him. He ate as delicately as he had been taught, but drank more wine than usual. There was little to do other than look interested in the goings-on and resent the finesse of Jacques Brienne as he guided Christiana in the dance with the other similarly adroit men and their wives.

Blackstone seized the opportunity to approach de Harcourt. 'My lord, my dancing skills are not required this evening. I would like to take William Harness some food.'

'Thomas, you *have* no dancing skills. You've the grace of a rooting boar snorting and grunting on the forest floor,' de Harcourt said, smiling to ease his protégé's discomfort.

'I can't argue with that, lord,' Blackstone said.

'You should show us a peasant dance, Blackstone,' said de Fossat who sat close by. 'We would be amused and informed as to how your kind celebrate.'

'My kind, lord, would be in a hovel with a smoking fire from damp wood, because the local lord does not permit dry kindling to be taken from his forest. We would have a jug of ale from the priest and a snared hare if we were lucky. There would be little cause to celebrate, and barely enough room to sleep, let alone dance.'

De Fossat reached out with his knife and pierced a piece of meat. 'Then you should go on bended knee before Lord de Harcourt every day and beg his forgiveness for being foisted upon him, and thank him for the onerous task he has had to perform.'

Blackstone knew he was being baited.

'I would go on my knee to him whenever he stood before me, but he has been gracious enough to demand little of me. To respect a man like my Lord de Harcourt is an honour a simple man like myself rarely has the privilege of doing. For others, it's a case of watching them squirm in the mud with a yard-long arrow sprouting from their gullet.'

'Mother of God, Thomas, you go too far,' said de Harcourt in a pained and angry whisper.

'My kind usually does, lord,' Blackstone answered and bowed his head.

William de Fossat choked and spluttered the chewed pieces of meat into his beard, and needed assistance from a servant, whom he pushed away angrily. His face darkened as his lungs fought for air, but he kept his eyes on Blackstone, who, without being seen by de Harcourt, smiled.

A baited trap could be sprung.

De Fossat lunged, but it was a foolish attempt from unrestrained anger and Blackstone needed only to take a step back as his attacker sprawled across the table. The sudden disturbance made the others turn towards him.

'Manners, William!' Louis de Vitry cried light-heartedly. 'Too much wine and you'll miss midnight Mass! Or is that the idea?'

Some of the younger barons laughed, as did their wives, but de Mainemares scowled disapprovingly.

'No laughter at the expense of our Lord Jesus,' he said to de Vitry, who did not know how to respond to the public reprimand, so he allowed a smile and an inclination of his head to acknowledge the older man's authority and religious commitment.

While de Fossat recovered, Jean de Harcourt gave a small gesture of dismissal to Blackstone. 'Go, Thomas, and don't come back. Words can be more cruel than actions. It is something you should remember.' Blackstone bowed and left the room. The music had not stopped and few heard what de Fossat said to his friend and host.

'I'll not be insulted, Jean. He must answer to me.'

'No, William, I'll not have you fight him,' de Harcourt answered, leaning across to make sure his answer was understood.

'First blood and I'll be satisfied,' de Fossat insisted. 'First blood,' he insisted.

De Harcourt shook his head and gripped his friend's arm. 'William, you cannot beat him.'

De Fossat's shocked face showed that de Harcourt's warning had aggravated the insult. De Harcourt shook his head in almost sad confirmation at his friend's disbelief.

'No man in this room can.'

Blackstone laid another piece of wood on the fire in the room where Harness sat propped up in bed. Warmth had built up during the day from its constant burning, but a wounded man was still vulnerable to the night chills.

'Now will you eat the food I've brought?' Blackstone asked, having been bidden to stoke the fire.

'A morsel might pass my lips, Thomas.'

'Aye, you'd rip the haunch off a sheep and call it a morsel,' Blackstone said, and settled the tray with its plate of food on the man's lap. He held the cup of mulled wine to his lips and let him sip slowly, being careful not to let him gag and cause a coughing fit.

'That goes to the groin. Another day of this luxury and I'll take myself a whore. My God, Thomas, you've found yourself a nest. Like a damned cuckoo you've got them feeding you without thinking twice.'

Blackstone noticed that Harness had some colour in his face, though his eyes were still sunken and his cheekbones stretched the skin of his face. 'Yes, I've been well protected. My life was lost, but here I am.'

Harness nodded, chewing the meat with his mouth open. There were few teeth at the back of his jaw and those at the front were blackened. He gnawed on the cuts like a rabbit, saliva dribbling and tongue working the flesh into manageable pieces to swallow. Blackstone was surprised at his own reaction. The manners he had been taught and the delicacy with which those who sat at the table in the great hall ate were more a part of him now than he had realized. Harness slurped the wine, giving a contented belch and sigh.

'You'd be a smart lad to milk this whore's teat, Thomas. Oh yes, very smart. You'll put some fat on your bones that'll get you through the winter, then you'll be fit and ready to be coming home.'

Blackstone didn't answer. His birthday had come and gone weeks ago without mention, and the memory of his birthplace and life before the war still burned bright. 'Yes,' he finally said, 'I'd like to go home. I'd like to be a mason again. That means something. It has a value that a man can live by.'

Harness shook his head. 'Not these days. You need a lord's blessing and his purse. Builders are ten a penny. Men can't feed themselves or their families. No, no, lad, you do some fighting to earn your keep. That's how fortunes are made, let me tell you. I've seen knights ransom their enemy captives and buy estates. Men who were little more than squires. Piss-poor. Not a decent nag to ride nor sword that'd cut a loaf of bread. But...' he ate and drank again, gulping air so words could get past the tortured meat on his tongue, '... a few lucky strokes, and a wealthy bastard ready to put himself on parole until his ransom is paid, and suddenly they're drinking from glass or silver and marrying ugly women for their dowry and fucking maidservants for their pleasure.'

The effort of talking and eating caused him to pause to steady his breathing. The spittle in the corner of his mouth was tinged with blood. Blackstone had heard that a man on his deathbed might suddenly recover and eat like a starving man, and then be dead within a day or two. It was as if the body needed nourishment for its final journey. Harness settled back against the pillows, and placed his hand on Blackstone's arm. 'Good. That was good. You've done William Harness proud, Master Thomas. You've saved his life and given him succour, and he's grateful, he is.' He nodded, agreeing with himself. 'And look at us. Eh? Two scrag-end shanks of mutton lying in feather beds with linen and pillows. I've never known it before.'

'No. Nor me,' said Blackstone, easing away the tray. 'I still sleep on the floor when I'm alone.'

Harness had quietened, sated by the food and warmth. 'Alone? Then you've a woman in your bed when you're not,' he said.

Blackstone matched the man's smile. 'I have.'

'Even with a face that could make a horse shy in fright?'

'Even with.'

'You either pay her too much or you have her heart.'

Blackstone eased the bedding up onto the man's chest. 'I've never paid, William. Not yet at least.'

Harness closed his eyes ready for sleep. 'We all pay, lad. We all pay. Be it with pain or money. Satan's bait will ruin us one way or the other. You'll see.'

That night Blackstone waited for Christiana, but she did not come to his room. He realized he had probably gone too far when he was with her in the chapel, because her feelings of guilt were not his. It could have been that or the deliberate snub at the banquet that had given her the power over him because he could not deny the feelings that welled up inside of him. Being outspoken and, at times, uncaring could cost him more than retribution from the Norman baron, who could also tear away the woman who held his affection. It seemed to be another lesson to bring him out of the uncomplicated life he once had. It was obvious that if he were to succeed in his own plans and fight once more for his sovereign lord, then his affections must be controlled and reined in so that he would be in command. If not, he would fall to a woman's whim. There could be no thought of subjugation, nor was there much doubt in his mind that whatever road lay ahead it was probably a lonely one. He would fight for Christiana, because that is what he had done from the beginning, but there would be no bending of his will. He could not challenge the superiority of noble families, and would always have to bow before them. He reached out his hand to the sword that lay on the sill, then, resting his open palm on the cold steel, promised himself that he would never allow himself to be humiliated by the word or deed of others, and especially not of his own heart.

Surely, he thought, she could not have abandoned him so freely for another man, and certainly not one who danced like a girl? Blackstone remembered what it had felt like when he was a boy with the body of a man and one of the village girls had taunted him. His inexperience when they were having sex had caused him embarrassment, but there had been no jealousy when she had gone off with another of the boys. The moment with the girl had passed, and he remembered there had been no anger, only the desire to make sure his humiliation didn't happen again. He soon learnt how to be with a woman. Perhaps he and Richard, being the two strongest boys in their shire, stood out from other peasants. Both were better bowmen and both took every day as it was offered. A carefree freedom, punished only by hard work and those in authority. Being a freeman had already set him on a path different to most. And the war had plucked him from that small community and hurled him into the greater world. Now another kind of force was tugging at him. Christiana's rejection was nothing compared to what he had already endured, but the thought of her being with another man stabbed like a knife beneath his breastbone. And that was something he had never experienced before.

A few paces away from his door Marcel lay curled in another doorway. Blackstone nudged him with the toe of his boot and the servant quickly awoke and got to his feet. Darkness smothered both of them, but the shifting clouds allowed some light from the moon.

'Take me to Lady Christiana,' Blackstone said.

He saw the man's eyes widen, and then his head nod. The wind moaned through the corridor's open archways as Marcel reached for a tallow-soaked torch to light. 'You don't need that. It will alert a sentry on the wall. You know this place inside out; you could take me there with your eyes closed.'

'As you wish, Sir Thomas,' the man whispered obediently.

Blackstone followed him along the corridor and up one of the narrow staircases. It became virtually pitch black and Blackstone found himself reaching out with one hand to hold Marcel's belt as his other followed the rough walls. Like a blind man being led he stumbled once or twice, feet catching a sleeping servant, and then another narrow corridor opened before them and once again he could see brief reflections from the night sky. There was only one door. Marcel stopped.

'Sir Thomas,' he said, barely above a whisper, 'my lord and lady's quarters are on the floor below.' He took a breath. 'Sound travels,' he said, daring to warn the Englishman, who seemed so intent as to disregard any thoughts of discovery, which meant that the servant would face the more severe punishment.

'Wait here,' Blackstone told him quietly and felt the man stiffen from the unexpected command.

Would she have dared to take Jacques Brienne to her bed? Blackstone asked himself. And if she had, what was he going to do? He dared himself to go into her room. It was the knowing that was important. His hand closed on the wooden bolt; it was worn from years of use, but he slid it carefully, making the rasp of wood little more than a whisper. The dull embers from the fire gave enough light for him to see the bed. He stepped further into the room. The bed was empty and had not been slept in. She's gone to him, he said to himself, the bitterness of his own thoughts surprising him. Heady wine and music and the courtly attention of a nobleman was perhaps no different from a raucous alehouse with a fiddle player. Men drank, women flirted and both lusted for the pleasures of the flesh.

He stepped back to where Marcel waited, back pressed against the wall. 'Where is Count Brienne's room?'

Marcel shook his head. 'I dare not, Sir Thomas. If you do that everything is lost. You condemn yourself to breaking the code of trust given to you by my Lord de Harcourt,' he begged plaintively.

Jealousy gripped Blackstone as tightly as he now held Marcel's tunic. 'Is she there? You follow her like a dog. You know where she is. Is she with him?' As he muttered the words he regretted them immediately. He had exposed his true feelings to a servant who could betray him for reward. He let the man go, and steadied his breathing.

The wind carried the faint sound of a distant monastery's bell calling the monks to prayer, rousing them from their beds a bare few hours before dawn. Three hours earlier Blackstone had sat with William Harness as the bell for midnight Mass rang out. 'Angel's Mass, Thomas, we should pray,' the wounded man had said, and tried to get out of bed to go onto his knees. Tears had welled in his eyes. 'That poor boy still hangs rotting without a Christian burial. It's ungodly, Thomas. We must pray for his soul.'

Blackstone had lifted him carefully and eased him from the bed and Harness let his bare knees press onto the stone floor. He leaned across the bed for support, clasping his hands together in fervent thanks that the light of salvation would be granted at this, the darkest hour of the darkest night of the year. Blackstone remembered when, as a child, he had been whipped by the village priest for keeping his eyes open as he searched the church's grim darkness for both the light and the angels. Neither had appeared.

It's pagan, Thomas. The winter solstice has been celebrated before that village whoremonger of a priest ever uttered a prayer. His father's words echoed back to him as he treated the beaten boy. The dawn bell for the Shepherd's Mass would soon ring and more hours of prayer would consume the faithful. Had she slept with Brienne between the call for prayer? She was a virgin when he took her that night; had he released an uncontrolled passion within her? The persistent doubts muddied his thoughts.

'Master Thomas,' Marcel said, 'what must I do?'

The man's whispers brought Blackstone's mind back to the dark corridor. He sighed. There was a line a man should not cross, especially when a woman was involved. 'Guide me back to my room, Marcel. It's Christmas Day – there should be charity in a man's heart.'

As he reached the corridor that led to his room the wind gusted and made him turn his face from its stinging chill. As he did so he saw the thin line of flickering light across the courtyard. He dismissed Marcel, whose duty beckoned him to attend the household that would soon rise. Blackstone made his way down the passageways, guided by the intermittent light from the shifting sky. By the time he reached the courtyard his hearing adjusted to the sheltered area. The light he had seen was gone, but then appeared again as a heavy door creaked back and forth. It was the chapel. A figure stepped outside the door, briefly silhouetted and then plunged into darkness, only to reappear a moment later carrying a flaring torch. The hulking shadow of the devout Jean Malet, Lord de Graville, came towards him on the same path where he stood.

'Is that you, Blackstone?' the older man asked, raising the flame to cast its glow.

'It is, lord.'

'I thought you barbarian archers desecrated churches, not prayed in them,' he said, the wind fanning sparks from the tallow.

'I'm no longer an archer, my lord. Besides, I saw the light.'

'Is that humour or has Jesus' benevolence reached even your dark soul?'

'I meant I saw the light from the chapel,' Blackstone said, noting the scowl on de Graville's furrowed brow.

'Aye, well, I thought it too much to expect that you would

offer prayers before the morning's Mass. I'm off to piss and then get back on my knees. Leave the chapel be, Master Thomas, if you've no intention of begging forgiveness from the Almighty. De Harcourt's ward has been in there longer than I have and she shouldn't be disturbed or frightened by young men prowling like tomcats in the night.'

De Graville pushed past him, leaving him in the darkness of the windswept yard.

Blackstone closed the church door quietly behind him. The dozen candles flickering in the chapel added no warmth. It was as cold as a tomb. Of the dozen or so long benches and stools only one held a figure, who sat huddled in the corner. She was wrapped in her heavy cape, the cowl pulled over her head, her shoulders hunched, a murmur of prayer from her lips barely showed her breath in the chilled air. Blackstone moved closer, walking as quietly as he could and then sitting at the far end of the bench from her. He waited silently, gazing at the crucifix and the shadow it cast. Mankind was damned, he knew that, every monk and priest confirmed those of this world were conceived and born in sin. Life was a perilous journey with the sole aim of seeking salvation. That's why the rich shed their wealth and fine clothes and were dressed in sackcloth or the habit of a mendicant monk or nun when they died. Humble before the Lord. Blackstone snorted and his unconscious sound of disbelief caused Christiana to turn. She seemed to have been in a dream state; her eyes blinked at him and looked red from tears.

'Thomas, you've come to Mass,' she said, with a note of disbelief.

Should he lie? He feared God's unseen hand as much as any man, but would he be struck down beneath the shadow of the cross if he did? How far could Blackstone allow his defiance?

'Yes. I didn't know you would be here.' Only half a lie then.

She smiled with unconcealed relief and her hand reached out for him. He moved next to her, hating the chapel's dank smell and the threatening images of the wall paintings, wishing he could take her into the wilderness and let the winter months pass elsewhere – just the two of them.

'You didn't come at midnight,' she said.

'No, I was with the Englishman. He needed help to get out of bed and pray. So I stayed with him,' he told her, without mention of his jealousy. And no candle flickered or sky broke with lightning as the half-truths slipped from his lips. 'Why did you ignore me at the banquet?'

She bowed her head. 'I wanted to punish you. For your harshness towards me,' she whispered.

'When have I ever been that to you?'

'Here. You blasphemed. You ignored my wishes and my feelings.'

It was a simple choice, he realized. Either he asked for her forgiveness or she asked for his. He wanted her and perhaps that was worth the surrender. He was about to speak when she saved his pride.

'But now I see how wrong I was to do that,' she said, and held his rough hand in hers. 'Forgive me, Thomas. I know you carry pain at the loss of your brother, but by coming here you've shown a willingness to seek God's help.'

So, he realized, she thought him contrite. He could not have wished for a better outcome had he prayed for one.

She waited for his answer, frowning her concern that he might deny her.

He knew what he felt for her. That he loved her was beyond question and now his doubts about her were unfounded. All was well again, but if vows were made in a place of worship then his were that he would never allow those uncontrolled emotions to seize him again. He smothered her hand with his own. Remaining in this uninviting and penitent place for Mass would impress the noblemen and bind her to him better than any words he might conjure.

'There's nothing to forgive,' he told her.

The distant bell rang again, beckoning the Christmas Day dawn to bring light into the world.

CHAPTER TWENTY

Those who worshipped retired for the warmth of the fire and food before de Harcourt brought his guests together for the sacred day's celebration, although, Blackstone thought, it would take little to find some comfort from the droning liturgy of the invited priest who had conducted the Mass. He was impervious to the rain as he waited for Christiana to come out of the chapel with Blanche de Harcourt, who insisted on paying the priest with silver from her own purse. With a calm patience he believed his plan had worked, because the noblemen and their wives had acknowledged, though grudgingly, his presence. It was only when Guy de Ruymont escorted his wife from the chapel into the half-hearted storm that it seemed his subterfuge had not gone unnoticed.

De Ruymont said, 'A hard bench and a cold floor focus a man's mind like a hangman's rope, Master Thomas. I know which I prefer, but a man of rank should be able to pay a begging monk to take the penance.' He smiled at Blackstone before his wife turned back to see what held him in the cold rain and her glaring disapproval changed his expression to a scowl. 'Smiling at the enemy is a sin in our household, but the day will come, I hope, when you will not be considered as such. Good Christmas Day to you, young Englishman.' He stepped after his wife, but then turned. 'Praying with the enemy was a clever ploy,' he said quickly, and then caught up with his wife and escorted her inside.

Was it that obvious? thought Blackstone. Guy de Ruymont was shrewd and seemingly less malevolent than most of the others and Blackstone would happily gamble that no one else considered that his own attendance, seated humbly at the rear of the chapel, was anything other than it appeared. Perhaps, though, Guy de Ruymont's gesture was one of possible acceptance and forgiveness for the carnage wrought at Crécy. It was not unknown for knights from opposing armies to join together to fight for a common cause. Which cause? And when? he wondered. Moments later Christiana came through the door, her arm linked through the countess's. With short, quick steps, like two village girls rushing to get out of the rain, they ran past Blackstone. Blanche barely glanced in his direction and Christiana modestly kept her eyes down. This time he allowed the rejection to sweep over him. Just as Blackstone had to play a game, so had she. Blackstone abandoned the cold courtyard. If the French followed the English traditions de Harcourt would be gathering gifts of cloth and new livery for his servants to mark St Stephen's Day, once this day's feasting and prayers ended.

He decided he would let the Normans break their fast from the previous night, and wait until he was summoned. A pinprick of conscience, as sharp as a splinter from Christ's cross, insisted he apologize to de Harcourt for the remark he had made to William de Fossat. It was a calculated taunt, and ill-mannered. His decision came quickly: he would not do so. The belligerent Frenchman could choke on his own hatred. Blackstone's plan was to leave for Calais as soon as William Harness was able to travel. He had grown to like the man and felt a duty to return the King's messenger safely. Everything was now clear. King Edward would take the French crown, and he would take Christiana home to England. The rain eased and for a few moments the watery sun showed itself, spear shafts of light piercing the grey clouds. God's angels were showing him the way.

Christiana helped Blanche change out of her damp dress and the sombre woollen garment, worn for the Mass, slipped from her shoulders. A more colourful and elegant gown was chosen. As Christiana draped the jewelled necklace around her guardian's neck, she glanced out of the window, seeing Blackstone walking the ramparts.

'You know they're going to use him,' said Blanche de Harcourt, catching her attention.

'Who will?' Christiana asked, aware that her attention had wandered.

'Those who gather here with my lord and husband.'

Blanche de Harcourt fussed the necklace until it sat squarely. The largest stone was the emerald and she nestled it between her throat and her cleavage. 'He's an asset to them, and he has a fearlessness that they are prepared to squander.'

Christiana's fingers hesitated as she fastened the necklace's clasp. How much of her care or interest in Thomas Blackstone should she allow the countess to see? 'No one can make Blackstone do anything that he would not choose to do himself,' she said.

Blanche sat in a chair by the window, glancing down to see Blackstone preferring the bite of the weather to the comfort of his room. She pulled her needlepoint stand towards her. She would have an hour of privacy before the day's festivities began.

'He's a weapon in their hands,' said Blanche, easing the needle through the cloth.

'And he could beat any of them now,' Christiana said defensively, feeling a flush of emotion warm her neck.

Blanche de Harcourt noticed that her ward kept her eyes lowered as she splayed the damp dress across a screen in order to deter the creases, but that her hands trembled. These two young people were being drawn together and she had played a part in it. If Christiana was in love with Thomas Blackstone then a poor knight's daughter would be yielding to a man who, she felt, would one day achieve notoriety. If he lived long enough.

'Yes, Thomas is a fine swordsman,' said Blanche. 'I've watched him practise, but we women have to ask ourselves whether we wish that the men we love and honour should be more than blunt instruments that can club others to death.'

Christiana was becoming flustered. It was unusual, Blanche decided. She knew that when Sir Godfrey's men had captured the brigands those months ago, Christiana had denied them clemency.

She had the makings of a strong woman, of that there was no doubt. Nursing Blackstone and softening his rough edges with music and poetry had helped subdue the man's coarseness, and yet Christiana was barely able to contain her temper.

'He's more than that,' Christiana said, lifting her head to gaze directly at Blanche. 'He is... aware. Of beauty and nature. His father taught him many things and he cared for and loved his brother who was a deaf mute. He's more than you think, my lady.'

That was better, thought Blanche. Spirited, but controlled, a bold response. 'And you presume to know my thoughts, child?' she said coldly, deliberately wanting to see what kind of response she could elicit.

'I do not, but you don't know him as I do,' Christiana said carefully, knowing she could so easily blurt out her true feelings for the Englishman. 'I've seen his courage; he rescued me when my enemies almost captured me. He disobeyed orders to come back for me. He risked a flogging.'

'Then perhaps he's an opportunist, Christiana. Foolhardy acts of bravery mean nothing. There has to be more than a man being driven by lust.'

'No, you are wrong about him,' Christiana answered, desperately trying to keep the fog of anger from her mind. 'I was there when the English Prince told everyone that Thomas had honoured his word when he went back across the river to rescue me.'

'Like I said, a blunt instrument,' said Blanche, dismissively, keeping her eyes deliberately on her needlepoint. 'Coarse and rough.'

'He has honour, and tenderness! He has a kindness that you have not seen, a gentleness that is unusual in a man. He speaks softly and beautifully when we...' She bit her lip. Her mouth had gone dry, but perspiration beaded her brow. She needed to breathe slowly, to suffocate the passion that threatened everything.

Blanche looked kindly at her ward. 'When you – talk?'

Christiana nodded, helpless and obvious in her guilt.

Blanche de Harcourt made no further comment. Her fingers held the taut linen, the needle pierced the cloth, pulling the thread through as she finished a section of the embroidery: a dragon representing the threat to all women and the blood-red heart held in its talons.

The day went well, with entertainment and enough dancing and eating to last Blackstone a month. He kept his presence as far in the shadows as he could, never yielding to the dance, or being drawn into conversation by any of the barons whose aim would surely be to antagonize him and lure him into confrontation. There were moments when Christiana happened to find herself standing close to him as she waited for one of the wives or their husband to draw her back into the celebrations. The two barely spoke, though there was an anticipation between them, but Blackstone knew that the festivities meant that he would not have her in his bed again soon in the coming days. Jean de Harcourt and his guests played games; the older barons, de Graville and Mainemares, huddled over a chessboard; all gave him plenty of opportunity to slip away and return to William Harness where they would sit before the fire and talk of England. The injured man was still weak; at times his breathing was laboured and he often drifted off to sleep, sometimes in mid-sentence. Blackstone kept the fire going, content to be the sleeping man's guardian. Once when Harness awoke Blackstone was fingering the embroidered piece of cloth that Christiana had given him. Harness reached out his hand.

'A token, is it?' he said, in barely a whisper. 'Let's see it, then.'

Blackstone laid it in his hand and Harness turned it this way and that. 'That's very clever, that is. Whichever way you look at it the bird is swooping. Your lady give you that, did she?'

Blackstone nodded and let the man's insistence of being told the story finally make him relate the events of how he first met Christiana and then carried her across the river at Blanchetaque.

Harness sat, like a child being told a fable. When Blackstone finished he said, 'I was with the King then. You archers made him glow with pride, you and the men-at-arms that were at your shoulder. You lads did a grand job but I never saw you swim that river with the girl. I wish I had. That would be something to tell your children about. I had no idea who you were, young Master Blackstone.'

'There was no reason you should.'

He wheezed indignantly. 'Nah! What? Me the King's mouthpiece? Me what carries the messages? We heard of the young archer. We heard all right. We knew what had happened. Soldiers like nothing better than to spin a line and catch a fish or three. Your stature, and that's a word I've heard used by Cobham himself talking about our sovereign lord, the stature of the young archer grew like a beanstalk. You must have killed a hundred men by now if they're still talking about it, which they will be. And why not? Sir Thomas Blackstone, eh? But I know you now and when I get back I'll be telling them all about you and that you're alive.'

They talked of the war and how the King's messenger had seen so little of it, being held in the rear echelon waiting for the command to ride just like the other twenty or so men who were paid by the King's purse to carry his word. Harness was too lowly to know the great fighting earls, and the battles fought were a mystery to him. The sound of warfare and killing was what he remembered, the clash of battle and screams that came in a wave of anger and fear sweeping up over the hills. The conversations were stilted as it did not take long for Harness to tire, slipping away into sleep, and always with a sad exclamation of what the villagers had done to the young man who rode with him into that village.

St Stephen's Day followed Christmas Day and the servants were granted their favours and gifted with presents. Villagers brought humble offerings to their lord and he in turn, along with the other noblemen, handed out alms to the poor, the blind and lame. De Harcourt walked among them with Blanche as Blackstone watched from a distance. Some of the noblemen handed the coins to their squires to give to the outstretched hands, not wishing to have physical contact with the villeins. It was also a day of remembrance for Blackstone to reflect upon. His father had always made him pray before they set off for Lord Marldon's favour. St

Stephen the martyr was the patron saint of stonemasons and every artisan should honour his saint, insisted his father. Blackstone knew nothing more than that, but he would always honour the hour with a prayer for his father. And now for his brother. No vision of St Stephen ever appeared to bless him or thank him for his prayers, so Blackstone kept the prayer brief and the memory of father and brother bright.

De Harcourt and the others made no attempt to hunt or ride out during the holy week as one saint's day followed another, and meat was forsaken for fish, and fish for fowl and it seemed that whatever flew free in the sky ended up on a platter. Woodcock, pigeon or common housebird, swan or goose cooked in wood-fired ovens or nestled in their embers, they were smothered in honey and saffron, a delicacy for the noblemen. And Blackstone took a morsel from each meal, the rich palette of sauces more disagreeable than common fare, but he fed William Harness, and ordered less exotic fare from the kitchen for himself. It seemed by week's end that the surfeit of food and prayer tired even the most stalwart of de Harcourt's guests and none had raised argument against him. He hoped that the jester called Luck was turning the wheel of good fortune towards him.

He was walking the battlements, having a word or two with the soldiers on duty – unimportant matters: the weather, the possibility of approaching storms, the silence and the emptiness of the landscape in this, their place of duty – when a movement caught Blackstone's eye. It was not unusual for low-lying mist to cling to the belly of land, stubbornly refusing to shift until late in the day. A ghostly haze of lemon-tinged vapour lay beyond the landscape at the edge of the forest where the silver ground remained untouched by villagers or horsemen. Now, shadows moved across it. A banner fluttered, still too far away for him to make it out. He glanced quickly at the sentries who stood on the walls between him and the next side tower; another sentry was down at the bridge across the moat checking villagers who needed access to the castle.

'Horsemen!' he called, and saw the sentries scan the horizon.

Meulon ran out of the watchtower's guardroom, pulling on his helmet. 'Stand to arms!' he shouted, then leaned over the parapet. 'Below!' he called to the man at the bridge. 'Inside!'

The bridge sentry pushed the villagers clear of the entrance and ran for the gate. If this was an attack they would go under the sword before he would.

'I've lost them,' one of the sentries called, scanning the horizon.

Blackstone peered into the poor light, but his eyesight was keen and he saw the brief flutter of the banner as it showed itself from the undulating ground.

'Your lord's banner! North-east!' he cried, pointing out to where the column of horsemen would soon appear in the distance. It was the de Harcourt armorial flag of red and gold bars, followed by a half-dozen riders who turned and headed straight for the castle. Before the men's faces could be seen Blackstone already knew that it was the bull-like figure of Sir Godfrey who led them. Was the war won?

Blackstone pounded down the steps into the courtyard, a grim satisfaction that the tug of the leg wound was a tightening of his muscle and nothing more. As he reached the gatehouse he saw Jean de Harcourt moving down the castle's steps followed by the other noblemen.

The wind carried the thudding sound of hooves as de Harcourt peered through the spy latch in the gate, the soldiers ready to open the main gate once he gave the command. Blackstone stood back, watching de Harcourt's concern. Obviously his uncle was not expected.

'It's Sir Godfrey, my lord. I'd recognize him at five hundred paces,' Blackstone said.

'You've an archer's eye, Thomas, but dishonourable men can hide beneath a surcoat and a helm and bring enemies into your house.'

'It's him. I swear it,' Blackstone answered confidently.

De Harcourt peered towards the distant fringe of woodland,

waiting until the approaching men were less than two hundred yards away. 'Open the gates!' he commanded, and moments later when the great doors swung open the horses were already clattering across the wooden bridge. Noblemen and servants alike pressed back as the marshal of the English army rode into the outer bailey. The horses billowed steam, their flanks heaving. They had been ridden hard.

Sir Godfrey dismounted with the ease of a man half his age. He quickly embraced his nephew and glanced at the gathered men. Blackstone saw that a mixture of emotions ran among them. Sir Godfrey was their enemy but kinsman to their host. All had fought the English but here was the open traitor among them. Antagonism towards their own King was one thing, but for some of those present to welcome a man who had helped lay waste to their lands was another.

'Cool them down, then feed and water them,' Sir Godfrey commanded the stable-hands who ran forward to hold the bridles. 'Pack food and drink for my men! We leave within the hour!'

Then he turned quickly, taking Jean de Harcourt by the elbow, and limped towards the great hall, followed by the half-dozen mud-spattered men who fanned out protectively behind him. He had not glanced in Blackstone's direction, which made him feel an inexplicable pang of loss.

'You're safe here,' Blackstone heard Jean de Harcourt say to his uncle, glancing nervously at the men who came behind them, each with a hand resting on the pommel of his sword.

'Nowhere is safe for me, Jean. Not any longer,' Sir Godfrey told him without breaking his limping stride.

'Sir Godfrey!' de Fossat called after him. 'Are you here to give us the English terms of surrender?'

The noblemen bristled as the old warrior turned to face them. 'I'm here to see my nephew. If I'd have known you'd be here, de Fossat, I'd have brought more men to protect my back.'

'Damn you, Godfrey, we're here at his invitation and you know why!' de Fossat spat back, unafraid of the older man's status.

'Then you'll wait until you're sent for,' Sir Godfrey told him.

'Have you won?' Henri Livay asked. 'Has Edward taken the crown from Philip?'

'While you hunt and gossip the war has ground to a halt. The great King Philip is in Paris behind bolted doors,' Sir Godfrey told him, his emphasis on *great* heavy with sarcasm. 'Edward is with his Queen, starving out Calais. I'll summon you when I'm ready!' And with that dismissal he urged his nephew up the steps of the inner ward towards the great hall.

William de Fossat made as if to step forward and confront Sir Godfrey, but de Mainemares held his arm.

'There's trouble. Leave him be. He'll tell us in his own time. We're in this together. Like it or not, we have to wait for him,' he said.

Rebuffed by Sir Godfrey, the humiliated noblemen shook themselves like peacocks, choking on their anger; only de Mainemares and de Graville seemed unconcerned as they moved away together like two men who understood that patience was needed.

De Mainemares' words to de Fossat were not lost on Blackstone, but he ignored the flustered nobles and made his way discreetly behind Sir Godfrey and his nephew. What was the old fighter doing here now? he wondered. It had to be important and he offered little if any respect to the other noblemen. They may be enemies, but there's obviously a link between all these men, he thought.

Sir Godfrey's men looked efficient and alert despite what must have been a long ride. Blackstone desperately wanted to reach the small gallery that overlooked the hall from one of de Harcourt's private rooms before the doors below were guarded. He turned down the passageway where a small oak door gave access to steps up to a half-landing and then another dozen more that opened into the solar. He prayed that Blanche de Harcourt was not there with the other wives, or that personal servants were not in the family's private room. He paused, held his breath, and listened beyond the thudding of his heart. The solar was empty. He crossed the floor, then went up a few more steps. He pressed his back against the wall and carefully lifted the wooden spindle latch, closing the door behind him. A floorboard creaked under his weight. He froze, not daring to move and look over the edge of the gallery. The men had already entered, the heavy chestnut doors below buffeting the air as they shut.

'Mother of God, Jean, this is an unholy mess. But I had to come and warn you.'

There was the clink of glass, a bottle glugged its contents and a metal object – that had to be Sir Godfrey's helm, Blackstone thought – clattered onto the table.

'About what? My King can't doubt me or the others. We bled for Philip!'

'Aye, that'll keep suspicion at bay for a while. There's a death sentence on me now, Jean,' Sir Godfrey said after slurping the drink. 'More. I need it.' Again the sound of liquid being poured reached Blackstone. *You want to hear a rabbit move? Or a deer step ladylike through the forest? Open your jaw, lad – let the sound reach you. Every poacher learns that.* Blackstone slackened his jaw slightly, easing the tension, remembering his father's lesson. The words below became subdued but Blackstone could hear the muted tension clearly enough.

'Edward is not going to pursue Philip into Paris.'

'He's given up?'

'No, he's settled for the territory he wanted. Imagine fighting through that warren of streets – Christ, it'd be worse than Caen! Every pot maker and whore could trap and kill the men.'

'Then they've signed a truce?' Jean asked.

'Not yet, and there's no sign of one. So this grand war of conquest has turned out to be nothing more than a goddamned raid!' A glass smashed.

'Then Edward has abandoned you?' said Jean incredulously. 'After giving him the Cotentin, St Lô, Caen? And how much more slaughter could you have done against us at Crécy? We chose badly, but I couldn't convince Father to relinquish his duty to the King. You'll have more than bitterness to contend with here, uncle!'

These men were waiting for a treaty. They were waiting to side with you! Is there nothing you can say to Edward?'

'He'll take Calais eventually – that gives him everything he needs. It's his gateway into France. No, he's not abandoned me, but I'm adrift in the slurry of shit that will sweep down upon me. The garrison at Caen has broken out and slaughtered the men we left to guard the city. My men have been killed at home. What remained of my lands is seized. The French have regained much of what we took. Edward doesn't have the money to pursue this war and Philip is bankrupt. Christ Jesus! I have to go and beg forgiveness in Paris or we've lost everything.'

'The King will never forgive you. Never. He's a vengeful man. He'll want your head on a pike for us all to see.'

There was silence and the sound of a weary man slumping into a chair. 'It has to be done. It's more than my life that matters now. Edward will come back. Normandy must be sworn to the English crown. Then we control our own destiny.'

'I followed my father and saw him die. This family stands divided because of Philip and his weakness, but I won't give myself to the English, nor will the others. Not now!'

Sir Godfrey sighed. 'I know that. Sweet Jesus, I thought Edward was going to sweep all before him. Listen, Jean, we need to keep the others under control. If I am reprieved it means we take longer to coerce the King. He has lost this war, and if Edward cannot finish the job now the time will come when he will. One day he'll call on us again and we have to be ready.'

There was an uncomfortable silence. Then Jean de Harcourt said, 'I'll get the others. You tell them yourself.'

Blackstone heard de Harcourt move across the floor.

'Jean! Wait. There's a reason I needed to talk to you first. Blackstone, did he live?'

Blackstone could barely resist taking the few paces forward and calling down. *I'm here, Sir Godfrey*, he wanted to shout. There were questions tumbling from his mind. Who lived, who died at Crécy? Did any of my archers survive? He felt his heart pulse in his throat at the mention of his own name and what might be said about him.

'Thomas? Yes.'

'Is he strong? Capable?'

'He's a fighter. Crude, belligerent, and damned insolent. But he saved my life and I offered him my friendship. And you should tell your Prince and your King that the man he asked our family to protect is safe and well. We honour our pledges, Godfrey, even to our enemies. Let Edward mark that and remember us for it. For the future.'

'His presence could cause your arrest. Philip is using mercenaries to root out Englishmen and Gascons who hold French towns. They'll come here and they'll want him. A man who saved the Prince at Crécy is a prize. He's worthless for ransom, so they'll kill him and make an example of him.'

Blackstone's mind raced. Was that why Sir Godfrey had brought his men? To take him prisoner? Would he be offered as a sacrifice to the King of France to help Sir Godfrey save his own life? The voice in his head told him to calm down, but it fought the surge of anger that threatened to overtake him. Escape from the castle and back to the English lines was his only hope.

Jean de Harcourt said, 'They have no idea he's here. How could they know?'

'Because he killed some of the mercenaries who hold Chaulion and sent a message warning them to stay off your land!'

'Then so what? They're bastard skinners who don't need any mercy.'

'Jean, those who hold Chaulion do so at the command of Philip.'

Both men fell silent for a moment.

'He's using them to keep the English from taking towns,' said Sir Godfrey. 'He can't pay them so they take what they want without fear of being stopped. They offer protection to those who want it. It serves the King twice over. Why do you think I came here? To warn you. Blackstone let one of them live but he saw your men's livery.'

'How do you know this?'

'We intercepted one of their messengers. He spewed bile and information before we killed him but the other escaped. They've sent word to Paris that you harbour an Englishman favoured by Edward. The King will send a warrant of arrest and he'll have routiers riding for him. Those scum will be here, Jean. Be warned. They're coming.'

'I'll not hand him over to mercenaries,' said de Harcourt, 'even with a royal warrant.'

Blackstone's gratitude and relief nearly swamped him.

'You do what you want, but you'll have barely a few days to decide. Have you told Blackstone what role he was to play in our plans?'

There it was, Blackstone realized, the snare that held him was being tightened by the grand poacher himself.

'Not yet.'

'Then say nothing. If he's taken he could have every one of you hanged. All right, get the others in here; I'll tell them about Edward at Calais and try to keep them on the leash until fortune favours us again. But I wouldn't count on them helping you to shield Blackstone.'

Blackstone eased away from the gallery as gently as he could down the stairs into the lower corridor. He had heard enough. There was a conspiracy between these men and he needed to find out what had been planned for him. He did not yet know how he would find out, but when he did he would take Christiana to Calais and serve King Edward again.

Sir Godfrey's arrival caused a flurry of activity, but also unsettled the servants and the men who guarded the walls. That he had been allowed free entry into the castle showed that Jean de Harcourt was allowing the English King's ally into the heart of his enemy.

Meulon saw Blackstone make his way through the colonnade. He raised his hand to attract his attention and, when he stopped, ran down to him. 'Sir Thomas, can you tell me what's going on?

Are the English coming to attack us?'

'There's no attack, Meulon.' He hesitated. 'It's family business.'

'There are rumours that my Lord de Harcourt is in danger from our King. Some of the servants gossip that there's a conspiracy between Sir Godfrey and the other barons.'

Blackstone gripped the man's arm and turned him away from some of the soldiers who stood on the wall watching them. 'You're their captain. You know as well as I do that rumours can tear men apart. Keep them disciplined. Your lord will depend on you, as he has done in the past.'

Meulon nodded. He wasn't happy, but he accepted the Englishman's explanation.

'And if you hear anyone gossip, beat him. Protect your lord and his family from such rumours and keep the servants in their place.' As Blackstone gave his orders there was a voice in his own mind. *You, a common man, telling a soldier to beat a servant.* He dismissed the self-condemnation and turned on his heel. There was no sign of Christiana anywhere; she would be with the women, most likely the countess, so there was no point trying to find her. The barons had filed into the great hall and by the time Sir Godfrey came out an hour later the horses had been refreshed and food supplied for the onward journey. Once again Jean de Harcourt accompanied his uncle towards the main gate flanked by Sir Godfrey's men. Blackstone saw Blanche and Christiana emerge from a side door and the lady's call to Sir Godfrey checked his step.

'Blanche, forgive me, there is no time.'

Christiana held back as Blanche de Harcourt stepped forward to question him. 'Sir Godfrey, it seems you have always brought distress to my house – is my family in danger?'

'Blanche,' said Jean, aggrieved at her intrusion. 'My uncle is leaving – don't delay him.'

The feisty countess did not yield. 'I have young children and there are other families as my guests. So if there is danger following on your heels I need to know just as much as my lord and husband.' She tilted her chin slightly, as if declaring her own rank. 'I have the right.'

Blackstone moved closer to the old warrior, eager to be noticed by him.

'There is no danger for you or your family,' Sir Godfrey told her, 'I give you my word. I am the one in jeopardy and I came here to help Jean. You must believe me.'

She studied him for a moment and then nodded with gratitude. 'Thank you.'

Sir Godfrey looked beyond her and saw Christiana. And, just as he did the previous time, Blackstone saw the hard man of war soften. 'Child, come here.'

Christiana did as he commanded and bent her knee before him. 'You have prospered since I saw you last, and I will tell you what I have told your guardians: you are safe here.'

'Thank you, Sir Godfrey, for your kindness and your good wishes.'

'I knew your father well, and although we fought on opposite sides, it was I who told him to send you to the countess for safety's sake. So I'm pleased that at least one decision I made was the correct one.' The comment had no meaning for her because she had no knowledge of the difficulties Sir Godfrey now found himself in.

'Have you seen my father?' she asked hopefully.

Blackstone saw Jean de Harcourt turn his face away. Sir Godfrey stumbled for a moment as he too was caught unawares. Blackstone felt his heart go out to her and a sickening sense of ill fortune clutched at him.

'Have you not told her?' Sir Godfrey asked his nephew in a low voice.

The look of quiet despair on the count's face needed no further explanation. Christiana stepped back. 'He's dead, isn't he?'

Sir Godfrey nodded. 'In the early days when we came ashore. He fought for his sworn lord Robert Bertrand. My enemy. I thought he might have escaped into Caen, but there was no report of him fighting there and we swept through all those early defences. I'm sorry, child.'

The marshal of the army climbed into the saddle. Blackstone hesitated as Blanche reached out to hold Christiana's hand and comfort her. Tears welled in her eyes, but Blackstone knew she would not break down in front of the servants. His opportunity to ask whether Sir Gilbert had survived the battle had passed. To approach now would serve no purpose. Christiana's grief could not be usurped.

Instead he grabbed the horse's bridle, steadying it as soldiers jostled to open the gate. The grey beard stared down at him.

'Thomas Blackstone,' he said, recognizing him despite his scar.

'My lord.'

'Your day will come, but whether I'll be alive to see it is another matter. You owe a debt to your Prince and to the King, and you'll honour my nephew's commands. We don't need a rogue Englishman in our midst thinking for himself. You can leave those matters to others better qualified.' He nodded curtly and spurred the horse free of Blackstone's grip. The soldiers followed and the gates closed behind them.

Blackstone turned, but Christiana was walking away. More than anything else at that moment he wanted to hold her and comfort her pain. But he could not approach her in public. She caught his eye as Blanche eased her away to the solitude of her quarters. He knew she would come to him, but the anticipation of being with her again was tinged with dread.

An ambush, an archer's skill, and a dead knight bearing her father's livery was a memory that would never be erased.

CHAPTER TWENTY-ONE

Where there had been some feeling of light-heartedness among the noblemen there was now tension, taut as a bowcord. For two days the men buried themselves in the small library, leaving the women to their own devices. Blackstone had no opportunity to approach de Harcourt, who was never alone, but always earnestly in conversation with one or other of the noblemen. On one occasion as Blackstone crossed de Harcourt's path, he and Guy de Ruymont watched him for a moment and then turned their faces away, heads bowed in low-voiced conversation. What part in their lives was Blackstone to play, he wanted to know, and more importantly, when could he prepare to escape? If routiers were coming to arrest him on the French King's orders then these barons could not refuse the command without placing themselves squarely in defiance. Blackstone regretted not taking Meulon's advice to kill the mercenary. His own desire to send a warning, to raise his banner in a way, had blinded him to the possible consequences. His natural instinct now was to escape, even though de Harcourt had promised Sir Godfrey he would not hand him over, but he had risked much for Christiana and that held him.

On the second night Christiana slipped into his room, shivering with grief. He held her, calming her uncertainty and fear and made no attempt at intimacy. She slept like a child in his arms in front of the firelight. When she woke in the early hours he was not next to her, but was sitting on a stool in front of the flames, ensuring it stayed fed, keeping its warmth through the night. She whispered his name and he went to her. At first he did not understand what drove her hunger for his embrace or her demand for sex, but he quickly undressed her and lay between her thighs. She closed her eyes and it seemed to him that she had a desperate sense of pain and pleasure that forced her to move quickly against him, her hips thrusting hard, drawing him in, biting into his shoulder, her nails clinging to his back, gasping like a drowning child, afraid and desperate. She shuddered and wept when she fell into the void and felt his warmth seep into her. Blackstone realized her demands from him were nothing as simple as desire, but a crying need for their passion to exorcise her despair and grief.

When they were spent they lay without speaking, his hand resting across her breast, watching it gently quivering from her heartbeat. Neither spoke and he felt his own guilt torment him. Should he tell her? Would she ever find out if he did not? Was it not better to let the war take its own victims and bury them where they fell? Had he killed her father? Could he be certain the old man at the crossroads was her father? It could have been any of those who fought for Sir Godfrey's enemy. Why did it have to be him?

The dawn would soon be upon them and she began to dress. 'Christiana…'

She paused and looked at him, then kissed him tenderly. 'Thomas, forgive me. I needed you more than I can explain. I'm all right now.'

Blackstone knew events were moving his destiny beyond his control. 'Christiana, come with me. We need to leave,' he said.

She looked at him uncertainly. 'Why would I leave? We're both safe here. The war isn't over. No one has signed a truce yet. There's nowhere for us to go. What do you mean?'

'I want you to come to England with me.'

She stared at him as if she had not understood.

He said carefully, 'I can go to the King and I can ask him to let me serve one of the English lords. I will have employment and you will be safe with me.'

Panic widened her eyes and for a moment she struggled to find the words she needed and when she did it was his turn to try and stay calm. 'England? I could never go to England. How could you ask that of me? The English killed my father. I could never live with my father's killers.'

His heart nearly choked him. It was a cruel twist of fate that had brought him to this place. He bowed his head and she reached for him.

'Not you, Thomas, it's not you, I promise. I know you fought. I know that. I prayed every night not to love you. I prayed that my guardians' hatred of you would soften. And it has. You have shown yourself to be unlike any of them.'

In that moment Blackstone felt a gulf between them wider than the sea that had brought him to war. He could not tell her what he had overheard for fear that she might run to de Harcourt and challenge him. Then she would demand to know if it were true that the French King had ordered Blackstone be taken. Everything would unravel like a fallen bobbin of cotton. De Harcourt would have to tell her, and she would turn her back on them. And then what would happen to them both? How would they live if such a confrontation forced her to leave? If she would not go to England how could he stay?

'It's war,' he said. 'We have all lost those we love in this conflict. But I've been taken in by my enemy and you have loved your enemy. I came for you that day because I had to. I was compelled. And so are you. Isn't that true?'

'Yes,' she whispered. 'And I have not admitted my love for you to anyone else for fear they would send you away. They wouldn't allow it, Thomas, even though you have proved yourself.'

'Then that's another reason to leave. I am in favour with the King. He'll grant me a modest request.'

'Not England. I cannot.' She shook her head. 'Not with the English.'

She pulled her cape around her shoulders and brushed past him.

'Then what am I, Christiana?'

'Your mother was French. You are different.'

She went to the door and he did not try to stop her.

No one travelled at night. The darkness held terrors and the roads were too treacherous when the moon kept its glow behind storm clouds. Even for those who knew the landscape, it would have been foolhardy even to try. When the riders came it was three hours after dawn and the household had settled into its routine. A bitter gale blew from the north as sleet fell in great sweeping walls like a starlings' swarm, curving this way and that as the wind twisted across the undulating land.

Their voices demanding to speak to de Harcourt barely carried to the sentry on duty, who then called Meulon. De Harcourt was summoned and he strode out to meet the half-dozen horsemen with Meulon and the guard at his back. Christiana watched from Blanche de Harcourt's room as the countess sat and spoke about the duties demanded of a woman to her husband.

'Christiana,' she said. 'I've been talking to you.'

She stood quickly when she saw the girl grip the sill and her shoulders stiffen.

'What is it?' Blanche stared into the storm and saw her drenched husband talking to the leader of the men, who handed him a document that he snatched and then turned his back. The horsemen waited patiently, obviously unconcerned about Jean de Harcourt's ill temper. He said something to Meulon as he strode back into the confines of the castle and Meulon gestured the riders to stay where they were.

The King's men and the mercenaries were not invited into the castle for shelter or food and were made to wait in the storm.

'What is it, child?' Blanche asked softly in deference to her ward's obvious fear.

Christiana's panic made her step back from the window. 'Does he know I'm here?'

'Who? Does who know?'

She gestured to the men below. 'The man at the back. It's Gilles de Marçy. Did someone tell him I was here?'

Blanche looked as concerned as the girl. 'The man who pursued you last year? That's him?'

Christiana nodded. Gilles de Marçy was a priest whose family had bought his benefice. He was a cruel and wanton man, known for savage violence, and such had been his threatening pursuit of Christiana that her father had sent her to the de Harcourt family, deep in Normandy, for protection.

'He cannot know you are here. I swear to you, this is coincidence. Do you understand?' She turned the girl to face her. 'He cannot harm you. He does not know you are here,' she repeated reassuringly. She made Christiana look at her, grabbing her shoulders and making her realize the truth.

'But I've just learnt of my father's death. And now he *is* here.'

Blanche de Harcourt gestured to a servant and eased Christiana into a chair. 'Stay with her,' she told the servant. 'Christiana, I'll find out what's happening. Don't leave this room until I return,' she commanded.

Blanche swept out of the room. If Christiana was correct and had identified the man who had plagued her life all those months ago then his appearance at the gates of her sanctuary was either a frightening twist of fate or he had gained some authority to take her. There was no reason to suspect he had any such authority. He rode at the rear of the horsemen, an underling, or someone who had now joined the routiers.

'Jean!' she called when she saw her bedraggled husband. 'Those men.'

De Harcourt's beard held the rain, his hair plastered to his head, his cloak black with water on his shoulders. 'The King's men with a warrant.'

'For Christiana?' she asked fearfully.

His confusion was apparent. 'What? What are you talking about?'

'She says one of them is Gilles de Marçy.'

'He's one of them? Is she certain?'

'Yes.'

'Go back and stay with her, Blanche. Keep her out of sight. They're not here for her. They have a warrant for Thomas.'

Before she could register her shock, he eased her aside and signalled Meulon and the four soldiers with him to advance down the corridor towards Blackstone's room.

'Do as I ordered,' he told them, and then turned back into the storm.

Blackstone had trained in the exercise yard and returned to his room pouring the warm water that Marcel had provided to sluice away the sweat from his arms and chest. The shutters were closed against the storm and he had not seen the riders approach. As he pulled on his undershirt and reached for his tunic there was banging on the door.

'Sir Thomas, my lord needs you now,' Meulon called.

The urgency in Meulon's voice made Blackstone open the door immediately. There was no one else in the corridor except the veteran soldier.

'What is it?' he asked as he hurriedly finished dressing.

'Come with me,' said Meulon and turned on his heel, which made Blackstone follow him without further questioning. They had gone no more than a dozen paces when Meulon swung open the door that Blackstone knew led to one of the rear staircases of the castle. Meulon stood back in deference to Blackstone. 'In here, Master Thomas, my lord is waiting.'

For a vital few seconds the urgency to respond to Jean de Harcourt's request dulled his instincts, which alerted him to danger only as he stepped past Meulon and saw the man's eyes. It was a trap. The door at the end of the passageway was locked. As he spun around Meulon slammed the door closed behind him. Blackstone wrenched at the heavy wood, but it was bolted.

'Meulon! What's happening?'

Blackstone pressed his ear against the wood and heard the scuffling of other guards. In that instant he knew.

'No! Not him! Meulon! I beg you! Leave him!'

On the other side of the door Meulon's men had carried William Harness from his bed and the semi-conscious man had called out, 'What's happening? Where are you taking me?' He heard Blackstone slamming his fist against the door and cried out weakly, 'Thomas, they have me. Thomas, help me, for God's sake, I beg you.'

The soldiers hauled him away quickly and his cries soon faded. Meulon waited a moment on the other side of the door. He laid his hand on the solid oak, as if wishing to calm the man behind it. He understood the loyalty of men to each other.

'Sir Thomas, he dies so you might live,' he said simply.

Meulon followed his soldiers down the passageway pursued by the echoing sound of Blackstone's helpless rage.

Harness was placed on a horse, his legs bound to the stirrups, hands tied to the pommel. Meulon's men had, as Jean de Harcourt had ordered, dressed the injured man in his livery, making plain the fact that he was the Englishman favoured by the King of England. His rambling curses made it even more convincing that they had the right man.

Jean de Harcourt strode among the horsemen. Now that he had handed him over he berated them for taking a wounded man and declaring his own shame in allowing it to happen. But he emphasized that he had followed the command as issued in the warrant and signed in the King's name. And as he pushed his way through the horses so that he could look at each man he sought out Gilles de Marçy, whose black robes marked him to be different from the others. De Harcourt wanted to see more closely the man who had terrorized his ward. He made no particular gesture or confrontation to him but wanted to set the man's face in his memory. The one thing that he noticed, despite de Marçy's riding gloves, was that the little finger on one hand was missing.

The leader of the horsemen showed little respect for de Harcourt's nobility.

'We'll be sure to tell his highness that you have obeyed. But that you gave the man shelter in the first place might still cause displeasure.'

'Then you will respectfully remind him that I, my father and my brother fought at Crécy and defended his good name and cause with our blood. And if he sends scum like you to do his bidding then we pray we did not suffer and die in vain for him.'

The leader of the horsemen sneered, and spat to one side. William Harness was already slumped in the saddle and if the ride or cold didn't kill him soon then no doubt these men would. He served no purpose to them other than to be delivered to the King who paid their blood money.

Jean de Harcourt stayed on the bridge, watching the riders disappear into the storm. It was even colder now and the sleet fell more heavily. He welcomed the stinging punishment as a flagellant welcomed the flail.

'You should have told me,' Blanche told her husband when they were alone.

'I could not,' he answered, feeling her anguish. 'There was no honour in what I had to do, but it was the only way I could think of to save Thomas. But now I fear whatever trust has been built between us might be lost.'

De Harcourt left Blackstone locked in the narrow passageway for a day and a night, hoping that his anger would settle and there would be an understanding of what had been necessary. Christiana had been calmed and assured that the vicious man who had caused her exile from her home had no idea that she was in Castle de Harcourt.

Blanche eased herself across her husband's chest as they lay in bed. It was barely light and they were naked from the previous night's lovemaking. Her breasts pushed against him as he opened his eyes and turned on his back, throwing wide his arm so that she could be pulled closer to him.

'You're awake,' he said, and yawned. 'I heard you go to the garderobe in the night; couldn't you sleep?'

'Did I disturb you?'

'No, but you were fidgeting and I was going to kick you out but decided I would rather have you squirming next to me than landing on the floor and cursing me. It was a difficult choice.'

She smiled and enjoyed the stale smell of sweat from their night's exertions. She traced one of the white scars that ran from his shoulder onto his chest. 'I was thinking about us and the children, and what will happen if the King forfeits to Edward. Do you serve him or challenge him?'

'Since when does Norman loyalty trouble you?'

'You forget, Jean, I am Countess de Ponthieu and I have to make my own decisions about whom I should support,' she said quietly and rubbed a finger across the top of his nipple.

He groaned, less from pleasure and more from anticipation of where her questioning was leading. He turned so they faced each other. She raised her knee enticingly to his groin. 'So, my countess might join the other side and we would become enemies. Is that what you're saying?'

'I could always offer you an alliance,' she said and felt him harden against her leg.

'And I suppose there'd be terms.'

'I could tailor them to suit your needs, my lord.'

He did not flinch as she reached forward and held his erection. 'And I cannot be so easily bribed,' he said, easing her wrist from him, taking back control.

She winced because his grip hurt her. 'Must you always be the stronger of us both? Can't I rule for even a few moments?' she asked, deliberately letting her eyes well with tears as she held his gaze.

'No, Blanche, because then you would get the taste of power, and this is a game, because you never cry. You were no more thinking of Edward and the King than I was thinking of rebuilding the hovels in the village.' The playfulness had lost its edge slightly and he waited for her confession. He eased her back, pushing aside her arms and letting her breasts settle so he could lean across her and tease them with the lightest touch of his lips. He suddenly jerked his head back. 'Sweet Jesus! Those tears of yours. You're not pregnant, are you?'

'And whose fault would it be if I were?' she answered carefully.

'Yours! Blanche, my wounds have barely healed and I have a serpents' nest of Norman lords to untangle and you think I should take the news well? Another day perhaps, but now?' He watched her. 'Are you? Tell me the truth.'

'I'm twenty-six years old, I'm becoming an old hag, my breeding years are coming to an end.'

'Blanche,' he said sternly.

'I could be if you co-operated,' she said and once again reached out for him.

He rolled clear and walked to the garderobe; the privy was at the far end of their room, behind a curtain, a cushion plugging the hole in the wooden seat. 'I must piss and then my brain might work because you are after something, Blanche, you are manipulating your husband. It is Christmas season and we are hosts to our friends and allies, and yet you, I can tell, are after something.' He tugged the cushion free and sighed as his stream echoed down the stone channel.

Blanche knew that, as in a battle, timing could decide the outcome, and when a man stood relieving himself that gave his opponent the advantage.

'I have to know what it is you planned for Thomas.'

'Thomas? Why? It's complicated,' he said.

'Aha. I thought it would be. No matter. I'd like to know.'

'Does it concern you?' he answered without turning, enjoying the relief from the previous night's drinking when he had tried to deaden the act of betrayal.

'It concerns you more. You need him, don't you? That's obvious. And after what's happened you'll lose him.' She paused, easing towards the moment when she might use what she knew. 'He asked Christiana to go back to England with him.'

'Has she agreed?' he said cautiously.

'No.'

He knew the day would come when Thomas Blackstone would wish to return home, but his plan was always to make him an offer to entice him to stay.

'If the girl can't hold him, then neither can I,' he said fatalistically.

Blanche waited a moment longer before telling him of her

suspicions and watched as the shock of it jerked his head around, making him spray the seat.

Christiana pressed her face against the heavy door and whispered to Blackstone. 'Thomas, you must not bear ill feeling towards my guardian. He saved your life the only way he could.'

His voice was tight with anger. 'Did they send you to convince me?'

'No, no, they did not. I came because I am grateful to them for saving you. One of those who came to the gate was the man who had promised to cause me harm. I think sweet Jesus has blessed us because he had no idea I was here.'

The mention of the threat against her eased his anger. He knew the story of why she had been sent to the protection of de Harcourt and his family. If the man who once threatened her had happened upon her refuge then it gave him another chance to convince her to return to England with him. Once again destiny had given him an opportunity.

His voice lowered. 'Are you alone?'

'Yes.'

'Were you frightened?'

'At first. But then the count gave up your Englishman and they rode away. But it made me realize how an enemy can stumble upon you.'

'It was like a freak storm, Christiana. You have to let it pass.'

'But he could come back.'

'Then I'd kill him. But if you were in England he could never reach you.'

A door slammed at the end of the passageway and footsteps echoed on the stone floor.

'Thomas, someone's coming. I have to go.'

'Come with me!' he whispered desperately. 'I'm not staying here now. Decide, Christiana. I'll look after you.'

'No. I can't. Don't force me, Thomas. Don't abandon me, I beg you,' she said hesitatingly, the devil's own choice being offered her.

347

Blackstone had to risk everything. 'I'm leaving, Christiana. I won't stay here. You have to come with me.'

Blackstone could not see her tears as she steadied her voice to disguise her anguish. 'I cannot,' she whispered.

And in that moment he knew that he had to harden his heart and go home without her.

She moved away quickly, moments before Jean de Harcourt turned into the passageway. He hesitated outside the locked door, and then threw it open.

It was dark and airless in there and Blackstone blinked as the light flooded in. De Harcourt took a pace back to allow Blackstone to do whatever he chose. He expected the young archer to lunge and strike at him, and if he did he would be hard-pressed to save himself from injury. Blackstone's aggression was well known to him now and de Harcourt was unarmed and unaccompanied. Blackstone stepped into the corridor.

De Harcourt averted his eyes. 'There was no other way, Thomas. I offer my regret. You knew he was dying. His lung was punctured, he would not have survived.' He made a small gesture towards the corridor. 'There's a horse saddled for you, and another for provisions. They're yours to do with as you wish. The road to Calais lies to the north and if you travel first to Rouen you'll probably avoid any French skirmishers. Within a week you can be at your King's side.'

Blackstone remained silent. Jean de Harcourt had expressed his contrition. And despite Christiana's plea for him to stay he was ready to follow his desire and be free of the castle.

'You caused the death of a good man, who never raised a hand against any of your countrymen,' Blackstone said.

'I made a promise to Sir Godfrey that I would not hand you over to murdering scum, no matter whose warrant they carried.'

'And he asked you whether I had been told what it was you wanted with me.'

De Harcourt suddenly realized that Blackstone must have overheard everything.

'Where were you?'

'The gallery.'

De Harcourt pondered for a moment. 'So you knew that they were coming to arrest you and yet you stayed.'

'You gave your pledge to Sir Godfrey to save me but I never thought you would give them William Harness. Where's my sword?'

'With the horse.'

'What were you and the others planning?'

'To tell you would be to put our lives into your hands.'

'As you held mine,' Blackstone answered.

De Harcourt shook his head. 'It's too great a game, Thomas. Stay, and you'll be told.'

Blackstone let the desire to know slip away. 'Goodbye, my lord.' He turned on his heel to make his way to the stables.

'Did she beg you to stay?' de Harcourt called after him.

Blackstone turned to face him. 'I go my own way now.'

'As all men should. And I wish you well, Thomas.'

Blackstone took another three strides and then de Harcourt's next words bit like a bodkin point through his spine into his heart.

'Christiana is pregnant.'

CHAPTER TWENTY-TWO

Christiana worried a handkerchief between her fingers. She and Blackstone stood opposite each other in the confines of her room.

'I saw them saddle a horse. One of the pages told me it was for you. I didn't know if I would see you before you left.'

'I would ask you once again to come to England with me,' said Blackstone, keeping his distance from her, feeling the churning emotions inside him.

She smiled sadly and shook her head. 'I can't leave my people. This is where I belong and all I know.'

'I'm afraid,' he said.

She looked surprised. 'Not you.'

Blackstone felt they were caught in an invisible current that swirled between them. The wind still howled through the battlements and eaves, so the warm room was a sanctuary, yet they seemed unable to approach each other because of some force that kept them apart.

'I'm afraid because of what I now know. Why didn't you tell me?'

She looked confused and turned away from him. 'You can't know.'

'You must have told Countess Blanche.'

'I never breathed a word.' She sat on a stool by the window. 'Perhaps she saw I had changed.'

Blackstone moved closer to her. He had seen no change, what was there to see? What he suspected, though, was that women were like God's other creatures that had a sixth sense. A man's instincts could save his life but the unknowable world of women's intuition was as deep as a mire. 'I'm excited and I'm fearful because having a child is like stumbling through a dark forest. You can't see your way clear,' he said uncertainly.

'I would not use the child to hold you.'

'But you wanted to, outside that door, when you begged me not to abandon you.'

'I couldn't force you to stay. Besides, I have only missed my monthly time once.'

He sat next to her, unable to grasp that a seed had taken hold in her. After what seemed a long and awkward silence she placed her hand on his. 'You must follow your own instincts, Thomas. There's no need for you to stay because of this. Blanche will discreetly take the child in, and I will be its wet nurse and governess. Shame can be hidden like a swelling stomach beneath flowing robes. Your child will be safe, and you can come back whenever you wish to see it. No one need ever know. Perhaps that's better for us all, including the child.'

He waited a moment before answering, searching for the right words that made sense of what he felt. 'When you refused to come to England with me, and you told me how much you hated the English, I thought even our feelings could not bridge such a gulf. The father of your child is an Englishman, and nothing can ever change that. And my son will know about his father, and my son will know about his family because that will be his gift to carry him through this life.'

'It may not be a boy,' she said.

'It will be,' he told her. 'And I'll not let any man take my place. And no one will take our child. I don't know how we will live, but we'll do it here in France, so that you'll be safe and surrounded by those who care for you.'

She bowed her head, her hands gripping his tightly, as the tears spilled and her shoulders trembled.

He pulled her to him. 'I didn't pull you across that river to let you drift away from me now. And we won't let our child come into this world as a bastard. Go and see the countess and ask if the priest is still here.'

She laughed and wiped the tears from her cheeks, then buried her face into his shoulder. 'Oh, Thomas, I was so afraid to lose you.'

He held the warmth of her body close to him. How many twists and turns lay on the road ahead he could not know. But if he had unknowingly slain her father, now he had sired her child.

He and this woman were tied together as surely as his sword by its blood knot to his right hand.

Jean de Harcourt led the way into the library and gestured Blackstone towards the trestle table where rolled parchments sat snug against each other.

'Find the grubbiest parchment there. The one that's been handled the most,' de Harcourt told him as he poured two glasses of wine.

Blackstone fingered his way through the scrolls and noticed one with a wine stain. He had seen it before.

'That's it,' said de Harcourt, and handed Blackstone the wine. Then with his free arm he swept all the other documents onto the floor. 'Unroll it,' he said and lifted a paperweight onto the unfurled parchment. 'Have you seen this before, when you spent your nights in here?'

Blackstone looked down at the map. It had the crosses in circles on it, the same crude drawing he had seen before and which still made no sense. 'Yes, I've seen it.'

'Then you'll know it's a map of divided France,' de Harcourt explained, his finger tapping the markings. 'This is the Duchy of Normandy, this is Burgundy, Aquitaine, and every red cross denotes a walled town or castle held by those loyal to the French King. Those marked by a circle and a cross are held in the name of Edward and these,' his finger pointed to the small black dots that freckled the map, 'these infestations are held by independent captains.'

'Routiers?' said Blackstone.

'Which often change hands. They terrorize an area and bleed it dry; some of them cage themselves within the walls, not daring to come out in case local populations rise up against them. They are victims of their own greed and once they've ravaged the town they leave it.'

Blackstone studied the map. 'That's the coast to the north, this borderline here?'

'That's Brittany. There's been conflict there for centuries. It's a wilderness of discontent.'

Blackstone's eyes followed his finger that traced across the map. 'A lot of these towns are held by my King, these are French. Brittany is strong in his favour.'

'And the further south you go into Gascony, you can see that your King also has many well-placed towns,' de Harcourt said, and waited as Blackstone studied the markings, wondering if the strategic importance of what he had briefly explained meant anything to him.

'This is Rouen. And we are here,' Blackstone said, then let his finger travel south-east. 'Paris. Your King is tucked away like a swaddled child. He's safe there.'

'Everything else is what's important,' de Harcourt said.

Blackstone nodded, seeing the landscape in his mind, remembering again his march from the invasion and riding with Sir Godfrey as they skirted Rouen. I'm here, he thought, and further south was the village where they killed Edward's messengers. So, Chaulion is here and the border country is…

He looked up at de Harcourt who waited expectantly.

'These places are held by the French and routiers. Why don't the French take them?' he asked.

'Because the King lets them take what they want from the people. They raid and kill. It's cheaper for him than paying them, but they have his approval. As we have just witnessed with those scum from Paris.'

Blackstone saw how close some of the markings were to the border. His finger went down, left and right, a small pattern emerged.

'King Edward blockades Calais in the north, but when he

invaded he came through – here. The peninsula. That's why there was little fighting when we landed. Sir Godfrey knew that most small towns wouldn't resist. Except Caen, but that's different – it's a huge city.'

'And don't forget your King holds Gascony to the south, Bordeaux is his.'

Blackstone felt the thrill of understanding; like a building's design on a master mason's plan, the intricacies offered themselves up. He gulped the wine, excited by the discovery, eager to find out more. 'When we landed we were worried that the French would come from the south and trap us, but you couldn't get to us in time because we had men down there. If the King ever loses Calais he needs to invade from these two places again. Normandy in the north and Bordeaux in the south. This is where he's weak. Here, in this border country. There are towns that could harass any troop movements.'

He lifted his finger and let the parchment roll into itself.

'Why are you showing this to me?'

'You're an Englishman,' de Harcourt said and turned to sit next to the fire. 'And we had hoped to use that fact.' He paused. 'In time,' he admitted.

Blackstone followed him; de Harcourt had caught his interest. 'I'm a common man, my lord, and I have nothing to offer anyone other than my willingness to fight.' He sat opposite de Harcourt, but the man's face showed no reaction. He was waiting for Blackstone to grasp the reality of the situation. He stoked the fire and flames devoured the dry wood.

Blackstone said, 'Those towns pose a threat should King Philip try to impose more pressure on you and the others, to bring you more under control, to crush your – what's the word? – when you wish to govern yourself?'

'Autonomy,' de Harcourt said.

'That.' Blackstone hesitated, trying to see the sequence of events that could inflict themselves on Jean de Harcourt and his friends. 'You can't attack and hold those towns because you're still sworn to King Philip.' The reasoning unfolded in his mind like a map, each crease revealing a hidden place. 'But if my King had taken the French crown, Normandy would have sworn allegiance to him and with his help you would have been free to do what you wanted to protect your borders.'

De Harcourt relented and poured more wine for Blackstone. Could someone like him understand the great nation of France and its divisions? His own history weighed like an anvil. 'We swear allegiance to those we choose. But we are trapped now that your King has taken what he wants.'

'There are men out there who would fight for your cause if you paid them,' he said.

'And who would betray us to the highest bidder.'

Blackstone felt the tingle of excitement, similar to what he felt when closing in on hunted prey. 'You need someone you trust to take those towns and hold them without you being involved. Someone who would have the blessing of the English King, and who would not interfere, because those towns are the silken thread that hold those territories together. It could take years.'

De Harcourt looked at him with an expression of regret. 'Yes, my young friend, that's correct. And if such a person died or was captured trying to do those things, he would have no link to us at all. We would not be implicated and we would not offer any help.'

Blackstone's heartbeat settled. War had beaten out of him any foolish thoughts of conflict being an adventure. Battle and conquest were best approached with cold-blooded skill and determination. Blood-lust came at the sword's point, when death promised its agonizing embrace.

He sat and gazed into the fire, letting the flames entice him. He could offer his sword to Edward and remain an impoverished knight in France with a wife and child, or serve his King in another fashion and hold land in his name; be his own man.

'Sir Godfrey was wrong. What you need is a rogue Englishman,' he said quietly.

* * *

The noblemen gathered that night. De Vitry was surly, Guy de Ruymont cautious, and the most senior among them, de Graville and de Mainemares, who had hoped more than any other for a strong King to lead their nation, continually urged the bickering men to settle their differences, support the venture that de Harcourt proposed and await the outcome. If this young Englishman died it would not harm their long-term plans; if he succeeded it would be the first stone laid on the bridge that would carry them to success. This plan was not going to benefit them immediately; they had to give thought to the future. King Philip might reign for years. Henri Livay thought the gout would kill the King in less than a year, Jacques Brienne had it on good authority from a kinsman at court that the King had suffered an apoplexy, while another baron believed the King's son John would usurp the throne.

As the bantering went back and forth Jean de Harcourt and Blackstone waited silently. De Graville finally raised a hand to silence them all.

'This plan comes too early for us. We can't expect support from King Edward, so how are we to stay in the shadows and let an inexperienced man-at-arms ride out and begin an assault that seems doomed before it has even started?'

'He needs men, and the only way to get them is to pay them,' said Henri Livay.

'And they will take what they want and then desert, because that's the kind of scum you get for such an undertaking,' said de Vitry.

Blackstone hoped, when they all turned to look at him, that they were not still thinking that he was the scum in question. He said, 'My lords, sometimes inexperience can be a benefit. Seeing things in a different way can bring success. I would need men, but I would need those who would serve me in your name.'

Guy de Ruymont said, 'We cannot hide our livery and ride out under false pretences. No man of honour would do such a thing.

Such deception would bring disgrace once the ploy was discovered.'

Blackstone thought quickly, searching for the answer that would satisfy the men's honour and yet shield them from recrimination.

'All of you have men who have served and fought with you. If you release them from their duty to you, then they could fight as free men. They would wear no livery and they would fight under the captain of your choosing. And to secure their loyalty you would pay them as you do now.'

The room fell silent. It was a simple plan and one that could still offer them anonymity.

'Blackstone is right,' said de Harcourt. 'We have bankrolled the King on many occasions and all we have in return is defeat and higher taxation. I say we have nothing to lose. I'll speak to my soldiers and offer them their release. Their loyalty will still be to me, and Thomas Blackstone will, in time, gather those about him who will offer their loyalty to him alone.'

Each of them considered the proposal. It was William de Fossat who broke the silence.

'I have no lands, and my fortune is taken by the King. So I am the most impoverished of us all, but I still have wealth enough to support an adventure, and if a town falls then I will take my share of its possessions and the land it holds. Blackstone can ride under my command. I'll take ten of my own men with me. I'm not afraid for our King's mercenaries to see my colours.'

De Harcourt kept a rein on his impatience. 'No, William. That defeats the purpose of having an Englishman to be seen leading men. He holds any captured towns for *his* King. To all intent and purpose he's not our man. Surely that is obvious? He fights and secures territory for King Edward. Unless you offer fealty to Edward and ride openly in defiance of Philip.'

'Then I'll cover my shield because who in their right mind is going to follow Thomas Blackstone? Ask yourselves that!'

Blackstone knew that de Fossat was still smarting from the perceived insult at the dinner. He was spoiling for a fight, and if that happened and Blackstone beat him he might feel such bitterness and humiliation that he could defy them all and betray their plan to the French King. If, on the other hand, Blackstone lost, then the others would think less of his ability, which might cause them to withdraw their support. And where would that leave Blackstone? But how was he to achieve anything with the animosity of a Norman lord clinging to him like a rash on a whore's back?

'I'll take whatever men will follow me according to your generosity,' he said, and faced each nobleman in turn. 'But if my Lord de Fossat is intent on leading the assault on Chaulion then the game is up before it has even started. His honour is too great for him ever to deny his name if called upon to identify himself. Covering your shield and obscuring your coat of arms is not enough.' He turned to face de Fossat squarely. 'My lord, it is obvious I've caused you offence, and for that I apologize. But if you challenge any decision of my command, I won't back down.'

De Fossat smiled. 'Then consider your defeat already complete.'

De Harcourt was on his feet. 'No! William, I've warned you already. Don't make matters worse.'

'A scarred upstart of a knight carries no fear for me, Jean. In God's name! You've been training a pup.'

Blackstone concealed his nervousness, and determined to brazen it out, he stepped closer to de Fossat. It was no time to show any trepidation about facing down a man of superior rank. 'And what will defeating me prove to everyone in this room? That you are the better swordsman? That your pride is restored? What good is your pride to these lords' cause?' Blackstone said.

De Fossat lunged, aiming a blow to Blackstone's face, but he turned quickly, making de Fossat lose his balance, stumble across a chair and fall. The others shuffled back hastily. There was no avoiding a fight now; de Fossat had forced the issue and Blackstone had staked his claim for their support.

'Stop it, William!' Guy de Ruymont shouted. 'It serves no purpose!'

'It satisfies me!' yelled back de Fossat and drew his sword.

De Harcourt quickly stepped between the two men. 'William! Hear this! Give every man in this room your word that if you lose you will not pursue revenge; you will not stand in his way to do our bidding.'

'I give it!' de Fossat spat.

'Dishonour your word and we will kill you,' said de Harcourt.

The words struck de Fossat and seemed to sober his impassioned challenge. De Harcourt and the others waited.

'I understand,' said de Fossat. 'I pledge my allegiance; that will never change.'

'Then you fight outside,' said de Harcourt and led the noblemen into the night.

Each of them held a flaming torch and encircled the training yard. The wind whipped the flames but the flickering light made no difference to the two men fighting. Soldiers gathered in the shadows as Meulon permitted the men to watch. Squires and their pages left their beds in the stables and gathered as steel clashed against steel. De Fossat gripped his sword with two hands, cleaving the air with a blow that could be heard whipping the air despite the buffeting wind. Blackstone half turned his body and the blades clashed. De Fossat's weight turned him, but Blackstone's balance was solid. He allowed the blow to fall away, and took a step forward, ramming his shoulder into de Fossat, forcing him onto the defensive. Blackstone's weight and height were an advantage, but de Fossat was a big man, skilled in close-quarter battle, and went on the offensive with a low strike that Blackstone parried. The force of the assault was like two powerful mountain goats ramming into each other. They sweated, grunting with exertion. If de Fossat could use his skills and tricks learnt from combat he could beat the younger man. Blackstone's sword criss-crossed his body like a whip, so fast that de Fossat barely managed to close his guard. He staggered back a pace. Blackstone could have strode after him and finished it there and then, but he waited as each man drew the cold night air into heaving lungs. They had already fought for nearly half an hour and Blackstone wanted the man's defeat to be complete, to be seen as indisputable evidence that he could earn by his skill with the sword the respect he needed. The grunts and gasps were not only from the combatants, the noblemen's own fighting instincts made them twitch and shift from one foot to the other, shoulders half turning as each blow fell, was struck or parried. Every word and punishing blow that de Harcourt had laid on Blackstone was carved into his mind just as the leaping wolf was etched into the hardened steel. Blackstone moved rapidly but de Harcourt cursed him under his breath. Blackstone was not moving enough. His stance changed by only slight corrections, a pace here and there, but never yielding ground, whereas de Fossat was trying everything to break through his opponent's defence. However, it was a wall that could not be breached and de Fossat's efforts were as useless as a wave trying to smash a rock. And still Blackstone let the man recover, allowed him to suck in the air and wipe the sweat from his eyes, and waited for the next attack What was he doing? de Harcourt wondered. *Move man! Move!* And then it dawned on him that Blackstone was showing his strength. He was telling his enemy that he could move as rapidly as he wished or he could stand his ground and beat off an attack. He was humiliating de Fossat even further.

De Fossat feinted, the blade nearly slicing into Blackstone's crooked arm. The noblemen gasped. De Fossat had him! For a moment the Norman had the advantage, and every dead friend and humiliated Frenchman at Crécy was about to be vindicated with a decisive thrust. Blackstone caught the blade on his crossguard and twisted. It was enough to turn it away but the feint had given de Fossat confidence and he brought the full weight of his attack onto the Englishman.

As de Fossat crabbed, seeking an opening, Blackstone allowed his eyes to glance across de Fossat's shoulder into de Harcourt's stare. The implacable message in de Harcourt's eyes was obvious. Finish it.

Blackstone spat the phlegm from his mouth and felt the mail links bite through his undershirt as his bunched muscles gathered the power that until this moment had been called upon to do only what was necessary to halt or turn the assault. Now they would be brought into the fray like a surprise attack.

The dragon rose up, its talons tearing through his chest. Crécy's slaughterhouse, the nightmare that never left him, loomed in the broken torchlight. Bodies jumbled through his mind as horses screamed and the lone knight cut down his brother. Mouths gaped and spat blood. A knight laid the Prince's banner across his fallen body, silent, desperate screams to hold the line! Hold! But Blackstone had surged forward, cutting a wedge into the enemy, like a meat cleaver through a carcass, slipping in men's guts and gore into that carnage. Shattered bodies, ripped and trampled, screams and cries, curses and dying breath.

He punished de Fossat's pride with a relentless and calculated act of power and defiance.

And then he heard the grunting and smelled the sweat as he closed in on him, smashing him into the torchbearers, seeing a flame fall and splutter as he grabbed the man's belt, and tipped him into the dirt.

De Fossat's bloodied face stared up at him. Terror at the death about to claim him.

'Mercy! MERCY!' a disconnected voice cried.

'Thomas!' de Harcourt's voice. 'Enough!'

Arms grappled him.

'Lower the blade, Thomas. It's done.' De Harcourt straddled the fallen man in front of Blackstone's glaring eyes, protecting de Fossat. Then, more quietly, 'You've won.'

De Harcourt nodded to the others, who released their restraint.

The men shuffled away uneasily. Blackstone had gone in for the kill. Even if a wound had been inflicted on him they all knew that something would have driven him on.

'Jesus Christ,' de Fossat muttered, and spat blood. 'Jesus...'

De Harcourt helped the beaten man to his feet. There was

no anger lingering in him. And even humiliation had no place to rear its spiteful head from such a defeat. He seemed dazed at the outcome, took his fallen sword from one of the others and nodded gratefully to de Harcourt.

Jean de Harcourt eased the bruised and exhausted man away. The Norman lords looked at Blackstone. They knew about fighting, of how men would tear each other's eyes out or beat a skull with a helm when the terror took hold. And they also knew that what they had witnessed that night was a fighter possessed of a kind of power given to few. Divine or satanic they couldn't tell. But it frightened them.

They walked away silently. No one spoke and no one approached Blackstone. His sword hand sweated and the leather blood knot bit into his wrist. He pulled off his open-faced helm and let it drop into the dirt and then raised his face to the rain. The shadows moved as soldiers whispered among themselves and returned to their quarters. The only one who ventured forward was a page. Guillaume Bourdin stopped and picked up Blackstone's helm.

'I'll clean this for you, my lord.'

He looked at the boy and nodded. Then he walked towards the inner yard. *Mercy*, cried that voice again.

Blackstone knew there was no such thing.

Not from the beast that clawed within him.

Had he remembered the fight? de Harcourt had asked him. Yes, every stroke and guard. And had he deliberately let de Fossat dash himself against him? Yes. He knew the man would tire and then experience greater fear when he was set upon, realizing he would be beaten. Blackstone was aware of every thought and saw every memory and felt everything.

De Harcourt had gathered the others in the great hall without Blackstone present. They pledged what money they could and what few men could be spared after their losses at Crécy. It was agreed that Blackstone would have thirty men at his back, a dozen from de Harcourt, with Meulon as their captain. And no man present would utter a word of their involvement with the Englishman. Only he, de Harcourt, would keep a line of communication open. The next day the noblemen returned home and soldiers from their estates were sent to de Harcourt stripped of their livery. All were commanded by their sworn lord to follow Blackstone.

De Harcourt had explained as much as he could to Blackstone. 'Christophe-la-Campagne, where you found the Englishman, is under the control of Abbot Pierre. He is a loyal supporter of Philip. There's a small monastery – a dozen monks or so – on the crossroads a few miles from Chaulion. The key to capturing Chaulion is to control the road, but how you do that, and how you draw out this Saquet, is up to you, Thomas. The abbot is safe from attack because the Pope favours our King and he and the abbot pay Saquet to hold Chaulion, which means he's the abbot's protector of sorts. The Breton is a vile creature. Despite being on the King's payroll he's allowed to take whatever he wishes from villages that lie in the abbot's diocese. The godly Pierre, in his hypocrisy, urges the villagers to pay protection to save the blessed Mother Church and their own sinful lives.'

'How do you know this?' Blackstone had asked.

'When you returned I sent a trusted monk from my priory to Chaulion. Stay away from the village, Thomas. They're dyed-in-the-wool supporters of the French King, and Saquet will ride out and hunt you down before you've even formed a plan of how to take the town.'

'I made a promise to William Harness, my lord,' Blackstone had said. 'And those people will know of it.'

'You risk everything from the start,' de Harcourt had warned.

'I gave my word. What other honour is there for someone like me?'

When the noblemen had left the castle Jean and Blanche de Harcourt sat with Christiana and Blackstone. It was arranged that the following afternoon they would meet in the chapel and the priest would officiate at their wedding. De Harcourt and his wife would bear witness.

'Were we not permitted to marry with the barons in attendance because of my shame?' asked Christiana.

'No one knows you're with child. We said nothing to them because for now your marriage should remain private,' said Blanche. 'We did not want to risk them speaking of it. A Christmas wedding is something women will gossip about and if Gilles de Marçy is still in Normandy with those men we don't want him to hear of it.'

De Harcourt said, 'Half the nobles in France are probably born out of wedlock, Christiana. We care for you now as would your father. His sacrifice will not go unrecognized in this house.'

Blackstone averted his eyes from de Harcourt. There was no possibility that he could know of Blackstone's involvement in those early days of the invasion, but mention of her father made him uncomfortable.

'You have to realize that Thomas will be in danger, as will this family, if what he does is traced back to us. We've heard from Paris that my uncle was made to wear a halter around his neck and nothing more than an undershirt, and they paraded him through the streets like that. The King spared his life, but his humiliation is complete.'

Blanche said, 'There is no youthful joy left for you, Christiana. You're a woman now and you'll stay with us until Thomas returns.'

'And if he fails then he fails alone,' de Harcourt added. 'Your marriage must remain a secret for now. This contract between you would guarantee a life of penury were it not for what Thomas has agreed to undertake. His success determines not only your well-being but ours too.'

Christiana nodded her understanding. Marrying a man for affection or love alone was seldom allowed and never considered a good match. And Thomas Blackstone was dirt-poor. Had Jean and Blanche de Harcourt not been her guardians her own life could have ended in a convent or a whorehouse, or she could have been raped and murdered by Gilles de Marçy.

De Harcourt wiped the wine from his lips with a folded napkin. 'Besides, you should have been spoken for years ago. It was something your father should have considered more seriously. A girl past twelve or thirteen is going to find it difficult to be suitably matched,' he said, with a glance of disapproval from Blanche.

'My lord and husband knows only that affection grows over the years. He never experienced it in his youth.' She paused and then smiled. 'Only when he married me.'

'Emotions without restraint are a woman's business, Blanche. If Thomas had bothered himself to learn gentle words through poetry he might have understood that.' He looked at Blackstone. 'That's one thing you've failed in. Learning the skills of courtly love is a means of honouring your beloved, Thomas. We go to war and fight because of the love we have for our women.' He returned Blanche's look, which he knew well. *Stay silent and guard your words*, she was saying. 'He has nothing to offer the girl, as far as I can see, except his strength and courage and love for her. Though I daresay that will be enough,' he temporized.

'And they are both blessed with your friendship. They are richer than most, my lord,' added Blanche.

She was not going to let him heap more ruin on a wedding ceremony that could not be acknowledged. A day when a bride had to suffocate her own joy. De Harcourt had to give in gracefully. If he did not, the winter nights could grow colder and seem longer.

'Aye, and it was earned, Thomas Blackstone. You've a way to go before I can let you loose in polite company, but you've proved yourself to me, without question. But there won't be a wedding notice posted, or celebratory feast given. The minstrels have been paid off. So your day will be one of quiet and no different than any other. And that's the way it must be. I'll bargain with the priest to take us into the chapel and perform the ceremony without the usual custom of banns being read.'

Blanche raised her eyebrows. There was one more thing to be said, but de Harcourt scowled.

'Is this a poor bargain, Christiana?' Blackstone asked gently, as if seeing her doubts.

'For my part it's the best of bargains, Thomas, and you must never doubt it. You found me in this castle and took me to Sir Godfrey and then you risked your life again for me. There's more than gratitude involved. I'll treasure you for the rest of my life, as will our child.'

Blackstone reached out a hand and smothered hers. 'Don't listen too closely to what my lord says. There's much joy coming our way and we'll be together once I've secured a place for us. I'm responsible for you now, but my Lord Jean, and his good Lady Blanche, will protect you until I send for you.'

Blanche de Harcourt had waited long enough for her husband to finalize the arrangement. 'My lord and husband will also offer Thomas a dowry on behalf of your father.'

Christiana grabbed de Harcourt's hand and pressed it to her lips. 'My lord. God bless your kindness and generosity. I shall say a prayer for you every day for the rest of my life.'

De Harcourt sighed and eased her away, so that she and Blanche might embrace. 'We have done our duty, child. How God came to place the two of you under my roof is indeed a mystery, but we have honoured His wishes – though His ways mystify me more often than my wife.' He spread his hands in supplication. 'Now can we eat? Marriages are arranged for whatever purpose is suitable. All this talk of undying love and childbearing squirms in my stomach like a worm that demands feeding.'

The following day the four of them went into the chapel and knelt before the priest as if it were a regular time for prayer. The priest was well paid and did as de Harcourt instructed. Special prayers were said in thanks for Sir Godfrey's life and then the priest said the nuptial Mass. Blanche gave Christiana one of her lavender and grey velvet gowns, embroidered with silver and thread, set off with a necklace of precious stones. Over her braided hair, which had been washed with rosemary water, Blanche had arranged a filigree of gold.

Blackstone had surrendered to the ritual and bathed. He wore fresh clothes and tunic, and parted his long hair in the middle. De Harcourt instructed Marcel to trim Blackstone's whiskers that now stubbled his face and prickled the whitening scar. Marcel was the only servant trusted enough who knew of the ceremony and, without speaking of it, he suspected why the marriage had been so quickly arranged. These events held Blackstone briefly in wonder, and for their wedding night Blanche had prepared a guest room fit for a nobleman and his bride, embellished with dried rose petals and fragrant perfume.

'I have no gift of jewellery,' Blackstone told her as they sat naked before the warmth of the fire. He extended the palm of his hand, showing her the silver coin neatly cut in two. 'But this is a token of my love for you. Wherever the two halves may be, then there will we also be. Complete. As one.' He kissed her tenderly and hoped the words he had read in one of de Harcourt's books had been well remembered.

Days later, when he had embraced his new wife in farewell and accepted Blanche's good wishes for a safe return, he had been taken aside by Jean de Harcourt before he and the twenty armed men rode out.

'Honour and glory will be yours in time, but temper your killing with compassion for those who deserve it, Thomas. For those who do not, strike the fear of your name into their hearts.'

PART THREE

SWORN LORD

CHAPTER TWENTY-THREE

The Feast of Epiphany, twelve days after Christmas Day, celebrated the arrival of the three wise men, the Magi, bearing gifts for the holy child. But on this particular bleak day Blackstone bore no gifts of goodwill.

'You'll grant us mercy,' said the peasant whose twisted face Blackstone gazed down on from his horse. The man sneered and laughed as he turned to look at the thirty or more villagers armed with pitchforks, billhooks and axes. They were in no mood to pander to a lone impoverished knight with only two men at his side. Meulon and Gaillard looked uneasily about them.

'So you believe I should offer leniency to those who butchered an unarmed man and messenger of the King of England?' Blackstone answered.

The peasant took a threatening step forward, half raising the billhook. 'You'd best be on your way, bastard Englishman. Our protector Saquet, *le poigne de fer*, will be upset if we kill you ourselves, but he'll not chastise us if we lop off a leg or an arm.'

A few of the men laughed, their bravery growing every moment. Killing the English messenger was easy, but three armed men on horseback might cause some of them injury. Blackstone had not yet taken Wolf Sword into his hand as he eased his horse forward a stride. The peasant's uncertainty was matched by his own small retreat.

'This "Iron Fist" you talk about. I've heard of him. They say he's as strong as an ox and twice as stupid. I'm here to punish, not be threatened.'

'You've a nerve coming here. Leave before we set on you!' the man shouted, encouraged by the others, but their courage slipped away quickly when women's screams suddenly broke the early morning air. The men turned. Flames were taking hold of three houses as armed men bearing torches stepped from the forest in a necklace of fire.

'There's no gift of mercy today,' said Blackstone, wrapping his hand around the sword's grip.

The houses blazed fiercely as every man, woman and child who had not escaped the encircling men was herded into the muddy thoroughfare. The bitter smoke swept across them and their tears of fear and self-pity mingled with those from the smoke. Blackstone had little trouble in identifying the half-dozen men who had caged William Harness like a pig awaiting slaughter and who had butchered Harness's friend. In their fear the villagers quickly turned on each other, giving up those responsible for the emasculation and killing of the young messenger. They were made to cut down his violated body and bury him in a deep grave so that wild animals could not root up his remains.

And then, as his men held back wailing women, Blackstone hanged the ringleaders and set their houses alight. The village blacksmith who had branded William Harness was held and burned with the same fleur-de-lys branding iron onto his forehead. And after this justice had been meted out every man, woman and child knelt in the mud and begged Blackstone to spare them.

'I am riding towards the coast to find other villagers who mistreated my King's messengers,' Blackstone told them. 'Saquet cannot protect you now. Remember that. I have relented and shown you mercy. I should have every one of you branded and sent off into the forest to survive like the beasts you are. Remember my giving of life and my name.'

Blackstone led the men out of the village.

'Not much chance of them thinking you're the Virgin Mary in disguise. More like the Grim Reaper,' said Meulon.

'Either way they'll remember,' said Blackstone.

'We can't ride to the coast, Master Thomas,' Gaillard said, 'those villagers will have run like rabbits to Chaulion and we'll have Saquet breathing down our necks.'

'Of course they will. It's what I want,' said Blackstone.

'You think we can win a pitched fight out here? They'll ambush us at their first chance. And I'll lay odds they outnumber us at least three to one,' Meulon said, adding his voice to the men's concerns. The Englishman might have the balls of a bull but that didn't mean he couldn't be brought down by a pack of ravenous wolves.

'We're not going to the coast. Saquet will spend the better part of a week looking for us. I needed him out of the way for a while. We'll be waiting when he returns. We choose the ground where we fight. Find me a slow road to the monastery at Chaulion and give our peasant friend time enough to do his work.' He spurred his horse, forcing the others to follow.

Riding out with the men had brought an unexpected sense of freedom. As a ventenar he had commanded twenty archers and now there was a similar number in his charge. These ordinary soldiers were simple, uncomplicated men. This was an experience that filled him with hope, unshackling him from the confines of the castle with its rules of behaviour. Christiana was safe and he would have a modest dowry, and if he succeeded in securing even one town he would be able to justify de Harcourt's trust. He had already demonstrated that his actions were tempered with leniency, and as he hanged the ringleaders the ghost of Sir Gilbert rode at his shoulder and grunted agreement. It took a few more miles of riding before he realized what it was that had changed in him. He was happy.

By the next morning they sat on a low crest of a hill gazing down at the lifeless, frozen landscape. They could see quite clearly that the crossroads had not carried much traffic since the last sprinkling of snow. It was a small, single-storey monastery, conceived as a reclusive hermitage in ancient times and then built up over the years as others sought out the solitude and reflective life of a monk. Over the years such hard-working self-sacrifice had eased from the monks, who relied on their lay brothers to do all the manual work. Villagers paid tithes and tilled the land – labour they could well have put to better use tending their own meagre crops. Monks attended to prayer every three hours, day and night. It was a life that no fighting man Blackstone had ever known could contemplate, though there were benefits of ale and wine – and it was not unknown for a prior or an abbot to have a mistress for other worldly comforts.

Smoke curled from the monastery chimneys. They had warmth, so they weren't too uncomfortable in their seclusion. Some of the outer walls had crumbled, but the main structure still stood and was kept in good order by the monks. A wood and stone bridge lay across the river, which was shallow in places as indicated by the boulders keeping ice from forming. But the pockets of still water showed there were deep pools that were frozen. An attempt to cross without that bridge would be difficult. In the old days monks must have seen the value of building such a bridge and Blackstone thought that the abbot most likely charged a toll.

He could see that some of the old storage barns and stables had fallen into complete disrepair, so over the years the monastery had brought everything within the walls of the existing building. That made sense because then brigands or common thieves would have to scale the walls to steal grain or drink.

'Why are we here?' asked Meulon. 'The town is miles away.'

Blackstone pointed to the churned road that led away in one direction. 'Chaulion's down there, and it looks as though horsemen have travelled down this way in the last day or so.'

'Saquet looking for us,' said Meulon.

'The abbot is under Saquet's protection and the King favours him. His hands will be smooth, his belly fat. There's no resistance in a kept man. Weak with good food, wine and a warm bed.'

'That sounds all right to me,' Gaillard said, and the other men muttered their agreement.

'And when men like us come to take it from you, what then?'

said Meulon. 'You'd have your fat arse kicked and a begging bowl and a whore to keep you if you're lucky.'

'Jesus, Meulon, having a soft tit and a skinful of wine isn't much to ask,' Gaillard answered.

'Best keep your mother out of this, Gaillard,' said one of the men.

Gaillard took the insult good-naturedly and allowed the men's jibes as Meulon turned his attention back to the landscape, where Blackstone pointed out the features. 'It's a good location for a monastery – on the crossroads. If a man who knew about such things pulled down those old buildings and rebuilt a wall you could stop anyone using the road. A few men could control the passage of trade and anyone would find it hard to ford the river,' said Blackstone.

Meulon raised himself in his stirrups and looked left and right. 'The ground falls away, and rises across the stream, so it would be a good strategic place to hold.'

Blackstone smiled. Those were his thoughts exactly.

Meulon sighed, and blew the cold phlegm from his nose. 'You're taking a stick to a hornet's nest is what you're doing. You interfere in one of his villages, and now you're going to take the monastery. Saquet is going to be very pissed off with you,' he said, and then smiled. This Englishman was like a bed louse, he'd get under your skin and you'd scratch until you bled.

Blackstone and his men urged their horses downhill. It was getting colder and one thing Blackstone knew for certain was that men hated fighting in winter. It was a time when wars ground to a halt. Horse forage was scarce and men needed food and warmth to fight effectively. He hoped that Saquet's wild goose chase would give him the time he needed to secure the road that led to Chaulion.

The voice called from the main gate, 'You there! What are you doing? Be off with you! Off!'

Blackstone and his men were carrying the fallen stones from the old tumbled walls down to the bridge. They barely paused in their work. It was already three hours after dawn.

'You've been at prayer, good brother,' said Blackstone. 'It's going to be a fine day, I think. The sky's cleared. Cold, mind you, and the wind will pick up again, I suppose, so we'll have that accursed rain and snow again. No matter, we'll be finished in a couple of days.'

The perplexed monk left the gate open and, gathering his habit, traipsed down to where the men continued their labours. He saw that a couple of hundred yards away in each direction a horseman guarded the road.

'You're taking our stone,' said the monk, unable to grasp why anyone would do such a thing.

'Yes. And it's good stone,' was the reply.

'It's not yours to take!'

Blackstone wiped his hands on his tunic. 'But you don't need it. It's just lying out there in the fields.'

The monk's mouth opened and closed like a fish. 'The abbot must know about this.' He turned on his heel and Blackstone strode by his side. 'I think you'll find the abbot will be happy to donate the stone to the cause.'

'Cause?'

They were close to the open gate.

'Our cause,' said Blackstone. 'I'll explain to the abbot when I see him.'

'You can't see him. Who do you think you are? He wouldn't allow armed men in here,' the monk protested.

'In here?' said Blackstone as he stood beneath the gate and eased it open further. 'Think of us as pilgrims seeking shelter, brother. Only we're going to outstay our welcome.'

Blackstone took the dumbfounded monk through the gate as Meulon and the other men followed. They had seized the monastery near Chaulion.

No one had ever dared challenge Abbot Pierre's authority. Even the odious and threatening Saquet had given way because the abbot was favoured by his King, and the mercenary had understood the terms of his own contract. The abbot might well have argued with himself that he had placed villagers in danger by abandoning them, but Abbot Pierre had, in his own mind, given them life by aligning his own aims with those of the routiers. A simple justification for a simple, venal man. But now the comfort of his massaged conscience was about to be stripped from him. Abbot Pierre visibly trembled. Thomas Blackstone's face sent a chill like ice water down to his privates. The Englishman had introduced himself, but without due courtesy shown to the abbot's status.

'You're confined to your lodgings,' Blackstone told him as he sniffed the succulent aroma of roasted meat suffusing the air. 'And you've a good kitchen by the smell of it. Roast pig is far too rich for humble monks. No matter, my men need feeding.'

'You're mistaken if you believe that you and your brigands can escape retribution. You have no idea of the wrath you have incurred.'

'Not from you, I think.'

'Your arrogance is insufferable,' spluttered the abbot.

Meulon said, 'A leader of men has to be arrogant, Brother Abbot – you set a fine example yourself.'

'Don't worry, your silver plate and artefacts are safe from plunder,' Blackstone told him. 'King Edward hanged men who looted churches and monasteries. We won't pillage your sacraments. You've splinters of the cross, though, have you? To sell to peasants? To give them hope?'

'Of course,' said the abbot warily. 'Do you intend to take them?'

'I'll burn them when I find them,' he said.

'May God forgive such violation,' the abbot whispered and crossed himself.

Blackstone seized a handful of the abbot's cloak that he wore over his habit, pulling him to where Gaillard waited. 'Worthless shards of wood, peeled from any scrap timber and used to prey on an ignorant peasant's fears. You offer them hope for salvation and don't even have to uncurl their hand to seize their hard-earned coin. If every splinter of the cross was gathered from every monastery or church our Lord Jesus would need to have been crucified a thousand times on as many crosses. Pray for your own forgiveness. Off to your quarters, my big fat crow, and I'll have one of the brothers bring you bread and water.'

The abbot's jowls wobbled, his prissy mouth unable to utter a word.

'Your lips are as puckered as a cat's arse,' Blackstone said and pushed him towards Gaillard. 'Understand this: your life of ease has now ended. You have how many monks here? Ten? More?'

The abbot had always had a simple understanding of where power lay and who wielded it. He steepled his trembling fingers together and lowered his eyes. A man of low breeding like this Englishman obviously needed his status as leader of his men acknowledged.

'Sir Thomas. This humble monastery can be of no interest to your English King. Surely?'

'That is for me to decide. Now I can either search every nook and cranny and drag them out, or you can tell me how many monks are here. Or would you prefer a starvation diet for a week to lose some of that blubber?'

The abbot swallowed hard. If he co-operated, then at least he might be fed meat, something he had become accustomed to. Not for him the modest food of a humble monk. The kitchen smells made him salivate. 'Fourteen monks and as many lay brothers.'

'Good. I'll need them all to help my men.'

'What can possibly be done here?'

'I have only a few days to build a wall and if I thought that having you carry rocks would be of benefit I'd have you whipped into the fields, but you'd be too slow and cumbersome.' Blackstone nodded to Gaillard, who stepped forward to escort the abbot to his quarters.

'A wall?' His incomprehension, as if Blackstone spoke in tongues, only added to his look of stupidity. 'The days are short. A wall?'

'You have tallow and oil so we'll have torchlight. You'll see. It will be a fine wall.'

Gaillard grabbed the confused abbot and forced him to quicken his step.

Blackstone turned to Meulon. 'Have the men fed, the horses stabled. Then take an inventory of food and supplies. Keep everyone behind the walls until we organize work parties. And ignore tradition – keep them armed. Two sentries at all times. Day and night.'

Meulon nodded and turned away without question. Whatever this young Englishman had planned he'd know soon enough and he was happy to be left to deal with the men. None had yet asked too many questions about why they had been put under Blackstone's command, but they would, so he decided to bring them together and, in a soldier's way, cut out any discontent that might be brewing. Thomas Blackstone commanded, but Meulon was their captain and he would make sure there was no chance of dissent.

Blackstone stood in the empty room and imagined the abbot's corrupt life of comfort and warmth when it should have been one of humility and hard work, of going among the verminous poor to offer healing and alms. He wandered alone through the monastery, noticing that the kitchen fires were well tended, the flour sacks in the bakery were dry, the flour coarsely milled. Not yet finely ground as for a nobleman's taste then, he thought. Perhaps the abbot had not elevated his aspirations as high as he might. The chapel was modest but functional; the infirmary clean, with boiled linen bandages neatly folded, the tinctures, herbs and ointments stored and labelled. An elderly monk bowed before him and when asked his name cupped a curved palm to his ear. He was Brother Simon; his eyes clear, his back bent and although age pulled the skin taut across his hands, there was no tremor in his fingers. Blackstone knew he would be able to stitch a wound with skill. He would not work in the fields, Blackstone explained to him, and he would not be asked to do anything other than what he did. Muscles would bruise and bones could break when working with rocks, and backs would need liniment, and shoulders would need putting back into place when pulled out of joint.

Wherever he went, everything was in an orderly state. The lay brothers were leather-skinned men used to hard work in all weathers, compared to the flabbier monks, mostly stooped and pale from bending over their manuscripts. The manner in which the lay brothers held back and bowed their heads respectfully when he walked past made Blackstone think that they were probably harshly disciplined on the orders of the prior as instructed by the abbot. These were the men who laboured to serve the self-indulgent monks as they scoured scripture and copied their pages in the warmth of the scriptorium. After inspecting the various parts of the monastery he walked the base of the walls until he was finally satisfied that they were in good order and gave little chance of being breached because of poorly laid masonry. There was always the risk that Saquet could mount an attack before Blackstone could find a way of seizing the town. The monastery was his men's safe haven and would remain their sanctuary until he could defeat the mercenary, Iron Fist.

The men's spears and shields were stacked against each other so that they could be reached quickly should the alarm be raised. Each man carried stone from the fields and the ruined buildings, which Blackstone had ordered torn down. The monastery's two donkeys were saddled with pannier baskets and used to carry more of the boulders. Blackstone's days in the quarry with his master mason had taught him how to organize work parties, and the monks worked obediently once they had made their protests at having their prayer times restricted to matins and vespers for the next few days. The monks had become lazy in their coddled life of prayer and scripture reading and they would have to sweat more to match their lay brothers. A monk's life was one of obedience, Blackstone had told them, and their prayers could be said while they worked. God would still hear them and the Lord admired those who laboured. Was it not a monk's duty to build something that would last? Then he, Blackstone, would give them the opportunity to please God and reacquaint themselves with obedience and humility. And, he promised them, for those who faltered a knotted rope would remind them of how weakness of the flesh could be banished.

He and Meulon worked out a roster so that everyone would be fed and have four hours' sleep in every twelve-hour period. The monastery's grain stores were full and there was enough salted fish and mutton to carry a whole village through a winter, let alone a couple of dozen monks. Blackstone ordered the kitchener to prepare and cook cauldrons of pottage and ensure that the bakery provided rough grain bread for the men. The kitchens were to be kept in use around the clock. A main meal of nourishing grains would be served at midday and the same warming food given at midnight to those who worked through the hours of darkness. A cup of hot, spiced wine would give the men fortitude against the icy rain, swept along by the north wind, that could sap a man's strength after only a few hours. There would be salted fish after matins and cheese and bread after vespers; then the work parties would continue by torchlight. By the time the winter sky darkened on that first day a stone cairn had already grown near the bridge, and another between it and the monastery gate. Torches flickered throughout the night. Those monks who proved too frail to carry out heavy work he sent to the kitchens to help their lay brothers, and to suffer the indignity of being under their control as they were instructed to prepare food, wash pans and scrub floors.

Blackstone gathered the men and explained what had to be done. He took small stones and pebbles and marked the outline of the monastery, then the bridge and how the roads crossed and disappeared into the forest towards unknown destinations. All soldiers, no matter who they served, would be used to building fortifications of one kind or another; they did not have to be sappers in order to build walls. A good stone layer could put down three or four yards a day of double-skinned wall, and he had thirty men and as many monks.

'We work with the monks and lay brothers. We have two, perhaps three days. We can all lay rocks and boulders, but I need someone to supervise the work and make sure the damned thing stays up. Are there any among you who have worked with stone?'

Two of the men raised their hands.

'I'm Talpin, I built my father's barn with him when I was a boy.'

'And you?' Blackstone asked the other, who was one of de Graville's men.

'Perinne. I built a wall for my village to keep thieving Bretons from raiding us and they never breached it.'

'Good. Then you two will be in charge of each shift of men who work,' said Blackstone, noting that their elevation in responsibility pleased them. 'If I had a choice I'd build an earth-rammed, double-skin wall.' The men nodded their agreement. 'And then plant whitethorn in it to repel intruders. But we can't, the ground is hard and this is only a temporary defence.'

Perinne hawked and spat. 'No, Master Blackstone, this wall will be here for years to come. The way I build walls, that is. Don't know about Count Livay's man,' he said, meaning Talpin. 'I bet that barn came down the first time his old man farted in the cow byre.'

The men threw more good-natured scorn and jibes at each other. That was fine, Blackstone thought. They were coming together as a body of men despite being soldiers from different sworn lords. Talpin smiled. 'I built a barn, my friend; a double-height, vaulted barn. Even the English couldn't pull it down when they came through.'

The men laughed, but then suddenly realized who it was that commanded them. They fell silent.

Blackstone filled the moment of unease with a quick response. 'If the English couldn't pull down that barn and the Bretons couldn't cross that wall, then you're the men for the job.'

This cheered them again. He went on, 'All we can do is make life difficult for anyone trying to bypass us or breach the wall. Double stone the base, bigger stones for support, dry wall, no mortar, no cut stone, pick your shape and lay. Show the monks if they've never done it before, though I'll wager some have, and those that don't learn quickly enough – use them to load and carry the stone. Build the wall chest high...'

'Your chest or ours!' one of the soldiers called out, causing the men to dare laughter again. Meulon waited patiently and said nothing. Like Blackstone, he knew that each time these rough and ready men insulted each other and then carefully, but respectfully, prodded a man of rank who was their leader, it bound them together. It was not something any man would dare say to a French lord; nor, he guessed, would an Englishman risk it with one who held rank. But this Englishman had a way with the men, and seemed able to take a fighting man's humour.

'Four and a half feet high...' said Blackstone.

'Ah, that's short-arse Renouard, then!' one of the men said, and the jeers rose again.

'With nine-inch-high copes,' Blackstone said, quieting them down. The promise of hot wine and roasted pig had already smoothed any sharp edges of doubt about the hard task that lay before them. 'Twenty-four inches wide at the base above the foundation stones and thirteen inches wide under the coping stones. Scatter unused rocks outside the perimeter along with cut branches and fallen timber – that should slow anyone trying to breach it at the run.'

Talpin and Perinne nodded their agreement. The Englishman knew what he was talking about.

Darkness was Blackstone's friend. He knew no one from Chaulion would venture several miles on a forest track at night. The ghostly wind that moaned through the trees would carry fear into many a soul, no matter how devout. And even if Saquet was to ignore the frightened villagers' warning of this band of English and French routiers then he would come hours after first light. Blackstone waited patiently as Meulon positioned some of his crossbowmen in an ambush on the approach, despite Blackstone's concern that once they had fired their first salvo they would be vulnerable because of the time it took them to reload. His thoughts made him yearn for the rough-hewn archers he had once been a part of. If only he could have had a half-dozen of them now he could fight off three times as many raiders. Meulon assured him that if an attack came the first horsemen would be brought down, and by the time anyone behind them forced their way through the low branches, his bowmen would have retreated to safety. As the building of the wall continued he and Meulon stayed watchful. Chance could always surprise even the most careful commanders, so he was happy to take the time for such precautions. Men of violence seldom exercised patience, but for those who did, victory could be gained more readily. At first light there were no riders and no one appeared on the skyline. It was time to reconnoitre the town.

Within the hour he and Meulon were on the heights that rose almost a hundred feet above Chaulion, the undulating hillside curving like a limestone-faced wave. Blackstone and Meulon had taken a circuitous route, dismounting and then walking their horses through the low branches. A hundred yards from the edge they tethered their mounts and crept forward to lie on the forest's floor to study the town. The brisk wind whipped away woodsmoke from house fires, and the sentries who stood hunched in the two watchtowers, which stood diagonally across from each other on the town's walls, would only be alerted by anyone approaching through the clearing in the forest.

'Do you know how many people live there?' asked Blackstone, without turning to face Meulon next to him. He sensed the man shrug.

'No idea. It could be a thousand people crammed ten to a room or a third of that living in the houses. There'll be tradesmen, blacksmiths and bakers and the like, but look at it, just like a village behind walls. The main square is where Saquet would live, probably in a merchant's house. This was a good trading route before he seized the town, but no longer.'

Blackstone watched for any movement beyond the town's walls. It was quiet enough to believe that Saquet had already left in his pursuit of the Englishman. 'Do you think he's bedded down for winter?' he asked.

Meulon nodded. 'No one likes to raid and fight at this time of year. He'll have stored his grain and feed just like the good abbot – most of it for his men – which means the townspeople are on poor rations and that keeps everyone weak enough not to try anything.'

The sentries had barely stirred from where they jammed their backs into the watchtower walls so as to gain whatever protection they could from the biting wind. They'd feel it more in those towers, Blackstone thought, and were likely to keep their heads down in their misery. He was about to tell Meulon to go back to the crossroads when the wind lifted a cry of pain upwards from the town's walls. The sentries turned lazily and looked down into the square that neither of the two watchers could see, but the sentries' lack of alarm meant that the sound was not unusual in Chaulion and posed no threat to the remaining mercenaries. Within moments of the agonized shriek muted laughter reached them from the square.

'They're hurting some poor bastard,' Meulon said. 'And enjoying it.'

One of the sentries called down to those below him in the unseen square, but his words did not reach Blackstone.

'Did you hear?' he asked.

Meulon shook his head. Another scream of pain rose above the sound of the wind.

'He's telling whoever's down there to hurt him again. Bastards. For once I wish we had a couple of your English archers, I'd have 'em skewered where they stand.'

Blackstone lay silent, chin resting on his fists, looking down into the town.

'How do we take Chaulion?' he asked. 'We can't lay siege. I don't see any repaired walls on this side to undermine. I don't know. I could ambush Saquet before he gets back. But then... I don't know how many men he has.'

'Are you asking me or talking to yourself?' Meulon asked.

'Asking.'

Meulon sighed and let his eyes linger on the walled town. Thomas Blackstone had enough courage and madness in him to scare the devil out of hell, but he was prepared to ask advice from an old soldier like him. 'Escalade is best,' he said. 'We build ladders, get them up on the wall at night and kill as many as we can while we have time. Before Saquet comes back.'

'Have you done that before?'

Meulon pulled off his helmet and scratched his scalp, then dug a horny fingernail into his matted hair and eased out a louse. 'A couple of times. My Lord de Harcourt didn't hold with it. He thought it a dishonourable way to fight, fit only for brigands.'

'But you think differently.'

Meulon rubbed his fingers together, crushing the louse. 'Why do you think he sent me with you?'

Blackstone studied the walls again. The watchtowers lay east and west, one giving a view of the approach road from the monastery, the other of a single track that disappeared into the rising ground and forest after two hundred yards.

'Those walls are twenty feet high.'

'Twenty-five,' Blackstone corrected him. 'Where do we go over? This wall closest to us, do you think? It's the one most shadowed by the forest, and will cast the darkest shadow at night.'

Meulon studied the sky and sucked on a piece of fallen twig, rubbing it like a tooth cleaner. 'No. Not there. The wind's from the north.' He pointed. 'That north-east corner is the coldest, wettest part of the town. And there's a gully that drops another five feet down. That's good concealment. If a sentry walks the walls, which I'll wager they won't because they're lazy, half-asleep bastards who think no one could ever threaten them, they wouldn't linger there. They'll turn their backs to that bitch of a wind. We go over there and both watchtower sentries will be looking the other way.'

'I can't take men into a town unless we know how many we're up against. We know there are sixty or more of them, but how many would Saquet take to chase us?'

Meulon flicked the chewed stick away and eased his helmet back on. 'You challenged and threatened him. Thirty of us – he'd take at least forty. If there's twenty or thirty men left in there it would be good to know where they are, because we need surprise on our side, otherwise we'll be hard-pressed to gain the advantage. And there's no telling how the townspeople will react.'

Blackstone thought it through quickly. It was his responsibility to gain the town. No, it was more than that, he told himself. It was his ambition. If anything was going to be lost or gained it would fall on him. He didn't want to go back to the Normans leaving most of their men lying dead on a winter's field.

Blackstone returned to the monastery, where Meulon had lay brothers build the scaling ladder. Blackstone's wall was taking shape. Wooden frames had been made, wider at the bottom than the top, as templates to get the height as consistent as possible. The turf had been broken to lay out the shape of the wall and then lengths of twine were strung taut between the frames to guide the stone-layers. Talpin and Perinne used plumb bobs to make sure it stayed vertical. Course by course the wall would grow and be interlocked with tie stones every yard or so. Blackstone liked what he saw. The men knew what they were doing. Stones were laid with a slight downward angle that would shed the rain, and as each yard went up a group of older monks spilled baskets of smaller stones and pebbles into the void. It would never be as solid as Blackstone would like, but the speed at which the men worked boded well. As each shift took over from the other they saw how many stones had been laid. Neither Talpin nor Perinne wanted to be outdone by the other and that competition took hold with the men. The work rate had increased as the soldiers formed alliances to outdo each preceding shift and that in turn caused despair among the monks until the prior, Brother Marcus, saw salvation in their more demanding work. The competition was God showing them the way, he told them. The sooner they completed the wall the quicker they could return to their life of prayer. Arduous endeavour would grant them relief from the Englishman's yoke.

Blackstone noticed the change; so did Talpin and Perinne.

'Do they follow the prior willingly?' he asked his two wall builders.

Talpin said, 'It seems so. From what I understand the abbot was put here a year or more ago when the Mother house got rid of him. The monks didn't want him – when the old abbot died, they'd voted for the prior. Somehow Abbot Pierre had connections and got the favour of the King and he was placed here. Who could challenge that? The villagers farm the land; he collects their tithes and sits on his fat arse.'

'They seem to listen to the prior, though,' Perinne confirmed.

'Good. Are you satisfied with their work?'

Perinne gestured with a sweep of his arm. 'You can see for yourself, Sir Thomas. The night work has doubled our efforts. Aye, they're working well.'

Blackstone was as pleased as his wall builders. 'Then encourage them. Don't beat them.'

The two Normans looked at each other.

'A rope across a lazy back is no real punishment, Sir Thomas,' said Talpin.

Blackstone nodded. 'I worked in a quarry from the age of seven. The quarryman thrashed me every day until the master stonemason saw my efforts and eased the whip. See that we do the same for them. Praise their work. And for every extra yard laid ahead of schedule we give the men and the brothers extra rations of bread and at the end of each shift extra wine or ale. Make sure the kitchener is told.'

For a moment it seemed Talpin and Perinne would question his order, but they understood the value of fresh bread to a man, and the promise of extra ale was better than an apple in front of a donkey. Their sworn lords' promise of full pay while they served Blackstone and the possibility of making more from this venture had been reason enough to step forward and swear the oath of silence and obedience. The first, to deny where their true allegiance lay, and the second, to do the bidding of this young Englishman. All these men had followed their lords into battle. They had seen stupidity and careless disregard for their lives take many of their comrades. So far Blackstone had avoided both pitfalls. That he was French-speaking didn't alter the fact that he was still a bastard Englishman, and an archer to boot, although that was slowly being forgiven as they began to see a man like themselves emerge – a soldier who had gained rank through skill and courage.

They could live with that.

CHAPTER TWENTY-FOUR

Before darkness fell Blackstone led twenty men into the forest. He had left ten of his men to guard the monastery and to ensure the monks were confined to the dormitory. Those he took with him carried two scaling ladders to take them over the walls under cover of black, troubled clouds driven by a harsh wind, tumbling across the sky. There was a dark gulley at the base of the wall, chilled from never seeing sunlight, and where mist would cling the better part of the day and night. It was a dank place with the smell of a tomb about it.

Blackstone had made a decision that Meulon thought stupid and had argued in strained whispers in case his voice carried down to the sentries. Blackstone was going to go over the wall alone to reconnoitre the town. And then, once he had a better understanding of its layout, he would return and take the men inside its walls. It was madness, Meulon had told him, and as Blackstone eased himself over the wall and onto the battlements, he was beginning to wonder if Meulon had not been correct. Perhaps he would have been wiser to bring the men over and seek out their enemy in the confines of the town's streets. A lantern swung in the corner of the square. Its faint light barely showed the three shadows that stood static near the middle of the open space. Blackstone crouched, letting his eyes follow the lines of the wall and the shape of the sentry who stood in each watchtower. Meulon had at least been correct about them huddling in their cloaks with their backs to the wind. He quickly moved forward and went down the steps leading into the square. The town seemed to be a jumble of various buildings with narrow alleyways between them. Here and there some houses were double height, better built in stone and wood, while others were squat and thatched, with smoke-holes cut into their roofs.

He skirted the walls around the main square, using the shadows to keep his movements unseen. His heart beat rapidly with the thought that any minute he could bump into someone sleeping or disturb a sentry, and then the alarm would be raised and he would be hard-pressed to race back up the steps to where Meulon and the men huddled at the base of the outside wall waiting for his command to put up the ladder and attack. He was alone in a hostile environment and he cursed his foolhardiness. But luck had always been with him and as he thought of the silver talisman on the chain around his neck he skirted the far side of the square and got closer to what he now saw to be three upright stakes in the ground, and tied to each stake was the slumped body of a man.

He moved closer and tried to hear if they were still breathing, but the wind and the clanking of the lantern overwhelmed any sound that may have come from them. He placed a hand on each man's face. Two were stone cold, but the third had warmth in his neck. Blackstone could feel the stickiness on his fingers and knew that it was blood. This must have been the man who had been tortured earlier and whose cries he had heard. There was barely any life in him and there was nothing Blackstone could do to help him. A gust of wind suddenly extinguished the lantern. The nearest sentry shouted, but his voice was carried away by the wind. Blackstone imagined the man cursing to himself as he turned from his post and clumped down the wooden steps that brought him into the square. Blackstone moved quickly back to the wall of the nearest building and watched as the sentry's shape slipped in and out of the darkness of the walls until he kicked at a door in anger and then pushed it open, shouting for those inside to relight the lantern. Those rooms must be where the guard slept, thought Blackstone, and sure enough, moments later, as the sentry made his way back up the steps a dull glow flared from inside the room and a man, stretching and scratching from sleep, came out and relit the street lantern.

As the light swayed again in the wind the door closed behind the guard and the light inside was extinguished. If nothing else Blackstone had discovered where some of the routiers were. Dare he go on further into the alleyways and risk alerting a dog or a townsman who could raise the alarm? His moment of indecision allowed a hand to snake out and grasp his ankle.

Blackstone almost cried out, but managed to choke back his alarm. He fell back, rolling in the dirt, his hand reaching for his knife. Before he could get back on his feet he heard a desperate whisper: 'Stranger, help us. For pity's sake, help us.'

Blackstone looked quickly towards the sentry in case his tumble had been seen, but the man still had his back to the square – what threat could there be from within? Blackstone peered into the darkness and less than six feet away, where he had been standing moments ago, was a grid in the ground that covered a pit. The gaps were large enough for a man to push his head through, and Blackstone could see that someone was there and that it had been a hand that now gestured to him that had snatched at his ankle. Blackstone wasn't sure what to do. How many men were caged below ground? If he didn't go to him it would only take a yell of despair to alert the sentries. He had no choice. Bent double, he took the few strides to the man whose features he could barely make out in the darkness. The swaying lantern gave just enough light to see that he too had been beaten.

The man whispered again, 'Stranger, there's a water bucket to your left. Reach for it, I beg you. There are more than a dozen men in this hole with me. Give us water, in God's name! help us!'

Blackstone glanced behind him and saw a wooden bucket with a ladle. What to do? If he gave these men water would they cry out or fight among themselves? The best he would be able to do would be to pass only the ladle down into the pit. 'Who are you?' he asked.

'Guinot, my name is Guinot. I served here. They take one of us out every day and beat us to death. Help us,' the man whispered, in a voice barely audible from the strain of his dry throat.

'Very well. I'll get you water, but how many men are there here? Routiers, I mean? How many did Saquet leave?'

'Here... I... I don't know... think he left with about... fifty men...'

It was still guesswork. Saquet could have a hundred and fifty men for all anyone knew. The town could be crawling with them back in those darkened houses.

'You came here to kill him?' Guinot asked, his hand reaching to grasp Blackstone's cloak.

Blackstone eased its grip. 'Will you and the others stay quiet if I give you water?'

'They're my men. We're Gascons,' he whispered with determined effort. Gascons from the south-west of France saw Edward as their natural lord, the descendant of their ancient ducal house.

Blackstone quickly turned and brought the water bucket to the edge of the caged pit and then handed the injured man the ladle. He could just about see Guinot's parched lips open with desperation as the thirsty man took the ladle and then handed it down to the men below with a warning whisper to stay silent. Each man, one sip. The ladle soon came back. Blackstone gave more water until finally, after vital minutes had passed, Guinot drank.

'I have men outside the walls. Can I take the town?' Blackstone asked, worried now that either of the sentries would glance down into the square. Rain fell, light swirls of it that within moments suddenly turned to sleet. Blackstone ignored the stinging attack on his bare head.

'How many men?' the imprisoned man asked.

'Twenty.'

Blackstone could almost see the look of disappointment on the man's face. It was certainly in his voice.

'Twenty?'

Blackstone heard the sentry stamp his feet, trying to drive out the cold.

Guinot said, 'I don't know. There's at least that many here. More, I think. Thirty – forty even. More men arrived and joined Saquet.

There are ten of them in there,' he said, meaning the guardroom. 'Others with their whores. Scattered in the town. Twenty men, you say?' He extended his hand and grabbed Blackstone's arm. 'I hope you survive. We can't help, even if we could break free. We're too weak. Good luck, stranger.'

The effort to stay upright through the cage bars took their toll and Guinot eased himself down into the dank pit.

It was either time to abandon the daring attack on the town or retreat to the monastery and draw Saquet into the open when he returned from his wild goose chase. Blackstone raced for the steps that would take him to where Mculon and the men crouched shivering in the cold on the other side of the wall. The short, sharp sleetstorm had passed, the cold blast easing as the sky filled with a descending swarm of snow. It was a good omen. The snow would camouflage the attacking men.

The sentries' muscles were cold and stiff from such a bitter night and their minds numb from the tedium of guard duty. They were the first to die. Meulon left two of his men with crossbows in their position, knowing there would soon be enough light for them to pick out short-range targets. Blackstone told Meulon his plan, but the older man suggested a different tactic. If Blackstone and a half-dozen men could deal with the guardroom he would torch a couple of buildings and then hide in the shadows across the square to cover Blackstone's back. Once the alarm was raised the bastard routiers would run into the square from the alleys. Blackstone would bear the brunt of the attack but Meulon would reinforce him.

Blackstone ran quickly to the guardroom with eight men and one of the sacks they had carried from the monastery stuffed with sheep's wool and felt, tied and soaked in lamp oil. A sack flared from the square's lantern that Blackstone broke over it, and as one of the men kicked in the door another threw the blazing bundle into the room. They pulled the door closed and rolled a barrel into place to slow their victims' escape. It took only moments for the fire to take hold and cries of alarm from the guardroom could be heard across the square. The guardroom door finally yielded as the smoke-choked and burnt men stumbled into a night where fire swept down from heaven. There were snowflakes tumbling out of the black sky and across the town's roofs, tinged with red from another burning house that Meulon's men had torched. It was a controlled burning to save the whole town from going up in flames, using the wind to fan the flames across another three or four buildings before they reached the stone walls. This bewildering conflagration of ember and snowflake was the last thing the soldiers from the guardroom saw as Blackstone and his men cut them down.

Blackstone deliberately kept his group in the open and the looming firelight. Shadows crawled across the walls as the alarm bell rang and his men opened the gates to allow the townspeople to escape. Those living nearest the burning buildings ran across the square in ones and twos as routiers dashed into the square. Blackstone and his men blocked their path and cut them down. Some turned to run for the steps onto the walls but the first few fell to the crossbowmen, who now had clear targets from the light of the burning houses.

Saquet's men were a ragged, disparate group of mercenaries, who had tumbled from the alehouse and whores' beds when the town's bell rang out its alarm, but a dozen men appeared suddenly as a fighting group, and then another fifteen or more from a dormitory close by and they called out to those others who stumbled from the alleyways. Now this body of men could resist more effectively and they charged, yelling their abuse and rage at Blackstone who was already fighting in the square. The men clashed, spectral figures cursing and slipping in the bloody snow beneath their feet. Blackstone had positioned himself forward of the others, who flanked him in a spearhead, and as he stood his ground and parried the blows of the attackers, those who survived his sword stumbled into his men, who hacked the routiers down. But more of Saquet's men appeared from the town, alerted by the cries of the fight in the main square, and they outnumbered Blackstone's.

'Now!' Blackstone yelled. 'Now!'

But there was no sign of Meulon.

A sudden shock of abandonment and fear took hold but he spat it out and threw more weight into his sword arm.

'On me!' Blackstone shouted, and the men drew themselves closer to him, forming as tight a line as they could against the onslaught.

Fires still burned but the flames battered themselves against the stone walls and, finding no purchase, began to falter. Seeing that the fire was being contained, some of the townspeople began to draw water and douse the flames, but others still panicked and ran for the gate to escape the slaughter and it was they who impeded Meulon and his contingent across the square. Women's screams mingled with cries of alarm as Saquet's mercenaries hacked their way through them. Pressed hard by the vicious attack, Blackstone and the others retreated. Blackstone took a blow across the shoulder but the sword failed to bite through his chain mail. He shouldered the man, ramming him aside, and then, cleaving downward with Wolf Sword, he shattered his opponent's collarbone. He stepped quickly to one side and thrust the sword into the man's chest, then turned again, sensing the next attack, twisting away as another routier struck down on him from the high guard. Blackstone had only a moment to strike before the blade took him across his exposed shoulder. With no time to turn his own blade he brought both hands up on his sword's grip and smashed the pommel under the man's nose. His attacker's momentum met the full force of Blackstone's strength and the double-fisted blow shattered his skull and threw him back into the gore-splattered snow. Vital seconds bled away. They were losing. They couldn't hold their line much longer.

And then a swarm of shadows charged across the square and Meulon's men began their slaughter.

The turmoil swirled about Blackstone. One of the attackers caught him a glancing blow on his head and a trickle of blood ran into his scar, making his face look even more fearsome. He snatched at a terrified woman who ran between him and an attacking routier, seeing her unmistakable terror as she caught sight of his scarred face when he shoved her away from the strike. He was too exposed. The blade could not be parried. Meulon took a stride forward, his sword low, striking from waist height into the man's stomach.

The attacker's momentum faltered and Blackstone took a stride forward and then another, taking the fight to the enemy, cutting through the curtains of white that fell and the men who squinted into the storm's blinding snowflakes – he had the wind at his back. One man came at him with a battleaxe, his beard caked with snow and blood, his eyes wild and focused. There was something familiar about him, but Blackstone didn't know what it was until he saw the stitched leather binding on the stump whose fingers he had severed weeks ago.

Blackstone's feet went from under him, slithering in the snow as the flat surface of the axe's blade struck him on the side of the head. The axe-man's effort brought others, ready to counter-attack, but Blackstone's men quickly formed a barrier around their stunned leader, their spears lunging at the mercenaries, whose surge faltered. Blackstone stared up at the one-handed man who suddenly folded in on himself as a spear ripped into his stomach. He crashed into the snow not an arrow shaft's distance away. A moment later his contorted face was spluttering blood, his eyes glazing as the soldier who killed him stamped a boot into his chest and yanked his spear free.

A hulking shadow whose eyes stared past his helmet's nose guard broke the darkness of his beard with a snarl. 'Am I always going to have to do this?' Meulon said, heaving Blackstone up. 'In Christ's name, stay on your feet!' And then he pressed on with the men who had protected the Englishman.

He had known the weariness of battle before. An exhaustion that could claim a man to the point where he could not raise another sword stroke, but this was different. It was a short, vicious fight and the killing was rapid. It was over in less than an hour. The surviving routiers threw down their weapons and

were herded into the square, forced to kneel in the snow, their
wounds splattering the whiteness. Some lay into the wet coldness
and let their blood seep away until they died.

By daylight the snow had diminished to an occasional flurry.
The captives were chained with the same shackles that had held
Guinot and his men, who had been released from the pit. Charred
timbers from the burnt houses smouldered and stank like the
fur of a wet dog. There had been forty-three routiers left in the
town. Blackstone's men killed thirty-seven with a loss of four
and that, he realized, was thanks to Meulon's ability to think of
how he might inflict the most casualties. Meulon, though, had
begged forgiveness for his late entrance into the fight, explaining
how the fleeing townspeople had impeded his attack and that he
had not wished to cause them injury. In that moment Blackstone
understood that Meulon stood before him as a subordinate. He
clapped the apologetic captain on the shoulder.

'It was a good plan, Meulon, and you came in time. That's all
that matters. And I swear I'll do my best to stay on my feet next
time.'

Meulon grinned sheepishly for having said what he had in the
heat of the fight, but also knew that Blackstone had once again
been generous in his praise.

Snow crunched beneath Blackstone's boots as he walked along
the bodies laid out in the square. Guinot and his fellow prisoners
had been moved into a building where a fire was stoked and food
prepared. They were weak, but Blackstone sent a rider to the
monastery to bring Brother Simon and his medications. It did not
take long for Blackstone and Meulon to scour through Saquet's
quarters. The house, which had once been well furnished, a
symbol of the owner's success in his trade, now looked more like
a whorehouse. Wine and ale had been spilled, bits of scorched
cloth showed where some linen had caught fire, and wall coverings
and mattresses strewn around the rooms suggested that Saquet
and his lieutenants had spread themselves throughout the house.
The cellar doors were bolted but were soon broken open.

Meulon gaped at the amount of booty stored in the room.

'He must have raided every monastery and nobleman for miles,' he said, tipping open boxes of coin and gold plate.

'Except that of Abbot Pierre,' Blackstone answered.

It was not enormous wealth that lay before them, but it was a sobering sight and was more than enough to buy men and favour for months to come.

'Bolt and seal the doors, Meulon, and then bar the entrance. I want this here when we return.'

A delegation of burghers stood waiting respectfully for an audience with the scar-faced soldier who was obviously in command and who now held their town. They had not been threatened by Blackstone's men but encouraged to bring those who had run from the fighting back into the town. Of the six surviving mercenaries, Guinot and the leading townsmen identified four who had taken delight in torture.

Meulon was at Blackstone's shoulder. 'The gates are secure and I've men on the walls. What about the prisoners?'

'Find a carpenter. Build a gallows,' Blackstone said.

By the time Brother Simon arrived under escort, Blackstone had gone among Guinot's men. He determined that three would soon die from their injuries, but the others would recover quickly enough with rest and food. Those who lay recovering from their imprisonment and brutal treatment mostly slept now that their ordeal had ended. He stopped at one, and then another, lifting the men's hands and rubbing his thumb along their fingers, feeling that familiar ridge of callus. He didn't recognize them but he could swear they were archers. One of the bearded soldiers had long hair that clung to his face like seaweed. He was barely conscious and the wounds from the whipping inflicted by the mercenaries festered. The man shivered, a sure sign that the wounds caused the fever. There was something about him, though, that Blackstone recognized – a strength in the man's physique, that slab of corded muscle that lay across his shoulders. He pulled back the hair from his face. It was that of someone who, months before, had stood at his side, unyielding when the wolves of war tore them apart at Crécy.

Matthew Hampton was one of Warwick's men who had served Sir Gilbert Killbere loyally as one of Elfred's archers and was one of the more experienced men in Elfred's command, a man who had offered advice to the young Blackstone. How had he ended up here?

'Matthew?' Blackstone said gently, wiping his face with a wrung-out cloth from a water bucket.

Guinot half raised himself. 'You know him, Sir Thomas?' he asked, having been told by Meulon the name of their saviour.

'Matthew Hampton. I fought across Normandy with him.'

'We had a dozen archers sent to us by King Edward. We were to hold towns in the south and by the time we got here we thought we'd beaten the French King all the way back to Paris, but we hadn't reckoned on routiers. He and a couple of other archers are all that survived Saquet's attack. Matthew's a good man, and if he's a friend of yours, then he's a fortunate one.'

Blackstone beckoned Brother Simon and the younger monk who had travelled with him as his assistant. 'All of these men need your skill, Brother. When you've tended to them here and given what aid you can I want them taken to your infirmary where you'll care for them.'

He laid a hand on the semi-conscious man's face. 'Matthew, if you can hear me, it's Thomas. Thomas Blackstone. You're safe now.'

There was no recognition or word from the older man. Blackstone stepped away to allow the old monk to examine the archer. He needed to question Guinot and find out how the mercenary had breached the town's defences held by the Anglo-Gascon soldiers.

It had been easy.

Guinot was on duty when one of the Englishmen in the mixed force called for Roger Waterman, the man-at-arms charged with holding the town with his fifty men. The new abbot of Chaulion monastery was at the gate with a gaggle of thirty villagers who had been attacked and whose homes had been destroyed by routiers. He begged shelter on their behalf. Waterman hesitated. Half his force was off duty and he didn't trust this French monk, who perspired with desire at the sight of spring lamb on a spit. The abbot pleaded for a full half hour and it was only when a band of horsemen appeared on the road and began to ride towards the unarmed villagers that the commander of Chaulion ordered the gates opened to avert a massacre. The helpless peasants were no sooner inside the walls when they drew weapons and set about killing. They were mercenaries disguised in the clothes of those they had already slaughtered. The riders whose approach had triggered the act of mercy rode straight into the town. The terror lasted a full day and Waterman was cut down, his body dragged around the town. Guinot and his men barricaded themselves in a street but the force against them was too strong and one by one they fell. Some of the Gascons had their women in the town and they were dragged out and used to blackmail the survivors into surrender. Of the twenty-one men Guinot had gathered to resist Saquet's raiders, only he and the men in the pit were still alive. The others had been taken out, one by one, then beaten and tortured to death in the main square.

Time was short. Saquet would return and Blackstone needed to be ready. Leaving only ten men under Meulon's command to patrol the walls of Chaulion he prepared to take what was left of his force back to the monastery, taking Guinot and the ailing survivors with him.

'Saquet will be gone three days, no more, and will then turn back,' Meulon told him. 'You've got a day left, maybe two at the most. You'll need men at the crossroads. These townsmen will hold the walls with anything they can pour down on them if he splits his force and attacks, which he won't, because when he rides back and sees what you've done at the monastery he'll need to kill you, all of us, if he's to retake this place.'

Meulon pressed his argument. If Blackstone was to return to the monastery with so few men it would be a gamble, especially now that he held Chaulion: the risk was that it could be lost.

Blackstone realized it made sense, and had the guildsmen, who held council in the town, summoned before him. The grain and food stores were to be opened and the food distributed. Half of the coin and plate that had been looted by the routiers would be returned, the remainder was his men's spoils for taking the town. A bargain was struck, rather than a threat being made. Were the townspeople prepared and able to protect their own walls over the coming hours until Blackstone could leave a garrison of men to hold the town permanently in his name and, by default, that of the English King? The councilmen, thankful to be rid of the mercenaries, and with no particular love for the high taxation that would be placed upon them by the French King if they fell back under his rule, readily agreed. The Anglo-Gascon force that had been in place before Saquet came had caused them no injury other than their demand to be fed and *patis* to be paid.

'Are there weapons here?' Blackstone asked.

'They had a half-dozen barrels stored with swords and falchions, some spears as well,' answered one of the men.

'And archers' bows,' another added eagerly, 'a dozen of them. They tried to draw them but couldn't.'

Blackstone stepped to the man. 'Are there shafts for the bows?'

'Yes, lord,' the man answered, 'but only a handful, a dozen at most.'

If any of those exhausted archers could have a bow put in their hand and they found the strength to use them, then even those few arrows would give Blackstone a great advantage for his outnumbered men. 'Fetch them. Keep the swords and spears for yourselves,' he ordered. 'What assurances do you give me that you can keep the gates closed and the walls manned?'

The men conferred worriedly, their shoulders hunched. There were outbursts of disagreement until one, who was not the eldest but a young merchant, settled their differences. It was agreed that they would give a child from each of their families to be taken by the Englishman and held to ransom. If it was to be a choice between Thomas Blackstone and Saquet, they would take the Englishman. All they begged of the vicious-looking knight was that he kill the mercenary, because if he did not their lives would be forfeit.

Instructions were given to lay the dead mercenaries in the cold gulley and cover what was left of them in the spring. Those towns-people who were killed were to be buried in their own graveyard, despite the hard ground. Blackstone had Meulon gather his men and the prisoners. Meulon, satisfied that his reasoning had prevailed, organized a wagon for the wounded. 'Where are the hostages?' he asked Blackstone as they prepared to leave.

'We don't need them,' he answered. 'They were prepared to give their children; that's proof that they'll do as they say.'

Meulon shook his head. 'You trust too easily, Master Thomas.'

'I trusted you with my life, Meulon. Was I wrong then?'

There was nothing more the seasoned fighter could say. The Englishman had an answer for everything. And the right one at that.

CHAPTER TWENTY-FIVE

It was a wall to be proud of. It ran in true lines to the road, forming a low defensive curtain to the front of the monastery, fifty yards each side with a front wall, all in all a hundred and thirty yards already built, according to Blackstone's experienced eye. It was not yet finished, but even if Saquet returned that day, Blackstone thought, the wall would be sufficient to form a strong defence and deny anyone ease of access over the crossroads. The men stopped working and cheered when they saw the survivors return from Chaulion, but their good humour settled when the monks unloaded the dead and took them into the monastery. These soldiers may have served different lords but they were in this place to fight together under one man, and each was dependent upon the other.

Gaillard recognized an old friend's body being taken from the cart. 'That's Jacopo. Jesus, he was a stupid bastard. He'd trip over his own spear if you didn't watch out for him. I'm not surprised he got himself killed,' he said. Gaillard had served with the slain soldier since they were boys. 'Did he fight well?' he asked Blackstone.

'He was at my side,' said Blackstone. 'We were outnumbered, but he stood his ground.'

'There you are, then. I always told him to keep moving,' Gaillard said and turned back to placing rocks into position on the unfinished section of the wall. Sentiment and prayer for the dead could wait until he was alone in his bunk and the night candle blown out.

The town's carpenters hauled their timber from the carts and the six prisoners were shoved unceremoniously to the ground.

'You four will hang for the torture you committed,' Blackstone told the condemned men. 'And you two, he pointed to the other prisoners, 'will hang because I've no need for you or your kind.'

One of the men snarled like a dog on a chain. 'Do it then, you scar-faced whoreson,' raising his voice so all of Blackstone's men could hear, 'because when Saquet sees what you've done, he'll gut you all, slow and even, a knife to your innards and your cocks sliced and stuffed down your throats. He'll put you on a spit and make you eat each other. And then he'll burn Chaulion to the ground. Do your worst. My body might swing in the wind like a tavern sign, but we sliced those feeble curs at Chaulion and took their women and we lived like men should live. Death is coming to every one of you. A bad death! Get on your knees and pray for your souls because—'

Meulon took a few strides and slit his throat. A final curse gurgled as blood spurted and splattered those chained to him as they attempted to pull away when his body kicked and spasmed.

'He talked too much,' he explained to a scowling Blackstone as he wiped his blade. 'There are lads here who haven't seen vicious fighting yet. Can't have a turd like him putting thoughts in their head. They've not much room up there as it is.' Meulon turned and ordered the men and monks who had stopped their labours, 'Finish the work! Saquet is an evil bastard who slays women and children for his pleasure. You'll be killing him and the scum with him when they get here. We've taken Chaulion and you've booty coming your way, thanks to Sir Thomas!' Meulon raised a fist and the men cheered, though the monks looked more worried than ever. Throat-slitting was easy work for men like these.

Brother Simon tended the weakened men in his infirmary as Blackstone came to check on Guinot and the others. The men sat propped on straw mattresses as a couple of the monks went among them spooning the pottage's liquid into them. 'Will they be able to fight?' asked Blackstone.

'They have been starved, my son. And beaten. I have medicine in the broth. Give them time.'

Blackstone knew that even though a killer whose men out-numbered his own was soon to be on them, men could not be raised from their exhaustion because of it. 'Tell me what you need and you shall have it,' he said.

'We have God's blessing now that you have come,' the old man answered simply.

Blackstone felt a heaviness building in him, something he had not experienced before. It was not fear, but it carried the same sense of trepidation that clenched his heart. And then he knew what it was. It was others' expectations. 'Brother Simon, I'm nobody's saviour. Don't have any thought that I am. I'm a soldier. I can be dead by this time tomorrow and then I'm only good for worm bait.'

The old monk looked at him a moment longer and then pointed a wavering finger at the silver effigy of Arianrhod. 'I was a pagan once, my son, I prayed to all the Gods including our Lord. One of them must have heard me, though I'm unsure which one it was. I'll find out soon enough, no doubt.'

'I'm no pagan,' Blackstone answered.

'No matter. What's important is who you believe it is that guides and protects you. Don't be ashamed to go on your knees and beg for their help,' he answered, and then went back to tending the sick.

Guinot swung his feet over the side of the cot, and tried to stand. 'I've heard a scaffold being built before. You're hanging them here, aren't you? That's a challenge to Saquet all right. He's a reputation to uphold and stringing his men up at a crossroads is going to make him come after you personally, but before he does I want to see them choke,' he said.

Blackstone eased him back onto the cot before his legs gave way. 'You'll see it. I give you my word. You and the others need to rest and let Brother Simon care for you. There comes a time when we have to surrender to those who can help us.'

Guinot nodded and eased back onto the mattress. 'You think you can stop the routiers here? You and a handful of men straddling the crossroads? Sweet Mother of God, you were lucky at Chaulion. Those men you killed were just the scum that settles on top of a shit pit. Prepare yourself because when Saquet breaks down those doors every last man of us will be put to the sword. I heard what the old monk said. Listen to him – give the men Mass. Put God on their side.'

Blackstone wanted more than God on his side, he wished he had another fifty men. A hundred would be better. As he walked past the cots he saw that Matthew Hampton's fever had broken. His eyes searched the torn face that gazed down at him. His breath rasped with effort through cracked lips. 'Thomas?'

Blackstone nodded.

'Look at you. We thought you dead. Bless you, boy. Where am I?'

'The monastery.'

The archer nodded. 'You got us out of Chaulion, then. We were dead men. They tricked us, Thomas, and killed us. Badly. My lads died badly.'

Blackstone rested a hand on Hampton's and squeezed gently. 'We'll avenge them together. I've got your bow.'

'No, they took it...'

'I took it back. It's yours. No one else carried a bow with such a dark band of wood that twists across the grain. I saw it right away.' Blackstone brought the war bow up from where he had held it out of Hampton's sight.

The archer's hands caressed the length of yew and his fingertips stroked the nocked horn tips. He nodded with an almost inaudible sigh, and then eased it back to Blackstone. 'You take it, Thomas, and kill as many as you can. There was none better'n you. Not even Richard, God rest his soul. Take it, lad.'

Blackstone extended his crooked arm. 'I'll never draw a bow again, Matthew. A sword stroke snapped me like a twig.'

Hampton's eyes followed the line of his arm. 'A sword stroke cannot break a mighty oak, Thomas. Give me and the others another day of the good friar's broth and we'll stand by you.'

Blackstone grasped the man's extended hand. He could see that no matter how willing Hampton and the other men might be they would need more than a day to recover. There would be no archers ready if Saquet's attack came the next morning as expected. Before that happened he would have a Mass said for his men.

They dragged Abbot Pierre from his room and kicked him out in front of those condemned to hang. As he fell his cassock was rucked up, exposing his bare backside. Blackstone's men and the lay brothers laughed at his humiliation. Blackstone saw that the other monks who had benefited from the fat abbot's rule looked concerned. They knew that if their penance of building the wall did not please the Englishman then they too could face ignominious banishment from their own monastery. And who would they turn to? Brother monks of the same order would have heard of the way they lived. They would most likely be shunned if forced out from the safety of these walls, and penance at another monastery could be harder than staying where they were. They all knew that the time of Abbot Pierre was over and that their future lay in the Englishman's hands.

Blackstone's men hauled the abbot to his feet as the Englishman stood before him. 'Those who want it can have the sacrament before they hang. And you can lead your brothers in prayer for your own safe deliverance before I send you on your way.'

Abbot Pierre's eyes darted back and forth among the gathered soldiers and monks. 'You cannot send me away, this is my monastery. I have the favour of the King and he has the favour of the Pope. You can't send me from this place; it's miles to the nearest village.'

'If you reach it alive you can beg for food and shelter like a true mendicant. Though I suspect that every door will be closed to you for allowing Saquet and his men to strip them bare. Your blessing to him became their curse.'

'You cannot! The weather is closing in.' The abbot's jowls quivered.

'You led Saquet and his routiers into Chaulion. I should put you on the scaffold with the rest of these men, but I doubt we have a gallows strong enough to bear such a barrel of lard,' said Blackstone.

Abbot Pierre fell to his knees, hands clasped, and begged for his life. 'Sir Thomas, I have no chance of reaching even the nearest village before nightfall. The cold will kill me, the coming snow will bury me and I will lie in unconsecrated ground. Recant, I implore you.'

'What about these men who are about to die? Have you no wish to beg on their behalf?'

The abbot struggled to his feet, sweeping his arm in a gesture to encompass the condemned men. 'Blasphemers and murderers. Their end was determined when their whore mothers dropped them from their fouled wombs. I was at their mercy. I had no choice in what I did!'

'Then forgive them their sins when they receive their last sacrament before I send you on your way. Hurry, the day is already shortening. Darkness will soon be your only companion. Get to it.'

One of the routiers stepped forward and gobbed a mouthful of phlegm at the abbot, splattering his shoulder and face. The abbot recoiled in horror.

'I'll not have a creature like this pray over me. I'll meet the devil on my own terms,' the routier said, and tried to land a kick on the fat abbot, who stumbled back, turning this way and that, searching the faces around him for any sign of compassion. There was none. Some of the monks turned their faces deliberately away from him.

Blackstone said, 'I wouldn't be able to face my King if I put you to the sword, or hanged you from a tree. I have given you your life. Do with it what you will.'

The abbot trembled as tears welled and spilled. Like a blind man he stumbled, not knowing which way to go. He was beyond the wall and his beseeching gesture as he reached out to those on the other side did nothing but graze the skin from his arms on the coping stones bristling like teeth along its top.

Everyone watched as Abbott Pierre moved further away, his sandalled feet finding a path to tread once he was across the bridge. He fell once or twice and then, almost on all fours, clambered like a child up the rising ground towards the forest. No one watching doubted that his fat carcass would soon become a feast for the creatures of the woodland. It had been a harsh winter and the wolves would find him.

Blackstone asked the routiers if any of them wanted the sacrament. They all accepted except the man who had spat his contempt at the abbot.

'Brother Marcus,' he said, gesturing the prior forward, 'you held Mass for my men last night, and now you're in charge of this monastery. Step forward and ease these men's souls into the next world.'

Guinot and the others were carried from their beds to watch the execution. When Matthew Hampton saw the gallows he knew that the boy who had become a ventenar and now a man-at-arms would never lose the inherent skills of an archer. The six men captured at Chaulion were hanged at hundred-yard intervals from the edge of the wall. The dead men marked out the distance for his archers, be they French crossbowmen or the English with their long, curved war bows. Ailing or not, he and the others would loose as many shafts as they could at the men who would soon fall upon them.

Some Norman lords had turned against King Edward; others were as yet undecided where their loyalties lay. The violent William de Fossat, seeing an opportunity to regain his pride and reputation, had offered his services – and thirty men – to the French King. He had vowed to the King that he would track down the marauders led by the Englishman. But then he stumbled upon the mercenary Saquet.

Saquet and his men had camped in the forests in rough shelters made from hacked branches and dead ferns, then finally picked their way through the forest's tracks until they came to where the road should be beneath the snow. They had not enjoyed a hot meal for days and their slow progress home was becoming a further irritation. The French King's warrant to kill the daring Englishman gave William de Fossat no status among the brigands he had joined and he and his men dutifully followed the mercenaries at the rear, acknowledging that the Breton was master of the routiers under his command.

As luck would have it the defenders at the monastery were granted another three days before the mercenaries broke the sky-line. Heavy snow fell during that first night and into the next day, and it took another two to die away into flurries. A blanket of snow a foot deep covered the approach roads to the monastery and smothered the obstacles that Blackstone's men had laid before their wall. No broad front of horsemen would be able to approach, only two or three men abreast, tentatively easing nervous horses forward through snow that hid uneven ground. Blackstone had marked out the road in the direction from which he wanted the mercenaries to come. The executed men's bodies hung in the cold air, barely moving from the breeze, caked with snow, clumps of which fell from them like rotting flesh. The man whose throat was cut took his place among the dead, a rope under his shoulders, the gaping wound blackened, his clothes stripped, leaving his naked body a meal for scavenging ravens and crows. His would be the first body that Saquet would see as he turned the bend in the road to bring him in sight of the monastery and the crossroads to his town. It would bring him down the track exactly as Blackstone had planned.

Blackstone's footprints led to the small bridge where he stood watching the river wash the snow from its boulders. The weather was fickle and warming; the snow might soon melt. He would rather Saquet arrived when it was still on the ground. He wanted the fight over and its outcome settled. His men were inside the mon-astery on his orders because he knew that when his enemy came they would be cold and stiff from a long ride and the discomfort of sleeping cramped in the open. He wanted his men warm, well fed and strong, ready to kill.

'You think he'll come today?' Gaillard asked Meulon, who stood with him at the front wall, watching Blackstone pace across the bridge.

The big man nodded, and pulled his beard. 'He has to. No one travels in winter; there'll be no food for him to scavenge. This snowfall bought us time.' His eyes scanned the distance. The dark figure of a horseman broke the grey horizon. 'It's today,' he said.

Saquet reined in his horse and gazed at the mutilated bodies. Anger pumped warmth into his frozen limbs. He spat and cursed. He had been pursuing a ghost through the forests and now the Englishman taunted him with the hanged men. So be it. He would slaughter Blackstone like a beast in the field and then send his butchered body back to the King, limb by limb, using the Norman lord as a lowly messenger. Those few pathetic defenders would soon lie in the bloodied snow and then every man, woman and child in Chaulion would die. He would smear the countryside with a streak of blood a mile long and no man would ever challenge him again. The French King would reward him handsomely.

William de Fossat brought his horse up next to Saquet's. 'He's got behind you and taken what you held. I told you he was cunning. Are those yours?' de Fossat asked, meaning the hanged men. There was no need for an answer; the look on Saquet's face was enough.

'Then if he's taken the crossroads he's taken Chaulion as well. Look, twenty-odd men behind a makeshift wall and not a bowman to his name. It looks as though your arse will freeze for more days to come. Shall I kill him for you?' the nobleman sneered.

'Stay back!' Saquet snarled. The Norman lord had already been kept in his place. He needed no help from a baron, or whatever he was; these earls and counts were no different from him, but they hid behind a cloak of nobility. As far as Saquet was concerned they were just better dressed brigands who trampled the poor and sought favour with the King. Saquet knew exactly what his code was: a man had to kill and spread terror to make a mark in his world. He spurred his horse down the path marked out by the hanging men and what remained of their executioner's footprints. Saquet's horsemen shoved de Fossat and his men aside. And as the last of the fifty or so mercenaries spurred their horses on, de Fossat turned to his men. Whatever the outcome of Saquet's murderous attack, de Fossat knew he would achieve his goal.

'Get ready!' he commanded, and drew his sword.

Five hundred yards away Blackstone stood at the head of his men. They were behind the wall, their shields on their arms, spears and swords ready as the horsemen came recklessly along the narrow road. Crossbowmen stood poised on each side of him, their weapons held out of sight. Matthew Hampton was ten paces back with the half-dozen English archers. They had few arrows between them, but they would bring men down more quickly than the crossbows.

Meulon stood next to Blackstone. 'You see that? Mother's tears. That's de Fossat up there on the ridge. He's joined the bastards. With Saquet's men there must be eighty or more of them.'

They were outnumbered by Saquet's forces alone; with de Fossat and his men, the sheer weight of them would easily break through their thin line of defence. Blackstone glanced at his men's faces. Their eyes widened as the horde got closer. *Four hundred yards.* Who could blame them if they broke and ran?

'Curse the bastards!' he yelled. 'Curse them for being whoresons and turds! They'll die condemned! Curse them! Let them burn in hell!' and then yelled abuse at the top of his lungs, clenching Wolf Sword above his head, clambering on top of the wall so all could see him. 'Burn in hell!' he bellowed.

And the chant went up as Meulon and Gaillard strode along the line screaming the curse.

Burn in hell! BURN IN HELL!

Blackstone twisted around and looked at Matthew Hampton. The archers looked sick and weak. Their sallow faces and flecked lips told him that they couldn't loose more than a volley or two.

Saquet's men were closer, their voices urging their horses onwards.

Blackstone waited. Watching those horses struggle downhill, seeing the men's urgency to kill them.

A few more strides was all he needed from them. Stay on the track, stay on the track, he urged silently.

It was time.

'Archers! At three hundred paces! Nock...' The men readied their shafts, arms trembling from ailing bodies, but a lifetime of training and skill steadied them. 'Draw...' Blackstone looked back to the horsemen being channelled down the narrow road as they came next to one of the hanged men. 'Loose!'

Though there were no more than a handful of archers the twang of their bowstrings and the sudden rush of air made the Norman soldiers at the wall turn and gape at the arrows' flight. The first fletchings were still quivering through the air when another volley chased them. And another. Blackstone couldn't hold back the yell of triumph that burst from him. It was England's killing machine doing its work again. Horses and men fell in a tumble, cartwheeling and sliding, veering away only to fall from unseen hazards beneath the snow. Some of the mercenaries pulled their horses up short for fear of more arrow strikes and dismounted, running forward in ragged numbers, tripping and making hard work of the assault, their lungs heaving in the cold air. They would be weakened by the time they reached the wall.

Two of the archers sank to their knees – the effort had taken the last of their strength. Hampton and the three others let fly their final volleys and were then out of arrows.

'God bless you, lads!' Blackstone yelled and then shook the walls with his yell: 'Normans! Gascons! Ready!'

The mercenaries were two hundred paces from the bridge when Blackstone's men brought up their crossbows and levelled them at the attackers. 'Wait! Wait!' At a hundred and fifty paces they were on level ground, some wading across the stream. 'Loose!' And a hum of armour-piercing bolts struck like a mailed fist on the first wave of men. The mercenaries faltered but recovered. The crossbowmen needed two minutes to reload and in that time Saquet's men would be over the wall. That knowledge gave them strength and courage.

Meulon stood at the end of his line of men, Gaillard was on the flank, and the ailing Guinot stood propped, sword in hand, against the main gates to steady himself: it looked as though he would be the last man they would have to kill in order to gain entry. Matthew Hampton and his archers had dragged themselves to stand with him. The mercenaries ran with wild abandon, thirsting to close for the kill. No one behind the wall moved. Blackstone leapt down to be with them. *Fifty paces.*

'Spearmen!' Meulon yelled. And where crossbows had been, spears now bristled across the saw-toothed wall. They had no intention of losing time reloading the weapons. The mercenaries tripped, stumbled and fell on the scattered rocks and branches that the wall builders had placed there on Blackstone's orders and which slowed their advance. Bruised and broken, the ragged horde of men got back on their feet and kept attacking, but those who had fallen lost momentum. Blackstone sought out Saquet. No man looked more vicious than another. Which was the routiers' leader?

He turned and yelled, 'Guinot! Which one is he?'

Guinot took a pace forward and looked desperately at the attacking men thirty paces away. Saquet was in the middle of a group of men running with shields half covering their bodies and faces. 'The boy!' Guinot yelled, and pointed with his sword.

Blackstone thought he had misunderstood. His eyes went from face to snarling face and settled on one of them – a clean-shaven lad who looked no older than most of the boys in his own village, but who towered head and shoulders above the others. A steel-rimmed leather helmet capped flowing fair hair, and blue eyes glinted beneath the shield's rim. For a moment Blackstone felt doubt drag at him. Could this be Iron Fist? The boy was big and he ran, powerful and lithe, behind the front rank of attackers. His sword was half raised in a gloved fist. He made no sound. He uttered no curse. He had no need of a battle cry to urge him onto the spear points. Blackstone suddenly understood. The men in front of this boy were there to breach the wall. They would die if they had to, as many of them would, but they would carve a space for Saquet. Blackstone saw the intensity of those blue eyes. They were locked on him. Blackstone was the target.

The mercenaries struck the wall. Spears jabbed and drew blood, but the routiers were too many for the defenders to stop – some of them clambering over the dry-stone wall, spilling the top stones and hurling themselves with great ferocity on men who had little experience of close-quarter killing. There was a clash of steel and the sickening dull sound of blades cutting through bodies, like a butcher's cleaver on the block, caused pitiful cries and screams from wounded men. Perinne and Talpin fought side by side, a torrent of abuse adding power to their spear and sword thrusts, as Meulon and Gaillard formed a shield wall to seal the breach.

Guinot saw a knot of men forcing their way towards Blackstone and somewhere behind those shields Saquet had lowered his head and the force of the charge was like a bull trampling those before it. Guinot knew he would be unable to reach the Englishman in time and Blackstone was becoming more isolated as he twisted and turned, sword striking and killing those nearest in the attack. The Gascon yelled a warning to Meulon, bellowing two or three times to be heard over the shouts and screams. Meulon finally half turned and saw what was happening. With a concerted push with the shield wall and with half a dozen men in support as Perinne and Talpin added their weight, they pushed back the assault, forcing mercenaries to clamber back over the wall so that the defenders could not pursue them. There were already twenty or more dead and half as many wounded. Meulon's surge had broken the tide of men. A strange silence fell. No shouts of rage or screams of agony tore the air; only the repeated thud and blows of sword on shield and metal.

Meulon and Gaillard had stopped the advance, but as the wall shield was turned it gave Saquet an open corridor, letting him stride forward with fighting men to hurl himself at Blackstone. Like a battering ram he smashed into the Englishman, rocking him back on his heels. Blackstone used the force of the attack to let his weight spin away, moments before Saquet's sword thrust came up from below his shield. There was no denying the man's power and strength and still Blackstone could not believe that this youngster led a band of killers. That doubt did not stop him from slashing down towards the boy's exposed neck, but where that charging bull had been seconds before he had now spun away and Wolf Sword slashed thin air.

There was no moment for either fighter to brace or find a solid stance, each reacted instinctively and they clashed again. Saquet smothered Blackstone's shield with his own and beat down on his helm with the base of his sword, its pommel hammering with such force that Blackstone felt as though he was being hit with a mace. Saquet, a slaughterman's apprentice from the age of five, had waded in gore all his young life. The brutal manner of a beast's death was a daily occurrence and, just as Blackstone had been taught to carry and cut stone, so too had Saquet been tutored in butchery. A hammer blow to stun a cow into submission and stop its panic from the stench of other slaughtered animals became a personal test of strength that grew ever more powerful until it was said he could stun a beast with his bare hands before using his knife. The boy's gentle looks belied a born and bred killer.

Blackstone felt that brutal power, managed to raise his shield, heard and felt the strikes and thought his knees would buckle. He rammed into Saquet, smashed muscle and fibre and roared a battlefield curse to wake the dead. Time and again he beat against Saquet's unflinching shield, feeling his shoulder muscles gorge with strength as he wielded his own attack. Saquet took the punishment, but Blackstone saw that the blows rocked him. No one until now had matched Iron Fist's strength blow for blow, as once again Blackstone used his crooked arm to give him the angle of attack. He had been taught how to move quickly, never allowing an enemy the advantage of having him in one spot. He shifted his weight, brought his right foot back slightly, then dipped his shoulder and angled the shield, then heaved his weight as if he were breaking down a door. The force of it took Saquet by surprise and caught him on the edge of his helmet. He rocked back, shock registering in his eyes. He was wrong-footed as Blackstone pressed home his attack and, despite Saquet being taller and heavier, he began to fall back from the blows rained on him with a rage that took Blackstone into the heart of an opponent and destroyed him. Saquet resisted, and caught Wolf Sword's blade on his crossguard, with the unmistakable glint of triumph in his young face. However, his killer instinct and fearlessness were not enough to match Blackstone's strength and skill. He had made the strike deliberately, forcing Saquet to bear the weight of the attack, giving Blackstone the chance to kick his legs away from beneath him. As Saquet's limbs floundered, eyes widened in surprise at his fall, Blackstone lunged and rammed his blade through the boy's open jaw, holding it there with a foot on the killer's chest, his face welling with blood until the writhing demons that dragged men's souls into the afterworld ceased their struggle.

It was finished.

No sooner had the routiers seen Saquet fall than they turned and fled. William de Fossat and his men could finish off Blackstone. Iron Fist was sprawled dead, bloody jaw still gaping and those intense blue eyes lifeless. Blackstone spared no thought for his victory. Some of the men began to clamber over the wall in pursuit of the twenty or so mercenaries who ran towards de Fossat's distant horsemen.

'Let them go!' Blackstone shouted. 'There's more to come!'

Meulon and Gaillard hauled soldiers from the wall and cuffed them into position.

'Stand fast!' Meulon spat at them. 'Hold your positions!'

Sweat trickled down their faces, and Blackstone took a moment to pull off his helm and wipe his face. Men sagged, breathing hard, while others lay unmoving. The archers were unscathed, as was Guinot, but he must have fought, Blackstone realized when he saw his blood-slicked blade.

'Meulon!' Blackstone called. 'How many have we lost?'

'Four dead, two wounded,' he answered. 'My God. It's nothing. Defend the house of God and He holds a protective hand over us, eh, Master Thomas? We've been blessed.'

'By a stone wall worth fifty men,' Blackstone answered. The men raised their heads. He was right. Their efforts with that wall had given them the advantage. Gaillard picked up a fallen coping stone and laid it back in its place and then others followed his example. The stone wall had saved lives.

'Look to your front,' Meulon said when he saw de Fossat's horsemen begin trotting towards them. No hail of arrow shafts would greet them, and if they got close enough with their mounts some of those men would jump the wall. If they did get inside, and de Fossat and his men were experienced enough fighters to do just that, then the defenders would have little chance of survival. They had turned back one onslaught from mercenaries but if a Norman lord and thirty mounted men got inside it would be as devastating as a fox in a chicken coop.

'Listen to me!' Blackstone called. 'They can't bring their horses over here if we stand fast. Every other man on this front wall. Crouch below the wall, ram your spear shafts into the ground and keep their blades on top. You'll rip their bellies open. The rest of you, ten paces back, with me. We'll take on those who get through.' The grim-looking men shuffled into position. The mayhem had only just begun.

Blackstone lowered his voice and walked among them. 'Ready yourselves. Spearmen to the front, shield wall to the rear. They'd be stupid to try. But then, some of our noble lords are not known for their clear thinking.' There was a murmur among the mixed bag of soldiers.

Matthew Hampton called out, 'What Sir Thomas means is their horses have more sense!'

That caused a ripple of laughter. Blackstone knew they would settle and hold.

'All right,' he said. 'Take your positions.'

The older, more experienced men ushered the others. The wall would do its job again, but a horse, even if it ripped its belly open, would bring down a low stone wall. They all knew that but no one spoke the thought aloud.

Once the men were ready, Blackstone pulled on his helm, and rested Wolf Sword.

His eyes held the far ridge as the mercenaries and de Fossat's men met.

And then the utterly unexpected happened.

Screams echoed down the road as the slopes were suddenly sprayed with blood. De Fossat and his men trampled and slaughtered the mercenaries. Horses whinnied and slithered as some riders came out of the saddle, but it made no difference, they suffered no casualties as they stood on the torn ground, blood-churned beneath sword and hoof.

De Fossat rode clear and brought his horse slowly towards Blackstone and his men. He stopped fifteen paces away and raised his visor, his dark-bearded face and hawk eyes glaring from the helm like a caged raptor.

'Well, Blackstone. This is a fine day. You're alive and well, I see.'

Blackstone clambered over the wall, but stopped short of going too close. 'I am, my lord. As are you.'

'Barely. My arse is freezing, my sword needs cleaning and I have a warrant for your arrest and execution. And I need a drink.'

The antagonistic Norman was invited into the monastery and settled by the fire in the abbot's old quarters. There was to be no act of violence between de Fossat and Blackstone.

'No wonder the King favoured this abbot; he lived in some comfort,' de Fossat said, sipping mulled wine and selecting pieces of meat with his eating knife. Blackstone had ensured that Meulon and Gaillard kept the men alert, in case de Fossat was laying a trap. But it was soon obvious that the soldiers who had defended the monastery were compatriots of the men riding with de Fossat. Food and drink was supplied to them. Despite this mixed bag of men having served their own lords, Meulon kept a wary eye and had sentries posted. He moved among them as fires were lit and those who knew each other talked of the fighting and how Blackstone had taken Chaulion with few losses. His reputation was already being enhanced as the men who had fought gilded their stories with extravagant claims of his fighting skills and how they, numbering so few, had slain so many in hour upon hour of fighting. The greater their stories of Blackstone, the greater their own exaggerated role and glory became.

William de Fossat accepted another mug of spiced wine. 'This is how it is, Master Thomas. When you left, Jean de Harcourt sent me to the King on behalf of the Norman lords. We are a self-governing Duchy which has always been in the hands of the King's son. And we needed some security, protection if you will, now that your English King has stepped back from seizing the French crown. And so Jean suggested that I ride to Paris and tell them that an English independent captain – that's you,' de Fossat said, tipping his head slightly towards Blackstone, 'intended to seize Chaulion and that I, and the soldiers offered by my Norman lords, would ride south and make sure you failed. We would seize you and lop off your head and display it on the end of a pole.' He sipped the wine. 'That is what I promised, not necessarily what I would deliver. Circumstances change a man's intentions, like a rock diverts water in a stream. Saquet was that rock.'

Blackstone waited in silence, studying the man he had humiliated at Castle de Harcourt, so who better to promise revenge to the King? 'And is that still your intention? You've helped kill the routiers you sided with. In what position does that place you now?' He could not deny the sense of unease he felt, still wondering if de Fossat's arrival was part of a more elaborate plot. Were there men in the forest just waiting for him to lower his guard, and then ride down on them because the enemy was already within?

William de Fossat was weaned on conspiracy and honour that curdled together like sour milk and red wine. Norman lords had their Norse heritage chanted to them while they suckled. A lifetime of hearing *La Chanson de Roland*, the epic poem of valour recounted at feast days, celebrating French honour, was as much a part of their heritage as Rollo the Viking. And now de Fossat sat, once again, opposite a peasant stonemason who now bore arms. The world turned mysteriously. The scarred face gazed at him.

'Why not kill Saquet before he attacked?' Blackstone asked.

De Fossat showed no sign of pretence. 'Why risk my men? The oaf thought himself better suited to the task of killing you. So, I let him try. Once I saw your defences I knew you would prevail. But, if by some chance he had killed you I would still be in the King's favour,' he said matter-of-factly. 'Your life or death is important to me only as long as either serves a purpose. I am not Jean de Harcourt, Blackstone; I would lose no sleep over your death.'

'Then you're not to be trusted,' said Blackstone.

'See it for what it is. I return with sackfuls of heads and I tell the King that they are your men and that I helped slaughter them. Unfortunately you had more men than we anticipated and that brutish Saquet was no tactician, but an uncontrollable peasant. His mercenaries fled or are dead, leaving me and my brave troops to engage you in battle. It was impossible to root you out of Chaulion and we retired with honour, having slaughtered thirty or more of you,' he sipped his wine, 'depending how many heads I take back. And the mean-spirited King's son, the Duke of Normandy, will return some of my lands that he confiscated because I have proved my loyalty to his father, the mean-spirited King. We shall all come out of this with our lives and lands intact.'

It was an effective deception and Jean de Harcourt's plan had given the Norman lords protection now that Sir Godfrey had been disgraced. 'And what happens to me and my men? Will your King send another force against me?'

'The King will not concern himself with losing a few walled towns this far from Paris now that I have tried – and failed; he has bigger worries than that. It means that another pawn has fallen in this game of war, but that you are master of what you hold.'

'I hold it for Edward,' Blackstone said, 'not myself.'

'And he will hear of it. You're no fool, Thomas, in time you will have control of this area; there are more small towns for you to take, and root out those that can cause us all problems. You will have enough money – the Norman lords will make sure of that, to start with at least – to keep your men paid, but then you'll take a share of the crops and livestock and raid and take booty.' De Fossat finished his explanation.

'Then our business is done, my lord.' Blackstone stood – an act that once again told the Norman that although Blackstone was in the presence of a superior, this was now his territory and he would do as he wished.

De Fossat's dark eyes flashed; a superior glare of authority. He lowered the pewter mug and wiped the excess from his bearded lips. 'Bear this in mind. Your men are paid by Norman lords, so you're a man-at-arms in our service,' he said. 'Do you have any message for those who secretly support you?'

'Our actions here are message enough.'

De Fossat pulled on his gloves and turned to leave. He had taken only a few strides when Blackstone's words stopped him. 'There is one thing: I have no further need of their money. I now have land and supplies.' He paused to let de Fossat take in his words that denoted his independence. 'And a cellar full of booty.'

De Fossat nodded. 'Then you're no longer a man-at-arms in our pay, but a knight of your own standing... Sir Thomas.'

Blackstone knew there was still an issue that needed to be broached.

'And what of you and me, my lord?'

The Norman held his gaze. 'You bested me in a contest. My pride was wounded – it still is. And if you had not been restrained by Jean the madness in you would have slain me. To that extent I am in your debt.'

'There isn't one, my lord. Had there ever been a debt it was wiped clean by the role you played in killing the routiers. Even though it was not done for my sake.'

'A gracious gesture is a sign of good manners, Sir Thomas. Is it possible you aspire to dine at high table?'

'You once said I fight like a bear-baiting dog.'

'And so you do.'

'Then it's unlikely that courtly manners will calm such a savage mongrel, wouldn't you say?'

De Fossat smiled. 'I *would* say.' He paused. 'We're from different worlds, Blackstone, but you should know that you have my respect as a knight and I would ride with you against a common enemy. But if we find ourselves on opposing sides I'll kill you when you least expect it.'

The bodies were gathered and laid in the snow, to be kept until spring when the ground softened and they could be buried in a pit. De Fossat's men cut off their heads and put them in sacks. They left Saquet's horses and weapons for Blackstone. Those men who knew each other from being in the service of the same Norman lord bade farewell and watched as the horsemen rode up past the hanged mercenaries and disappeared up the track through the forest.

While de Fossat's men had gone about their grisly work Blackstone had gathered his men together and offered them the chance to return to their own masters. It was an opportunity to leave the service of the Englishman and return to their garrisons and the protection of whichever lord they served. It took only a few moments, as men looked at each other; some shrugged; others passed a comment between themselves. It was Talpin, one of the wall builders, who stepped forward.

'You've bought us a stronghold here and Chaulion, Sir Thomas, and we've food in our bellies and money in our purses. I think we could make this wall bigger and stronger, so I'm thinking I'll stay and see if it can be done.'

'Aye, and he'll need me to make sure he keeps it straight and true,' Perinne said.

A murmur of approval ran through the survivors.

Meulon said, 'We stay with you as long as you need us, Sir Thomas.'

Blackstone turned to Matthew Hampton standing with those archers who had not been taken to the infirmary.

'You're asking me to fight next to Frenchies,' said Hampton, and glowered at the gathered men. 'Me and the lads don't much care for them. The Gascons we know about; they're like us,' he said, leaning on his war bow, 'but this bunch of Normans seem to have taken to you and that's good enough for us.'

CHAPTER TWENTY-SIX

After two weeks at the monastery where the ailing men recovered, plans were made to demolish more redundant buildings and agreement was reached with the prior, Brother Marcus. The monastery would be given another defensive wall and a rotating contingent of four men who were God-fearing and who welcomed the prayers offered by the monks. Blackstone and his men would honour the monastic Rules of St Benedict, as they were called, in that no man would carry a weapon inside the monastery, and to adhere to this a place would be built adjoining the walls where these men might live. They would eat with the lay brothers, and if trouble passed their door or tolls were refused, then the monastery bell would be rung and men from Chaulion would ride to their aid. It was an enclave held by men who months earlier had never imagined that they could not only co-exist but even fight shoulder to shoulder.

Prior Marcus would send chosen brothers out to the local villagers to proclaim that the killer Saquet was dead, slain by Sir Thomas Blackstone, and that they would no longer be raided. Chaulion and the monastery were held in the name of King Edward of England and no messenger or Englishman who served him was to suffer. In return for their tithes, which would feed Blackstone's men, they would share the same protection as that offered to the monastery. When spring came there would also be a market held in Chaulion each month where trade and barter would take place and where a tax of two per cent would be levied on each trader from beyond the area. Crime would be punished, enforced by Sir Thomas or his captains. Hangings of miscreants would coincide with market day as a warning to others and for the entertainment of the people. No slaughter of animals was to take place within Chaulion's walls and no river upstream from the town or monastery would be used for slurry, the washing of carcasses or as a privy. It was to be a new beginning.

Blackstone rode at the head of his men towards Chaulion. It was time to see if the townspeople had honoured their word. The gates were closed as he drew to a halt.

'Inside!' Meulon bellowed. 'Open the gates!'

A dozen faces appeared on the walls, spears and swords were displayed to show the men were armed. It was a good sign and the men knew that Blackstone was now the master of town, monastery and surrounding villages. Within moments of Blackstone being identified there were shouts from within and the gates were opened as the same delegation who had offered their ransom hurried forward to greet the man who had rid them of Saquet and his killers.

Now to make sure the town stayed in their hands.

The weeks passed by rapidly and news came that the King of France had failed to raise an army to challenge Edward's siege of Calais, thus reinforcing many noblemen's belief that Philip was a spent force and that the Estates General, those who controlled the government's purse, were voicing their disappointment more openly to their monarch, insisting that he had not pressed the English hard enough. A hearth tax was raised in Normandy, but unrest spread into the Duchy of Burgundy, where the King's brother-in-law was challenged by rebels in the pay of the English King. More nobles, ruined by the war, offered their services to Edward, making it increasingly difficult for French revenue collectors to travel across the countryside and raise taxes from the hard-pressed lower ranks of nobility.

In his own corner of the troubled kingdom, Blackstone oversaw the building of a new dormitory and stables at the monastery to house his guards. These men ate in the lay brothers' refectory, leaving the monks to their privacy, their manuscripts and their prayers. But there had been a notable alteration since Blackstone had taken control. On two days a week Brother Marcus sent the monks into the fields with the others, and by the season's end the crops and animal husbandry had doubled in value. The acreage under crops was extended and the monastery began to reclaim disused land and increase its wealth. By the end of that first summer goat's cheese and other products were sold and bartered at Chaulion's market, alms were distributed to the poor and the area became known as a place of safety and refuge for those seeking the Englishman's protection.

Thomas Blackstone's accomplishment was all the more remarkable given the few men he commanded, but as the stability of Chaulion and the surrounding area grew others travelled to offer their services. Most were from Edward's army now that the siege of Calais was over and Edward held his gateway into France. But Blackstone took few men into his company and used his captains Guinot and Meulon to assess the newcomers' worth, leaving him to make the final decision as to who should be allowed to join the group of men who had come to rely on each other. Logistics of food and pay determined how he could sustain his soldiers, who now numbered seventy or more, with still only fifteen English archers – now led by Matthew Hampton – most of whom had come from Edward's reserve battalion, their services no longer needed. While convalescing at Castle de Harcourt after Crécy, Blackstone had learnt patience, and now his daring was tempered with caution as he extended his territory. He avoided any drawn-out siege that could sap his meagre force.

'How many fighting men can the town support?' he had asked the captains.

'Easily a hundred,' said Guinot.

'There are new quarters for them. Some have taken in women, they'll be breeding like rabbits,' Meulon told Blackstone.

Blackstone laid out the map that Jean de Harcourt had given him. 'I don't want too many men in any place we hold. Fifty here at the most. It can be defended with less. Others will come now the war's ended and there'll be those who will challenge us. Soldiers without war are like a pack of wolves. I want to go further south, pluck what we can and bring whoever's there onto our side.' He paced the room that he had taken for his own use in the merchant's house, containing a simple cot and a table for the maps and a plate of food. He knew they had been lucky so far. The nagging uncertainty of how to fulfil his promise to those he had offered to protect was always with him. Men now looked to him for their welfare and reward, and since he had rejected the Norman lords' stipend they had raided further away from the security of Chaulion. Blackstone's name and reputation had grown, but the coffers had shrunk as French loyalty had been fractured by the war, spawning other bands of routiers who would tear the heart out of an area that lacked protection.

'We've achieved much this year, but we need to secure provisions for winter,' Blackstone told them. 'Start choosing men the others respect and give them the responsibility of command. We need to rely on the men we have.' He tapped the map, which showed several smaller hamlets and manor houses. 'Choose those places that are scattered within a few miles of the walled towns. By taking them we keep those who command the towns from using the roads and moving across country. Seize and hold.'

For those first few months his men had raided beyond Chaulion, ignoring walled towns and concentrating on smaller fortified manor houses whose defences could be quickly overwhelmed and then improved enough to be held by only a few men. His strategy of picking off these easily captured manors and hamlets meant that the smaller garrisons of the lesser nobility were hampered in their movements and their access to food when their villages were brought under the English knight's protection. Two of these towns, smaller than Chaulion, with ancient, crumbling walls offering little protection, fell by the autumn. Their men had been barely able to travel five miles without being attacked and harassed by Blackstone's marauders. It was this slow and deliberate plan, executed by surprise attack, and the ability to change tactics rapidly that often caught the French off-guard. Despite their small numbers – the raiding parties were often no more than a dozen men – they were used to attacking trade routes and traders and Blackstone rode and fought with his men until towns and hamlets further south were held. It was this capacity to strike an enemy in different places that he likened to inflicting multiple wounds on a stronger opponent. Sooner or later the bloodletting would weaken them and they would fall to their knees. Blackstone's incursion became the silken thread that held these places together and festered in French flesh. It had been a daring start to a campaign, but now the men were becoming weary and it would soon be time to secure what they had.

'We can't fight through another winter,' Meulon said. 'It would exhaust us.'

'My men fight as long as I fight, Meulon. I eat what they eat. I take no special favour for myself,' Blackstone said, but knew as he said it that the edge to his voice was due to tiredness.

Meulon stood his ground. He was the one sent by Lord de Harcourt as Blackstone's right-hand man, and had been at Blackstone's shoulder in every attack. 'We are not you, Master Thomas. We've lost men, some are still wounded. Too far, too fast and we could lose some of what we've gained.'

Blackstone looked at Guinot, who shrugged. 'He's right. We're secure, we've food. It would rebuild the men's strength. And the horses are being punished harder than the men.'

Blackstone knew that man and horse could be pushed further but he also knew that he was in danger of abandoning his own strategy of seize and hold. Before he could make his decision a messenger from Castle de Harcourt was announced and one of de Harcourt's soldiers was ushered into the room. He bowed his head to Blackstone, and acknowledged Meulon who had once commanded him. The messenger had obviously ridden without rest. His clothes were wet and mud-splattered and he had the gaunt look of a man who had not slept for a couple of days.

'I serve my Lord de Harcourt,' he said.

'We know that, you idiot,' Meulon chastised him. 'What is it you want?'

'I have a message for Sir Thomas,' the courier said.

'Then hand it over and get to the kitchen for food,' said Meulon, a sense of despair creeping into his voice at being reminded how slow-witted some of the garrison soldiers were.

'It is not written, it was given to me by my Lord de Harcourt with orders to speak only to Sir Thomas,' the man said.

'And you remember your lord's words, Bascard?' Meulon asked, remembering the man's name.

'I do. I was made to repeat them many times before my lord sent me.'

'Aye, well, I'm surprised he didn't hang a slate around your neck to remind you,' said Meulon, as he and Guinot left the room.

Blackstone had given little thought to de Harcourt because time had passed quickly. When he slept he dreamt of lying across Christiana, and that arousal would wake him to the cold reality of whatever floor or cot he slept on alone. Some of his men had taken women and others had made use of the town's whores, but Blackstone had busied himself with making war.

'Give me your message and you'll be fed and quartered until your return,' Blackstone said.

The man stood rigidly, gazing straight ahead so that his eyes did not meet that of a superior and began reciting the words that had been drilled into him. 'Your absence for these many months has caused concern and as this year draws to a close my lord notes that you have made no effort in another regard.'

'What regard?' Blackstone asked.

The man looked perplexed, not expecting his orders to be questioned. 'I don't know, Sir Thomas. But my lord commands you to attend the wilful neglect of your duty.' The man swallowed nervously. 'That's what he said.'

Blackstone had no idea what the message meant. He had secured territory in the name of his sovereign lord, Edward, and had extended the buffer between the Norman barons and those who might threaten them. Long, hard months of raiding had forged a small company of men who fought as if they were twice their number. What other duty? And then it became obvious where his neglect lay. Christiana.

'How does my Lord de Harcourt command me?'

'By returning until the matter is settled.'

With a sickening wrench Blackstone realized the master was pulling the leash on his dog. After months of freedom it was being curtailed and despite the sudden reminder of his lust for Christiana and de Harcourt's goodwill, he could not help feeling resentment. He was being taken from his men. He knew them as well as he had known the English archers with whom he had served. And he did not wish to lose such a close bond again. Could he defy de Harcourt? Why not? He was independent of them, he had proved his worth. But honour and a promise made to his wife that he would return had to be reconciled.

He gave his instructions to Guinot and Meulon to do as they suggested and give the men rest. Then, on the following day, he rode back to Castle de Harcourt.

The castle's imposing walls loomed before him, and as he clattered across the wooden bridge memories of time lost flooded over him.

Jean de Harcourt looked at the man before him. His wild hair was matted like a dog that had hunted its prey through bramble and hedgerow and his gaunt, unshaven face was weather-beaten, the skin taut against his cheekbones, tightening his scar like a bowstring. He had seen that haunted look in fighting men's eyes before; it was one of constant wariness, of always being alert. He stepped forward and embraced Blackstone.

'Thomas, it's good to see you after so long. I'm pleased you're well and have suffered no injuries.'

Blackstone felt a familiar comfort within the castle walls. In one sense it was like coming home and yet there was also the feeling that they were imprisoning the part of him that wished to ride freely across the countryside and strike at his enemy.

'I've been fortunate, lord. How is your standing with King Philip? Has everything gone as you had hoped?'

'Thanks to you, yes.' He poured wine as Blackstone restlessly went to the window. 'De Fossat came back with enough evidence to convince the King that we were hunting you in his name. If there had been any suspicion that Norman lords had connived at your success in the towns to the south it was a doubt soon pushed from the King's mind when the severed heads were tipped from the sacks with great ceremony by our friend William. The King's chancellor vomited because of their putrefaction, but Philip was keen to see if your scarred face was among the heads that rolled around his courtyard. William de Fossat has regained some of his lands, although the King's son resents him for it, but it's politics and de Fossat knows how to get the best yield from a well-sown crop.'

'Then your plan worked, though you might have warned me, lord. I thought we were about to fight our last when he appeared.'

'Better not to signal where you place your knight on the chessboard,' said de Harcourt, handing Blackstone a glass of wine, which he swallowed down as de Harcourt sipped his own. 'I had prayers said for you, Thomas. But what had happened between you and William was common knowledge and I used that because he was the only one of us the King would believe.'

'Then you gambled with my life. He'd have killed me if he had to.'

'No, I knew that he would not because he owed you a debt.'

'Which is now wiped clean.'

'Listen to me, Thomas, what happened at Chaulion with Saquet and de Fossat bought us time.'

'Perhaps so, but I don't understand him. He said he would fight alongside me in a common cause but if we faced each other on the battlefield he would kill me. And that can be done by a crossbow easier than a sword.'

De Harcourt laid a hand on his friend's shoulder. 'William will choose whatever course best suits him. Treat him as you would a chained war dog. Don't get too close and don't make him strain against it. He's strong enough to make it snap.'

Blackstone had been caught up in the Norman lords' web and although his friendship for Jean would hold him, they both knew he had already cut himself free from their entanglement.

'Now, Thomas… there are other matters that must be attended to.'

Blackstone felt another kind of trepidation, different from the brief moments of fear that gripped him before battle. He had to face Christiana after months of absence.

'Where is she?' he asked.

'In her rooms. She knows you're here.'

'She's well?'

'Yes. She and Blanche accompany each other every day. She's happy here. But she misses you, though she never complains. It was time to bring you back, Thomas. It's been too long.'

'I had work to do. We've secured a corridor that gives Edward an opportunity to strike through the heart of France should he need to.'

'And he's aware of it. We have our ways of telling the English King what he needs to know. You refused our payments, Thomas. Is our money not good enough?'

'I wanted to be independent and to save you and the others from being associated with me, but, unless I can find someone to capture and ransom or strike lucky with another attack, then I shall come back with my begging bowl. I have enough to get through another winter.'

'You'll never be seen as a beggar by anyone in this house, or those associated with me. We've watched you hurl yourself through the countryside like an angry storm. We could never have acted with such abandon.'

Blackstone allowed the warmth of the compliment to calm him. 'I have good men. Every one of them. Tell the barons that they chose well when they sent them. And I should be with them.'

'Every man has more than one duty, Thomas. Christiana was under our guardianship, but you can't abandon your wife and child.'

De Harcourt's words caught him like a flail. 'Child? Already?'

The Norman lord looked at the man he had taught to fight, the boy who went out a mercenary and returned a seasoned leader. 'Sweet Jesus, Thomas, you can count the months.'

Blackstone looked blank, trying to recount how many sorties and attacks he had undertaken. The months went hand in hand with conquest. How many men lived and died, and when, was his calendar. 'Eight?'

'Ten, damned near eleven.'

'A child,' he whispered to himself. 'What am I to do now?' he asked like a fool. And then, 'What kind of child?'

'Well, there are no signs of horns or cleft hoof, so most likely one sent by the angels. You should see him.'

A son.

Christiana was different. Her face had softened and there was a warmth to her skin like a blush; she looked somehow younger; childlike, he thought as he gazed at her. Her body pushed more against the soft cloth of her dress and her breasts, he noticed, were fuller and the taste of desire for her caught in his throat.

As he stepped into the room she was blowing gently on a cord to which were tied a dozen or more strips of coloured material that swayed above a small bundle lying swaddled in a crib. She whispered a soothing sound that would have caused the wildest heart to quieten. Except that when he saw her his heart beat faster. She turned as he made a movement, a sudden look of alarm giving way to surprise and joy as she ran and leapt at him, her lips covering his own with that unmistakable taste. She whispered his name a dozen times and then lowered her legs to the floor, gazing up at him, holding his face in her small hands, and letting her finger trace his scar.

'Thomas, my beloved husband. I have missed you so much and prayed every day for your safe return.' She tugged his hand. 'Come, come and see your son.'

She lifted the sleeping infant from its crib and handed the

swaddled child to him. He held it awkwardly away from his body, his big hands like grain shovels compared to the tiny bundle. 'It's like a loaf of bread,' he said curiously. Bringing the child to his face he sniffed. It was a delicate smell that he had never experienced before.

'I've just fed him,' she said and eased the baby from his arms. She kissed the infant's forehead and Blackstone could see that she was like a child with a new kitten.

'There's a wet nurse here?' he asked, because there had never been women servants at Harcourt.

'I feed him. I've enough milk for every child in Normandy,' she said, without any coyness in her voice and an impish look in her eye.

'What do we call him?' Blackstone asked, imagining the child suckling at her breast, lying in her arms as she stroked its face and cooed a sweet lullaby. And wishing he were that child.

'Henry, to honour your father, Guyon, to honour mine, and Jean, to acknowledge his godfather.'

Blackstone realized that he had never known her father's name. And learning it now made the circumstances of his death more painful than it had been before. She saw the shadow that fell across his face.

'Did I do wrong in my choosing?'

Blackstone recovered quickly. 'No, it's perfect. Henry Guyon Jean Blackstone. Just that it's a mouthful,' he lied, covering himself, 'I hope I can remember them.' He broke her frown with a smile, and bent down to the petite girl who had become his wife and mother to his child and kissed her. He reached out for the baby.

'You're filthy,' she said, putting a restraining hand against his chest. 'You stink of horse sweat and greasy leather.' And then kissed his lips lightly and whispered, 'We should bathe.'

The following days were easy. They made love frequently and the tension of commanding men and seeing to their welfare gave way to languid nights after vespers, where she would return from her prayers and satisfy their lust for each other, so that she would have to spend even longer praying for forgiveness for her lascivious thoughts and acts. Blackstone would have none of it, and begged her not to pray for him, or she would be all night in the chapel.

Hours of the day passed slowly; soldiers begged leave to approach him and ask about their comrades who now served with him, to learn who lived and who had not. He slept in Christiana's feather bed with her in his arms, but most nights after their entangled bodies eased away from each other into sleep, he felt the bite of his back muscles, more accustomed to a hard cot with a straw mattress, and she would wake and find him curled on the mat with his cloak over his naked body. Each day seemed to pass more slowly than he had remembered. The way he lived with the men at Chaulion had smudged his memory of how quiet and simple life could be within the castle walls. Marcel still hovered as his mistress's servant and, Blackstone suspected, informer, but he showed a particular skill with the baby, and would often be sent by Blanche to bring mother and child to her rooms. Christiana seemed not to give it a second thought when Marcel went down onto the carpet where Henry lay on his back mewling, small arms and legs wriggling, like a beached fish with limbs, and plucked the child into his arms, wrapping him in a shawl. Servant, mother and child seemed like a family unto themselves, as Blackstone watched the ease with which his son was embraced. Blackstone had not yet gauged how much tenderness should be applied to a body that felt like a boned chicken. That it was his seed that had grown into the bleating infant was still a cause for wonderment. Part of him lived in another creature now, just as he had been spawned by his father. A regret caught him unawares: he would not be able to pass on his archer's skills as his father had done. But, he told himself, there was little sense in becoming too sentimental about the child. If it lived a year it was lucky, two was fortunate, beyond that it had a chance. Arianrhod came to his lips, as he closed his eyes in a silent prayer to the two mystical women – the Celtic goddess and the Virgin Mary, Mother to all children – and asked that the infant might live so he could share its life.

* * *

'Hoi! Hoi!' Jean de Harcourt cried as one of his falcons battered through the dull sky in pursuit of a doomed woodpigeon. He doted on his new falcons, with their perches in almost every room of the castle except the bedchamber, the one place where Blanche's prohibition was inviolate. De Harcourt stroked and pampered them, cooing tender sentiments as if to a child on his knee; an unlikely sight. The hunting season was as good as over, but he wanted Blackstone to ride out and see the beauty of his birds. Blackstone had always felt what he could only describe as resentment when he was a boy watching Lord Marldon hunt with his falcons. It was a nobleman's sport, easy kills that came with little effort, so different from the woodsman skills he and his brother had learnt. If they could not snare a cony or bring down a bird with a sling, they might not know the taste of meat for weeks, and using a sling brought eye and arm together, perfect training for bowmen. That same feeling had risen again when he was convalescing at the castle and had watched de Harcourt ride out with his birds. Now, though, as the hooded raptor on his master's glove was given sight of its prey and released, Blackstone had a different thought: he was like that bird – trained, held and sent in pursuit.

He was relieved to ride without the company of women, for after being regaled by Christiana and Blanche with the events of the past months he had quickly tired of their chatter. During his absence there had been visits by other lords and there had been feasts that brought with them all the attendant gossip. De Harcourt's summons provided a welcome escape from the two women, who had begun to talk yet again of the protracted labour pains that Christiana had endured.

When Blackstone and de Harcourt returned home the birds were settled by the falconer and de Harcourt guided Blackstone into the library, where they warmed themselves by the open fire, dogs at their feet and a map beneath their fingertips. Jean de

Harcourt and the other Norman lords enjoyed relative safety in their heartland even though the war between the French and Anglo-Gascon forces in the south went on regardless of the treaty made between the two kings at Calais, while to the west conflict continued unabated as independent captains, mostly loyal to Edward, fought and gave weight to the opposing side in the civil war that sapped resources and men with its unrelenting violence against the dukes of Brittany.

'Edward has little interest in the west,' de Harcourt explained as his finger traced a map. 'The ports are his but the Ushant Reef is treacherous and Brittany offers no convenient port of entry into France, so he continues his support simply to stop the French from going south to his lands in Bordeaux. If they ever struck there they would deny him his shipping routes to England and make the defence of Gascony more difficult and expensive than it is already. Both Kings jockey for position. Both seek revenues to pay for others to possess territory in their name.'

Blackstone pointed out the scattered outposts he had secured inland. 'These are my towns and villages. I'm vulnerable from here and here,' he admitted, his hand sweeping east and then west to the marches of Brittany. 'But those that I hold, be they manor houses or hamlets, are defended and within easy distance of the others for reinforcements.'

'But you don't have enough men, Thomas. You must be prepared to take those of low character into your ranks. Prisons are being emptied, footsoldiers and horsemen roam in bands taking what they can.'

'I don't want scum. Those I have wouldn't grace a halfway-decent tavern, but alehouse whores like them and they pay for what they take. Besides, as I told you, money goes quickly. Perhaps I should go to Edward and ask.'

De Harcourt let the map roll into itself. 'The cost of keeping his garrison at Calais puts a strain on his coffers. Take those who offer their services and let them live from *patis*. It's how men like that survive.'

Blackstone knew more of how these soldiers of fortune lived than did de Harcourt. *Patis* was nothing less than protection money – a contract between mercenaries and surrounding towns and villages to take what they wanted, when they wanted it and with the agreement that the villagers would not be attacked by them. The trouble was that it gave those men independence and allowed them to live by their own rules. For Blackstone to allow groups of men to do so meant he would have no control over them. His own *patis* was protected by his sword arm.

'If I do that it would take only a few incidents to have the locals rise up and attack my men. I have a core of soldiers that serve me and those I have given authority to. I can only do what I can with those that I have. It was never your intention for me to ride at the head of an army. Small groups of us in strategic places are worth more to me than hundreds scavenging the countryside for food.'

De Harcourt knew it was dangerous to be too ambitious. Sir Godfrey had miscalculated the King of England's ability to finance war away from home. Blackstone was right, it was better to have control over a smaller and more vital area than to gain a greater territory and risk losing all. But he thought he knew how Blackstone could strike a blow for the Norman lords and seize enough French coin to buy himself the kind of men he wanted.

'We'll talk more of this later,' he said, wanting to think on it further. 'You'll stay for Christmas, Thomas. The other lords will be here.'

Christmas was something he dreaded. The whirl of coloured dresses and jewellery would brighten the heavy walls and bring gaiety and laughter to a house that had nurtured him. He would always be grateful to de Harcourt, Blackstone knew, but to have to endure another Christmas would feel like a punishment.

'Lord, I cannot leave my men that long. I'll return with Christiana and my son and we'll make the best of it there. Isn't that why you summoned me from Chaulion – to do my duty to my family?'

De Harcourt nodded his agreement. 'As every man must, Thomas. But don't let those responsibilities hinder your enterprise.

Let Christiana have the boy until he's old enough to serve as a page. I'll take him when the time is right; when he's able to read and write and wipe his own arse. But do you understand how this places a greater burden on you?'

'I have to support them, that's natural.'

'And if you die?'

'Then they take what I have.'

'And what you have are scattered places of land with modest crop yields and ignorant peasants who'll give themselves like whores to the next man with a sword who can protect them. Your son needs an inheritance; if you have more children, a girl perhaps, then you'll need a dowry. Poverty is not for the likes of us, Thomas. You're no aristocrat, but you've a better understanding than most of what survival is about. God did not spare you at Crécy to remain a yeoman archer; he took that from you and gave you a greater gift.'

'He took my archer's arm and a brother in my care.'

'And in exchange he brought you here and gave you anger and ambition. For a murdering bastard you have a sense of honour, and I dare say that came from your father and your sworn lord, but you've crossed a line, Thomas.'

Blackstone's possession of the dark secret of Christiana's father made him feel like a thief in the night who dreads a sudden knife to his throat. He poured himself more wine as a diversion, in case his guilt was apparent.

'How so, my lord?' he asked, raising the glass, his eyes watching de Harcourt over its rim.

'Those who travel the roads, tinkers and monks, merchants and scavengers, they all have stories to tell. And your name is already known. Yours is a strange way, Thomas Blackstone.' De Harcourt stretched his legs in front of the fire and rubbed one of the dog's ears. 'You're more complicated than I took you to be. You burn and you kill but you don't allow women to be raped or children to be slaughtered. You have no breeding and you mocked our notion of chivalry. And yet you practise it.'

* * *

They left Castle de Harcourt with extra provisions and a bag of silver coin, provided by de Harcourt as a dowry for Christiana. Promises of an early reunion between Blanche and Christiana were made, women's tears were shed and de Harcourt's priest was summoned to give them a blessing for a safe journey home. God's protective mantle was bolstered by another ten men, who were to follow at a discreet distance and then return when their charges were in sight of Chaulion.

'We should have stayed, Thomas,' said Christiana. 'It's Christmas season, and it would have been my last chance to see everyone.'

He glanced at her. She seemed happy enough but who could tell with a woman? She wasn't pouting, which was good, and her lip did not curl in self-pity, which was better.

'I know you don't like to dance, and perhaps you feel some envy of the lords who speak beautiful verse, but it's soothing to one's soul, like a prayer said in humility,' she went on, seemingly without taking a breath. 'And the weather will be upon us, I feel sure of it, and my cloak will be soaked. I wish it would make up its mind. Rain or snow. Nothing is as it should be. Did you know they lost their harvest last autumn in the south? It rained so hard. There'll be famine.'

He did know. It was why de Harcourt had told him his plan. The further south, the greater the conflict. Rival captains on the same side fought for town and castle, and the French King's soldiers engaged in running battles from citadel to citadel in a continuous war of attrition. De Harcourt knew that the regional mint was secured in the town of St Aubin and a large sum of money was being put together, most likely to pay one of the French garrisons. If Blackstone and his men could find a way to slip through the warring factions and secure the mint or waylay the money in transit, he would inflict a heavy blow against the French King's ability to pay his troops in the south. What better way to serve one's own King, hamper the enemy and secure much-needed money for his own men? It was a plan fraught with danger, but a plan that Blackstone would consider nonetheless.

Christiana was not yet prepared to let him free of her gentle chiding. 'And Henry was safe at Harcourt. Safe and warm. Marcel was wonderful. Like my right hand. No, Blanche was my right hand; he was like my left. I shall miss them.'

He had learnt forbearance while at Harcourt and knew he was asking much of her. He remained silent, watching her lips that enticed him as much as when she spoke, as when she kissed him. Blackstone pulled up his horse. She didn't notice. Her monologue continued for a few more strides and then she realized he was not at her side.

He glanced back to where the escort shadowed them a few hundred yards away. They too stopped, watching their charge to see what he was doing.

'Is the baby all right?' she said with sudden concern.

Henry was swaddled in his crib, fastened on one side of a pannier saddle that carried Christiana's trunk of clothes on the other. There was no sound from the child and Blackstone assumed the swaying of the palfrey's gait was as good as a rocking cradle. He let his gaze wander, taking in the spindly boughed woodland.

'When I snatched you from those Bohemians in the forest and we nearly drowned you were feisty, like a peasant's ratting terrier; and then when you cared for me you were brave and selfless and subdued your own suffering. But since you've been with Blanche it's been like a tide creeping upriver. The dark water swallows everything that was once there. That's what's happened to you. You've become a housebound woman drowning under frivolous gossip and fine clothes.'

She scowled in protest. 'Thomas, I have spent—'

'Christiana. I haven't finished speaking yet,' he said firmly, without anger in his voice. 'I wish I could offer you more. I cannot. And our fortunes will be mixed. You shall have everything that is mine but you're a soldier's wife, not the lady of a nobleman, and there will be hardship and danger for us all. You'll have no gentle company and at best a merchant's wife to help with the child if that's what you need. There will be weeks when I'll be away. My heart and my bed are yours, but everything else demands my attention. Accept this life or go back and be with Blanche. She'll take you gladly. I'll visit once in a while. You'll have the child until he's seven and then he's mine. You must decide what it is you want. And I pray it is me.'

He handed her the palfrey's reins, then heeled his horse forward. It was a gamble, but one that had to be taken. It was up to her if she followed. And if she did then she would have turned her back on the comforts afforded her at Harcourt and they would face their uncertain future together.

By spring Christiana had long rid herself of the despair at the state of the house that Blackstone had taken as their home. He had lived in one room, ignoring the distressed state of the others that Saquet and his men had occupied. She demanded from Blackstone, and got, a dozen townsmen and their women to remove all traces of filth and scrub the house with vinegar from top to bottom. And once chimneys were cleaned and fires lit she scoured the area for rosemary and other herbs to burn and sweeten the fetid atmosphere of unwashed men and dogs and the fouling they had left behind. Fresh reeds alone would suffice for those rooms she visited infrequently but for all others she insisted on woven rush matting laid over the floors. No woman could trail her skirts across loose floor coverings until they had been crushed flat underfoot over months. Blackstone realized to his quiet satisfaction, and amazement, that Blanche de Harcourt's influence had played a role. Christiana was mistress of her own house, though without putting a resentful distance between herself and the townspeople. That she was the daughter of an impoverished French knight gave her an advantage in addressing them, artisan or labourer, washerwoman or seamstress, with a simple dignity that demanded respect. Brother Simon shared his knowledge of herbs and she scattered wormwood and fleabane, crushed with chamomile, throughout the house to keep infestations under control. Servants were interviewed and put to work, as was a steward to supervise them. He was given responsibility for the household accounts and, as a member of the town's council, he presented Blackstone with the expenditure and requirements for sustaining the town and its people through the coming year. In a few short months Christiana created a home and organized a small workforce to sustain it and its vegetable gardens. When Blackstone returned from reconnoitring for a way to secure King Philip's mint he found a house that may have lacked tapestries and ornament, but was nonetheless a place of warmth and comfort, befitting a man who had taken the town and now gave it his protection.

During the following weeks Blackstone prepared his plan. The mint was held in a small castle at the head of an escarpment, above cliffs rising two hundred feet. The road to the main gate was guarded by a small garrison of about fifty men, which allowed no direct assault, and a siege was out of the question. Before Blackstone's force could reach the objective they had to strike into the heartland of the warring factions, a raid that had to be swift and carefully executed. Either side might see his incursion into their territory as a direct threat. During his reconnaissance he had bribed a goatherd to show him paths scratched into the hillside by which Blackstone's men could approach from below the castle's most vulnerable wall and where they might scale the cliffs. Once they had breached the walls, the archers, who would stay concealed in nearby woodland, would strike at those guarding the road, and drive them inside. Matthew Hampton would hold the road and Blackstone's men would hold the keep. Their enemy, trapped between two hostile forces within the inner and outer walls, would be held fast, unable to advance or retreat. Blackstone put the plan to Meulon and Guinot, who, since recovering, had been placed back in command of Chaulion. They would halve the garrison in early July when the weather warmed and grazing was plentiful. By then their horses would have regained their strength after winter. Chaulion and the other places held in Blackstone's name would be bringing in their winter-sown wheat and he wanted to be back for the harvest to ensure the crop was safely stored and protected from any scavenging routiers. It seemed a good plan.

And then one day the monastery's bell rang out its distress.

CHAPTER TWENTY-SEVEN

Prior Marcus stood at the crossroads with a family of travellers. They looked exhausted. The man and woman carried their worldly possessions on their backs, and five children, their ages somewhere between three and seven, Blackstone estimated, sat huddled at their parents' bare, blackened feet supping from a wooden bowl of pottage. Talpin was guard commander and came forward to hold Blackstone's bridle as he and the half-dozen men who rode with him dismounted.

'They're the fifth lot this morning, Master Thomas – came up on the road from the south. We thought nothing of it at first, but now these wretches tell us there's another horde following on their heels. Something's going on. Brother Marcus isn't telling us anything.'

Blackstone nodded, scanned the hillsides, but saw no sign of anyone else. 'Keep the gates closed, Talpin. No matter what Prior Marcus wants, you follow my orders.'

Blackstone strode across to the family, who quickly got to their feet and bowed at his approach.

'Sir Thomas, these people have travelled from the south where there's pestilence. Many have died, they say hundreds, perhaps thousands,' Prior Marcus explained.

It was doubtful the peasant could count the fingers on his hands but if he had seen a lot of bodies it did not matter.

'Have you fed others today?' Blackstone asked Prior Marcus.

'They were all needy. Of course,' the prior replied.

'Who approached them?'

'I don't understand,' Brother Marcus answered, perplexed at the question.

446

'Did you attend them? Feed them?'

'I and Brother Robert. Why?'

'Have any looked ill? Fever, or raging thirst?'

'No. They move ahead of the plague. It has come from the ports. They say Bordeaux burns the bodies in vast pits and in Narbonne they are blaming the Jews and hanging them. The Pope has issued a decree to stop them but terror grips the people.'

Blackstone knew how virulent the plague was. 'My men and I were riding south a few weeks ago, we heard of a pestilence sweeping up the Rhône valley from Marseilles but I didn't think it would turn towards us.'

'God will prevail,' said the prior.

'God has abandoned us like some of your religious brethren. The Pope may well stay at Avignon, but the cardinals have fled. Lock the doors. Stay inside. Help no one,' Blackstone told him and turned back towards Talpin and the guard. The prior tugged at his arm.

'Not help? We cannot let these people pass without food. Look at them. They have nothing. Most haven't eaten in days.'

Blackstone signalled Talpin to him. He answered the prior, 'If you are lucky then these refugees haven't brought the plague with them. You and Brother Robert will be kept in the cow byre for two or three days. If you don't succumb you'll be allowed back inside the monastery.'

The prior's jaw dropped. Blackstone did not know whether it was the thought of being contaminated or the fact that he was to be kept in the stench of the byre. It didn't matter.

'You understand, Brother Marcus, that this pestilence will be on us quicker than the wind, and most likely carried on it. I have heard how people died. Check your armpits and groin for lumps. You have two days before the signs appear. I suggest you pray as you have never prayed before. For your life.'

Talpin stood waiting.

'Did you touch or go near any of the travellers today?'

'We kept them at spear length,' he answered.

'Keep it that way. We barricade the road.'

There was a drawn look of fear on Talpin's face. 'Plague?'

There was no need for Blackstone to answer.

'And you'll leave us out here? Alone?' Talpin asked.

'What you risk, so will I,' Blackstone answered and then he told Talpin what he wanted done.

Blackstone's father had once shown him a diseased cow with a pestilence that had killed the beasts in three of the local villages. The infected animals were isolated and left either to recover or die. It was the same with people. By the end of that day a barricade of wicker palisades, taken from the vegetable gardens, was used, along with fallen timber, brush and bramble, to cut off the road from the monastery to Chaulion, and then the bridge was closed. Two of the English archers were added to the monastery guard with orders to bring down anyone who tried to breach the palisades before they could even reach a spear's blade. In Chaulion a ripple of fear ran through everyone when they learnt of the invisible assassin that sought them out. Many thought God had sent the dark angel for them, for past and current sins.

Blackstone had a pious monk taken into Chaulion where a chapel was made inside an old stable block.

'We'll clear the stench for you,' Blackstone told him. 'Those who wish to pray can stand in the yard. It'll be cold and wet, but there's nothing else we can do.'

The young monk had calluses on his hands and a weather-beaten face. He was no stranger to hard work, having been a late arrival at the monastery.

'The stable is appropriate, Master Thomas, wouldn't you say? And God's love will ease their discomfort in the yard.'

A wave of devout prayer soon followed when the monastery rang out the prayer times during the day and night. Blackstone was thankful for it. It kept the townspeople's minds focused and lessened the chance of panic. Blackstone gave strict orders that the gates of Chaulion would remain closed until the plague passed them by. At first he thought there would be panic, but they listened to what he had to say and the councilmen supported him. They had two good wells in the town and enough food for weeks ahead. If anyone fell sick they would be taken to a house especially chosen and kept isolated.

'What can we do to protect Henry?' Christiana asked.

'Brother Simon told me to keep the air scented. Use whatever herbs you have. He said juniper should be burned and we should drink apple syrup, can you do that?'

She nodded and then eased into his arms. 'We have a new son born that could be taken back by God,' she whispered into his chest.

He could not disguise the irritation in his voice. 'Is this God's work? To smite down the lowly who have so little in the first place? It's not God, it's nature. Like a pestilence that smites the cattle. God doesn't hold a grudge against a poor cow. It's beyond our reasoning. We can do nothing more than wait it out.'

'Do nothing? Is that what you expect of me? Burn incense and drink sweet apple water? There are doctors in Paris, many of them Jews. They will know what to do,' she said, her voice rising in exasperation.

Blackstone closed a window. 'Christiana, when this pestilence reaches Paris it will slay pauper and nobleman alike, quicker than a horde of barbarians. You stay in the house and garden and keep the servants in their own quarters, away from you and the child.'

'And where will you be?'

'Everywhere,' he said, 'and there will be days when I cannot come back inside these walls. I daren't risk bringing it in so I'll stay outside and make sure I'm free of it.'

'You're going outside?' she said in disbelief.

'The villagers need warning,' he told her. 'My men need re-assurance.'

She turned on him angrily, like a she-wolf protecting her young. 'No, Thomas! I won't allow it! You're the boy's father! They're peasants who live and die in their own filth on any given day of the week. Your responsibility is here with us. To protect us!'

She wiped the tears of anger from her eyes and Blackstone made no attempt to calm her. He saw that she had let the fear take hold. He understood that; had seen it in men who caved in under its muscle-sapping virulence. It was as powerful an enemy as a battle-crazed soldier wielding a war axe. And to see someone close to your heart succumb to the panic was little different than seeing them swept away on a tide. He grabbed her wrists and let her struggle, his voice soothing her, bringing her back from her panic and anger.

'Christiana... Christiana... hush now... listen to me... listen... take a deep breath... and listen to me.'

She stopped writhing, unable to move this way or that because of his strength. He kissed her tears, and then released her, cradling her face in his hands.

'I am the protector of these people. It's my duty, as much to them as to you. They have to be warned, otherwise I am as worthless as the man who held this town before me. These people will look to you when I'm not here. They'll see a young mother who's as frightened as they are, but who's strong and who puts trust in her faith. Be that woman, Christiana, not only for me, but for the townspeople and our son.'

Her body relaxed and she stepped away from him. 'Blanche asked me to be strong when they brought you to the castle. I vomited when I saw your wounds, but I put my hands into them and cleansed them. I cared for you. This is different.'

He said nothing more and gathered his cloak and sword belt.

'I'll watch for you from the walls,' she said gently, relenting from her anger. 'God protect you, Thomas. All of us.'

Past experience reminded Blackstone that God was often busy elsewhere.

The townspeople shared responsibility for their own safety and Guinot made sure that his guards on the city walls were reinforced by men from the town. At first light Blackstone rode out with four other men, including Meulon and Gaillard, and although he wanted to take two archers with him for distance killing he did not wish to risk losing them to the pestilence. A couple of English archers with half a bag of arrows were worth a dozen hobelars and were too precious a resource. When Talpin and the guard at the monastery barricades saw that Blackstone was prepared to ride out it strengthened them against the fear that sat heavily in their chests and which could soon creep into their minds and blind their reason. Abandoning their posts would be like running into a haunted wood at night where wraiths of the dead would seize them. One of the archers, a man known as Waterford, watched the horsemen disappear across the skyline and then took to wiping his stave soothingly along its length with an oiled cloth, a slow, calming caress. The scarred knight could scare the shit out of Satan himself, he told Talpin and the others, and if the pestilence saw him coming it would turn back to where it came from. And who among them could argue with that? Blackstone's reputation and fierce looks were all that stood between them and the devil's seed. Matthew Hampton twirled an arrow shaft in his fingers and eased an errant goose-feather fletching into place.

'Aye,' he said quietly, 'but I'm glad he didn't take me out there with him.'

The first two villages were still safe havens and Blackstone instructed the villagers how to block the pathways. Palisades, cut brush and sharpened stakes would be warning enough to any itinerant refugee. No helping hand could be offered to anyone outside of their own community. They should slaughter what animals remained and ration their corn and smoked fish stocks. Perhaps, Blackstone hoped, the plague had bypassed them altogether. Small villages were usually safer than towns or cities when disease took hold. Fewer people meant less chance of contagion.

Several miles on, woodcutters' tracks led them to where five families of thirty or so people lived and who had not yet seen travellers on the road. Most likely their isolation had so far saved them. Once Blackstone told them of what might be approaching down the rutted track that led to their hamlet, it ignited terror as if a flaming torch had been tossed into their reed-covered hovels. Meulon barged one man with his horse as he tried to run free. Blackstone shouted his orders. Run into the woods and they would die, he told them. Stay and keep strangers and other villagers out and they had a chance to live. No trade, no bartering. If one man's wife or her family lived in another village there was to be no contact. He had them cut wattle and make six-foot fences to block the tracks leading to them and then to hang dead crows as a warning to anyone who thought to approach. Those who sickened and died must be burned in their houses.

'And when will we know if the plague has passed?' one of the woodcutters asked.

'When I return and tell you,' Blackstone answered.

'Lord, if you are taken, how will we know?' the man persisted.

'If I die another will come. And if no one comes, then it makes no difference.'

Before they reached the next village Blackstone pulled up.

'Gaillard, dismount,' he said, getting down from the saddle. Gaillard looked perplexed, but did as he was told. Blackstone handed him his reins. 'I have the best horse – take him and ride to my Lord de Harcourt and warn him of the plague. Tell him what we're doing here, and that he should blockade the road to his villages and keep those within the castle from leaving. Ride hard and stop for no one. Stay in open country as much as you can. If anyone gets in your way, kill them. It doesn't matter whether it's a priest or a monk, or a nobleman running for his life. Don't hesitate. Lord de Harcourt and his family must be warned. You stay and serve him till this is over. Do you understand?'

'Yes, Sir Thomas,' Gaillard answered, the burden of responsibility for the safety of de Harcourt now placed squarely on his shoulders.

'I trust you with this, Gaillard.'

'God bless you, Master Thomas; no man has ever treated me so well. And God bless you, my friends,' said Gaillard.

Gaillard's distressed look prompted Meulon. 'You serve Sir Thomas, Gaillard, and you've done well for him to choose you. Spit on the devil and when he blinks, ride past him,' Meulon said as the men laughed, easing the tension.

'With a horse like this, he'll never catch me anyway,' Gaillard answered more confidently.

'Ride him steady and find him water. Give my respects to the count. Tell him I will pursue the matter we discussed once this evil has passed. He'll understand.' Blackstone took the waterskin from Gaillard's horse and wrapped it around the pommel. 'Don't stop, don't accept food or shelter.'

He stepped back and let Gaillard kick the horse away.

'And no whores either!' one of the men called after him. Gaillard raised a hand showing he had heard. The men laughed among themselves. Gaillard was all right, he had the strength to fight two men at once, but the brains to know when he should run.

Meulon nodded at Blackstone; that was why he had been chosen.

Riding back to the main route that flowed like a stream of mud between the villages and town they saw the first signs of death on the road. Four bodies lay no more than three hundred paces from each other. They were peasants from God-knew-where, and Blackstone hoped they were not those who had passed by the monastery. It was doubtful, because he and the men were now more than a half-day's ride away and those he had seen at the monastery were already exhausted. They would have reached the woodland and settled there until what little strength they had had returned, he thought.

'Give me that,' he said to Meulon, extending an arm for his spear. He dismounted and prodded the face-down corpse, which was that of a man. The body was not long dead, the flesh and the limbs gave way to the pressure but there was a rigidity to it that spoke of an agonizing death. The man's hands were clenched. Blackstone wondered if that was because his soul had been dragged gasping from the body. He turned the body over. A grotesque face glared back at him. As the head lolled a black swollen tongue squirmed from the open jaws. The man's bloodshot eyes were frozen in horror. The stench caught the back of Blackstone's throat and he smothered his face with his crooked arm.

'Sir Thomas! Don't touch him!' Meulon shouted from where he and the other men stayed safely with the horses.

Blackstone laid the tip of the spear against the man's shirt and sliced through the worn material. The arms were splayed and once the shirt fell free Blackstone could see the buboes in his armpits. Some were small like overripe crab apples; others the size of an orange, and they had burst, weeping a black slime that stank like nothing Blackstone had ever smelled before. Even a battle's gore was less offensive.

He pulled back his head as if struck, and after a few paces went down on his knees and vomited until his stomach muscles knotted. There was no prayer yet uttered by the holiest of men that could save anyone from this malignant enemy.

Going quickly to another body he knew it was unnecessary to see if they had all suffered the same fate; his purpose was to try to identify any of the fallen and establish which village they came from.

He turned a big man over with the spear and saw a face like a church's gargoyle. Perhaps this look of terror on the dead was the devil's imprint, he thought.

'It's spread fast,' he called as he walked back to his horse. 'It's missed the villages to the east. It's travelling north,' he told them.

'You're certain?' Meulon asked.

'These people were heading towards Chaulion and the monastery,' Blackstone told him.

'They needed prayers said for them by the monks,' Meulon replied.

'Nothing to do with redemption, Meulon,' he said.

They spurred on their horses, leaving behind the suppurating body of the big bearded man who carried not only the dark angel's mark, but also that of the fleur-de-lys that Blackstone had branded him with months earlier.

The village of Christophe-la-Campagne had not learnt the lessons from Blackstone's punishment after killing the English messenger and beating William Harness. They had done as he expected and betrayed him to Saquet, but they were still riven with hatred for the Englishman. And when the pestilence had struck they had turned in on themselves like a snared wolf chewing off its own leg.

'It came here first,' said Blackstone as they stood off from the village watching for movement among the houses. 'Came here like an enemy through a back gate. They weren't seeking a monk's prayers, Meulon, they wanted to strike back at me. They wanted to get inside our walls before the plague showed its full force on their bodies.'

The men crossed themselves.

'Sweet Jesus on the cross! That's hatred, Sir Thomas,' said one of the men.

Meulon looked up and down the muddied road. 'This is the main highway for most anyone in these parts. If a pilgrim steps across that threshold they'll be dead within a week and infect others.'

The men remained uneasy, some looking over their shoulder as if malign spirits could sweep down from the treetops. They could see animals untended in the fields; the cow byre was empty. Only one or two houses seeped smoke through their thatch. No dogs barked; no babies cried.

'Many of them will lie where they fell,' Blackstone told the men. 'Wild boar and carrion will feed on them, the disease will spread. Get a fire going, make torches. We'll go down and burn them out.'

Blackstone and his men tore strips from their shirts to cover mouths and noses and rode slowly into the sullen village. He and Meulon carried the burning torches as the other two men acted as guards with their spears at the ready. Every mud and wattle house they went to calling out for anyone still alive, was in darkness, the stench of human and animal waste rising up to meet them, mixing with the foulness of the putrefaction of the scattered bodies that lay in the muddied track. It was as if a sudden, silent blow from Heaven had slain them where they stood. In reality some had tried to crawl into their hovels but succumbed in the gaps between them, or fell straddled half in doorways; others simply lay in the street. The wealthier villeins' houses were half-timbered and had windows covered with oiled cloth, but the privilege gave them no protection, and inside families lay in grotesque embrace.

As the men worked their way through the village they counted fourteen houses, some with reed roofs, others little more than shelters with animal skins stretched over them. There had probably been seventy or so people living in the village. Broken pigpens and scattered chicken feathers from an unlocked chicken house told a story of predators and untended animals for at least a week.

Meulon suddenly pointed: 'There!'

A group of men, women and children sat huddled at the far end of the village, their haunted eyes staring fearfully at the approaching men.

'Speak to them,' Blackstone told Meulon. 'Find out how many have survived.'

Blackstone stood back as Meulon cautiously advanced and spoke to the cowering villagers.

'Twenty or more went into the forests,' he reported. 'Others were buried in a pit in the meadow. They don't know what to do so they've kept themselves back here. No food to speak of, but there's water.'

Blackstone turned and cut free a stretched goatskin from its curing rack and then carefully grabbed a corpse's wrist by its clothing and dragged the body onto the hide. He called to the spearmen. 'Take down some of those roofs and use them,' he said, dragging the corpse to the threshold of a hut. The men were hesitant, but seeing how Blackstone gathered the dead they soon followed.

'Get their help!' Blackstone commanded, pointing at the villagers. 'At spear point if necessary.'

Meulon dragged a body onto a cow hide cut down from one of the roofs. 'We can't do this in every village we come across. The risk is too great.'

'I know,' Blackstone admitted, realizing their task was going to prove too difficult, 'but this place is a danger to others and if there are more survivors then we give them a chance. We can't know how far or fast this plague has gone. We burn everything. If any of these people survive they can rebuild what they had.'

By the day's end they had gathered thirty-seven bodies of men, women and children and placed them in one of the houses. They pulled down the reed roofs of other houses and laid them over the bodies. Blackstone wiped the sweat from his face, and dreaded the thought that the tang of salt he felt on his lips might harbour the disease. Meulon approached him once the last of the bodies was covered.

'The villagers ask permission to speak to you, Sir Thomas,' he said.

Blackstone looked to where they stood, heads bowed, caps taken off respectfully.

Blackstone gave Meulon a quizzical look, but the man could only shrug.

Meulon herded forward the reluctant men and women who, unlike the children who gazed fearfully at his scarred face, kept their eyes lowered.

One of the men prodded another, urging him to speak. The reluctant spokesman shuffled another half-step forward. 'Lord, we have paid dearly in this village. There has been no priest here for years, and no monk from the monastery at Chaulion has ventured this far.'

'There's nothing I can do about that,' Blackstone told them, a fragment of memory reminding him of the villagers' brutality.

'Lord,' the man continued, 'we beg you to speak for those who have died. Without a priest or monk, only a man of rank like yourself would know the words to bless their souls and to bear witness to our sins.'

Blackstone could not grasp what they asked of him. Meulon raised his eyebrows.

'They want you to say a prayer for the dead and confess them. They're scared of dying without confession,' he said.

Blackstone pulled Meulon aside and kept his voice barely above a whisper. 'I'm no confessor or priest. Why do they ask it of me? I'm the one who hanged and branded them.'

'I've heard of this before. Better to be confessed even by a common man than die burdened. You'll be their saviour, Sir Thomas,' he answered, and then dared to add, 'that would make a change, would it not?'

His men retreated to their horses as Blackstone sat on a milking stool and heard each confession from those who knelt in the mud before him. And then as he and his men thrust the torches into the huts he said a boyhood prayer for the dead, barely remembered from his own village priest's incantations.

That night, a mile or more from the village, Blackstone and his men sat naked, wrapped in their cloaks, their own clothes washed in the river and drying by a campfire. In the distance the sky glowed as flames from the burning pyre released flickering sparks of departing souls into the dark heavens.

CHAPTER TWENTY-EIGHT

Days passed as the men rode across miles of deserted countryside. Bodies lay scattered in fields and on roadsides, groups of travellers lay dead around a cold campfire. Some of Blackstone's villages fared well, and he instructed the inhabitants how to protect themselves; others were wastelands of ghosts and were burned. Their journey yielded food and abandoned livestock and in exchange for some of the supplies two more manor houses yielded to Blackstone without a sword being drawn as impoverished knights swore loyalty to hold their land in Blackstone's name. Every day they made camp he had the men strip and show themselves to be free of buboes or rashes, and he did the same so that each knew the other was not infected. By the time the weary men returned to Chaulion they had two carts drawn by villeins' palfreys and loaded with sacks of grain, barrels of smoked meat and pickled fish, and caged chickens. They arrived at the crossroads with a procession of goats and cows. Blackstone had allowed no swine to be taken and slaughtered those that were found in the infected villages. He called Perinne to the bridge and ordered that the men keep back as they made their way to the gates of Chaulion. Once there he summoned Guinot and ordered him to take the supplies and animals in hand. He and the men then dismounted and hobbled their horses. Soldiers and townspeople gathered on the walls.

'Guinot! Put food and drink out. And vinegar water! We'll stay over there for a few days,' Blackstone said, pointing to an area a hundred paces away.

The Gascon barked his orders and Blackstone's instructions were carried out. Meulon and the two men were already building a fire as Blackstone moved closer to the walls where Guinot leaned down.

'Is there news from anyone? Messengers?' Blackstone asked.

'No one. Not a damned word from anywhere. No pilgrims, no travellers. Is the world dead?'

'Damned near enough,' Blackstone told him. 'Thank God for the walls.'

'Aye, well I'm glad for them, but I've been rotating the guard at the monastery more often than you said because the men are going wall-crazy. Much more of this and we'll have fighting on our hands. Some of the whores are complaining!'

'Complaining or moaning?' Blackstone said.

Guinot laughed. 'Yes, all right, I can handle that problem, but we need these men out of here.'

Blackstone knew what it meant to be caged behind walls.

'All right. I'll do something. Get fresh clothes for us. These still carry the stench no matter how often we wash them. My wife and son?'

'All well. We've had no plague in here, but we'll be glad of that food.'

Guinot turned away to arrange Blackstone's demands and Christiana suddenly appeared, leaning over – looking for him.

'You're safe?' she cried.

He smiled. 'We're blessed. You've been praying!'

He saw her nod and smile, and caught the glint of tears that she quickly wiped away. 'Day and night. Guinot has kept good discipline. Everything here is as you would wish.'

He wanted to tell her how he yearned for her. How the fear of what he had felt beyond the safety of the walls had brought her even closer to his heart than she had been before. There was so much to say, but the walls were crowded. He nodded and turned back to where Meulon and the other men were already stripping off and tossing their clothes into the fire. The cold wind shivered the forest but the naked men ignored it.

Meulon seemed as big as a bear as he dropped the last of his clothes into the flames. Four townsmen came through the gates

460

carrying buckets and left them thirty yards away. Blackstone took two of them, another of the men loped forward and grabbed the others. By the time Blackstone had undressed the four men were in full view of those on the wall. None of the men looked that keen to begin their scrubdown with the astringent-laced water.

'Christ, that's going to sting my arsehole!' one of the men said.

'At least your shit will smell sweeter,' the other told him.

Blackstone bent and scooped water over himself, then raked his fingers through his soaked hair. He gasped as the vinegar stung his lips.

Meulon tried hard not to flinch. 'My cock feels as though it's being thrashed with nettles.'

A voice from the walls carried on the wind. 'Hey, Meulon! Wash that weapon of yours! The whores need it to rid themselves of cunny crabs!'

A ripple of laughter spilled over the walls.

Matthew Hampton added his own insults. 'That's big enough to use on the butts. Let it swing, Meulon, I can use it for target practice!'

The laughter increased and Blackstone laughed with them.

'We're home and we're alive. That's good, isn't it?' he told the scowling Meulon, who finally gave in to the jibes and opened his big, bearded face in a grin.

'It's good,' he agreed and then turned his back to those on the wall, bent over and slapped his buttocks.

No plague entered the walls of Chaulion or the monastery.

As weeks turned into months Blackstone allowed the inhabitants and monks to begin, under strict control, a slow return to their normal lives. The monks were allowed back into their fields under guard by Talpin and Perinne's outriders. Those few travellers who came towards the crossroads were kept at spear point and moved on. They would find no sanctuary on the road north and none cared whether they survived or fell by the way. There were towns and villages that never knew of the plague, their isolation a protective cloak against the outside world. The Norman lords were as vulnerable as any peasant, but their castle walls saved most, although fighting in the south between Philip's territorial strongholds and those held by the English King's seneschals went on sporadically despite the pestilence. Gaillard had reached de Harcourt without incident and, as the year drew to a close, the baron sent riders with written messages to those who were in alliance. The messengers understood they were not to enter any stronghold and that the letters should be left in plain sight in exchange for food and water for rider and horse. Then an answer could be written and sent back by the same means. It was this method of couriers that allowed the towns, and the lords who controlled them, to know of events. One of the first such letters arrived months after Blackstone had returned to Chaulion. No name appeared on it in case the courier was stopped. It was simply a letter of news about the state of the Norman towns.

'Thousands died in Rouen and in Paris. The cities ran out of burial space,' he told Christiana.

'But they are still safe? Jean, Blanche and the children?'

'Yes. Others not. King Edward's sister died on her way to marry a Prince of Castile.'

Christiana put her hand to her mouth in shock. 'We must pray for her, Thomas. As you must for your King.'

'Prayers won't help him. That marriage would have given Edward an alliance with the Spanish kingdom. The plague has taken more than a princess; it's probably snatched peace from him.' His eyes followed the scratchy writing and once he saw their meaning he carried on. 'King Philip is trying to raise another army, but now there are not enough taxes. Too many have died. And – there's still a price on my head.' He handed the letter to her. 'Blanche writes to you.'

She kept from lowering her eyes to the page, as eager as she was to hear from Blanche de Harcourt. 'Will they hunt you?'

He gestured to the letter. 'It's in there. If they capture me they regain the territory and the towns. I'm a threat. So it looks as though Jean's idea worked.'

'It was not my Lord de Harcourt who suggested you undertake to risk everything. It was you. Blanche told me.'

'What good would I have been without my bow arm? There's no need for you to worry. You're safe here, anyone would be hard-pushed to get past the monastery, let alone breach these walls now.' He knew in his heart that any determined enemy with sufficient numbers could smash their way through to Chaulion, but it was unlikely, given the ravages of the plague. He wondered how much more he could do.

Time was measured only by the ringing of the monastery bells. Day turned into night and then day again as month after month passed. It was as if they had been cast into a wilderness, remembered only by the occasional messenger. Blackstone had changed the face of Chaulion by putting every man and woman in the town to work. Idleness bred fear and under Guinot's guidance they did as he ordered, because by now they had recognized that he was their master. They not only laboured in the fields under the watchful eye and protection of the soldiers but he used them to dig a broad ditch around the town whose spoil made a protective bank several feet high. Blackstone himself laid the stone foundations for a narrow bridge, which the town's carpenters built, wide enough for a wagon. It was added protection for what would become a key town in his defence of the territory. The withered corpses of the headless routiers went beneath the shovelled dirt, and by the time Henry Blackstone was walking and pulling tablecloths and ornaments from tables in their home, the Englishman had diverted the small river that flowed around Chaulion. It was only a narrow moat, but it would deter attack by escalade and the fortified town could be held with a small garrison aided by the town's inhabitants. Blackstone had allowed no rest for his men. Soldiers who were used to garrison duty alone were of no use to him if he led a raid, and he had berated both Guinot and Meulon, a ploy to spur competition between their men. The two commanders had drilled the soldiers in lance and shield wall, defence and attack; battered them with mace and sword and culled the weakest by shaming them until they begged to be released from sentry duty and allowed to return into the fighting group. Blackstone spared no one, including himself, from the rigours of training.

One morning, before daybreak, Blackstone was already up and about when he heard the monastery bell ring for matins. It was another day that promised a bitter wind and he was thankful that, over time, he had sent soldiers into the forest to guard the townspeople as they loaded carts of fallen timber. They had cut fresh logs, but it was the seasoned timber that would give them the warmth they needed. They had stored chestnut wood in the byres and barns, but that was useless unless it had been kept for two or three seasons. He had given orders for them to seek out ash wood because it would burn well whether it was wet or dry – that and slow-burning oak. But this morning the bell rang with a different urgency and it took him a few minutes to realize that it was not the call to prayer but a summons for the guard to turn out to the monastery.

Meulon had already kicked men from their beds and sent stable lads to saddle the horses. By the time they were out of the gates the bell had ceased its demands. As they rounded the bend in the road that brought the monastery into sight it began again, only this time in a different rhythm, for matins. As they drew closer they realized that no threat awaited them, only a dishevelled figure on horseback wearing a tunic and who looked barely able to stay upright. Another palfrey held by a trailing rein carried a knight's shield and sword. Although Blackstone could not make out the coat of arms, he did not have to. He knew the rider.

'Let the men have their breakfast here, Meulon,' he said, staring at the drooping figure.

Talpin came forward as the men dismounted. 'He called for you and you alone. Said he knows you and that he wouldn't move until you were here. I can't tell whether he's sick with pestilence or not, but we warned him off. Had one of the archers put a shaft close to him.' Talpin looked concerned.

'You did everything as I've ordered. There's no favour for anyone in these times,' said Blackstone and strode past the men who stood their guard at the wall. Blackstone walked as far as the bridge. The horse had not moved and the rider's head drooped on his chest, exhaustion claiming him.

'Guillaume,' Blackstone called. His voice made the horse shift its weight and the boy raise his head.

Like a man being pulled from sleep in the darkness, Guillaume Bourdin looked uncertainly towards the figure who stood across the bridge. 'Sir Thomas? Is that you?'

'I'm here.'

'Forgive me. I had no choice but to come to you,' he said with a voice that breathed weariness.

'That's all right, boy.' He turned and called to Talpin. 'Bring a basket of food and drink. Hot food with bread and spiced wine. Tell Brother Simon to put a potion in the drink, something to help the boy, tell him what you see.' He looked up at the sky. Rain or snow was coming, either one would finish off Henri Livay's page if he didn't have shelter. 'And I want canvas and ropes.'

The wind cut at them but the boy showed no sign that he felt it. Blackstone knew that meant he was beyond exhaustion. He turned back to Guillaume who swayed in the saddle. 'Guillaume! Listen to me, boy! You hear me?'

Once again he raised his head. 'I must sleep, my lord. I must.'

'You will not. The cold will kill you unless you eat first. Obey me or you'll die! And you did not come all this way to die at my door. Tell me what's happened. Come on – talk to me, lad.'

'My Lord Livay is dead. And his household. Servants and squire. All of them.'

'How? The pestilence?'

Guillaume's head sagged again.

'Guillaume!' Blackstone bellowed, desperately wanting to reach for the boy.

Blackstone's voice snapped the boy's head back. 'Pestilence. Yes. He took in a merchant... gave him shelter and... in days... they were all dead. I brought his shield and sword so that they were not stolen.'

Talpin hurried back with a basket containing a small earthenware pot cradled by bread and a hand-sized piece of cheese wrapped in cloth. Two other men followed with a folded sheet of canvas and ropes. Blackstone took the food and pointed to an outcrop of rocks.

'Make a shelter there. Tie it fast, batten it with wood and stone and then bring straw from the stable.'

He walked closer to the horses. They didn't shy at his approach and by the look of them they too had not eaten for days. He searched the boy's face. Wind and dirt had pitted his skin but there was no sign of boils. But that did not mean the lad was not infected. He put the basket of food down.

'Guillaume, ease yourself down and eat. And then get yourself into that shelter where you can sleep. Understand?'

The boy nodded and, like an old man, slowly lowered himself to the ground. His legs trembled and gave way. Blackstone instinctively took a step forward but then checked himself.

'Do you have any sign of red buboes? Have you had fever or thirst?'

Guillaume shook his head and eased himself down onto the ground. 'My master died in terror, Sir Thomas, he writhed like a wounded beast... his wife too... it was the merchant who... brought it... the sickness... and the warning... so I came to warn you...' the boy said haltingly, his voice now barely above a whisper.

The boy is dying, Blackstone thought. His body had deflated like a pierced football in what seemed to be a final sigh of breath. He stepped around Guillaume's body and eased the horses away and then handed the reins to one of the men. He took the man's spear and turned it to use the blunt shaft to ease Guillaume's body over. If the lad had come all this way to warn him of the pestilence then he had sacrificed himself needlessly. The boy flinched. There was life still trapped in his body, a reluctant spirit refusing to die. He prodded him again and, as the boy stirred, took off his cloak and threw it over him.

Guillaume gazed up at him.

'Forgive me, Sir Thomas, I fell asleep.'

'And I thought you dead. My cloak will keep you warm, and I'll have blankets brought for the straw. Now do as I say and eat. Then you sleep. I'll be over there beyond that wall.'

'No, Sir Thomas, I must tell you something...'

'Later,' Blackstone commanded and waited to make sure that the boy put food into his mouth, no matter how feebly it was done.

He returned to the monastery wall where Meulon was waiting.

'Does he have the devil's kiss?' he asked.

'I don't see any sign of it. We'll wait a few days. There are two of Livay's men here, aren't there?'

'One died last summer, when the clumsy bastard fell from his horse. Talpin's the other.'

'Yes. I remember. Tell him his lord and master is dead,' Blackstone told him.

'You forget, Sir Thomas, months turn into years. You've been his lord and master for more time than you remember. But I'll tell him. And don't worry about that boy out there. If he hasn't got the plague he'll live. Looks to me as though he's been in that saddle for more than a couple of weeks. I'll wager he's a hard little bastard.'

'He's a page who will one day be a squire. Remember that, Meulon,' Blackstone said.

Meulon's face dropped and he bowed his head for his indiscretion.

Blackstone smiled and reached out and grasped the man's shoulder. 'You're too serious, Meulon! You're right; he's a hard little bastard. He was prepared to kill me once.'

Guillaume Bourdin had survived the Blanchetaque battle and then helped his lord to safety at Noyelles castle where he then faced the English archer. And now that his new master Henri Livay had died in agony he forced his young body to cross the empty and hostile terrain with little sense of where the small town of Chaulion might be. A mendicant friar he passed on a track knew of the monastery and sent him in the right direction, but finding anywhere inhabited in that unknown landscape was down to luck and his horse's ability to find water. Where there was a river or stream people would live, and if they were not afflicted they would know of the monks of Chaulion.

Blackstone stood every day at the wall and waited for the boy to die, but by the third day he was on his feet and as the sky cleared he had made a fire and busied himself drying the damp blankets, and by the fourth he was washing in the river and calling for Blackstone. When Blackstone got within thirty paces of him, the boy stripped away his tunic and shirt and raised his arms. There were no boils.

'I was locked in the cellar,' he told Blackstone as they sat in the monastery's refectory and ate breakfast, a meal tolerated by the monks for their lay brothers before the midday dinner and insisted upon by Blackstone, who had taken food every morning since he had worked in the quarry as a child. He waited as Guillaume took a last slice of apple and swallowed the cup of warm goat's milk.

'I had spoken out of turn and was knocked to the ground by my squire,' he said.

'What did you do to deserve the punishment?'

'I served at my master's table and the merchant told Lord Livay that a Norman lord had been promised a bounty for you because you were known as a vicious killer of women and children,' Guillaume told him. 'I couldn't help myself and shouted out that that was a lie.'

'A foolish act. Brave but foolish. He could have had you flogged,' Blackstone said.

'As you know, Sir Thomas, my Lord Livay was a good and kind knight and he spared me that.'

'And the cellar saved your life,' said Blackstone, quietly pleased with the boy's bravery in finding him and bringing the warning of the Norman who hunted him. It had been two years since he had last seen Guillaume ride out of Castle de Harcourt with Henry Livay and he had grown taller and broader, but still with the gangly arms and legs of a youth.

'I know about the bounty. Count de Harcourt and William de Fossat created a pretence of hunting me. It's long over.'

Blackstone rose from the table and Guillaume quickly got to his feet.

'Sir Thomas, it was not William de Fossat who was commissioned to hunt you down; it was Count Louis de Vitry. He was given a great payment from the mint and an army. He promised that he would retake the towns held by the Gascons and English. He's already done that with places in the south. There was a plan to trap you at St Aubin where the King had his coin minted, but the pestilence caused them to move it somewhere else. I don't know where.'

Blackstone felt a pang of alarm. It had been Jean de Harcourt who had suggested he attack the King's gold and silver. Was that information planted by de Vitry or was de Harcourt abandoning him in favour of the French King? It seemed the plague or the Celtic goddess had saved him.

'What else do you know?' he asked the boy who must have served at Livay's right arm like a sharp-eyed falcon who missed nothing.

Guillaume shook his head. 'I'm not sure what I heard but there are other French lords with him and someone in Calais will betray your King and open the gates.'

The information would have little meaning to a page like Guillaume. Calais was just another city to be taken from the English, a part of the chequerboard of war, but to Blackstone it was more vital than knowing that he was a prize to be taken. The months of plague had passed over, and it was already across the water in London. What better time to strike at Edward? A double attack in the south where so-called English allies argued between themselves to the point of conflict, and when England stumbled almost to her knees from pestilence. The Captain of Calais would have insufficient men to protect the gateway to France if de Vitry and the others got inside the walls.

Blackstone gathered the bulk of his force. Their winter fat had been shed, the sloth of peace was banished.

Guillaume Bourdin begged to serve, but the thought of having a page attend him was too big a leap for Blackstone. And besides, he told himself, he would not be able to complete the boy's training to the age when he became a squire. Once this fight was over he would be sent to a noble lord to complete his apprenticeship.

'How old are you now?' Blackstone had asked.

'Thirteen, Sir Thomas – nearly fourteen – and I'm proficient in sword and other weapons, and I can read Latin and know verse.'

'Then you will stay here and be a companion to my wife and son and when I return we will discuss your future.'

The boy had been insistent. 'You'll need someone to hold your horse when you fight and bring you food and water.'

'I can look after myself, Guillaume. You'll stay. There's no telling how the fight will go and I've fought in city streets before.' He raised his hand to stop further argument. 'I promise you, when this is done I'll seek advice of what to do with you.'

'My lord,' Guillaume said, bowing his head and going down on one knee. 'I beg you! Give me your word that you will allow me to stay in your service when you return. I have no desire for yet another master.'

'Goddamnit, boy! I'm not here to reason with you!' Blackstone said, irritated with the boy's persistence.

'I apologize, Sir Thomas. But if I cannot serve you, then I would ask permission to leave Chaulion and find my own way in the world.' He kept his head bowed, knowing it would be reasonable for Blackstone to strike him.

Blackstone cursed him. Time was short. But the damned boy secured his word.

Leaving Guinot as Captain of Chaulion, he led the men onto the north road and Calais. As Christiana had embraced him in farewell she did not tell him that her belly was already swelling with another child.

CHAPTER TWENTY-NINE

It was a long, cold ride north. They had stopped at the monastery and received their blessing from Prior Marcus. They were a mixed bunch of English, Normans and Gascons; a band of men who would have fought each other in different times, and might still do so again. Blackstone had gathered them together in the town square. Meulon, Guinot, Matthew Hampton, Waterford, Perinne, Talpin – all of them. He knew every man's name. He spoke to them, offering them the chance to stay at Chaulion. He did not expect the Normans to fight their own countrymen or the Gascons to go deeper into French territory where, if captured, they would be slain without hesitation. The same fate would await the Normans. Retribution from a French King would be without mercy for any of them.

'We're Normans,' Meulon told him. 'Our lords give their loyalty to those they choose, and they chose you to lead us. That's good enough for me.' He had turned and looked at the men who stood without argument. Dukes and counts and kings were born to nobility and breast-fed the milk of dissent. Greedy, selfish bastards, most of them. A fighting man could fall beneath their war horse's hooves and his family would starve. Blackstone was different. He was of peasant stock and had earned the right to lead them.

Matthew Hampton called out from where he stood at the head of the archers. 'If your head's to end up on a pike then mine will be next to it; that way I can keep an eye on you, like always.' That caused laughter and a cheer.

'Aye,' shouted Waterford, 'I've always wondered what it's like to be tall!'

'I could stick my spear up your arse now and hoist you up!' Talpin jibed.

'Piss on them,' one of the Normans cried in English.

Hampton smiled. 'He's learning right well, is our Frenchie friend. Come on, Thomas, let's be at them, it's a hard ride to Calais.'

The men had cheered, eager to get beyond the walls and try their strength. There would be silver belts and coin to be filched and taken off the French dead.

Blackstone had the loyalty he needed.

'You have to take Gaillard,' Meulon told him. 'It's marshland around Calais. He was born and raised near there. If there's a fight to be had he knows the causeways and paths to firm ground.'

Doubt clouded Blackstone's thoughts. Could he risk going back to de Harcourt? There was still the matter of the plan de Harcourt had devised to seize the mint. Like a foul case of dysentery, mistrust griped in his gut.

He took them to within sight of the castle and then he and Meulon rode forward alone and called to the sentries. The gates soon opened and Jean de Harcourt rode out in full armour with twenty or more of his men. For a moment Blackstone's hand went to Wolf Sword, but Meulon turned to him.

'Sir Thomas, I served my Lord de Harcourt for many years, and I know he would not harm you. It would be insulting to draw your sword.'

Blackstone let his hand rest on the pommel as Jean de Harcourt pulled up his horse.

'So here you are again, Thomas. Back at my door.'

'It's been a long time, Jean.'

'It's Christmas again, Thomas, I always see you at Christmas! Would summer be such a hard time to visit? Are you my Christmas-time gift? You're a wanted man and there's a fair price on your head for those who would deliver it.'

'I'm at your mercy, my lord,' Blackstone answered to the smiling de Harcourt.

'Well, I cannot be seen to welcome you back until King Edward settles matters once more. You know the truce is broken and that Geoffrey de Charny and Louis de Vitry plan to attack Calais? And there are some mighty names of France who ride with them.'

De Charny's reputation was one of the greatest in France. His chivalry and courage were legend, and if he led then Blackstone knew that other great knights would follow him.

'Word reached me of Count de Vitry's agreement with the King. If Calais falls then everything is lost. It's the key to Edward's plans for France,' Blackstone answered.

De Harcourt smiled. 'Indeed it is. Is this you getting involved in politics? I thought such things were of no interest to you.'

'I don't care anything for intrigue or conspiracy. I serve my King and *his* interests. But I don't know how many of the barons have gone over to King Philip. Henri Livay is dead, taken by the plague, but they tried to buy his support. Who else besides de Vitry has turned?'

'None that I know.'

'De Fossat?'

'William's a law unto himself. I can't tell. I think he's already in Calais swearing allegiance but to whom I don't know. If Louis de Vitry takes the citadel, he's reclaimed the key to France and the rewards will be great. Who knows what our Lord de Fossat will accept if tempted to sell his loyalty to the King? De Vitry hates you, Thomas, but de Fossat... I don't know... both men would benefit from your death. You humiliated them both. What better place to reclaim their pride than on the battlefield?'

'And you, Jean? Where do you stand?' Blackstone said without taking his gaze from the man's eyes.

There was no sign of dishonesty when he answered. 'With Edward, when the time is right.'

Blackstone nodded. The answer was good enough, and one he expected. 'I need Gaillard.'

De Harcourt hesitated, not understanding for a moment, then he realized the man's value. 'Of course.' Without turning in the saddle he commanded that Gaillard be brought from the castle. 'Christiana is well? And Henry?'

'Yes. She appreciates your letters and misses you and my lady Blanche.'

De Harcourt looked at him for a moment as if he were addressing his brother, and could barely keep the regret from his voice. 'And we you, Thomas. There's affection for you both in our home.' The moment passed quickly. 'Meulon,' he said, 'there's grey in your beard. Has Sir Thomas aged you that much?'

'And more, my lord,' he answered.

De Harcourt laughed. 'You're learning to answer like him! Yes, I can imagine, but you've honoured me with your loyalty to him. You were my best captain.'

Meulon's chin lifted in an unmistakable surge of pride from such praise.

Gaillard rode out from the castle and waited at a respectful distance.

De Harcourt nudged his horse forward. 'Thomas, I see your sword is without that expensive scabbard I gave you, so obviously you are ready to fight anyone who tries to stop you. In which case I shall escort you and your men from my lands, by way of safe passage in case others try to impede you, though you understand, I am not helping you. As you outnumber us there is to be an honourable agreement between us that you will not raid or plunder. You will agree to this for the sake of formality so I am not obliged to lie to the King's officers if I am questioned.'

'Of course. You have my word.'

'Then let us ride together as far as we can and I will show you the quickest and safest route to Calais.'

De Harcourt escorted the men north beyond Rouen, into Ponthieu and the castle at Noyelles, and then bade his farewell. The road ahead would stir too many memories, he told Blackstone. It was a place that Blackstone had no desire to revisit either.

They skirted the woodlands above Crécy, where the charred

remains of the windmill stood as testament to the burnt-out lives of those thousands who lay buried in the fields below. Matthew Hampton cast a glance at Blackstone. It was the last great battle they had fought and the place where so many of their friends lay dead beneath the undulating ground. Blackstone's eyes lingered on the site as they rode past. He saw Hampton's grim expression and gave a nod in his direction. The past would always haunt them and to experience it meant they were alive. Ghosts would always accompany them no matter how far they travelled.

On the fifth day they halted on the heights and looked down across the marshlands surrounding Calais. Its streets could clearly be seen, laid out neatly within the rectangular walled town, and the citadel with its keep and curtain walls sat snugly in the north-west corner that faced the inlet whose harbour Edward had successfully blockaded, three years earlier, starving out the thousands of inhabitants. Once Calais was in his possession Edward had brought in hundreds of English merchants to occupy the town, which was well fortified with high double walls surrounded by a moat and a long, fortified dyke that could be flooded, not unlike the one that Blackstone had built at Chaulion. There was no sign of Louis de Vitry and Geoffrey de Charny or their army. It was the first time Blackstone had seen Calais and now he understood why his King had besieged it for so long; a direct attack would be impossible. Other than being starved out, having a traitor within the walls would be the only way to seize it. Blackstone studied the shifting sands and marshlands. They gave little choice of approach for an army and he reasoned that de Vitry and the others would line up on the wet sand banks between the castle's gate tower and the sea. Once that drawbridge was down and the portcullis up they would be inside the walls and the slaughter would begin.

'You're going into a part of England now, Meulon,' Blackstone told him, pointing out the town.

'Sweet Jesus save us, then. I hear your food is terrible,' he answered.

* * *

They gained entry and were met by twice their number of men-at-arms who defended the inner walls. John de Beauchamp, Captain of Calais, had been in Prince Edward's division at Crécy and knew of Thomas Blackstone, but his caution was understandable when allowing a band of armed riders into the city walls. King Edward and the Prince of Wales had sailed secretly from England and were in the citadel.

'Then my Prince and my sovereign lord will vouch for me. We came to defend Calais,' Blackstone told him, and repeated the names of the towns and manor houses he held in the south for the benefit of the men who remained with arms at the ready.

'Put your men there,' Blackstone was ordered. 'And wait.'

'Do you know who has betrayed you?' Blackstone asked.

'We do and it's of no consequence to you, Sir Thomas. I'll tell the King you're here. Every man will have his place when the French come.'

Blackstone settled with his men on the wet ground, backs against the inner walls, their horses taken by others to be stabled. No food was offered and none asked for. As far as Blackstone was concerned there was no point in showing any need for comfort. The men rolled out their blankets and made do with the salted meat and fish they carried with them.

'Like old times,' Matthew Hampton said and he cut a slice of meat and fed himself.

'And as wet and damp as it always has been,' Blackstone answered.

Hampton lowered his voice so that Meulon and the other Normans didn't hear. 'Good to be killing Frenchies again, Thomas,' he said, knowing Blackstone would most likely allow the familiarity. 'But if we're stuck in here we won't get much booty.'

Blackstone chewed on his own food. 'Don't you worry about that, Matthew. You just keep your bowcord dry. There'll be enough killing for us all.'

Hampton grinned, teeth ragged with meat, and tapped his leather helmet. That's where his bowcord was and it would stay there until the Frenchies came within range.

Within a few hours there was a flurry of activity as the inner gates were opened and an entourage of knights and men-at-arms came towards Blackstone's men. The man who led them, wearing full armour, was the same age as Blackstone and almost as tall, and wore his hair long and parted in the middle and, unlike the last time Blackstone had seen his Prince, he now sported a short beard. But the striding confidence of the King's son had not altered. He was a fighter like his father. How many sovereign lords would have sailed secretly through the night to aid even a key town like Calais that was under threat? He could have stayed at home like Philip, Blackstone thought to himself as he quickly went down on one knee, followed by the others.

'You arrive like will-o'-the-wisps from the marshlands, Thomas, but far more frightening than creatures of superstition and nightmare. Get up.' The Prince of Wales looked critically at the band of men who stood before him.

'To defend our lord's good name and safety of his city, my Prince,' Blackstone answered.

'And your Prince. You've come to defend me, I hope? You seemed rather good at that,' he said and stepped forward to gaze more carefully at the archer's ruined features.

Blackstone faced the man who had honoured him at Crécy, but averted his eyes for fear of being thought impertinent. 'My lord, you need no help in that matter. Your fighting skills are known across the land.'

'As are yours, Thomas. We hear that mothers tell their children that if they don't behave, the scar-faced-devil of an Englishman will come for them in the night and carry them away to purgatory. Merciful God, Thomas, we didn't expect you to live after Crécy, perhaps you *have* come back from the dead to terrify us all?'

He laughed and his entourage visibly relaxed. 'There are so few of you. What? Sixty, seventy men? A mongrel bunch, Thomas, by the look of them.'

'It's not how many, lord; it's how they fight.'

'A good answer. You please us. And if memory serves, your mind is as quick as your impertinence. So, my knight, you ride here not knowing we were already hidden behind the walls. We accept your loyalty and daring with gratitude.' He paused and looked slightly askance at Blackstone's men, who appeared little better than brigands. 'You have no colours, no coat of arms. Unless you are part of the conspiracy and have found a way to exploit our trust and gain entry by subterfuge.'

There was no hesitation in Blackstone's answer. 'If that were the case, my Prince, you and these men would already be dead.'

Some of those in the entourage visibly flinched. The Prince also looked taken aback for a moment as Blackstone's eyes dared to look into those of his lord.

'Yes, we believe that would be the case as well,' he said. He held out his gloved hand. 'We see you still carry the sword.'

Blackstone's hand reached for the grip and as he drew the blade from the metal ring that held it some of the men behind the Prince went to draw their own, but the King's son made a small gesture that stopped them.

'We know this man. We knelt with him in the mud at Crécy. Many of you were not with us that day, but we shared a moment that will only be forgotten when death takes us. Not so, Thomas?' He paused and then took the sword that was offered, hilt first. The Prince felt its weight and balance. 'It's as we suspected, Thomas. As perfect a sword as could be made. When you lay injured you gripped it as a man going to the grave clings to life.'

The Prince turned the sword and held the blade in front of him, holding it like a crucifix. 'You were God's instrument, to save our life. Will you give us this sword?' he asked quietly.

'Everything is my sovereign lord's,' Blackstone answered.

'We are not your King, Thomas. Will you give *me* your sword?'

'Gladly,' said Blackstone without hesitation, and hoped the flutter of apprehension he felt at losing Wolf Sword did not show on his face.

The Prince of Wales still held the cruciform forward. And then after a moment he said, 'In truth, we think it would see better service in your hands, Sir Thomas. Take it from us.'

Blackstone grasped the blade above the Prince's hand. It was a gesture of unspoken fealty.

Prince Edward released his grip and stepped back. 'Very well. Remember our King's orders. The leaders of this army must be taken alive. Ransom and shame in defeat are bedmates to a French King. We wish to exploit that. So, choose your ground.'

'Where will the enemy strike first?'

'Here. Between these walls. Through those gates. And then we pursue them and finish them off so that Philip doesn't dare try again.'

'Then this is where we fight,' said Blackstone.

The young Prince studied him for a moment and then, in a rare gesture, laid his hand on Blackstone's shoulder.

'Thomas, you cannot defy death forever.'

Days later Blackstone learnt that the traitor was an Italian mercenary, Aimerac of Pavia, who was King Edward's galley master. He had betrayed his King for money and then betrayed the French for safe passage. Before dawn on the following morning Blackstone stood in the chill gloom of the two walls' shadows. They had been told that a French army had come in the night and waited in battle order on the stretch of sand beyond the castle's walls and the sea – exactly where Blackstone had thought they would be. As the grey light brought the day closer those on the battlements saw what appeared to be as many as four thousand infantry and more than fifteen hundred men-at-arms, who readied themselves to lead the assault.

Blackstone was five paces in front of his own front rank and three paces behind him stood Meulon, ready with shield and spear.

The walls were narrow and allowed twenty men abreast to stand. Blackstone's few English archers took the rear ranks with enough clearance to draw their war bows. Blackstone and his men were too far away from the tower gate to identify the shadowy figure who went forward, but soon afterwards the sound of the drawbridge being lowered was heard as the portcullis was hoisted up.

Blackstone turned to face the men. 'Make no sound. They'll send scouts in first. They're not the ones we want.'

Minutes later indistinct figures of armed men ran beneath the portcullis and quickly checked left and right that no ambush awaited them. Deep in the grey gloom Blackstone and his men waited. The scouting party signalled for others to follow. Blackstone looked up as he heard the wind off the sea catch the fluttering French royal standard being hoisted above the tower. Two other banners were hoisted. One Blackstone did not know; the other was that of Louis de Vitry.

Blackstone and his men raised their unmarked shields.

Feet thundered across the drawbridge, creaking armour clattered as men ran forward shoulder to shoulder to be the first to strike into the heart of Calais and its unsuspecting garrison. Blackstone raised his sword, and heard the rattle of sword and spear as the men behind him readied themselves for the attack. More than a hundred men swarmed beneath the tower's gate and then, the moment before the portcullis dropped, trapping them inside, and a sudden fanfare of trumpets signalled the attack, the French men-at-arms saw the darkness race towards them as Blackstone and his men hurled themselves silently into their midst. Two volleys of arrows from the rear ranks flew over the men's heads and brought down men-at-arms at the rear, which gave the others little chance to retreat or to form themselves into defence. Metal clashed on metal and then the devil's brew of fear and the urge to kill became a sudden roar from Blackstone's attacking men – a sound even more terrifying after the silent attack – that echoed between the two high walls, which now trapped the leading French units. Blackstone smashed and cut his way forward at the point of the phalanx; Meulon's spear thrust past his face as its length jammed into the open helmet of a Frenchman at his right shoulder. The heavy figure of Gaillard forced his way forward, plunging his spear into a flailing man, whose body-weight took the spear down with him. Gaillard made no attempt to retrieve it, but drew his sword to hack others. Blackstone barged a French man-at-arms, turned, locked crossguards and twisted, kicked and brought the man down, then rammed Wolf Sword between breastplate and thigh and trampled onwards, as writhing men were gutted and despatched by those following.

Gaillard was down. A knight hammered a mace across the back of his helmet, covering any retaliation with his shield. Meulon's huge form forced his spear beneath it, and when Blackstone saw blood suddenly spurt, he reached down with his crooked arm and grabbed Gaillard's shoulder. The stunned man rolled to one side and a sword suddenly plunged through the tightly fought mêlée and pierced Gaillard's shoulder. His mail took most of the thrust but blood oozed. Blackstone came up from his half-crouched position and slammed his shield upwards, sweeping the man's sword arm away, exposing his chest, and then, as if Meulon and Blackstone were one, like a chimera spawned for war, Meulon shortened his grip and rammed his spear beneath the man's gorge. Then they moved forward: stab, cut and thrust, side by side. Unstoppable. Gaillard got to his knees and was swept up in the surge.

Faceless spectres loomed from the grey stone walls wielding battleaxe and sword as they tried to halt Blackstone's advance, but his spearmen jabbed and wounded, as Matthew Hampton's archers kept their distance and sent another storm of shafts into the French. Blackstone angled the attack, catching those with their backs against the portcullis, caged with nowhere to go except finally onto their knees to yield. The inner gates opened and garrison troops led by the Captain of Calais pressed forward in a steady rhythm.

'Hold!' Blackstone yelled, keeping his men from rushing forward and finishing off the surrendering men. They had already killed more than thirty of the enemy; murdering the rest would have no further effect on the failed attack. And he wanted his men still strong, because there was no sign of Louis de Vitry in this first assault. The sweating, bloodstained men ripped buckles and swords from their enemy. Booty was their reward. Some of the surrendered were felled by blows to quieten their insults at being bested by men who wore no coats of arms. Trumpets and drums sounded in the distance, heralding an attack. Blackstone pushed through the scavenging men to John de Beauchamp.

'Where's the King?' he demanded, knowing his men's work was done between the walls. The portcullis groaned upwards as de Beauchamp barked his answer and horses clattered from the inner walls across the drawbridge.

'He's attacking from the south gate, the Prince from the north!' de Beauchamp shouted, and jumped clear as the horsemen pressed between them.

'Sir Thomas!' Meulon cried as he saw Blackstone grab the bridle of one of the bustling horses and haul its rider down. The man fell heavily on his back, but rolled to avoid the dancing hooves. Blackstone was in the saddle and was carried through the tower gates by the swarming horsemen.

Beyond the citadel Blackstone saw many of the French retreating under the English King's onslaught. There must have been more than two hundred English archers with the King, Blackstone realized, as a swathe of Frenchmen fell from a sudden dark cloud. He scoured the French lines for Louis de Vitry's banner, but the mayhem of the battle obscured it. And there was still no sign of William de Fossat. Was he biding his time, waiting to strike when the clamour of battle allowed him the chance?

Beyond the marshes on the spit of sand, horses galloped at full stretch as Frenchmen stood their ground and bravely met the Prince of Wales's assault. It would be a miracle if they held against Edward's pincer attack. But where was de Vitry? Where? Neither flank carried his banner, so Blackstone urged the horse forward into the centre as the other horsemen split and joined each of the flanks.

And then he was suddenly pitched forward. Crossbow bolts thudded into the horse. Its momentum carried it forward barely a dozen paces as its vital organs were hit. Blackstone fell into the marshy ground, the horse rolled across him. Visions of Sir Gilbert Killbere going under his horse at Crécy flashed into his mind. *Don't let me die like that!* the voice in his head shouted. He was trapped. His left leg was pinned. Kicking and pushing with his free leg he began to drag himself clear. He was in the eye of a great storm, where an unearthly quiet prevailed. It took only a moment for him to realize that mud and turf had rammed itself between his helmet and ears and that was what had caused the battle to become muted.

He pulled the helmet free and shook his head, pulling his mud-sodden hair from his eyes. A handful of Frenchmen had seen him go down and were running towards him, accompanied by a knight on his war horse, half a dozen strides behind them, its lumbering gallop kicking clods of mud into the air. Sword raised and visor open, it was impossible not to recognize William de Fossat's hawk face. Blackstone's leg sucked clear of the quagmire and, with less than twenty paces before the men were on him, he pulled himself upright and readied Wolf Sword to strike.

De Fossat dropped his right shoulder and let his sword scythe down, feeling it bite through exposed head and neck.

Meulon yelled at the men to get clear of the castle and follow Blackstone. Matthew Hampton ran from the back of the group and caught up with the bigger man whose stride was twice that of the stocky archer.

'He's down! D'you see that?' he gasped. The going was already soft, but Meulon pushed forward onto one of the broad paths that offered a causeway through the soggy ground. They were still too far away to use their bows and Meulon seemed to be in a race with Gaillard as they ran through the middle of the men on each side who were being pressed from the flanks. Englishmen turned, thinking Meulon and the men were attacking French coming from their rear, but Hampton plucked a fallen pennon from the ground and punished his legs and lungs to catch up with the spearmen.

'Saint George! Edward and England!' he yelled as loud as his gasping lungs would allow.

It was enough for the English troops to turn back and fight their way towards de Charny's standard.

Their advance was halted by a knot of Frenchmen who burst from a mêlée on their right, and Meulon pushed Hampton clear as one of them thrust his pike between them. Gaillard's sword slashed the pikeman's throat, and Talpin and Perinne quickly formed a shield wall with others either side of him and Meulon. The wedge they formed allowed them to edge forward step by step. Heaving and cursing with effort, some stumbled and fell on the uneven ground, but sheer brute strength drove them on until the French lay slashed and dying beneath their feet.

'He's there!' Gaillard cried, as fighting men parted showing the knight on horseback bearing down on Blackstone.

Blackstone had no shield, so he reached for a broken spear. Wolf Sword's blood knot held, and the horse was seconds away from trampling him. He heard de Fossat grunt as his sword severed bone and flesh of the attacking men. Two went down and a third had no chance beneath the war horse's iron-shod hooves. He was not there to kill the Englishman after all.

'Move on! Man! Move on!' de Fossat cried, yanking the horse around as Blackstone parried a sword blow from one of the men with the broken shaft and then cut him and the other man down. 'Louis is there! There!' he cried, pointing with his sword. 'He comes for you!'

Blackstone spat blood, his dry mouth barely able to hawk the clot from it. He'd taken a blow to the face at some stage, but had no memory of it. He moved forward towards the company of men that bore down on him and the half-dozen horsemen in their midst who rode next to Louis de Vitry and his banner.

'Sir Thomas!' a voice bellowed behind him. He turned. Matthew Hampton and Meulon with Gaillard, Talpin and Perinne led the others like a horde of barbarians, their eyes staring wide through mud and blood-spattered faces, their beards matted with snot and spittle.

'De Vitry!' he yelled at them and turned to begin his lone attack. Sidestepping the bodies he ran for the drier ground to his left, as the causeway paths across the soggy ground would let him get closer more quickly and force de Vitry's men to alter their own direction. Half of them would still be running straight and, as they turned to curve back, the middle body of men would be closer to Blackstone. And that was where Louis de Vitry rode.

William de Fossat pushed his horse next to the running man. 'Take hold!' he yelled, casting aside his shield, changing his sword arm, allowing Blackstone to grab hold of the stirrup strap with his left hand and to keep his own sword arm free. The horse could only sustain an erratic trot as it found its footing, but Blackstone's feet barely touched the ground. Man and horse were propelled into the seething mass as arrow shafts fell among them. Matthew Hampton had steadied the archers as Meulon and the others threw a protective shield wall around them. Now they moved forward again when they saw Frenchmen pull de Fossat down, the speared horse whinnying, eyes rolling back in agony as it crashed to the ground. Blackstone danced away from the thrashing hooves, saw de Fossat honour his word as he fought a common enemy at Blackstone's side. De Vitry yelled something, but Blackstone could not hear amid the mayhem. The banners had turned, they were sweeping behind the two knights. A baying howl rose up from Meulon and Blackstone's men. They were being cut down as they forged towards their master's side. Waterford died from a spear thrust, Talpin had two Frenchmen beat him to death with mace and axe. Blackstone watched as his wall builder fell under the men's savagery. Then, by some miracle, Meulon's lead took the men forward.

Blackstone had stood his ground, picked up a fallen shield and moved closer to de Fossat. Neither looked at the other as the hordes seemed to increase rather than lessen despite their having taken a vicious toll on de Vitry's men.

'Down, Thomas! Down! Down!' a voice suddenly cried behind Blackstone's right shoulder as Matthew Hampton lunged forward. Blackstone turned, four of de Vitry's men levelled crossbows. Too late, Blackstone brought up the shield as Matthew Hampton ran forward and took two of the bolts into his chest. A third ripped through Blackstone's shield and pierced his side. It burned like acid into his skin and muscle. He sucked in air, tested his weight. Could he still stand? Move? Attack? Three steps and then five – the pain blistering his mind, the sword swinging, as the scalding wound drove him on, spurring his strength. De Fossat lay unmoving in the mud, blood spilling across his breastplate.

Trumpets sounded somewhere close. The Prince's men were closing the net. Louis de Vitry had promised to kill the man who had humiliated him. His lands had been returned, a bounty would be given. And he, among all Norman lords, would hold more power and control than any of them. But even as he spurred his horse forward towards the wounded Blackstone, he knew the battle was lost. Now there would be only ignominy. He had chosen the wrong side and sold himself to a French King who could never win. There could be only one satisfaction left to the embittered count: kill Thomas Blackstone.

A shockwave ran through the French troops. The English King had trapped them and his son had cut their feet from beneath them, and Blackstone's strike into the very heart of their army had severed their strength. They suddenly faltered, and then the last of them turned and ran. Blackstone saw Louis de Vitry's look of abandonment as he cried out for his men to stand. Fear and desperation closed their ears to his pleas. Among the thousands it must have seemed to Louis de Vitry that he was completely alone. He spurred his horse. Blackstone stood in its path, unable to move quickly enough. From several paces behind him Meulon hurled his spear straight into the beast's chest and its legs crumpled. De Vitry clung to the pommel but was thrown. Sixty pounds of armour slowed him getting to his feet. His sword, like Blackstone's, was tied to his wrist. Blackstone could almost smell the suffocation within the man's helmet, its narrow slit limiting his vision. He stood back as de Vitry got to his knees and then his feet, staggered, then found his balance, shoving up the visor and sucking in air. There was no hesitation as he attacked with such ferocity that Blackstone fell back. He saw Gaillard take a pace forward to help, and shouted for him to stand his ground. De Vitry would be ransomed by the Prince, sold back to Philip, or sent to the French King in disgrace. A perfect victory for the English that would rub salt into King Philip's wounds for years to come.

If Blackstone did not kill de Vitry first.

They clashed. Blackstone's bare head put him at a disadvantage and de Vitry neatly turned on the balls of his feet, nimbly changing direction and catching Blackstone a tooth-rattling blow with his sword's pommel. Blackstone spat blood, blocked, parried and felt his strength being drained with the blood running down his leg, the bolt still embedded in his side, impeding his sword strikes. Before he died, Blackstone wanted nothing more than to drink a bucket of water. To drown in it. To die not thirsty.

Louis de Vitry had the attuned senses of a man trained in hand-to-hand combat and this peasant archer, who had been honoured and treated as an equal by the great and noble de Harcourt family, was a stain on Norman honour. A wrong would now be righted. Blackstone was nothing more than a brute-strength fighter who now staggered, head sinking to his chest, hair smothering his face, mouth agape, desperate for water, shoulders yielding to the burden of his wound. He was going onto his knees. He was down! Count Louis de Vitry pressed both hands onto his sword's grip and raised the blade.

It had become nothing more than an execution.

Blackstone lifted his head, and de Vitry saw his eyes stare coldly through the blood-soaked hair. He swung the blade down – too late. Blackstone turned Wolf Sword and, as he had when killing the wild boar, rammed upwards beneath de Vitry's breastplate into his heart and lungs.

Louis de Vitry fell, sprawling, only this time Blackstone twisted clear and let the body thud face down into the sodden ground. What little breath remained bubbled blood into the trampled grass.

CHAPTER THIRTY

Barber-surgeons cut, sawed and stitched the wounded. It seemed to Blackstone that more blood flowed from their hands than had been let by the enemy. They took cutters and snapped the bolt below the fletchings. He wished the infirmarian from the monastery, Brother Simon, was with them. His care for the sick and wounded would keep a man in this world rather than punish him into the next. The barber-surgeon used an arrow spoon to draw out the bolt and prepared his cautery iron.

'Let the blood run,' Blackstone insisted. Another lesson from the old monk was to let blood flow and carry with it any impurity before sealing the wound. Finally they pushed the steel wire needle, its eyelet threaded with gut, into the wound. Gaillard brought the sack that hung from his horse's pommel and handed him the small clay jar, sealed with beeswax, prepared by the old monk. The balm was the colour of lemons and very fragrant, which in itself gave a sense of healing. Blackstone used it on his wound and made sure that others smeared it across their injuries. He and his men were kept two weeks within the city walls, attended to and fed. Despite their injuries they buried their dead themselves, caring little for strangers who threw corpses into pits.

Matthew Hampton had rushed between Blackstone and the crossbowmen and now the veteran English archer lay cradled by the earth. Prayers were said and blessings given, and then Blackstone went among his men. They had come off lightly, but losing two archers was a grievous loss to Blackstone. He knew, though, that in time, others would come.

'Talpin was a good soldier,' Meulon told him, nursing a cut

to his arm. 'Still, better him than me, is how you have to look at it. I think you pissed off your English Prince, though, Master Thomas. He was counting on keeping the French leaders alive.'

'He wasn't on my mind at the time,' Blackstone answered.

Blackstone had lost fifteen of his seventy-five men, and a dozen others were wounded, including himself. It was a time for prayer and giving thanks, and he knelt with his company at the men's graveside. There was a sombre place in his heart for those who had died at his side on the battlefields of France, and he knew the memory of them would ride with him forever.

Blackstone and his men were quartered in the town, but kept close to the stables and the garrison's quarters. The seneschal of Calais had ordered de Beauchamp to keep fighting men well away from the merchants and inns. A battle won beyond the walls could soon be lost within them. Gold- and silversmiths offered more temptations than tavern whores.

By the third week after the battle he could ride without seeping blood. It was time to go home. He shared a cooked meal with the men, who were given fresh bread for their efforts. If nothing else, the King and the Prince fed their men well.

Gaillard sucked the broth's juice from the bread. The lump on his head had risen to a mighty bruise that made wearing a helmet painful. A couple of weeks of letting the lice escape would do no harm, was the common consensus. 'I hear that Italian, whatsisname... the one who did the deal, he got paid. One of the garrison guards said he overheard that he'd taken a holiday to Rome, said it was a Jubilee year. If there were a few spare coins to be had I'd travel through Avignon and see the Pope myself.'

'Gaillard, the Pope would choke on his fine cuts if you showed up. He would have to take a year off his duties to confess you,' said Perinne, lifting the men's mood.

There had been some booty, but not enough to make the fight worthwhile, though it made little difference to most of them, because they would soon be back home where raiding gave them modest but acceptable pay under Blackstone's command.

Blackstone stood and wiped his hands on his leather jerkin. He could smell his own stench and longed for a bath, promising himself to bathe when they came across the first freshwater stream.

'We leave tomorrow after matins,' he said and then made his way to where William de Fossat lay, resting in surroundings more fitting for a Norman baron who had decided to throw in his lot with the English. He had taken the fourth crossbow quarrel in those deadly moments when Hampton died and Blackstone was wounded. It had punched through his armour and embedded itself in his shoulder. He looked gaunt behind the dark beard because the surgeons had bled him even more than the wound itself.

'Butchers. That's what you English are. I ask for a French surgeon and I get an Englishman who stutters my language, and farts while he stitches me,' said de Fossat.

'I'm told that was because you held a knife to his throat in case he took your arm.'

William de Fossat grunted indifferently.

'What will you do now? Edward can't grant you protection here. Will you go to England?' Blackstone asked.

'No. Did you not hear? I found myself a rich widow with estates that need looking after. And I think she's some connection to a long-forgotten bastard of the royal family. He will leave us alone – and besides, I hear he's ailing. He'll be dead before I give myself to the worms. That's if your English butchers haven't done for me.'

'I came to thank you,' Blackstone said.

'Don't be a fool, Blackstone. I didn't do what I did for you. Louis de Vitry betrayed us. Had I confronted him he would have surrendered to me. He needed to be dead.' He smiled. 'You were – convenient. You're the one who mocked our code of chivalry, Thomas, but it's a code nonetheless. Surrender only to a man of equal rank.'

'Which I am not.'

'Which you most definitely are not. And he wanted badly to kill you. You humiliated a Norman lord. Sweet Jesus! Did you think he would ever forget?'

'No,' said Blackstone. 'But I doubted you. For a moment only. But I doubted.'

'That I was coming to kill you,' he said

'Aye. You had the perfect opportunity out there. And now I am in your debt.'

'I gave my word that I would stand at your shoulder against a common enemy,' de Fossat said quietly, adding weight to his sincerity.

'A pledge can be broken,' Blackstone replied.

'It depends who you give it to,' said the Norman lord.

John de Beauchamp strode at the head of a company of pikemen, who outnumbered Blackstone's men two to one. They stopped where Blackstone and his men were garrisoned.

'Is this trouble?' Meulon asked as he saw the men outside form up as escort.

Before Blackstone could answer, the Captain of Calais made himself known. 'Sir Thomas Blackstone, you and your men are summoned to the market square. I am sent to escort you there now.'

'By whose orders?' Blackstone asked, knowing his men were wary of the English.

'Your Prince,' de Beauchamp answered.

Meulon muttered beneath his breath. 'Disobeying a sovereign Prince is a hanging offence. Maybe they've already got the scaffolds built in the square.'

'Because I killed de Vitry?' Blackstone asked him.

'How would I know? He's *your* Prince.'

The soldiers marched as Blackstone's men shambled between them. There had been no command to disarm but to be taken like this into the confines of the town created suspicion. They turned into the market square and saw it was boxed by troops, keeping the townspeople at bay as they gawked at the assembly of noblemen and their rich tapestry of banners. The Prince of Wales, resplendent in armour and unsullied surcoat, was in conversation with his entourage. It seemed that he and his household were preparing to leave for England. John de Beauchamp halted the men.

'Sir Thomas, you will accompany me,' he commanded, and went forward to where the Prince spoke with his seneschal and other officers of state who controlled Calais.

Blackstone stayed a respectful two paces behind de Beauchamp, who waited until an officer approached him. The Prince of Wales looked up and nodded and the officer indicated that they should move forward. Once close enough, both Blackstone and de Beauchamp went down on one knee and then stood before him.

The Captain of Calais stepped away, leaving Blackstone to face the stern-faced Prince alone.

'We leave on the tide, Thomas. Back to England. Our King has already sailed,' he said.

Blackstone could not determine why he had been summoned. Thoughts dashed through his mind. Was punishment due? Surely the Prince did not want him to return to England, abandoning his territory, his wife and child?

'You hold towns in your King's name, Thomas. Come the day we will no doubt have need of them.'

'They're yours to command, my Prince,' Blackstone answered.

A frown of irritation crossed Prince Edward's face. 'Do you always have to kill so readily, Thomas? Count Louis de Vitry was a Norman we could have used in our favour.'

Blackstone remained silent. To answer might stir a hornet's nest of recrimination.

The heir to the throne of England let the moment pass. 'What's done is done,' he went on. 'Your action drove a wedge through the enemy centre. It was... helpful... to us. Has the yeoman archer become a military tactician as well as a knight?'

'I do as I see best, my Prince,' Blackstone said, watching Edward's movements as he made a barely noticeable gesture and a nod of his head to no one in particular, but it was enough for a knight in full armour and a groom on the periphery of the square to take hold of a pack horse's bridle and begin its swayback gait towards them.

'Then make sure that you continue to do so,' the Prince said and carried on, indicating that he did not expect a response. 'Did you know we have given the wool Staple to Calais, that our Flemish allies to the north are almost within hailing distance? Their looms hum with trade from the wool off our sheep's backs. It makes no difference whether you do or not, Thomas, there was strategic and political importance in holding this town.'

Blackstone saw that the approaching knight and groom wore the royal livery, so whatever was packed onto that palfrey had something to do with the Prince's household.

'And hold it we did. And you would have stood alone in our name had we not known of the plot to throw open the gates. Your action deserves to be honoured. And Thomas, you are making a habit of this!'

The rebuke seemed genuine and Blackstone bowed his head.

'We jest. For God's sake, Thomas, we are not an ogre, we are your Prince and we value you. Did they cut away your English humour at Crécy as well as your face?' he said, and with another flick of his wrist the knight responded by taking something from the side of the horse. He held up a plain woven surcoat, its sanguine dye as rich as blood. The outline of a shield was sewn onto the left breast and it bore the black stitched image of Wolf Sword, pommel and grip distinct above the curved-down crossguard. The narrowing blade was held in a gauntleted fist. Blackstone remembered meeting his Prince's eyes across the sword when both men grasped its blade before the battle.

'If you are to be known as other than that face of yours then you need a coat of arms. Our King thought this appropriate,' he said and nodded to the groom to give it to Blackstone.

'There are sufficient to clothe your ruffians, and more for those who will no doubt seek you out. And five hundred pounds a year will come from the treasury to sustain your efforts,' he said.

The honour had surprised and embarrassed Blackstone and he stuttered his gratitude.

'You are too generous, lord.'

'Yes. We know. But honouring you reflects well on us. We bathe in the warmth of your name and success – and we would wish it were more fragrant,' he said and smiled.

Impatiently he looked to the groom, who fumbled with something on the blind side of the horse. The knight quickly took over and unlaced a shield. The Prince stepped forward and took it from him. He turned the shield and the same blazon of sword and gauntlet faced Blackstone.

'We chose the motto ourself,' he said. 'You were close to death that night, and yet you would not yield to it. The King, our father, uttered the words that you were defiant unto death.'

Blackstone looked at the words written beneath the gauntlet: *Défiant à la Mort*.

He took the shield from Prince Edward's hands.

'Thomas, go home and stay alive; we will have need of you again. Now show your men their coat of arms.'

Blackstone hooked his bent arm into the shield and raised it to his men.

They saw it and roared their pleasure.

'Thomas,' the Prince beckoned, and spoke a few final words despite the deafening cheers that the crowd now saw fit to share.

Blackstone rejoined his men as the Prince's entourage left the city gates. Within the hour, wearing their new coat of arms, they clattered across the drawbridge. The solemn look on Blackstone's scarred face prompted Meulon to question him.

'We've been honoured, Sir Thomas. Have no regrets about the men we lost – they look down on us and share our pride. They're beyond harm and our time has yet to come. Is that such a bad thing?'

Blackstone remained silent as they drew away from the citadel.

'Did your Prince chastise you for killing de Vitry? Is that what happened?'

'Killing de Vitry was little more than an inconvenience to him. And we'll mourn the men in our own way. No, what the

Prince told me was that King Philip and his son John, Duke of Normandy, have quarrelled. Some of the Norman lords will side with him and no matter who becomes the strongest they'll want revenge against those of us who stay and fight here.'

Behind them wind-filled sails pushed the Prince's ship towards England as Blackstone spurred the horse forward and galloped for home.

THE END

HISTORICAL NOTES

When King Edward III invaded France – a country twice as large, far wealthier and more densely populated than his own – it was the leading military power in the West. Edward's army, men from poor families as well as members of the nobility, had opportunities to secure wealth and status through plunder and ransom – if they survived the savagery of battle. But what happened to those men once these great battles had been fought and they were discharged from service? Their skills were in high demand by those who had no armies of their own – most notably the Italian city-states. Before they reached the Italian paymasters they had to have proved themselves in warfare, and it was the lead-up to the day when these hardened men were contracted that I wanted to explore, and discover how a humble boy from an English village could become a Master of War. I discovered that many independent captains who fought as mercenaries would have themselves knighted by their fellow routiers. But there were some men from a lowly station in life who were honoured because of their bravery and who seemed to have a natural talent for war. And I set Thomas Blackstone off on his journey so that he could earn such honour.

English and Welsh bowmen dominated King Edward's major battles in the fourteenth century. Young men practised at their village butts, a unique army, trained for service in war, that could not be matched by any other European monarch. One such young man was Thomas Blackstone, who would overcome his fear of killing and the terror of a heavy cavalry charge in battle, and whose courage would create an opportunity for recognition that went beyond the usual reward of war booty.

To begin my acquaintance with that violent period I reached for my well-worn copy of Barbara W. Tuchman's *A Distant Mirror*. The brutality of the age and, in particular, the appalling savagery of its mercenaries made it difficult to find any redeeming features for Blackstone. At that time there was a great desire to behave in a chivalrous manner, especially for those of noble rank, but a knight's word of honour to a peasant counted for nothing. Chivalric endeavour was an insistent ghost from the days of old, most notably the Arthurian legends and *The Song of Roland*, the mid-twelfth-century heroic poem that celebrated the deeds of Charlemagne. The sheer demands of fighting and the necessities of war usually swept away any semblance of compassion. Despite going to war to gain riches and honour and carrying the ideal of chivalrous behaviour, prisoners were massacred, churches pillaged and women raped.

But many of the knightly classes and nobility were literate and accomplished in poetry and courtship, so perhaps there *was* a chink in their armour. There were instances where courtly and gentle manners won the day – especially with women. A routier, Andrew Belmont, fell in love while serving in Italy and stopped the destruction of the town where his beloved lived.

Modern society can barely comprehend the privations and culture of a contemporary army at war, so a true grasp of the experience of those who fought in a medieval conflict can lie only in our imagination. It was a cruel and savage time. Children were working at hard physical labour by the age of seven. The offspring of craftsmen might be apprenticed if there was money to pay the master whose skills were to be acquired. A boy of noble birth would be sent to another family and trained as a page from the time he was nine years old and then, from his early teens, would serve as a knight's esquire, already trained in swordsmanship. Men-at-arms, strapped into sixty to eighty pounds of armour, could fight for hours on end in hand-to-hand combat, which might seem superhuman to us today, but the medieval capacity for absorbing and shrugging off pain appears to have been extraordinary. One knight who had his helm and nose pierced by a crossbow bolt, which stayed embedded in his face, fought on, suffering some 'discomfort' each time a blow was delivered against him that struck the offending quarrel. The medieval man's strength and endurance is unlikely to be replicated today. There are accounts of knights, clad in full armour, who could somersault, and run and leap into the saddle of a war horse.

Many of the events in *Master of War* took place. There are few names known of the common men who fought during that invasion, but two archers who are recorded, Henry Torpoleye and Richard Whet, fell during the street fighting at Caen. Few incidents of resistance from the local peasants against the heavily armed English and Welsh invaders are recorded, but one such event took place at the village of Cormalain when English troops sheltered in a barn. That night locals blocked its entrance and burned it down. The troops suffocated and died – an event I used and which resulted (in the story) in the execution of young John Nightingale.

King Edward's son, Prince Edward of Woodstock, fought as a sixteen-year-old in the vanguard at the Battle of Crécy. He had experienced commanders at his side, but his youth, like many of the common men in the ranks, was no impediment to his aggressive defence of his position. He would later be known as the Black Prince, but that sobriquet did not appear until several centuries after the events in this book. The two most decisive battles fought against the French, which gave the English prestige, wealth and territory, were Crécy and Poitiers. The English and Welsh archers inflicted arguably an even greater defeat on French nobility at Crécy than at Agincourt nearly seventy years later. The killing field at Crécy meant that the flower of French knighthood faced

a terrifying storm of arrows that fell at sixteen thousand a minute
– nearly three hundred per second.

Medieval women of the nobility had clearly defined roles to play
but there were some remarkable women who shouldered the whole
burden of being the heads of their households when their husbands
were killed in war. One such stalwart was Blanche de Ponthieu,
a noblewoman in her own right, and married to Jean V, Count
of Harcourt. The Harcourts of France played a dangerous game.
The family was divided between those who supported the French
King and those who did not. History records that after recovering
from his wounds suffered at Crécy, Jean became embroiled in a
plot to kill, or at least replace, the King.

The outcome of this conspiracy forms a turning point for
Thomas Blackstone in the second book of this series – *The Savage
Priest*.

As Castle d'Harcourt – to use the correct French spelling
– itself plays quite a substantial role in *Master of War* I
include a link to a few photos I took during my research trip:
http://ven.so/masterofwarphotos.

Historical novelists, in particular, are dependent on many
fine scholars whose diligent research and knowledge allow an
author to place his characters in a more vivid setting than would
otherwise be possible. I acquired (or, as a routier, plundered) many
historical articles for this novel, but continually returned to an
informed and brilliant work that covers the Hundred Years War,
Jonathan Sumption's *Trial by Battle* and its companion volume,
Trial by Fire. It's a work of enormous appeal and information
and is possibly the most comprehensible account of the war. *The
Road to Crécy*, a more recent book by Marilyn Livingstone and
Morgen Witzel, is an excellent read and an invaluable source
of information. The two authors list more names of those who
fought in the invasion and their book gives an insight into the
day-to-day conditions experienced by Edward's army, from food
and logistics to weaponry. Its narrative history gives a very vivid
and close-up account of what happened from pre-invasion to the

Battle of Crécy. I first discovered the brilliance and courage of King Edward III in Ian Mortimer's *The Perfect King*. This author offers a wonderful portrait of one of England's greatest founders. There are contentious, though fascinating, issues discussed in his book that fell outside the scope of research required for *Master of War*.

For personal weapons of combat, and especially in determining the origin of Wolf Sword, I turned to Ewart Oakeshott and two of his books: *A Knight and his Weapons* and, more particularly, *The Sword in the Age of Chivalry* (revised edition). When it came to understanding that most lethal weapon on the field of battle – the war bow used by the English and Welsh archers – there were many articles available, but the book *Longbow – A Social and Military History*, by the actor and author Robert Hardy, is probably the definitive work on the subject.

Medieval surgical procedures were taken from various articles, most notably from the *Annals of The Royal College of Surgeons of England*. The Great Pestilence that became known as the Black Death is a fascinating study in itself and I can recommend that any interested readers or researchers pick up a copy of *The Black Death* by Philip Ziegler.

Wherever I have deviated from any expert's view it is either from choice, to allow me to tell the story the way I wish to tell it, or because, at times, the experts themselves offer different explanations of events that took place.

David Gilman
Devonshire
2013

ACKNOWLEDGEMENTS

I owe a special thanks to Nic Cheetham and his unstinting enthusiasm for *Master of War*. Creating two novels from the first draft, at his suggestion, was a huge undertaking, but everyone at Head of Zeus has been most generous in their praise and support for this book and the following series. I am extremely pleased to be part of their new venture. My friend, and 'unofficial' editor, James McFarlane, is a stalwart commentator whose considerate suggestions improve my efforts.

As always a huge thank-you to my tireless literary agent, Isobel Dixon, and everyone at Blake Friedmann Literary Agency.

David Gilman
Devonshire, England
www.davidgilman.com
Follow me on: http://twitter.com/davidgilmanuk